LOUISIANA BLOOD

MIKE DONALD

This is a work of fiction. Names, characters, organizations, places, events, and incidents are either products of the author's imagination or are used fictitiously.

Published by Inkshares, Inc., San Francisco, California
www.inkshares.com

ISBN: 9781947848078
e-ISBN: 9781947848085
LCCN: 2017956962

First edition

Printed in the United States of America

For Dorrie.

PROLOGUE

ON OCTOBER 2, 1893, the second-largest hurricane ever recorded hit Louisiana, killing over two thousand people. Whole villages, including Saint Malo and Cheniere Caminada, were swept from the face of the earth. To this day it remains one of the greatest natural disasters in American history and is known as "the Evil Wind."

ONE

SPIRIT'S SWAMP, LOUISIANA – October 2, 1893

TONGUES OF LIGHTNING flickered across the sullen clouds overhead, bleaching the dark swamp waters on either side of a muddy track. Trembling shadows silhouetted the desolate landscape. Mangrove roots writhed in the howling wind like gray tentacles. Through torrents of rain, a carriage with black coachwork and a steamer chest roped to its back, raced ahead of the approaching storm. From inside, the pale, frightened faces of five women stared out into the gloom. The driver whipped the horses with grim desperation, his face a ravaged mask framing coal-black eyes. He wore a studded leather collar that barely covered the livid rope burns around his throat. The carriage shuddered to a halt. The wind and rain ceased. They were in the eye of the storm. A skein of cloud tore across the moon and revealed a ghostly, silvered landscape. Swamp water shimmered beneath its pale light. Beside the banks of the track the hooded eyes of an alligator stared into the night. The horses lunged against their harnesses, eyes rolling with fear. The alligator sank back below the surface, leaving nothing behind but ripples. The weary women huddled together inside the carriage.

They wore identical red scarves. One of them, blonde haired and with an ethereal beauty, looked out of the window. A gust of wind ripped the scarf from her neck, sending it floating up into the sky, a blood-red wound that slashed the dark clouds above. The driver climbed down from the carriage. Reached into his jacket and pulled out a pistol. He headed purposefully toward the carriage door. The blonde girl started to scream, but her voice was quickly snuffed out as a maelstrom of gray water engulfed everything.

TWO

LONDON, ENGLAND – Present day

CHANDLER TRAVIS WALKED alongside the gray water of the Thames. In the distance he could see the vast square structures that supported Tower Bridge's immense deck, its history palpable in every inch of its monumental stonework, and the surface of the river like a blurred photograph as the rain swept across the city. Chandler had taken to walking to work from his flat in Shad Thames and had grown to love the city at that time of the morning.

At just over six feet, with his distinctive loping walk and boyish looks, he'd struggled to be taken seriously during his early years in the Met. The result of this was that he'd had to work twice as hard to get a promotion. He'd joined the Metropolitan Police Force straight from university, reached the rank of detective, and was considered to be on the fast track for the post of inspector. But the 2005 terrorist attacks on London changed his life forever. Though his body had recovered well, and the physical scarring was minimal, his career as a detective on active duty was effectively over.

It was ironic, he reflected, that the past—somewhere he inhabited a lot in his free time—had come to his rescue and helped to secure him a future. Chandler's great-great-grandfather had been a reporter during the reign of Jack the Ripper, and his own father had been fixated with the case. Chandler had inherited the family's obsession with the Ripper, and it had proved invaluable during his recuperation. The department had managed to find him a desk job in what was known as the Black Museum, or room 101 of New Scotland Yard.

As well as his general duties at the museum, he gave lectures on modern policing methods and how they might have been employed during the time of Jack the Ripper. His colleagues knew of his obsession and had taken to calling him "Springheeled Jack," a title they felt aptly summed up not only his obsession but also his characteristic gait.

As he made his way along the glistening cobbled streets through Butler's Wharf, he thought about the talk he was to give later that morning. There wasn't a year that went by without someone claiming to have revealed the Ripper's true identity. Not surprisingly, most of them were all neatly tied in with a book launch.

He passed the iconic New Scotland Yard sign, headed through the front entrance, and downstairs to room 101. As usual, PC Jenny Sedgeway was in early. She possessed some kind of built-in radar and already had a cup of fresh steaming coffee ready for him as he entered the room. Jenny was one of those people who always had a ready smile and a quip at hand, no matter how dreary the day outside. She handed Chandler his mug, emblazoned with an ironic Sherlock Holmes silhouette. He took a grateful sip of the strong brew.

"Morning," he said.

"Ready for battle?" Her eyes sparkled with humor.

"Of course. How many are we expecting?" She scanned a sheet of paper, pursed her lips.

"You have a small group of tourists and police trainees at ten thirty and about the same numbers for the facial-recognition lecture this afternoon."

He nodded. The facial-recognition lecture was proving popular. With the advent of more powerful computers, the ability to produce 3-D projections meant a multitude of different possibilities could be generated within seconds. The days of using a skilled clay modeler to work up details from a skull were long gone.

He took another sip of coffee. "I guess there's no point in putting it off any longer."

Jenny smiled and held out a computer tablet.

"No chance of just using an overhead projector and a blackboard then," he said with a smile. Jenny gave him one of her looks: the sort that mothers reserve for troublesome teenagers.

"The tablet's linked to the video projector. Just hit 'Run' and the slides will pop up in sequence." Chandler took the tablet from her like it was an unexploded bomb.

"You make it sound so simple," he said nervously. Jenny rolled her eyes.

"Just because the nineteenth century is your specialist subject, doesn't mean you have to live there. I swear you'd have a Bakelite phone installed if you thought you could get away with it."

Chandler headed toward the door before pausing to deliver his parting line.

"Yes, well, sometimes the past can be an interesting place to live." And with a wink he was gone.

THREE

SPIRIT'S SWAMP, LOUISIANA – Present day

A RED CAMARO stacked on a jacked-up frame with bulbous truck tires blasted through the oily swamp waters, jockeying for position among twenty or thirty other swamp buggies. CHILLY FISH – SWAMP GATOR was painted down one side of its body, while an alligator design with snarling teeth flared across its hood.

Deputy Sheriff Duke Lanoix clung to a grab handle inside the bucking machine, each landing sending shudders through the vehicle's chassis and reminding him that his back wasn't what it used to be. He was headed for the big four-oh, and though his muscled frame was still in good shape, he hadn't been spending as much time working out as he used to, and he was feeling it.

"Man, this is a blast!" the driver, Deputy Wayne "Chilly" Fish, yelled over the howl of the powerful engine as it overtook another competitor. Chilly, a decade younger, was enjoying the ride far more than Duke. The sheriff gritted his teeth and reminded himself that the annual race was for charity, and a way of mixing with the local community. The swamp had been the site of oil-drilling operations during the so-called black gold rush and had sat badly polluted for decades. There had been uproar after the clean-up contract was awarded to Blackburn Industries. The Blackburn family had owned oil refineries during the boom years and were responsible for a lot of the resulting pollution.

Governor Roman Blackburn saw himself as a modern-day Huey Long, with big plans for the county—and, some said, even bigger plans for himself. Duke braced himself as the Camaro hit another clump of vegetation and soared through the air. Each time it hit a patch of mud, pockets of "swamp gas" were released, filling the vehicle with fumes strong enough to make his eyes water. Duke wiped his face and looked behind. They were in the lead and pulling ahead.

Chilly punched the air in triumph. "It's in the bag!"

Duke forced a grin, being careful not to open his mouth too far in case he bit his own tongue off as the machine twisted and bucked across the swamp. Up ahead, he could make out crowds of people cheering from the causeway as they headed for the finish line. And then he saw it. Rising out of the swamp like some prehistoric monster.

"Look out!" He yelled to Chilly, but it was too late. There was a dull thud as the Camaro smashed into it, spun one eighty, and rocked sideways onto two wheels before miraculously righting itself and coming to a lopsided halt. The rest of the field roared past. Chilly sagged back into his seat.

"Dammit, we just lost an axle—and the race!"

Duke stared at him, grinning ruefully. "Axle? We just hit a damn horse."

FOUR

LONDON, ENGLAND – 1888

A PAIR OF horses tugged at their harnesses in front of the carriage. Its shining black coachwork and dark velvet curtains reflected the wealth of its owner. It was parked behind a four-story Georgian house on Cleveland Street. The horses snorted vapor into the freezing night air and pawed the ground impatiently. The normal street bustle had subsided as night fell, and a blanket of virgin snow now coated the grimy streets. Pale yellow light spilled from the upper windows of the house, illuminating the snowflakes swirling past the carriage.

Nearby, Mary Jane Kelly, a young prostitute with blonde hair and a face that had not yet lost its innocence, huddled against the cold. She'd taken shelter in the alleyway behind Cleveland Street, hoping to pick up some trade from the house's occupants when they left later in the evening. The establishment, known as "the club," was frequented by people of high standing and had a reputation built on total discretion. She stamped her feet on the freezing ground and rubbed her hands together as she tried to get some circulation going. Mary had never envisioned herself in such a situation, but fate had dealt her few cards and none of them were of much value.

She had been blessed with good looks and a blossoming figure, and with that being her only advantage, life led her down the obvious path. She remembered the gray, damp weather on the day she'd left

Limerick, her home in Ireland. Along with her six brothers and her sister, she'd set off on the long journey across the sea to Wales. There, she'd met a kind man, a coal miner, and was married at sixteen. But two years later she found herself a widow when he was killed in a pit explosion. With no money and no way to support herself, she and her sister had drifted into prostitution on the streets of Cardiff. The life was hard and the money available in such a run-down area was poor. She managed to learn the basics of reading and writing when a customer of hers had offered to teach her in exchange for her more carnal skills. She'd heard tales of vast sums to be made in London and out of desperation had taken the risk and moved to the city's West End.

With the advantage of her still-fresh looks, she was able to get work with a French madame in Knightsbridge. Within a few months she'd met a wealthy client who told her she could earn enough money to set up her own business if she moved to Paris, and had offered to pay for her passage. At first, things seemed to go well, and with her looks and lilting Irish accent, the customers were more than happy to pay a little extra. Soon she had earned enough to rent a small apartment in the Montmartre district, and made plans to become the madam of her own establishment.

Excited with the thought of her new venture, she went to Le Chat Noir, a nearby nightclub, to see if any girls were interested in joining her new business. She had stayed late, watching the cabaret, marveling at the amazing shadow play of Henri Rivière. But when she returned home in the early hours of the morning, she walked into a nightmare. Her apartment had been ransacked. All her money was gone. She later discovered that her benefactor had become jealous of her success and set out to ruin her. Penniless once again, she had no choice but to leave Paris and return to London. Things hadn't improved while she was away. There were now so many Irish immigrants in the East End that it was known as "Little Dublin." She switched to her Welsh accent to stand out from the other prostitutes and changed her hair color and name more times than she cared to remember.

The black carriage with the dark velvet curtains was now the only one remaining at the rear entrance. The driver dozed in his seat, face muffled behind his cloak to keep out the cold. Inside the carriage, a man leaned forward and drew on a cigarette. The light from outside caught his face, revealing an aquiline nose and dark, intelligent eyes. Even sitting, he had an alert quality and a military bearing. He was a man of action, used to taking decisive steps to control situations. Sitting in the cold, babysitting the rich and privileged while they indulged in their sordid habits didn't please him at all. He'd joined the Secret Service a few years back, when protecting members of the royal family had assumed national importance. Since the Fenians had started their campaign of violence against the British people, the undercover work of the service had grown considerably. Once absorbed into the service he became a code name, and he was now referred to only as Triton.

He had caught Queen Victoria's eye years earlier, when, as an Irish Special Branch officer under William Melville, he had infiltrated the Fenian Brotherhood and prevented an assassination attempt on the royal family. He'd learned of a plan to attack the royal yacht *Victoria and Albert II,* with the queen and prince on board. With a crew of 240, there would have been a catastrophic loss of life had the Fenians succeeded.

The Fenian Brotherhood had been funding John Holland, an Irish teacher based in Cork. He was developing a new kind of submersible weapon. He'd submitted his first design to the Royal Navy in 1875, but they had turned it down as unworkable. The Fenians, however, continued to fund his experiments until in 1881 the first submarine, nicknamed "the Fenian Ram," was launched. Triton had been undercover in the organization for just over six months when he learned of their conspiracy. They'd planned to fill the craft with explosives and dive below the royal yacht before detonating it beneath the hull.

The plan required a suicide team. There was no time for Triton to alert his superiors. He had to make the decision on his own. He'd volunteered for the mission and was accepted along with two other Fenians. Once below the surface, he overpowered the other crew members and surfaced next to the yacht, where the Fenians were arrested. As a result of his bravery, he'd been awarded the George Cross and become one of the queen's favorites.

Looking after Victor Albert, or "Eddy," the Duke of Clarence, was now something he couldn't avoid. The duke, described as "abnormally dormant" by some members of the royal family, had proved to be a loose cannon. Triton leaned back into the shadows as a group of men and women left the club. His mind may have been dormant, Triton thought, but Eddy made up for his lack of mental activity in other departments. He'd been to the Cleveland Street club three nights already that week, and Triton had to admire the duke's stamina.

He'd waited for Eddy outside brothels before, but this one was different. Triton was well aware that all forms of sexual depravity took place behind those expensive and discreet doors. Once, while incredibly drunk, the duke had told him that though he was as red blooded as the next man, he got a bit of a thrill watching men with men, especially if he was entertaining a woman at the same time. Being with prostitutes was something that society could gloss over. But even a whiff of homosexuality could be the kiss of death to the royal family's reputation. It was a situation that couldn't continue, and Queen Victoria had expressed her concerns to Triton personally.

He pulled out his fob watch and checked the time. Eddy had already been in there for two hours; surely he wouldn't be much longer.

Mary jerked awake. Her fingers numb from the cold, she fumbled with her buttons and wrapped her coat closer around her. The back door of the club burst open, sending light spilling across the street. A barking laugh echoed through the night. Mary would have recognized that laugh anywhere. It was Fay's. Mary had known Fay back when she was a common little tart working the streets. Irish born, with a mane of curls that cascaded down her back in a chestnut waterfall, translucent skin and emerald-green eyes, she'd become a big hit with the toffs.

Fay stood swaying in the brightly lit doorway. Behind her Mary caught a glimpse between two open doors, before the inner door was slammed shut. But in those few seconds Mary was afforded a glimpse into another world. A world of fine wines on silver trays, naked men and women coiled against each other like Greek statues. The flash of decadence was so quick it felt like an illusion, but Mary knew this was one of the busiest brothels in London, and the most expensive. Fay kissed the man who clung to her as they exited the club. And then he turned toward the light. He had sensitive features and a neat, waxed mustache. Fay had hit the jackpot; the man she was with was Eddy, the Duke of Clarence, heir to the throne of England.

Triton extinguished his cigarette on the floor of the carriage. It was time. The couple staggered out into the crisp night air, and the door closed behind them. He watched as they lingered on the steps. A shadow detached itself from the darkness and flew across the road, an arm raised against the light. Triton saw the glitter of steel as it scythed through the air, sweeping in an arc, plunging into the woman's soft flesh, again and again. Triton was out of the carriage in a flash, his gun drawn. But by the time he reached the duke, the assailant had vanished into the night. Eddy stood there, stunned. The woman lay on the soft white mantle of snow, now stained crimson beneath her. The light faded from her emerald eyes, and she was gone. Triton moved quickly.

"This way, Your Grace." He dragged Eddy by the arm. The duke looked down at the pale figure at his feet.

"Why?" he wailed. Triton kept him moving.

"You have to get away from here, for the sake of the nation."

The duke strained to tear away from him. "Damn the nation! We need to help her. For God's sake, man!" His lower lip trembled, his eyes bright with tears. "I loved her, we were going to—" He stopped abruptly at the look in Triton's eyes, nodded, and climbed into the carriage, his face a mask of pain.

Triton pursed his lips and whistled sharply. There was the clatter of horses' hooves, and another carriage came into view. Two men jumped out carrying a heavy blanket. They ran over to Fay's body, wrapping the blanket around her and hefting her up and over to the cab's open door. They laid her inside before climbing in and slamming the door behind them. The carriage thundered off into the night.

Triton always made a point of having two carriages available when he was on any kind of surveillance or babysitting duties. On several occasions he'd had to use one as a decoy while he made his escape with his charge in the other. Triton headed toward the remaining carriage and spoke to the driver.

"Paddington Station, as quick as you can." The driver nodded and took up the slack on the reins. Triton jumped into the carriage. Eddy was slumped in the corner, his eyes red and swollen, tears running down his cheeks. Triton squeezed his shoulder.

"Sir, we're going to Paddington. You'll go to Windsor on the night train. No one must know you were in London tonight." Eddy stared at him, struggling to focus, still absorbing the horror of the attack. Triton had a hat and a cloak in the carriage, and with a pair of glasses and a scarf, he was confident he could get Eddy across the platform and into the train unnoticed. Triton produced the cloak and slipped it around Eddy's shoulders.

"I'm sorry, sir; there was nothing we could do. She's gone. If anybody had seen you—" He left the statement hanging, because as the carriage clattered away from the club, he saw something move in the alleyway next to it. A pale face framed by blonde hair. His eyes met Mary's as the carriage swept past, and he knew from the look on her face that she'd seen everything.

FIVE

LONDON, ENGLAND – 1888

"COMPLICATED. HOW COMPLICATED?" Victoria said, her eyes narrowing. They sat facing each other in the plush velvet interior of the royal carriage in a quiet mews near the palace. Though it was dark outside, Triton could see the silhouettes of the armed peelers he knew to be guarding the entrance to the street.

"Eddy was badly shaken up by the event, as you'd expect. I don't think he'll be revisiting the habits that have recently given you such concern, Your Majesty." He paused.

"And?" Queen Victoria said. Her eyes fixed on his. She sensed this was only part of the news that was coming.

"Unfortunately the incident was witnessed."

Victoria nodded. She'd guessed there was a problem.

"By whom?" she asked.

Triton took a slow breath. "A street girl."

Victoria shifted in her seat. "A prostitute?"

"Yes."

"Go on."

"My agents followed her, so we know where she lives…" Victoria waited. "She has some friends."

Victoria knew what that meant. Gossip was habitual among the lower classes.

"How many?"

"Four." He went on, "Obviously we can control the situation . . ." He looked at Victoria for acquiescence.

Her voice adopted a steely tone. "You can skip the podsnappery with me. I'm not some asinine politician. I'm your Queen."

"I'm sorry, Your Majesty. Only sometimes it's best we don't involve you in the more base issues of national security."

She shook her head.

"They may be worthless to you, but if you intend to murder five women for being in the wrong place at the wrong time and gossiping, that's something I can't and won't condone."

"I understand, Your Majesty. But should news of the incident and Eddy's involvement spread . . ." He left his statement open for Victoria to draw her own conclusions.

"I know. Public disgrace for Eddy, political dynamite for the Fenians, and irreparable damage to the monarchy."

"It's a very real possibility, Your Majesty," Triton said.

Victoria shifted in her seat. The night air wasn't doing her aching legs any favors. Triton saw the pain flicker across her face. He reached over and handed her a thick blanket. She nodded thanks and draped it over her knees.

"I've had a very successful reign so far, and should you 'control' the situation and were the results of your actions to come out—and trust me, they eventually will—what do you think history will remember me for?" Victoria said.

Triton nodded. "The murder of five innocent women to protect the reputation of the monarchy."

"Exactly," the Queen replied. "I understand the situation has to be dealt with. I just want you to do it in a way that will enable me to sleep at night and history to view me favorably." She fixed him with a stare. "Do you think you can do that?"

Triton's mind had been racing from the second he'd realized that Victoria wasn't going to go with his original plan. And he was quite sure that something that had already proved itself could be successfully employed on a larger scale.

He leaned forward.

"I think I may have a solution that will satisfy Your Majesty."

Victoria smiled. "Good. I rather hoped you would."

"It will require considerable resources."

She looked at him. "Rewriting history is always expensive. But, as is usual in affairs of the state, to hell with the cost."

Triton gave her a smile of relief and sank back into the heavy velvet seats. But inside his head, he was anything but relaxed.

SIX

SPIRIT'S SWAMP, LOUISIANA – Present day

DUKE NURSED A flask of coffee as the winch whined. The morning mist hung like a yellow shroud on the surface of the swamp as the sun rose behind it. The divers gave the thumbs-up for the crane to swing its load across to firm ground. The corpse of a horse already lay on a tarpaulin spread out on the causeway. Perfectly preserved by the mud, it looked like it was sleeping. The visibility in the heavily polluted swamp was so poor, they'd had to drag the area, working by feel, to locate anything at all.

The crane took up the slack as two large wooden spoked wheels rose out of the water, followed by an old Victorian carriage with a wooden chest strapped to its back. The empty stays where the horses had been harnessed were still in place. Duke watched as the whole thing swung through the air and was lowered down onto the causeway. Chilly munched through his third Twinkie of the morning and gestured to the carriage.

"I'm guessing we ain't gonna find this in no vehicle database." He dragged out his syllables in a deep Southern drawl.

Duke took a slug of his coffee, wiped his lips.

"Nope. Been all kinds of shit coming out of the swamps since Katrina and the rest ripped through these parts." Sadness flashed behind the eyes in his amiable face and then, as quickly, was gone.

He watched as one of the officers struggled to pry open the carriage door with a crowbar. Encrusted with weeds and swamp mud, it resisted his best efforts.

Chilly finished off the last piece of his Twinkie and looked over at the dripping carriage.

"How long do you reckon that's been in there?"

Duke shook his head. "I'd say this has gotta be over a hundred years old."

Chilly let out a low whistle. "Jeez, how come that horse ain't a damn skeleton?"

Duke smiled; this was something he knew about.

"It's to do with the swamp mud. The acidity in it preserves things, halts the natural decay—I gave a talk on it a while back."

Chilly inclined his head. "No shit."

The carriage door burst open. Black mud and wriggling fish spewed out onto the ground. The officer peered inside and recoiled. He turned his face toward Duke, his expression more eloquent than words.

"You need to take a look at this, Duke," he said.

Duke ambled over and looked inside the carriage. Inside were five mummified corpses, entwined by roots. A grotesque human sculpture.

SEVEN

LONDON, ENGLAND – Present day

CHANDLER LOOKED OUT AT the rows of intent faces staring back at him as he neared the end of his lecture. The usual mix of police cadets and Ripper fans had crowded the lecture room at New Scotland Yard. His talk, "The Future of Crime: Learning from the Past," always pulled in a good crowd. On a large screen behind him, a 3-D facial-modeling program cloaked a skull with cyber flesh. Chandler waited for it to finish before turning back to the audience.

"So, to sum up: this type of reconstruction, combined with advanced DNA techniques, enables us to solve cold cases from decades ago, and the boundaries of science are continually being broken. It may be possible in the future to go back hundreds of years and get posthumous convictions. Any questions?"

A bright-eyed cadet flung his hand skyward. Chandler nodded at him.

"Do you think the police forces of today could have caught Jack the Ripper?"

Chandler smiled; it was a perennial question and one he had learned to vary his answers to. Today he went with one of his favorites.

"There's still time." He was glad it got a ripple of laughter.

Another hand shot up. "Who do you think it was?"

He paused. “Good question. Never been asked that before.” More staccato laughter. Chandler continued. “But seriously, I don’t think there is any conclusive proof that it was the work of one man—or even one Jill the Ripper.”

A Japanese tourist gabbled excitedly. “How come police never catch Ripper with so many suspects?”

“There are many theories,” Chandler said. “Some people think that the police may have actually interviewed the murderer but never knew they had him in their grasp. After all, they had no DNA back then, or even fingerprinting. It wasn’t until 1905 that the US military adopted the use of fingerprints as identifying markers, and it was some time after that before the police began to use them.”

A tall American with a Texan accent butted in. “I heard he was some kind of snake oil salesman, passing himself off as a doctor.”

Chandler nodded. “That was one theory—the police followed a Dr. Francis Tumblety to New York, but they didn’t have enough evidence to extradite him.”

Another cadet jumped in. “I read it was a member of royalty, so they couldn’t arrest him.”

You set them up, I’ll knock them down, Chandler thought as he answered.

“Eddy, the Duke of Clarence. It’s a popular misconception—he was at Balmoral Castle when the murders took place.”

A geeky-looking individual with a mop of unkempt curly hair waved a chocolate bar in the air. Chandler pointed to him. “Man with lunch in his hand.”

The geek smiled. “If they never caught the Ripper, then that means his ancestors could still be walking among us. They may even have inherited his unpleasant habits.” He sat down, looking pleased with himself.

Chandler didn’t really want to start a long discussion. He was feeling tired and hungry and was looking forward to lunch.

“I imagine that’s a possibility. But you would need to know the real identity of Jack the Ripper to follow his or her familial DNA back through a hundred years of history. And as we don’t know that, then there’s as much chance that you’re related to the Ripper as there is for anybody else." There was laughter at the geek's expense, and a few people made knife-slashing gestures in his direction. Chandler felt a mixture of guilt and satisfaction at shutting him down. But lunch was lunch.

A female cadet waved her hand. He nodded at her and she beamed.

"You must have a theory; after all, you're writing a book on it. Who do you think did it?"

Chandler switched off the projector. "My family has spent the last century trying to answer that, and I'm not quite there yet."

The girl smiled sweetly, packed up her books. "So there's still a chance it's Jill the Ripper?"

Chandler shrugged. "Anything's possible."

EIGHT

BUTTE LA ROSE, LOUISIANA – Present day

DUKE AND CHILLY watched as the forensic team wrestled with the large copper-bound wooden chest that had been roped to the back of the carriage. Their base of operations was an old abandoned refrigeration warehouse on the outskirts of Baton Rouge off the I-10, near Butte La Rose. Duke had pulled some strings and stretched his discretionary budget by getting some criminology students to work on the case during their spring break. Two of the assistants lowered the chest to the floor, levered the lid open, and tilted it. The contents spilled out onto the plastic sheeting spread across the floor: sodden clothes, shoes, a hatbox, some cheap jewelry, and a small wooden box.

One of the assistants, a mousey-haired girl, carefully prized the box open. Inside was an oilskin-wrapped bundle secured with a piece of string. She cut the string, unwrapped the parcel, and found a leather-bound diary, a collection of envelopes, and some old photographs. They were damp and showed signs of deterioration. The assistant looked up at Duke. "We'll have to stabilize these."

Duke looked down at the envelopes. "Is that copperplate writing?"

She nodded. "I'd say these are from the late Victorian era and from England."

"How do you know that, er . . . ?" He struggled to remember her name.

She smiled. "Emily."

Duke nodded. "Emily."

She pointed to the small, faded red stamp on the corner of one of the envelopes. "This is an English jubilee-issue stamp." She tapped the silhouette of a woman in the middle of the stamp. "That's Queen Victoria, and the four-and-a-half-pence stamp was first printed in 1892."

Duke looked at her. "I'm impressed."

Emily flushed. "My dad was a philatelist. My mother came from England, and he wanted to impress her, so he learned all about her country's stamps."

Duke chuckled. "And did it work?"

Emily grinned. "They're still together."

Duke looked more closely at the back of the envelope.

"So we have a rough time frame?"

"The stamps were in circulation from 1892 till the end of the century. Once we've been able to stabilize the envelopes, the letters inside may give us a more accurate date." She paused, pulled out a magnifying glass. "It's faint, but I can make out the postmark." She squinted at the marking. "Yes. This was posted from East London on the tenth of September 1889."

Duke nodded. "That's great. So we have a good timeline."

Emily nodded. "Yes."

Duke pointed at the faded writing on the back. "Does that say 'Dr.'?"

Emily peered through the magnifying glass. "It looks like 'Dr.,' yes." She studied it closer. "The surname looks like 'Tumblety.' We'll get a clearer view once the chemicals have done their work."

Duke rubbed his face. The coarse stubble reminded him he hadn't shaved in a while. "Good, thanks Emily," he said. "I know someone who's going to be mighty interested in what we have here. Let me know when you have any more detail from the letters."

"Sure thing," Emily said, carefully placing the envelopes and the diary into plastic bags and sealing them before turning back to Duke.

"How do you think these women got here?"

Duke shook his head. "Beats me."

Emily paused. "There was a big storm out here, wasn't there—around that time?"

Duke turned, looked at the other assistants, pallbearers to the five mummified remains, as they carefully carried the twisted corpses over to a workbench.

"They called it the Evil Wind. Swept across these parts on the second of October 1893. At the time it was the second-largest hurricane ever recorded in Louisiana. Over two thousand people lost their lives. There was nothing that deadly until Katrina hit us in 2005."

Emily studied him. "You know a lot about storms."

Duke's eyes grew distant. "Far more than I ever wanted to know."

Emily nodded and headed off with the envelopes and diary.

Duke watched as she went back to work, full of enthusiasm, young and bright, with her whole life ahead of her. Julie, his wife, had been like that, before Katrina hit.

When the storm came, he'd been inside their house, packing their most valuable possessions into boxes, getting ready to leave. It was unusual for them to have time off together. She worked in the local school, and as a deputy he was on shift patterns that usually meant they missed out on weekends together. But with the approaching storm and mass evacuations taking place, neither of them was at work that day.

It had been barely a week since Julie had been to the hospital for her second-trimester ultrasound scan. They'd both decided that they wanted to know the sex and were overjoyed to learn that she was expecting a baby girl and everything was going well. They had spent weeks deciding on names, and prior to the scan, had settled on Jimmy if it was a boy, and Gemma for a girl. Duke had already redecorated the spare room and made extra space by shifting his collection of old guitars into the garage. He paused from packing for a moment, and wondered if he dared hope the storm might miss them, or whether he should face the possibility that they could lose everything.

He looked out of the window and saw Julie. She was collecting roses in an old wicker basket. She'd nurtured the rosebushes since they moved in and was determined to take some clippings and the last of the current blooms before the storm hit. Duke had wanted to leave immediately, but Julie had persuaded him to wait. She felt the risk of being caught up in a mass panic was worse than waiting to see which way the storm was going. The governor had still not committed to a full-scale evacuation, and so she thought they were doing the right thing. From his time in the force, Duke knew it was always a hard decision when people's safety and money hung in the balance. If you ordered an evacuation and people were injured or killed in the panic, and the storm changed direction, then you were hung out to dry by the press. Conversely, if you did nothing and people died in the storm, you were held responsible.

Duke had kept the TV on while he packed, and nothing on the news made him feel anything other than worry. There was talk of jammed freeways, while the hurricane was upgraded to a category five, and the mayor of New Orleans had called for an evacuation.

It grew darker inside the sitting room, and the automatic nightlights in the garden flicked on. Duke looked out of the window. The sky had turned black; it was as if night had arrived early. Julie's face was a pale smudge next to the lurid red of her roses. She looked up at him. He signaled for her to come in, as a sudden feeling of dread swept over him. Then a roaring sound surrounded the house. He saw the persimmon tree at the edge of the yard was now bent over in a ferocious wind. Duke ran to the back door, yelling for Julie. She strained toward him, still determinedly hanging on to her roses with one hand while clinging to the tree with her other. She shouted something at him, but he heard nothing above the wind. In the days that followed, he'd convince himself that she had been saying, "I love you."

He heaved at the door handle, but before he could get it open there was a tremendous crash as the tree tore free and slammed into the back of the house, blocking the door to the garden. And then it hit.

A wall of gray water smashed into the house, and the windows exploded. Their glass shards peppered the room, cutting Duke's face with their needle-sharp edges. The power died, and the water was up to his waist in seconds. It surged through the house, sweeping furniture and possessions out through the broken windows and into the raging torrent outside. Duke desperately shouted for Julie, but the force of the wind drowned out his cries. The water kept rising, and soon he was struggling to keep his footing. He half walked, half swam to the stairs, pulling himself clear of the swirling water that churned through the sitting room. He remembered news reports from other storms of people reaching their attics and chopping their way through the roofs of their houses. If he could do that, maybe he'd be able to see where Julie was and get to her.

He reached the top of the stairs and pulled the attic ladder down from the hatch. He climbed up through the open trapdoor and fumbled for the flashlight he kept near the hatchway. He found it, switched it on, and swept the beam around until he located a large metal toolbox to one side of the opening. Inside was a pile of rusty tools. He grabbed a claw hammer and frantically smashed at the insulation on the underside of the roof. He managed to create a small opening and began to widen it, punching through the shingles to access the roof. Eventually he had a hole big enough to pull himself up through.

The wind was ferocious. He screamed Julie's name, but his voice was snatched away by the wind. The water surged past the second story and was soon climbing above the guttering. Where the yard had been, there was nothing but foaming water. The persimmon tree lay jammed against the door, the water rushing past it. He glimpsed a flash of red in the distance. A basket of roses. A crimson blob in the muddy torrent. But there was no sign of Julie. Bracing his feet against the jagged opening in the roof, he pulled his cell phone out of his pocket. The network was down. He looked around him. There was nothing but water for miles. Flooded cars and trucks, their roofs barely visible, were swept past in the surging water.

For two days he clung to the roof, existing on rainwater and some dry cereal he had stored in the attic. And then the helicopter came.

Duke hunted for weeks after the storm had passed, checking every shelter and hospital that had survived in the surrounding areas, even searching through the hordes of people sheltering at the Superdome in New Orleans.

He never saw Julie again.

NINE

LONDON, ENGLAND – Present day

CHANDLER LET HIMSELF into the cramped basement flat he'd inherited from his father. Every available shelf was crammed with research and materials that he had yet to organize. Books were piled against the sides of the narrow hallway and threatened to topple over each time he squeezed by. He knew that if his wife had been alive, she would never have allowed things to get this out of hand. He went into the small box room that served as a study. An untidy pile of paper sat on a table, a manuscript: JACK THE RIPPER: MONSTER OR MYTH? by Chandler Travis and Peter Travis.

More piles of research notes spilled onto the floor next to a laptop. A thin film of dust clung to the screen, a nagging reminder that he hadn't written for a while. One wall was festooned with laminated newspaper clippings from 1888, all of them about Jack the Ripper. Another wall was covered with modern-day magazine articles and Internet printouts, all of them offering different theories about the Ripper's identity. A sheet of cardstock with a hand-drawn family tree stretching back to the 1800s was pinned on one wall. It had lots of question marks and frustrated crossings-out.

Since his father had died, far too soon, from a particularly pernicious form of cancer, the flat had remained untouched. Travis had promised himself he would sort things out, spread his father's possessions between the various charities, secondhand bookshops, and recycling bins. But a sort of creeping malaise had set in. He moved a buff folder marked "MEDICAL RECORDS" along the desk to create some space. Some pages spilled out and he picked them up. There were letters from the specialist, details of blood tests, requests for more tests, as well as all the usual illegible scrawled notes and referrals. He didn't know why he hadn't binned all of the records a long time ago. Maybe it was just too final.

He stacked the folder on top of some other papers and switched on his laptop. The dusty screen flared to life. The mouse arrow winked reproachfully at him halfway down a page. He stared at it for a moment, then headed for the kitchen. He procrastinated by making himself a cup of fresh coffee. He liked to grind the beans himself; that was at least one thing he could control. He tapped the power button on an iPod dock that sat on a nearby window ledge: a small concession to the twenty-first century. He'd needed to make space for more research, and the shelves full of CDs had to go. His fingers hovered over "Play," then landed. The flat filled with the eerie opening chords of the Beatles' "I Am the Walrus."

Before he'd gone into the hospital, his father had played it a lot. Chandler had heard it first thing in the morning and last thing at night when he'd stayed overnight in the flat caring for his father. He'd thought that at some point it might mean something to him like it obviously did to his father. But so far, nothing had materialized. He finished making the coffee and carried the mug back to the study, squeezing himself again between the books.

He took a sip from the steaming mug of coffee, wiped the dust from the laptop screen with his sleeve, and looked around at the piles of notes strewn about. The family had inherited some of them from Chandler's great-great-grandfather, Edward Richard Travis, who'd been a cub reporter at the time of the Ripper's murders. The fragments of notes they had managed to unscramble always alluded to some great artifice perpetrated by the British government during Queen Victoria's reign. Chandler was convinced Edward had removed some of his notes and stored them somewhere for safe-keeping. Wherever that was had remained a mystery. His father was convinced that Edward had a personal connection to the Ripper case but could never find any proof of it.

After the murder spree ended, Edward went to America and struck up a relationship with a woman, who gave birth to a son and a daughter. The only information Chandler had concerned the daughter, Evelyn Travis, born in Louisiana in 1889. She'd traveled to England in 1914, fallen in love with a soldier, and become pregnant. But before the baby was born, Evelyn's lover was called up and lost his life at the front. Unmarried, Evelyn kept the name Travis and gave birth to a boy, John, who married and produced a son, Peter, Chandler's father. Meanwhile, documents from the Ministry of War showed Edward had been a correspondent for them. After the war, he returned to America and worked in New York as a columnist for the *Times*, giving an Englishman's perspective on American politics.

During all this time, Edward continued to pursue his obsession with Jack the Ripper until his death in 1946. An old trunk filled with his papers and notes had remained in the Louisiana side of the family, unopened until it made its way back to Peter in the UK. Chandler had enjoyed writing and researching the book with his father, but as Peter became too ill to continue, the project had ground to a halt. Even though he'd promised his father he would finish the book alone, he hadn't made much progress. Travis knew deep inside why that was: Claire, his wife.

She'd wanted the flat cleaned up and the boxes of notes and books put into storage to create room for a nursery. Ultimatums had been levied. Either the boxes went or . . . they'd still been simmering from a particularly nasty quarrel that morning. It had been her thirtieth birthday. Once again, the discussion about time passing and the ticking clock caused tempers to flare. Chandler's plans for their special birthday meal had hung in the balance.

He'd dropped Claire off at King's Cross on his way to work, her face cold and stiff to his peck on the cheek, neither of them willing to back down. He knew that by the evening she would have thawed out, and that perhaps with a bottle of wine and a good meal in their favorite restaurant they could reach a compromise; he could move some books around and show some enthusiasm for the nursery.

Then, just as he got into work, his cell phone rang. A terrorist bomb had ripped through the early-morning commuters' train, between Liverpool Street and Aldgate. Claire's normal route. His blood ran cold at the news.

But in one of those ironies that he would replay over and over again, Claire had rung him to say she'd missed her train. Above the screaming and the chaos, she told him she was catching a bus. She was heading home. She was safe.

Traffic was already a nightmare as Chandler made his way through the backstreets in an effort to avoid the jams and get to Claire sooner. His phone rang again. There'd been an explosion in Tavistock Square, minutes from where he was. A bus had been blown up: another suicide bomber, they thought. Every available member of the force was being pulled in. Immediately, Chandler rang Claire's cellphone. It went through to her voice mail. He tried again, and this time the network was down. He abandoned his car and ran the last few hundred yards toward the flaming wreckage of the bus. Its roof had been torn off. People were still trapped inside.

Claire had told him the number of the bus she was on. She'd only mentioned it because it was the same as her age on that day. As he raced toward the bus he saw its number, and his heart stopped. The smoking remains of the roof had been thrown across the road, but the number on the front of it was still visible, and it seared into his brain. Number 30.

Ignoring the shouts of the emergency services, he flashed his warrant card, pushed past them, and ran toward the smoking steel skeleton of thc bus. The passengers in the back had taken the brunt of the blast. There was hardly anything left of them. His nostrils took in the smell that he would never forget as long as he lived. His eyes searched the dark smoke. He felt his foot squash something soft. He looked down. It was an arm. But it was what the arm clutched that shook him to the core—a brightly colored carpetbag, just like the one he'd bought for Claire at Camden Market the week before.

His mind went into overdrive, spewing out protective thoughts. Lots of people probably had exactly the same bag. But then he saw the wedding ring on the finger . . . the ring that matched his.

Later he was told he'd run into the bus and torn at the red-hot metal with his bare hands. The responders had managed to drag him away from the smoking wreckage and took him to the nearby burns unit in the Royal London Hospital. He'd suffered second-degree burns, but the doctors told him he'd have minimal scarring. His mental wounds would take longer to heal.

Gradually his mind had found a way to cope. But now, sitting in the study, surrounded by his research and the accusing screen of his laptop, he knew that he'd either have to finish the book or give up on it entirely to find any kind of closure. He picked up the mug, drained the last of the aromatic brew, and wondered if he could delay things any more. A slice of toast . . . maybe a look at the papers. There was always a way to put aside the task at hand for another few minutes. He headed toward the kitchen and was staring at the bread crisping in the toaster when the phone rang.

TEN

LONDON, ENGLAND – Present day

BACK AT THE Black Museum, Chandler stared at the image on his computer screen. Duke Lanoix, an old friend of his, had rung from Louisiana with news and emailed him some photos. Chandler had raced over to the museum to view the images on their large screen. As usual, Jenny grabbed him a preemptive cup of coffee. She handed it to him as he downloaded the attachments in Duke's email.

"I haven't seen you this excited since you discovered that new brand of coffee."

Chandler smiled. "Duke's an old friend of mine. A deputy sheriff out in East Baton Rouge, Louisiana. He came to London to give a talk on the significance of polysaccharide in long-term body preservation a couple of years ago."

Jenny looked at the screen, put on an ironic expression of interest. "Mmm, I'm sorry I missed that. Sounds riveting."

Chandler grinned. "Do I detect a hint of sarcasm? We hit it off when I told him I could get tickets to Ronny Scott's. He's a jazz enthusiast, plays some himself, and as it turns out, he's a bit of a Jack the Ripper fan as well. Which is why he sent me this stuff as soon as he got it."

The screen filled with handwritten letters in a copperplate scrawl. Chandler tapped one of the pictures with his finger, pointed to the return address and the faded writing. "Do you recognize that name?"

Jenny smiled. "Of course I don't, but I'm guessing it's something to do with your favorite subject."

Chandler moved around the room, pulling down reference books, opening them, and comparing the writing in the photo to that in some of the books' illustrations. Jenny caught a tome that threatened to fall off the shelf as Chandler dragged more materials out. He flipped open another book.

"Look at the similarity in the penmanship." He pointed to the writing inside the book. Jenny looked at the spidery script.

"Didn't everybody write like that in those days?"

Chandler shook his head. "Only the educated. Literacy wasn't widespread back then."

Jenny looked at the picture accompanying the writing in the book. It showed a serious-looking man with a big walrus mustache. "Dr. Francis J. Tumblety? You think the letters are from him?" she said.

Chandler moved around the room, animated. "His name's on the return address, the handwriting matches. This is a big deal!"

Jenny nodded. "So this guy, Tumblety . . ."

Chandler hit "Print" and watched as the printer spewed the pictures into its tray.

"Tumblety was a quack, a man who pretended to be a doctor," he explained. "The police pulled him in for questioning, but they didn't have enough evidence to hold him. After he left London, he traveled between St. Louis and New Orleans. He was arrested at one point for trying to buy an exhibit from a museum."

Jenny flicked through the book. "What sort of exhibit?"

Chandler looked up from his printouts. "A human uterus."

Jenny pursed her lips. "And the police didn't think that was significant at a point when a serial killer was hacking prostitutes to death and cutting them open to harvest their reproductive organs?"

Chandler pulled down another folder, sending a cloud of dust billowing into the room. Jenny coughed and waved her hands as she tried to deflect the dust from the fresh mug of tea she had placed on the shelf.

Chandler smiled. "Sorry," he said. "We really should have a cleaner." Jenny covered the mug with the book she'd been holding.

"We did. She's probably still in here somewhere."

He pulled down another book. "Tumblety was writing some medical paper about growing a human fetus in vitro. He had some theory that a child could be conceived in an external womb. There were a lot of medical experiments carried out back then we wouldn't allow now: frontal lobotomies on the insane, unnecessary surgical sterilizations. There was a rumor, that he'd promised to send out a woman's uterus with each copy of his work."

Jenny wrinkled her nose in disgust. "That's some book promotion! Christ, I was happy with a plastic doll on the cover of my copy of *Jackie*."

Chandler smiled at her northern humor. "Apparently he had a collection of preserved ones he kept on display at his house in St. Louis."

Jenny shook her head. "You'd think that would be a bit of a warning sign, at least among his close friends . . . if he had any."

Chandler said, "Yes, it's not something that would pass unnoticed these days. When he died in 1903, he left a fortune in his will, so whatever he was doing, it paid well."

"Where did he get the money from?"

Chandler shrugged. "Nobody really knows. There are lots of theories. He was a bit of a con artist as well as a quack—"

"A sort of Victorian Dr. Shipman?" Jenny said.

"I guess so. He was also very charming, and a bit of a ladies' man," Chandler said.

Jenny stared at a photograph in one of the books. It was a graphic image of Mary Jane Kelly's mutilated body at Miller's Court. Jenny wrinkled her nose. "Looks like he had a great bedside manner." She snapped the book shut.

"So your friend, Duke, what else has he found that's got you so excited?"

Chandler flicked up some more pictures on the screen. "Well, along with the letters from Tumblety, they also found five female corpses, which they believe are from London." Suddenly, he had Jenny's full attention. She looked at the pictures on the screen—an old carriage being winched out of a swamp, along with various pictures of the corpses twisted together, cocooned by entwined roots.

"How on earth did they wind up in the swamp?"

Chandler looked at her, his eyes burning with determination. "That's what I intend to find out."

ELEVEN

LONDON, ENGLAND – 1888

EDWARD TRAVIS ALWAYS knew what he wanted to be when he grew up: a detective. He had an inquiring mind and, as a child, had sorely tried his father's patience with nonstop questions. His father had eventually hit on something to distract him. He read him stories. Edward had been enthralled, and he howled with frustration whenever his father came to the end of a story. His favorite author was Charles Dickens, and he'd devoured every book of his he could get his hands on. He loved the way Dickens weaved social commentary into his stories along with larger-than-life characters. Then he'd started reading newspapers. His plans to be a detective faded into the background as he reasoned that becoming a journalist was probably a better bet. After all, he could get paid to write, and it involved as much detective work to dig up a story as it did to solve a crime. Even at the tender age of fifteen, Edward was smart enough to work out it was also a lot safer being a reporter than it was confronting criminals down some dark alley.

He got his first job helping out on the printing floor of the *Evening Standard.* Sweeping up, making tea, and carrying the boxes of cast metal sorts from the typesetters to the compositors. He would also run errands for the editorial offices and absorb what was going on.

He soon learned which sort of stories the editors were interested in: stories of corruption and brutality in the police force, political stories, and articles concerning foreign policy. Royalty was another common topic, and if you could catch any of the high and mighty up to no good, then that was considered a scoop. But that didn't always mean the story would be run. Edward had seen many an article quashed by a small but powerful phrase: "Not in the public interest." He soon realized that the *Standard* wasn't going to give him the opportunities he needed, and that if he wanted to make his name, he would need to attach himself to a more prestigious publication. He applied for the job of cub reporter at the *Pall Mall Gazette* and was granted an interview with one of the editors. During the interview, the editor seemed distracted, and after some initial pleasantries and a few half-hearted questions, had promised he would send word if Edward had been successful in his application. Edward had thanked him for his time, and asked if he might be given a tour of the establishment. The editor promised to send someone down to show him around.

As soon as the editor had left, Edward set off on a tour of his own. Edward knew the editor wouldn't want to waste any time with him and would delegate the task to a junior. And that suited his plans perfectly. He'd seen enough offices to know that it was what the journalists were talking about that mattered, not their surroundings. He picked up a sheaf of paper and hurried down the corridor outside the office. Anybody who saw him would assume he was delivering copy to one of the editors. He headed toward the copy room and suddenly found himself following the familiar figure of Sir William Stead, the editor of the newspaper.

Stead was accompanied by George Monroe, the assistant police commissioner, and leading the way was a man with a military bearing and eyes that missed nothing. Edward dropped back, as if looking for a particular office. Stead had become a controversial figure after writing stories of white slavery and child prostitution. The controversy came from the fact that he'd actually arranged to buy a young teenage girl from her mother. This resulted in him being charged and serving time in jail. Whatever the men's meeting was about, Edward guessed it was just the sort of story he'd like to be involved in.

He turned around and bolted down the stairs leading to the basement. During his time at the *Standard*, he'd learned of some devices that could be used in entirely different ways to those envisaged by their inventors, and one of them was the Lamson pneumatic tube system.

TWELVE

LONDON, ENGLAND – 1888

CHIEF EDITOR W. T. STEAD paced his office. The newspaper was situated in an impressive four-story building that looked more like a palace than the home of the famous publication it housed, and Stead's office was clearly the throne room. A large leather-inlaid desk dominated the room and was surrounded by bookcases jammed with expensively bound first editions. An ornate and well-filled drinks cabinet stood to one side. Monroe sat opposite Stead's desk. The Lamson system—an impressive device for sending messages throughout the offices via tubes and air pressure—was installed on the wall in front of him. Monroe was a thick-set, intense-looking individual, and was not only the assistant police commissioner but also a secret agent and head of Section D, the political intelligence branch of the Criminal Investigation Department. Another man sat with his face in half shadow, smartly dressed and with a military bearing: Triton, secret agent to Queen Victoria.

Stead was furious, his face scarlet and sweating profusely, the veins pulsing in his forehead. He wiped his face with a sodden silk handkerchief.

"Do you have any idea what you are suggesting?"

Triton spoke with icy calm and absolute authority. "I am not suggesting anything. I am relaying a specific policy that you will be assisting us with—"

"Assisting!" Stead leaned over the desk, glaring at Triton. "Is that what you call it? It sounds like I don't have any options."

Triton steepled his fingers and fixed the editor with cold, appraising eyes. "That is the impression I meant to give."

Stead mopped his brow. "And if I choose not to assist you with your—policy?"

Triton motioned for to Stead to sit down. "Let me explain the reality to you."

"I'd be obliged to you, I'm sure."

Stead's sarcasm wasn't lost on Triton; nevertheless, the editor sat. Triton pulled out a small leather-bound pocket book, consulted it, and cleared his throat.

"Your publication appears to be a well-respected and profitably run business. However"—he ran his finger down a column of figures that filled one of the pages—"your latest bank position shows a deficit running at several thousand guineas—a condition your competitors might view as parlous, should they ever be appraised of the situation."

Stead sprang to his feet again. "How the hell do you know—?"

Triton fixed him with another icy stare. "Please sit down, Mr. Stead." The editor sat back in his chair, this time slumping like a deflated fairground balloon.

Triton continued. "Your involvement in the procurement of a thirteen-year-old girl for sale into prostitution as part of your research for an article was ill judged, and could, with the relevant testimony, still prove fatal to both your private and public life."

Stead looked up. "That's all dead and buried. I served my time for Eliza."

Triton shot him a thin-lipped smile. "Nothing remains buried if we wish to exhume it, Mr. Stead. We can bring witnesses forward who will crucify you. And believe me, there will be no resurrection."

Stead's face crumpled. Triton nodded. "I'll take your silence as acquiescence. Now, Assistant Commissioner Monroe, do you have any issues with our plan?"

Monroe leaned forward, cleared his throat. "I don't wish to be indelicate here"—he paused—"but the women, isn't there another way? Something . . . discreet?" Like all diplomats, he had a way of making the suggestion of cold-blooded murder seem like a mere implementation of policy.

Triton shot him a look. "I'm afraid not. Queen Victoria was quite insistent on that point. None of the women are to be harmed." Triton smiled. "Everybody clear now?"

Stead nodded. Monroe gave another cough, rubbed his hands together as if washing them clean of any responsibility.

"How do you know your plan will work? After all, it relies on the absolute discretion of a large number of people."

Triton fixed Monroe with eyes that missed nothing. "It will work because as an agent of her majesty's secret service, I have her full backing and all the resources necessary to ensure success. As to secrecy, the people involved have too much to lose were the truth to come out. Warren will not be commissioner for much longer—we'll see to that—and then the position will be yours. As a result of our endeavors, the police force will be adequately funded, properly staffed, and given the respect it deserves." Triton looked at their faces as they stared at him. "We have an opportunity here to change society, and to create some good from a tragic incident."

Monroe pulled at his collar like it was choking him. "I agree the force could do with all you are suggesting. It's just, well, if this ever got out . . ." He trailed off.

Triton straightened up in his chair. "The incident involving the Duke of Clarence was unfortunate. Had it not been witnessed by the Kelly girl and confided to her four friends, we could have controlled the situation."

Monroe nodded, licked his dry lips. "The Irish girl, Kelly. If the Fenians got wind of this, it would be a political catastrophe."

Triton nodded.

"One of the men assisting us is familiar with an area in Louisiana that should prove discreet enough for our purposes," Monroe said. "America is a big country. It's always a good idea to put as much distance as possible between a situation and the people connected with it."

Triton slipped his diary back into his pocket. "Quite. The Kelly girl will be the most sensational, our final performance, so to speak."

Monroe gave an embarrassed smile. "You sound like you're putting on a West End show."

Triton looked at him. "Indeed. 'All the world's a stage, and all the men and women merely players; they have their exits and their entrances.'"

Monroe nodded. "Shakespeare, *As You Like It*."

"Exactly," Triton said. "Only this time, we are in control. Their exits will be orchestrated and—well, you'll read about them in the papers."

Stead looked across at Triton as if suddenly realizing the depth of his involvement." For the love of God, this is insane!" he said.

Triton gave him a pitying look. "My dear William, you will be producing the copy of your life. You'll be notified of the time and the place, and given the most accurate details. Your paper will herald the birth of a new form of journalism, one that appeals to the masses. Your circulation will go through the roof, along with your bank account and personal fortune. You will, of course, be selling your soul."

Stead shook his head in disbelief. "Do you even have a conscience?"

Triton shrugged. "I save it for special occasions, and I never bring it out in matters of state."

Stead, quieted by Triton's certainty and commanding presence, calmed down. "Do you have a name for this phantasm?" he asked.

Triton stood up and moved toward the door. "I have some ideas."

Stead nodded. "Good. It helps to have an identity for the newsboys to bawl. And who will be, er, showcasing the work?"

Triton smiled. "I have a pair of likely candidates in mind."

Stead threw his sodden handkerchief into a waste bin. "And what about their trustworthiness? What's to stop them from selling their story to some other tabloid?"

Triton turned back toward the editor, his eyes glacial.

"Their fear of death, William. Their fear of death."

THIRTEEN

LONDON, ENGLAND – 1888

THE PNEUMATIC TUBES that sent messages shooting around the Gazette's building terminated in the basement. They filled a wall with rows of brass tubes capped by stoppers to maintain the air pressure. The system linked to offices throughout the building. In the gloom, Edward listened intently at an open brass tube marked EDITOR. The dim gaslight was reflected in his terrified eyes. Alert to the slightest sound, he strained to make sense of the conversation that was to change his life forever.

FOURTEEN

ST. LOUIS, MISSOURI – 1888

DR. FRANCIS J. TUMBLETY pulled his collar up against the chill of the evening wind and walked toward the Italianate townhouse on Hadley Street he called home. A few minutes' walk from Jackson Place Park and close to the port of St. Louis, its location suited his needs admirably. Amid the darkness of the park, he was able to indulge in the base acts that had nearly cost him his freedom on several occasions. He could still smell the sweat from the body of the young soldier whom he had recently bent to his needs, and didn't regret a cent of the goodly amount of coin he had lavished on him to slake his lust. He climbed the stone steps and let himself in through the wooden doors that led into the large entrance hall, then hung up his coat and headed down to the basement room. It had been used as a library by the previous owner and was ideally suited for his purpose.

He poured himself a drink and lit up one of his favorite Havana cigars. He let out a stream of pungent smoke and looked around. The walls of the room were shelved from floor to ceiling and displayed hundreds of glass jars containing the uteri of women, ranked by their class and age. Preserved by a bespoke embalming fluid he'd had made up by an apothecary, they still looked as fresh as the day they were harvested.

Collected from operating theatres, hospital morgues, and other sources he had managed to find, the uteri had become a fascination he never tired of. He had written many articles extolling his advanced medical theories—some of which he had submitted to *The Lancet*, all of which had been rejected. He had sent the publication countless sketches and descriptions concerning his work, and even though nothing of his was ever published, he saw no reason to give up on his research. For many years, he had believed that the process of reproduction could be carried out externally if only a reliable blood supply could be provided. He'd submitted diagrams along with his articles showing how a simple pump system might achieve that. The main problem he faced was that there wasn't a pump available with the accuracy of pressure needed. He'd had some thoughts on using animals to provide a temporary blood supply, but so far they had proved unsatisfactory. His blood boiled at what he saw as the male enslavement by the female species when it came to providing an heir. He was convinced that the act of birth could be achieved externally if his research work were properly funded by the Royal College of Surgeons.

But despite his constant submissions to various medical publications, no one took his suggestions seriously. He was convinced his theory was sound. And each rejection made him all the more determined to take his research to the next level.

He walked past the shelves and trailed his fingers against the cool glass of the jars, past the matrices of women from all walks of life. He reserved his hatred in particular for the uteri of the whores. His life had been blighted ever since he met a woman and fell hopelessly in love. He'd married her in haste, and for a while he was very happy. But he soon grew suspicious of her flirtatious nature, and had been devastated when he discovered she had once been a prostitute. One night he decided to follow her when she went out, and he saw her going into a brothel with a man. It was obvious she was still carrying on her filthy trade. From that day on, he swore never to trust his heart to another woman.

He took another pull on his cigar and studied one of the uteri. Placing his hand around the smooth glass container that housed it—so cool to the touch—he imagined the pleasure it would have given him to have hacked the organ from her body in revenge for her treachery. He owed it to the world to absolve mankind of the tyranny of women. As far as he was concerned, they were all whores and should be treated as such.

As he savored the idea, he thought he heard a muffled sound from the floor above. Maybe he hadn't secured the door sufficiently on the latch and it had been caught by the wind. He listened again. There was silence except for the distant sound of a horse and carriage clattering its way toward the port. He headed out of the room and up the small flight of stairs to the hallway. He saw a shadow in the street outside, visible through the front doors' stained-glass windows. It was soon followed by several more. There was no doubt: a group of people was standing outside his front door. He was about to go and open it when a discreet cough came from the front room. Someone was already inside the house!

He had a pistol in his study, but that was no use if some blaggard was already inside. A voice spoke from where the cough had come.

"If you were thinking of fetching your weapon, I can save you some time. It's in reasonable condition for a Thomas Fowler—and certainly very popular with the Fenians—but the main problem is that it rests in my hands and not yours."

Tumblety entered the room and found himself staring into the barrel of his own weapon. The man who sat in the shadows was in no hurry to show himself. Tumblety was angry and frightened, but he wasn't stupid enough to try anything when the odds were quite clearly stacked against him.

"Who are you, and what do you want?"

The man uncocked the pistol and laid it down on the desk. He reached across and turned up a small gas lamp on the side of the wall. With the light behind him and in Tumblety's eyes, he was a murky shape in the gloom.

"You will know me as Triton. My real name is of no issue." Triton waved a hand toward the chair in front of him. "Sit down. You may as well be comfortable while we talk business."

Tumblety relaxed slightly as he hesitantly took a seat opposite the man. It sounded like he wasn't in imminent danger—yet. Triton continued.

"Good. Now, let's just get a few things out of the way. We are fully aware that you are a murderer—"

Tumblety started to protest, but Triton held up a hand. "Please, don't insult my intelligence or that of my department by denying it. Your various remedies and professed medical skill have led to the sudden and unexplained death of many of your patients, so either you are a very bad doctor indeed, or it is part of your plan."

Tumblety leaned forward, straining to get a sight of the man in the chair.

"The behavior of the human body is not an exact science—we are still learning," he said.

The man in the shadows shook his head. "I don't disagree with that statement, but your learning comes at a high cost to your patients. The majority of those who have died have been female, and I'd wager a great many of their uteri are exhibited downstairs as part of a disgusting little display."

Tumblety said nothing. He could hardly deny the large number of specimens presently residing in his library.

"I think you would agree that your constant travel between Europe and America is not so much to facilitate your holiday or business arrangements as it is merely to keep ahead of embarrassing questions."

Tumblety acquiesced with a curt nod of the head.

"Good. Now we are getting somewhere. There's also the problem you have with your prurient sexual proclivities, for which you were recently arrested and charged with indecent behavior and indecent assault in Liverpool."

Tumblety shifted in his seat. "Merely a case of mistaken identity by some ruffians who wanted to cause me embarrassment."

Triton leaned forward, and for the first time Tumblety saw his face. He knew at once that he was looking at a man used to getting his way, and who could tell in an instant if he were lying. He felt his throat go dry and wished he had a drink in his hand. Triton's unblinking eyes stared at him.

"I think we both know that is a lie. My men have just witnessed your most recent adventures down at the park, and have secured a written statement from the young man involved."

Tumblety sagged in the chair.

"So to sum up, you are in a lot of trouble."

Tumblety felt the blood drain from his face. Whatever Triton wanted from him, he had no doubt at all he would be providing it.

"What do you want?" he asked. He heard the tremor in his own voice.

Triton continued. "You have a modicum of surgical skill, and some theories that might be considered highly dubious should they become common knowledge."

Tumblety straightened up in his chair. "My ideas are sound. I can't help it if I am ahead of the field in some specialist medical areas."

Triton leaned forward. "Maybe; they do say that genius is very near to madness. The problem is that the people who would condemn you are, sadly, not geniuses. Part of your predilection toward the collection of uteri is your need for revenge on the female species, on those who you believe have betrayed your trust."

Tumblety stood up. "What I do or do not believe is none of your damn business. What the hell do you want? Tell me now, or to hell with you!" He sat back down. He could feel the sweat on his face, and cursed himself for losing control.

Triton shook his head and affected an apologetic tone. "Oh dear, I do hope I haven't offended your sensibilities. The truth is, you married a prostitute—and as they say, once a prostitute always a prostitute. But you're not a man to forgive and forget, are you? You couldn't kill your own wife, so you channeled your hatred of her onto all women—and what better way to feel more in control than to collect their organs of procreation, the one thing man cannot achieve?"

Tumblety sat in silence. Triton continued, "But of course, you don't believe that, do you? I've read some of the articles you sent to

The Lancet and the Royal College of Surgeons. You actually think you can cut women out of the process."

Tumblety swallowed. His throat was parched, and a cold sweat ran down his back. Whoever this man was, he knew everything about him, right down to the smallest detail. Tumblety raised his hand and mimed a crushing motion with his fingers.

"She broke my heart."

Triton nodded. "And for that, you believe her kind must pay." He paused before leaning forward. "Imagine if there were a way for you to avoid the consequences of your past and recent crimes?"

Tumblety shook his head. Whatever was going on here, it had left him behind. "I don't understand."

"Of course you don't." Triton said. "But what we are proposing will allow you to be of service to queen and country whilst doing what you like best."

Tumblety managed to croak a reply through his dry lips. "Will I be working alone?"

Triton shook his head. "In some instances, yes, but we have another collaborator who, like yourself, has some problematic psychological issues." He reached across the desk and turned the lamp down before standing up and walking across the room to the door.

Tumblety turned to ask one more question. "How can you be sure that this other collaborator will agree to your demands?"

Triton looked back at him with his hand on the door handle.

"Well, sometimes you just have to give them enough rope."

And then he was gone.

FIFTEEN

LONDON, ENGLAND – 1892

DR. THOMAS NEILL CREAM felt the rough coolness of the rope as it slid past his left ear. He smelled the hemp and sensed its weight against his skin. The hangman was James Billington, chief executioner of England and Ireland, responsible for many high-profile hangings. As the rope was cinched tight around his neck, the doctor let his mind wander back over the events that had led to the grim fate that awaited him. He was guilty; there was no doubt about that. In fact he was proud of the number of women he had poisoned over the years, and especially happy that a good many of them were lowlife prostitutes. Though he had been born in the mean streets of Glasgow, he'd been raised on the outskirts of Quebec City, and graduated from McGill University in Montreal with a medical degree. He did his thesis on the effects of chloroform on patients and its possible uses in surgery. He soon learned that he could do exactly what he wanted to women by applying the right amount of the drug to a piece of cloth and then holding it over their mouths while they were drunk. As the body count grew, the police had given him a name: the Lambeth Poisoner. He'd laughed out loud as he read the newspaper reports about the murders, and how the police were baffled. Reading how little progress the police had made, he started to feel invincible. Emboldened by each new victim, he began to take chances, expanding his territory, operating in broad daylight rather than the darkness he'd favored . . . until one day, he made an inevitable and fatal mistake.

He'd been ordering a drink at the bar of the Ten Bells in Spitalfields when he'd overheard a man talking at a nearby table. While he waited for his ale, he learned that the man was Morgan Ogilvie, a detective from New York, in London to do some sightseeing. But he wasn't a normal tourist. He'd heard of the Lambeth Poisoner and was fascinated by the case. Cream went over and introduced himself to the man. He offered to give him a guided tour of where the various victims had lived.

It had given Cream a visceral thrill to point out the details and locations of the murders to someone who had no idea he was standing right next to the actual killer. After he had finished the tour, Cream bade Ogilvie farewell and walked away with a lightness of step and a smile on his face. But he soon realized he had made a serious error of judgment. Previously, he had tried to implicate two doctors he had taken a dislike to during his time at St. Thomas' Hospital medical school. They had mocked his Canadian accent, and he had promised himself he would make them pay. He'd poisoned Matilda Clover, a prostitute and heavy drinker, one night after a chance encounter down at the docks. He'd given her some whiskey dosed with poison and watched as she writhed in agony before breathing her last.

At the time, there was no suspicion that it was anything other than alcohol poisoning that had carried her off. But Cream still intended to exact his revenge with her death. He wrote anonymously to the police accusing the doctors of murdering her. The police dismissed the letter as rubbish, but it did get them thinking about Matilda's death. They had a postmortem carried out and found traces of strychnine poison. They added Matilda's death to the killings thought to be the work of the Lambeth Poisoner. And then they got a break. Ogilvie told an English policeman about Cream's detailed knowledge of the murders, and the policeman's suspicions were aroused. Scotland Yard put Cream under surveillance and soon noticed his habit of visiting prostitutes. It didn't take them long to learn of his conviction for poisoning a prostitute in the United States.

They wasted no time in arresting him, and once they'd discovered his many purchases of poison from local apothecaries, he was charged with Matilda's murder.

So there he stood, Dr. Thomas Neill Cream, alias the Lambeth Poisoner, the rough wood of the trapdoor beneath his feet and the noose around his neck. A guard guided him to the chalk mark scrawled on the surface of the trap, and the hood was placed over his head. He heard Billington moving around, making sure every detail was correct.

Cream had rehearsed the phrase he was going to shout before the drop dozens of times, and was sure he would be able to do it. But before he had time to compose himself, the trap opened and he hurtled through. He just managed to shout, "I'm Jack the Ripp—" as the noose snapped tight. And that's when he realized he was in real trouble.

The padded harness beneath his shirt was meant to have taken the strain of the steel cord woven through the hemp fibers. But now the rope was cutting into his throat, and he couldn't breathe. His vision swam as he fought desperately to draw air into his lungs. Then, just as he started to black out, he felt strong arms around his waist and the weight was taken off his neck. He fell to the floor as the sack was pulled back from his head. A face came into focus. It was Triton. The man behind his present predicament.

He'd offered Cream a deal that he couldn't refuse: either he did their bidding, or he would hang. Cream only realized later exactly what that entailed. Triton told him that they needed him to work on an enterprise of vital importance to queen and country. Cream had no loyalty to the Crown, but he did care to save his own skin. He would not only get to walk free but also be provided with a new identity and free passage out of the country. But right now he was just happy to be alive. Triton looked down at him.

"Sorry about that. The bracket supporting the steel safety line pulled free from its support. You'll have bruising to your neck, and some rope burns. But if you wear a support for a while, you'll be back to normal in no time." Cream sat up and winced as the pain lanced his neck. He gingerly explored the area with a finger, and tried moving his head from side to side. It hurt like hell. He looked up at Triton.

"I though you said it was foolproof?"

Triton smiled. "Well, obviously you're no fool."

He produced a newspaper. There was a picture of Cream on the front page and a headline: JACK THE RIPPER CONFESSES ON THE GALLOWS.

"You made the headlines."

Cream stared at the picture, confused. "How long have I been unconscious?"

Triton folded the paper. "Only a few seconds. This is just a test printing. It'll hit the streets tomorrow."

Cream laughed and instantly regretted it as pain seared through his throat. He croaked, "Well, I guess we just made history."

SIXTEEN

LONDON, ENGLAND – Present day

CHANDLER RUBBED THE sleep from his eyes. He'd been up half the night researching and going over the pictures Duke had sent. He must have nodded off at some point, because he'd woken to the smell of fresh coffee and found a mug steaming on the desk next to him. Jenny stood at his office door. She gave him a disapproving look.

"You need to get some sleep."

Chandler grunted and straightened his jacket. "I'll be fine."

Jenny smiled. "You might also want to sort your hair out."

Chandler ran an ineffectual hand through his tousled hair and caught sight of his reflection in the old Victorian pub mirror on the wall. He looked rough.

Jenny sniffed. "It also smells like a tramp's bench in here—quite an old tramp if I'm being honest."

"Okay, I'll have a shower and grab some breakfast."

Jenny produced a package wrapped in a paper napkin from behind her back like a conjuror pulling a rabbit out of a hat. "Thought you could do with one of Peggy's specials."

Chandler unwrapped the napkin to reveal a large and soggy bread roll. Peggy's breakfast buns from the police canteen were legendary. Filled with fried egg, sausage, bacon, and tomato, they were virtually impossible to eat without racking up a substantial cleaning bill. Chandler tucked into the messy concoction and mumbled his thanks. Jenny headed for the door before turning with Columbo-like precision.

"Oh, and just to give you fair warning: Harris is dropping in later."

Chandler grunted, his mouth too full of crispy bacon and greasy sausage to allow a full response. Jenny smiled at him and slipped out. Harris Jenson, his immediate boss, and an accountant at heart, saw the museum as an unnecessary sideshow and was constantly looking for ways to trim the budget. He was a saturnine character whose morbid atmosphere followed him around. He walked with a self-inflicted stoop, in constant fear of banging his head on the low ceilings of the old building, and what with Jenson's hangdog expression and pallid complexion, Chandler had always thought the man would have made an excellent mortician. Chandler finished his breakfast, topped up his coffee, and managed to grab a quick shower before Harris appeared like a Lowry matchstick man in the doorway. He walked up to Chandler's desk.

"Rough night?" Harris always had the ability to annoy Chandler just by opening his mouth, and today was no exception.

"Just heard something that could transform the finances of the department, from a friend across the pond," Chandler said, forcing a cheery smile in Harris's direction.

Harris opened his eyes a fraction wider. He'd listened to many of Chandler's plans for the museum, none of which had produced any income—quite the opposite, in fact.

"Really? This wouldn't be anything to do with Jack the Ripper, would it?"

Chandler bridled; things were already starting to head downhill.

"In a way."

Harris waited for him to continue. Chandler placed the printouts on the desk. "These letters turned up in a carriage pulled out of a Louisiana swamp."

Harris studied the pictures. "Ah, Dr. Tumblety. One of your favorite suspects. How does this help our finances exactly?"

Chandler stared at him. "Well, for a start, it could reveal new information about Jack the Ripper—but more importantly, there's the small matter of the five female corpses found inside a carriage buried in the middle of a swamp for over a century." Chandler placed the picture of the grotesque human sculpture in front of Harris like a cardsharp producing a winning hand.

Harris pursed his lips. Chandler sometimes thought that even if he'd brought Lord Lucan to him in handcuffs, Harris wouldn't have shown any reaction. Harris picked up the printout and studied it.

"I'm sure the Americans will enjoy unraveling this particular mystery," he said.

Chandler could feel his blood starting to boil. A terrible urge to strangle Harris with his bare hands came over him, and he tried to control his anger.

"What?" he demanded. "All the evidence points toward the victims being from England during the Victorian period: five women, in the middle of a swamp, along with documents connecting them to one of the main Ripper suspects. Why let the Americans take all the glory?"

Chandler stood very still, his hand clenched around the edge of the desk so hard his flesh was white. Harris cocked his head to one side.

"You can't just jet off on some departmental jolly. We have budgets to be approved, channels to go through."

Chandler looked at him in disbelief. "This could be one of the most significant discoveries of the twenty-first century."

Harris's disapproval oozed from every pore. "We don't have the funds. In fact, I've even been told to cut down on your lectures."

"But this could change everything we know about the Ripper case!"

Harris shook his head, another of his irritating habits. "Not everyone shares your obsession. I have budgets to trim, committees to report to—"

Chandler couldn't contain himself. He'd never liked Harris, and this was the last straw. "Don't be so stupid," he said. "Not supporting something that could add monetary value to the exhibits is madness, and you're an idiot for not realizing that." Chandler saw Harris's face redden. It was the nearest he'd ever got to showing any kind of reaction.

"I'm not the idiot here. No one's interested in history anymore. I'm not letting you blow thousands of pounds flying across the Atlantic on some wild goose chase."

Chandler shook his head. "This could be the making of us. We could open up to the public and have loads of visitors—*paying* visitors—but only if we had something sensational to show them."

Harris gave Chandler a hard look. "Do yourself a favor, give it a break."

Chandler glared back at him. "No. This is too important."

Harris went to go, and then turned back.

"I've tried to support you, let you do your research, use the department's facilities . . ." He threw up his hands and headed for the door. "If you want to chuck away your career, it's your funeral."

He shut the door quietly behind him, which was even more annoying to Chandler than if he'd slammed it.

SEVENTEEN

ATLANTA, GEORGIA – Present day

HIS JOURNEY HADN'T started well. They'd had to divert from Miami to Atlanta to avoid the aftereffects of Hurricane Matthew as it made its way up the southeast coastline of Florida. As it was, the aircraft had run into some particularly vicious bouts of wind that had thrown the wide-bodied jet around like a toy. Quite a few of the passengers were wearing evidence of the in-flight food on their clothes.

Atlanta Airport was packed. Passengers stood milling around beneath the departures board, staring at an ever-increasing list of delayed or canceled flights. Chandler was just one of the thousands trying to match up their luggage with their connecting flights. Having eventually found his bag and gone through security, he had seen his original three-hour window shrink to five minutes and had ended up running for his gate, which was reading LAST CALL on the departures board.

By the time he reached the gate, the boarding time for his flight had been put back by half an hour. A passenger had failed to show, and with the security as tight as it was, there was a choice between unloading all the plane's baggage or waiting for them to appear. He collapsed onto one of the unforgiving plastic seats, squashed between a man mountain with two fractious children, and a bearded traveler with a well-worn rucksack and Birkenstock sandals. He'd inadvertently made eye contact with Birkenstock man, exchanging one of those "another damn delay" expressions the way that air travelers do the world over. That was a mistake; the guy was a dam waiting to burst. He was one of those crazy people who sought out hurricanes, and now he was going to tell Chandler all about them. If there was a time when too much knowledge was a bad thing, it was learning about hurricanes when you were about to step onto a plane following one.

Birkenstocks filled him in on all of it. Katrina was one of the largest category-five hurricanes to make landfall in recorded history, with storm surges of twenty feet and winds reaching 125 miles per hour. But the highest recorded wind speed was from Cyclone Olivia in 1996, with a gust on Barrow Island, Australia, of 253 miles per hour. Meanwhile, the deadliest tornado hit Daulatpur-Saturia in Bangladesh in 1989, killing over 1,300 people. Birkenstocks was on fire.

Chandler stood up. He was going to have to break this cycle of facts and figures before his head exploded.

"I'm going to head off and get myself a cup of coffee," he said, preparing to sever the umbilical.

But it wasn't to be. Birkenstocks stood up. "Great idea. Mind if I join you?"

Chandler inwardly cursed. He could have said he was off to the toilet and never returned. Now, he was going to have his moment of savoring a coffee diluted by more mind-numbing facts.

He gave a tight smile. "Why not."

They headed for a large coffee chain and placed their orders. As they weaved their way past the line-up clutching their cups, Chandler thought he might be able to break free as there were only single seats available. But two seats opened up at a table in front of them and he was trapped once again. After enduring half an hour of Wikipedian intensity, Chandler looked up at the departures board and was relieved to see Now Boarding written next to his flight details. He hastily downed his coffee and stood up.

Birkenstocks nodded to the board. "Baton Rouge, huh? Have a good flight." He shot him a mock salute as Chandler hurried off toward his gate.

Chandler joined a small line of stragglers making their way past the boarding desk. The check-in clerk at the gate noted the stain on his pant leg—an unfortunate result of a small child drumming his feet against the back of the seat as his lunch had arrived on the last flight. He'd selected a dish with the word *Cajun* in it, and instantly regretted it. *Blackened shrimp, po'boy style,* the menu had listed helpfully. The airline official checked his boarding pass and nodded him through to the passageway leading to his plane.

EIGHTEEN

BATON ROUGE, LOUISIANA – Present day

CHANDLER DRAGGED HIS CARRY-ON down the endless corridors of the arrivals hub at Baton Rouge Metropolitan Airport. Outside on the tarmac, parked aircraft shimmered like blobs of mercury in the fierce heat. Chandler already felt overdressed in the sensible jacket he'd picked out. The plastic wheels on his bag had long ago given up their vow of silence and drew irritated glances as they shrieked their welcome to everyone within earshot. The airport was all steel and glass, and the centerpiece of banyan trees in the arrivals hall was impressive. Chandler wondered if they were there to remind the passengers what a tree looked like, since so many spent their lives surrounded by skyscrapers.

He stood in the middle of the hall and looked around. A lot of flights had been diverted to the airport, which now held a heaving mass of people. To one side he could see a group of protestors jostling with airport security. The placards they held aloft bore a variety of slogans: *Save our wildlife, Don't put oil before wildlife, Vote Governor Blackburn for jobs.* One of the protestors, a teenager with a freckled face wearing a tatty alligator costume, stood behind an attractive blonde girl shaking a placard that read *BLACKBURN OUT!*

All at once, Chandler saw a group of security men cutting a swath through the protestors ahead of a slick-looking man with black hair and silver sideburns. Wearing an immaculately tailored suit and a pair of gleaming handmade shoes, he looked like he'd just stepped out of a clothing catalog. His security detail cleared a path for him as he made his way across the arrivals hall. Some girls cheered as he swept past, while others booed. A smooth-looking man greeted him leading two large white hounds. The first man bent down to make a fuss of them.

A gap opened in the crowd, and Chandler spotted a tall figure with an open face across the hall. His physical presence stood out among the throng of bustling passengers. Deputy Duke Lanoix radiated a sort of slow-moving tranquility wherever he went, as if he brought the leisurely pace of the wetlands with him. His face creased in a smile as he spotted Chandler and headed toward him. He clasped Chandler around the shoulders as he looked him up and down, taking in the crumpled jacket.

"You expecting a cold snap?"

Chandler shook his head. "I thought Americans didn't do irony."

Duke laughed. "Irony? Hell, I was going for pity."

He made no move to take Chandler's bag as they headed toward the exit, and Chandler noticed he held himself as if he was in pain.

Duke stretched his hands up over his head and twisted himself from left to right, grimacing as he did so. "I've had a muscle spasm going on since the race. It'll probably pass in a few days."

Chandler shrugged, looked down at his battered case as he dragged it behind him. "No problem. I travel light." He looked at the circus surrounding the man being guided out of the airport. "What's going on with him?"

Duke looked around. "Who?"

"The suit and shoes fellow," Chandler said.

Duke gave a tight smile. "Governor Blackburn. He ain't too popular with the conservation groups."

The freckle-faced protestor in the alligator suit made a run toward the governor and was pursued by two overweight airport security guards. At the last minute, he swerved past the governor and headed straight for Chandler and Duke, before racing past them. Chandler nudged his case forward with a foot. The first security guard stumbled over it and ended up in a heap on the floor; the second, unable to avoid him, tripped and went flying. The freckle-faced protestor shot Chandler a grateful look, and raced out of the exit. Duke glanced at Chandler, not sure if it had been an accident or orchestrated. Chandler kept a straight face.

"Alligators are an endangered species," he said.

Duke smiled. "Not over here. The population's pretty stable right now. Louisiana has the largest number in the world at around two million."

Chandler watched the receding figure of the protestor in the alligator suit. "So now it's two million and one," he said.

He turned to see the man with Blackburn leading the two hounds outside and onto the concourse. "Nice dogs."

Duke snorted. "They're 'dogos Argentino,' apparently. Kind of pretentious, don't ya think?"

Chandler smiled at Duke's slow Southern drawl. A black Escalade swept up to the curb as they watched.

"He looks like a man who thinks he's going places," Chandler said.

Duke's eyes remained fixed on the governor as he climbed into the huge car. He shrugged. "That's what he thinks. How was your flight?"

Chandler tried to smooth a crease from his rumpled jacket. He soon gave up and slid out of the sweat-sodden rag it had become. "Okay, I guess. Thanks for putting me up, by the way. The department's budgets are pretty tight right now, and I barely managed to get them to cough up for the flight."

Duke halted alongside a battered old Buick—a classic Skylark custom convertible from the seventies—badly parked at the curb. He put Chandler's case in the trunk, slammed it shut.

"No problem. I'll be glad of the company," Duke said. He climbed behind the wheel as Chandler slid into the passenger seat.

"I've never stayed in an Airstream before," Chandler said.

Duke grunted as he fumbled with the ignition key, finally getting it in. "A friend loaned it to me after Katrina turned my house into a damn canoe, and it kinda suits me now. But I've booked you into a hotel for tonight. Thought you might like to get a good night's sleep before we start on the investigation. Once you've gotten over your flight, you can move to my place, maybe sample some of my legendary gumbo?" Chandler smiled.

"Looking forward to it."

Duke turned the key in the ignition—the motor eventually wheezing into life, a lot of tired but willing horses under the hood—before shooting Chandler a hopeful look. "We on expenses?" he asked.

Chandler remembered the stand-up fight he'd had with Harris before finally managing to settle on a cofunded research trip to Louisiana.

"Of course, especially now I'm not paying for hotel accommodation." This was a lie, but Chandler didn't want Duke to feel he was being taken advantage of. There was always a chance that Jenny could slip the receipts through once he got back to London. She was highly skilled in that area.

Duke grinned. "Well then, let's go celebrate with a meal at Crawdaddy's jazz restaurant."

Chandler forced a smile. This was going to cost him an arm and a leg. "Sounds great."

They started to pull away from the curb. A horn blared behind them, and the black Escalade swept past. Blackburn flicked Duke a look through the back window. Duke shook his head.

"Asshole," he mumbled, following it with something in French that Chandler couldn't make out, as they pulled away, belching smoke from the rumbling exhaust.

Chandler watched the Escalade disappear into the distance. "I take it you're not close?"

Duke grunted. "Wannabe senator thinks he owns everything."

Chandler sensed there was more to this story than Duke was letting on, but decided to let it go for the time being. Duke floored the accelerator, and the Buick rocketed forward.

NINETEEN

BATON ROUGE, LOUISIANA – Present day

INSIDE THE ESCALADE, Governor Blackburn turned to Agent Kale. The tinted windows and bulletproof glass partition between them and the driver provided complete privacy. He reached behind the back seat to stroke one of the dogs as he talked.

"We need to do something about that." He waved a hand in the general direction of the airport.

Agent Kale nodded wearily. "They can be a pain in the ass, but it comes with the territory nowadays. It's better to have them for you than against you."

Kale had been with Blackburn for five years now, during which time he'd managed to keep him out of trouble while the governor built a solid public profile. Now, with Blackburn's senatorial aspirations, it was even more essential to avoid any bad publicity. Though Kale worked for the government, he was permanently assigned on close protection duties for Governor Blackburn. He never asked how that was arranged, and it didn't do any harm that he was paid three times his normal salary for the pleasure.

Kale and the governor went back many years. He'd met Blackburn during a general meet and greet of the local law enforcement agencies. Kale had given the governor his card and pretended to admire his dogs. He'd learned that they were "dogos Argentino," and God help anybody who referred to them as just *dogs*. Apparently they were a mix of various breeds, including the Cordoba Fighting Dog and the Great Dane, and were specifically bred to protect their human companion to the death. Kale had no doubt that would prove to be the case should anybody make a wrong move around the governor. He'd tried to stroke one of them before they had accepted him, and he still bore the scars.

Given that close encounter, Kale was surprised to get a call from the governor in the middle of the night some weeks later. Blackburn was barely coherent, obviously drunk, and in big trouble. Kale arrived at the scene to find the governor's Escalade wrapped around a tree, a teenage girl with a nasty gash to her forehead slumped in the passenger seat. Another vehicle was on its side, its driver dead on the road. He'd gone through the windshield, and half of his face had been ripped off in the process. Fragments of bone and brains were smeared across the hood. It was a situation of Chappaquiddick proportions. It would mean the end of Blackburn's political career, and a long spell in jail, if Kale didn't act fast. Blackburn had a history of drinking and had only narrowly avoided a recent DUI charge when the liquor-measuring device had been shown to be faulty and a blood sample mislaid. Kale suspected it had taken a large amount of money to render that device as such. But this time around, the problem wasn't as easy to deal with. The governor had literally given Kale a blank check to make it all go away.

Within two hours, Kale had used up every favor he was owed and close to a million dollars in cash. The girl had been bought off; an apartment of her own, a pony, and a sports car had seen to that. A couple of ex-cons with a low-loader had disposed of Blackburn's car and transported the car wreck and the body to a well-known accident black spot, scattered a few empty bottles of J&B around, and torched the car with the body inside.

But there had been a problem. Some months later the man's family had hired a PI to look into the case, and he had unearthed some fresh evidence. A piece of glass from one of the bottles found by the side of the road contained prints that didn't match the victim's. Kale made sure it never made it into the courtroom, but it had been close. He kept other evidence from that night locked up in a storage unit, and sealed instructions with his lawyers to be opened if he died under suspicious circumstances. He considered this evidence as insurance in case things ever turned ugly in his relationship with Blackburn.

Kale jolted back from that long-ago night to find Blackburn staring at him.

"Well, what are we going to do about them?"

Kale had to come up with something fast; Blackburn wasn't known for his patience.

"The problem with their kind is, they're not interested in money." Blackburn scowled.

"I know that. It's all about saving the planet and the Goddess Gaia shit. The guards have seen them hanging around the plant on the security cameras. If they get inside—"

Kale tried to calm things down. "They won't get in. They're just kids waving banners around and getting all angst-ridden about protecting the environment."

The governor kept going, working himself up again. "One of the protestors had family working for us. We dodged a bullet there—they died before the case came to trial. But it would make them very happy to bring us down."

Kale knew the situation the governor was referring to. Blackburn Industries had oil refineries with less-than-perfect safety records. Some of the workers had mounted a tort case claiming they'd been exposed to dangerous levels of the toxic liquid benzene. Cases of leukemia had been linked to workers who'd spent many years in proximity to the substance, and someone had submitted evidence that pointed to a cover-up by the company. But the Blackburns were a family with enormous wealth, and a history of abusing their power. Kale suspected that this was why the lawsuits had gone away.

Blackburn was in Kale's face again. "The local deputy is poking around in Spirit's Swamp, and now he seems to have a friend here to help. Do you know what's going on with that?"

Kale shrugged. "He's a retired detective from London, works as an archivist in a museum at Scotland Yard. He's just some Ripper fanatic. It's all pretty harmless."

"Harmless!" Blackburn was practically shouting now. "Harmless? They've found five bodies. We haven't even processed that part of the swamp yet…" He trailed off, fuming.

Kale had seen the governor like this before. He'd have to shut him down fast before it got out of control. He spoke carefully, as if he were talking a suicidal man down from the roof of a high building.

"I know some of the students working on the project. They're pretty sure the bodies date from around the end of the nineteenth century. That English cop thinks there's a link to Jack the Ripper, so unless he's planning to pin those murders on you, I don't think you have a problem." He paused, hoping his attempt to lighten the mood had been successful.

Blackburn appeared to be thinking things through. His eyes had lost their angry look. Now he just looked thoughtful, or worried—it was difficult to tell which, or what, he was thinking, and Kale had misjudged him before.

Eventually Blackburn nodded. "Okay. But if need be, you shut them down. I don't want anything coming back to bite me on the ass during the campaign." Kale shook his head. He had to risk going against Blackburn at times, and this was one of them.

"We go in mob-handed and people are going to start asking questions. Next thing you know, they'll be talking about a police state and government interference, and then you'll be getting even more interest in the swamplands. We need to back off until we know what we're dealing with."

Blackburn's expression remained blank, though the temperature in the Escalade seemed to drop a few degrees. The dogos started to whimper. Then something changed behind Blackburn's eyes. He nodded, stroked the dogos until they quieted.

"Okay, put a team together in case we need to take things further. Until then, just monitor the situation."

Kale started to relax. He'd often thought the governor was bipolar, his moods were so mercurial. He'd always wondered why

Blackburn had such a high level of security out at the Spirit's Swamp plant. There had been some local opposition to Blackburn Industries' being awarded the contract to run the decontamination, especially as it owned the site the old oil refinery had been built on. But as the plans promised to eventually make the swamp a better environment for the wildlife, the backlash had been minimal. Kale suspected that the protestors at the airport were part of the same group that had tried to break into the plant earlier that month.

The driver dropped him downtown next to where he'd parked his car, and he nodded to Blackburn as the vehicle drove away.

TWENTY

BATON ROUGE, LOUISIANA – Present day

CRAWDADDY'S WAS A favorite haunt for visitors to Baton Rouge. It had a large outside courtyard with a wrought-iron trellis draped with pink bougainvillea that provided a blaze of color for most of the year and kept the hot sun at bay during the summer months. But what made it a special place for Duke was the jazz quartet that filled the air with its atmospheric music.

A waiter passed carrying a large tray laden with fresh lobster and bowls of the restaurant's famous turtle soup. At the table next to them, another server prepared a pepper steak flambé dish. Flames leaped into the air, bathing the diners' faces in an orange glow. Chandler tensed and rubbed at the old scar on his wrist—a reflex action that he'd never quite managed to control. Duke noted it but said nothing. He already knew the story and didn't need to bring up his friend's bad memories.

The waiter cleared their plates and slid another bottle of wine into the bucket on a stand next to the table. Duke filled their glasses. "Full?"

Chandler patted his distended stomach. A consequence of air travel and the large portions of fish he'd put away. "Never been fuller."

As the jazz music wafted across to them, Chandler remembered when he and Duke had first met. Duke had come to London to give a lecture to some recent recruits to the Met. Chandler started to smile at the memory.

Duke looked over, taking a sip of wine. "What?" he asked.

"I was just remembering that night we went out in London after your lecture," Chandler said.

"Oh yeah, that memory will never go away. You led me astray big time." Duke smiled.

"What was the name of that place?" Chandler asked. "The owner was an overweight Japanese guy with two gold teeth like fangs."

Duke nodded. "Big Bobby."

"That was it, Big Bobby's Kamikaze Karaoke Club." The memories came flooding back, and Chandler remembered the night like it was yesterday. Unlike normal karaoke clubs where patrons stood on the stage and sang along to a song they knew, Bobby's club added another twist to the proceedings. All the tables had voting buttons that allowed the audience to choose the most unsuitable songs for the victims up onstage. The audience's choice for Duke and Chandler had been inspired: Adele's "Someone Like You."

"I hope to God that there isn't a YouTube clip somewhere of the two of us singing." Duke smiled at the memory.

"To be fair, we almost hit the high notes." Chandler and Duke's friendship had been cemented that night, and after Chandler had managed to get two tickets for Ronnie Scott's Jazz Club later in the week, they'd become firm friends and had kept in touch over the years.

"Don't worry," Duke said. "I made sure Bobby deleted that file. There are too many smartphones these days—it would have been on the Internet before we left the club."

Chandler took a sip of wine and focused on the matter in hand. "So what do we know about the bodies?"

Duke put his glass down. "Swamp mud did us some favors there—"

Chandler held up a hand. "If I can quote you: 'with a fully submerged body, anaerobic conditions will halt decay, and the presence of a polysaccharide, such as sphagnum, reacts with the digestive enzymes of putrefying bacteria, immobilizing them and further inhibiting decay.'" Chandler prided himself on his memory, and even after a bottle of strong wine, he still felt confident in his recall.

Duke smiled. "I'm impressed. Not many people manage to stay awake at my lectures, never mind remember what I've said after all those years." He paused before picking up where he'd left off. "Well, from all the stuff we've found in the carriage, and the letters, it looks like these folks are from the late nineteenth century."

Chandler grew more animated. As far as he was concerned, this trip was shaping up well, and he was looking forward to feeding Harris a large slice of Victorian humble pie.

Duke continued. "The letters were postmarked between 1889 and 1893, the latest date being the year the great October storm hit Louisiana. So from the initial timeline, there's a strong possibility they could have been caught up in that storm."

Chandler listened to Duke intently, but the wine was making him drowsy and he was struggling to stay awake. "Maybe. I'm guessing the coroner will be able to tell us how they died?"

Duke smiled. "Jonas is looking forward to getting his hands on their bones, so to speak."

"That's good to know. But we're going to have our work cut out finding out who they are."

Duke finished up his glass of wine. "You're right. It may take some time, but eventually even the dead can be made to give up their secrets."

TWENTY-ONE

BATON ROUGE, LOUISIANA – Present day

CHANDLER GRIPPED THE grab handle as Duke's patrol car bounced down the local roads, leaving the outskirts of Baton Rouge behind it and heading onto the I-10. Duke had picked him up from his hotel in his patrol car, an old Chevrolet Impala with a lot of miles on the clock. It had seen better days, but it was a solid ride that Duke felt at home with. He'd turned down the chance to upgrade to a Tahoe with a laconic "if it ain't broke, don't fix it" attitude, and the department accountants were happy with that. He and Chandler were headed out to West Baton Rouge, and before too long the soft slap of the I-10 beneath the tires gave way to the rough gravel of the Henderson Levee Road. In the distance, Chandler could see the bridge that stretched across the Atchafalaya River.

The river ran for over 130 miles, and the name Atchafalaya came from the Choctaw word for "long river." The basin formed a wildlife management area and was the industrial shipping channel for the state of Louisiana, as well as the cultural heart of the Cajun country.

They left Henderson behind, passed Lake Bigeaux and the Plumb Bob oil and gas fields, and headed for the town of Butte La Rose, where the evidence was being housed and the investigation was based. Chandler straightened up in his seat and looked out at the miles of featureless swamp sliding past the window, occasionally punctuated by a distant oil field. Duke looked over and smiled at the state of his friend. Chandler was already regretting the third bottle of wine they'd downed at Crawdaddy's, and not just because of the eye-watering bill. In the harsh light of day, it was obvious his student drinking days had set sail many years back, and the dull throbbing behind his eyes was a painful reminder of that.

Twenty minutes later, Chandler saw signs welcoming them to the town of Butte La Rose. It claimed to have a population of 53,000, but Chandler saw little evidence of that in the deserted streets as they drove through. There had been a fort there in 1863, and he saw signs to Lost Lake and Cow Lake. Up ahead was a ramshackle barn. On its weathered gray boarding, faded yellow letters spelled out the words REFRIGERATED WAREHOUSE. The building had been vacant for many years, and the sheriff's department had managed to get it on loan from a local realtor. As they approached, Chandler saw six or more cars parked outside. The Chevrolet came to a halt alongside them, and Duke switched off the engine.

"Here we are. It ain't much but it'll keep things cool. And it's free."

Chandler twisted his arms from side to side to ease his aching shoulders as he climbed out into the hot, wet morning air. Sweat was already pooling in the small of his back and he wondered how anybody could take this heat for months on end. He saw a mud-splattered Camaro swamp buggy with a damaged front axle up on a support. Duke came over to where Chandler was standing and nodded at it.

"You can thank that, and Chilly's driving, for our recent discovery."

Chandler studied the large bulbous tires, the jacked-up space frame, and the big bore exhausts that flared up into the air to keep their openings out of the deep water.

"That's some beast," he said.

Duke nodded. "Got a thousand horses under the hood, twin axles, four-wheel drive, and shock absorbers so firm you think your spine's gonna go through your skull."

Chandler winced at the thought. "Sounds fun."

Duke walked toward the warehouse entrance and cricked his neck. He was still finding aches in muscles he didn't know he had. Thanks to Chandler's efforts to ease his own back, they looked like the world's worst two-man dance troupe.

"I think I'm still getting over the fun," Duke said.

Chandler looked at the name emblazoned down the side of the Camaro. "Who's Chilly?" But Duke obviously wanted to judge Chandler's first impression because he just smiled and said nothing.

Inside the warehouse, it was refreshingly cool. They'd gotten the old refrigeration machinery up and running, and the cooling fans wheezed and rumbled, the sound echoing around the cavernous space. The warehouse had been sectioned off with heavy sheets of plastic on tubular framing, and Chandler saw ghostly shapes moving behind the sheeting: Duke's volunteer staff, he guessed, hard at work. As he entered the main workspace, he saw they were all very young. Duke caught his look.

"Got myself a bunch of students to help out with this. Ain't got the budget for the real deal yet. Department won't fund a cold case unless we can prove it's a homicide, and I doubt that's gonna happen."

A stocky man with a fleshy face and a wide grin approached them. He was devouring a Twinkie, which he clutched in one of his massive hands. Duke introduced them.

"This is Deputy Wayne Fish. We call him Chilly. Chilly, this is Chandler Travis. He's a detective from London—New Scotland Yard. He's going to be helping us with the Babes in the Bog case."

Chandler smiled at the name they'd chosen for the investigation. He shook hands with Chilly and retrieved his mangled fingers, shocked not only at the sheer pressure of the other man's grip, but also the surprisingly cold temperature of his skin. He nursed his bruised fingers as Chilly smiled at him.

"They call me Chilly 'cos my body runs a few degrees cooler than most folk." Chandler made a note not to shake his hand again as he waited for the feeling to return to his fingers.

"Comes in real useful when there's a sweat on, which is pretty much all the time out here 'cept when it rains. Then it's hot and wet."

Chilly stretched out his syllables in a Southern drawl, then paused to take another bite of his Twinkie. "New Scotland Yard, huh? I always wanted to be around in Sherlock's time."

Chandler decided to sidestep the obvious confusion between fiction and reality. "Ah, so you're interested in history?"

Duke smiled. Chilly looked blank for a second. Then a slow grin spread across his face.

"Hell no! I would've just liked to be able to say, 'No shit, Sherlock,' to the real deal." He winked and ambled past.

Chandler watched as Chilly fed the last of the Twinkie into his mouth. He looked around the shed interior. "Shouldn't the bodies be in a proper mortuary?"

Duke shrugged. "Yeah, but we needed to preserve them fast," he said. "Seemed best not to risk transporting them to the city morgue till we got 'em down to bite-sized chunks. Jonas is going to check them over once we've got things under control here."

Chilly unwrapped another Twinkie. Duke nodded at the creamy sponge bar as it headed toward his mouth.

"Don't get between Chilly and a Twinkie—you could lose a finger!"

Chilly looked back at them and gave a deep belly laugh that shook his sizeable frame. "You'd better believe it. They're part of my calorie-controlled diet." He nodded toward the section where the assistant worked on the tangled corpses. "I think it was Mark Twain who said the swamp is a cruel mistress."

Chandler fixed a smile in place before replying, "He may well have done." *In another universe,* he thought. His mind immediately recalled a song by Celtic punk band Flogging Molly titled "Cruel Mistress" that had a "The sea is a cruel mistress" line in its lyrics. It was the sort of quote that he imagined would have come from the novel *Moby Dick*, but he wasn't entirely sure. Chandler had no idea why his mind was able to remember eclectic musical facts about esoteric bands, but it had always been that way.

He moved toward the carriage, which stood dripping on a plastic sheet. A student was treating the carriage with a handheld water spray.

"We're keeping the wood moist until we can stabilize it," Duke said.

Chandler looked at the volunteers as they worked. Considering the lack of funds, they were doing a pretty good job. Around the warehouse the students were already working on the various artifacts from inside the carriage with solvents. Others were using preservatives to fix the envelopes and paper, to prevent any further degradation now they'd been exposed to the atmosphere.

Duke waved a hand around. "This isn't exactly an episode of CSI here. Once we get results, I might be able to get some discretionary funding from the department. Maybe even enough for another meal at Crawdaddy's." He chuckled.

Chandler caught a glimpse behind a partition of a gangly teenager with designer glasses, a hawkish face, and a hank of hair that flopped across his forehead. He was staring intently at something on a computer screen. Duke pointed in his direction.

"We got a guy from Lafayette University processing the documents and photos. He's a little off the wall, but he's a genius with all that computer shit—name's Phaedon. His friends call him Google; if you haven't got Internet, he's the next best thing. Guy's a goddamn planet brain."

Duke headed toward the computer work area, pulled back the sheeting, and headed in. Chandler followed, looking around the makeshift computer-processing room. Racks of servers and computer towers were linked together and piled high on a bench at one side, along with a high-end electronic analytical kit. Some faded photographs and handwritten documents were displayed on the large monitors. Phaedon sat, mesmerized, in front of a screen full of whirling polygon shapes and colors, his hands flying across the keys like a concert pianist's. Duke coughed. Phaedon kept typing, in a world of his own.

"Hi—with you in a sec—just got to—there." There was a final swirl of color on the screen as a landscape appeared behind two figures. Phaedon swiveled in his chair and got up, grinning at Duke.

"Just had to nail some polygon texturing algorithms. They can be tough little suckers!"

Chandler listened. He had no idea what Phaedon was talking about, but he made a stab at pretending. "I know what you mean—damn polygons."

Duke shook his head and smiled at Chandler's attempt to show his technical skills.

Phaedon extended a limp hand with long, delicate fingers toward Chandler, who shook it.

"Chandler Travis."

Phaedon grinned. "Phaedon, though I'm sure people call me other things. I can't do much while the computers are rendering, so I'm working on my game. It's gonna be a kick-ass search-and-destroy killer-robot scenario—but with an emotional core. Kinda like *Terminator* meets *The Wizard of Oz.*

Chilly wandered over to them. "He's going to scan me into the game. I play a sensitive cop who becomes a sleepwalking serial killer."

Phaedon's cell tweeted as it received a text. He picked it up. Chandler saw the large screen was full of icons.

"Er, nice phone," he said. "I should really look into getting an intelligent phone." He pulled an old Nokia out of his pocket. The thing was barely able to handle voice calls on a good day, and its battered waterproof case made it huge in comparison to the sleek model Phaedon held.

He continued, "I just carry a basic one when I go abroad. Doesn't matter if it gets stolen, and with the case to protect it, I don't even have to get it insured."

Phaedon looked at the phone and smiled. "Trust me, dude, that ain't gonna get stolen." He held up his own cell phone.

"Smartphones are the way to go. I've written some really neat apps for mine."

Chandler realized he was slipping down a technical rabbit hole, but couldn't stop himself. "Yeah, I've done some stuff with mine as well—brought it up to speed."

Duke laughed. "I don't think downloading a clip of a skate-boarding dog counts."

Chandler grinned; as usual, Duke had seen right through him.

A sound like a strangled frog came from Chilly's pocket. He made no move to answer it. Duke looked over.

"Could be urgent?"

Chilly shrugged. "Nah, probably one of the gang—we're having a barbecue." Duke gave him a playful push. Obviously this was some running joke that Chandler wasn't in on.

"Better check—you never know." Chilly reached into his pocket and eased his cell phone out far enough to squint at the screen. Phaedon frowned.

"The hell happened to your cell, dude? Looks like it went ten rounds with a raptor."

Chilly sighed and pulled it all the way out of his pocket. It had a cracked screen and was covered in bite marks. Chilly stared at it ruefully. "My damn dog hates cell phones—he hears one go off, he nukes it. This is my fourth one this year."

Phaedon shook his head. "Bummer."

Chandler looked at the computer monitors. Some faint writing was materializing from behind an electronic fog. "These the letters?" he asked.

Phaedon nodded. "Yes. I used short waveform scanning, UV, infrared, and side band reflective information—"

Chandler looked at the words forming on the screen. "Do you have a timeline?"

Phaedon tapped a few more keys. "We're hoping to see something soon. We're starting on the diary next, but that might be more complicated."

"Why's that?" Chandler said.

"The diary uses a different kind of paper than the letters," Phaedon said. "More absorbent." Phaedon hit some keys, and a close-up picture of a worn and waterlogged diary flashed up on the screen. Phaedon pointed to the foxing and the water damage. "The front and back covers, along with some of the other pages, are meshed together. If we dry them out gradually, we might be able to save some of them. I'm hoping somebody on the team might come up with a better solution," he said, "but I've made some progress with the photos."

Phaedon moved over to another keyboard and tapped some keys. Five wire-frame heads appeared on one of the large monitors. "Okay, so we digitized the five heads"—he tapped the keyboard again—"and used the photo from the carriage." The screen filled with a sepia photograph of a group of women and a man wearing a large walrus mustache, a top hat, and suit. Two white carriage dogs sat in front of him. It was a typically awkward Victorian pose.

"Sure looks like Tumblety," Duke said.

"Yes," Chandler replied. "A lot of people wore walrus mustaches in those days, but with his name and return address on the envelopes, the evidence is pointing that way."

Phaedon looked at the screen. "Creepy-looking dude," he said. "I made a 3-D extrapolation from the women in the photo. Then I mapped their images onto the skull structures of our swamp babes." Phaedon tapped instructions into the computer tablet. The wire frames were digitized and electronically painted with the women's faces from the carriage photograph. Phaedon did some more adjustments. The facial tones of the women became sharper. "The colors are based on their reflectivity in relation to gray scale," he said.

Chandler stared at the screens as color suffused the women's faces. He was convinced he knew who they were. But the problem with computers was that they could make things look like anything you wanted them to. Especially if you already had a theory in mind. He wondered if anyone else was thinking the same thing. He didn't want to be the first to speak out. Maybe they'd realized the major chronological flaw in the conclusion. He decided to leave the elephant in the room undisturbed until they had more facts.

"So the bodies from the carriage," he began, "their general physiognomies match those of the women in the photo?"

Phaedon tapped some keys, and the picture sharpened up. "Yes, but I need more accurate data to be sure."

"If we can get any DNA from the bodies we might be able get a match from one of their relatives, if they're on any of the databases," Chandler said.

Phaedon nodded. "I guess that's something we'd need to run by Jonas."

Duke turned to Chandler. "I'll hook you up with one of the locals, Roxie. She's a bright kid, spends a lot of time up at the library out at East Iberville. She's studying for a degree in anthropology and I've asked her to join the team."

Phaedon grinned at the mention of Roxie's name. "Yeah, she's cool." He paused before continuing. "For a bone doctor."

TWENTY-TWO

ROSEDALE, LOUISIANA – Present day

ROXIE PARKED HER battered Jeep Cherokee outside her mother's small bungalow in Rosedale, on the outskirts of Maringouin. She'd wanted to buy her mom a place somewhere nearer Baton Rouge, and the hospital, but her mother had spent most of her life in Rosedale and refused to live anywhere else. Roxie's father had worked at the Opelousas oil refinery until he got sick. The refinery was long gone now and the area was run down, with only the occasional tourist visiting the surviving examples of antebellum structures or the local museum. The untidy garden was colorful, and bougainvillea clustered around the entrance to the porch, hiding the peeling paint and dilapidated wood.

Roxie sat in the Jeep for a moment, getting her mind into a cheerful place. She always tried to be as upbeat as she could when visiting. It was getting difficult to keep up with her studies and look after her mom, but she didn't want her to worry. Her mother had enough trouble in her life without anything else on top of it.

Roxie had realized early on that there were only two ways for her to afford a university education: to get rich or to win a scholarship. As a young girl she was the fastest at all her track events, and it seemed only natural to pursue that avenue when it came to aiming for a scholarship. She applied for a track-and-field scholarship at LSU, and thanks to her physical abilities along with her SATs, she got in. Before his death, her father had often read detective mystery stories to her. She'd become fascinated with the way murder cases were solved by forensic scientists investigating the remains of long-dead victims. So when she'd learned about the LSU Department of Social Humanities and Social Sciences, it seemed a perfect fit.

She joined the forensic anthropology course run by renowned bone doctor Mary Menhein and worked numerous jobs to keep the household going after her father died. She'd worked evenings at the local branch of Hooters, tending the bar, waitressing, and dodging the wandering hands just to keep the money coming in. She'd spent four years studying, observing archaeological digs, assisting local coroners at weekends, and getting practical knowledge with the local law enforcement, all while working toward her masters degree. But now with her mother housebound, things were getting tougher, and she wasn't sure if she would be able to continue with her education.

And then she got a call from Deputy Sheriff Duke Lanoix. He was working on a case that needed a forensic anthropologist and explained that it was an expenses-only job, but a good opportunity to build up her résumé.

As she climbed out of the car, she felt a pang of regret for the way her mother lived. There just wasn't enough time or money for Roxie to focus on anything other than keeping her mom safe and making sure she took the drugs that kept her comfortable.

Roxie jiggled the key in the lock, pulled the door toward her, and bumped it open with her knee. "It's only me, Ma," she called out as she went in through the door.

She scooped up the junk mail and headed for the bedroom. She heard the wracking cough as she opened the door. Her mother's weary face lit up in a smile as Roxie moved in and wiped her mother's forehead with a handkerchief.

"Hello, darling, how are you? You look tired."

Roxie squeezed her hand and gave her a kiss on the cheek. "I'm okay, Mom, just busy is all." She held up a flask. "Brought you some of my magic soup."

Her mother smiled. Roxie unscrewed the thermos flask's cap and poured its contents into a small bowl. "There you go. It's not too hot." She held the bowl while her mother took some tentative sips.

The room was a shrine to her mother's long-term illness. Jars and bottles of medicine crowded the bedside table, while the TV murmured in the background. The news showed pictures of Governor Roman Blackburn touring the state, drumming up support for his senatorial election campaign. Her mother fumbled for the remote, turned the volume up. A reporter spoke to the camera.

"Local feelings are mixed about his proposed bill to open up the wetlands for development, with some people believing it would result in large corporations profiting from the region at the expense of the wildlife and the natural beauty of the area."

The camera moved in on a group of protestors, focusing on one in particular: Roxie. The reporter held a mic out. "Can you tell us why you're against Governor Blackburn's plans for the wetlands?"

Roxie was a natural speaker, and the camera loved her. "The Blackburns have only ever had their own interests at heart. It's taken years to tackle the pollution caused by the irresponsibility of the oil industries, in which their family played a large part, and now it looks like they're going to profit from cleaning it up. The wetlands should be left as a place of natural beauty for wildlife to live in and for people to visit—"

The report showed footage of Blackburn's decontamination plant. A flare stack belched flames into the darkening sky. Dumper trucks rumbled out, piled high with rubble, while chemical tanker trucks lined up outside. A reporter pointed at the activity and spoke to the camera, "With the recent climate conference expected to give a boost to carbon trading, tackling pollution might just be the hot ticket to boost Governor Blackburn's bid for the Senate. I'm Johnny Desbois for WBRZ 2, live from Spirit's Swamp, Maurepas."

Roxie turned the TV off and moved over to the bed. "You don't want to be watching the news, Ma. You know how it upsets you."

Her mother put the half-finished bowl of soup on the bedside cabinet, wheezing as she struggled for breath. She fumbled for an inhaler and took a couple of puffs to ease her breathing.

Roxie helped her finish the last of the soup, and wiped her mouth. "There, how was that?"

Her mother smiled. "Thank you, dear. I don't know what I'd do without you." She squeezed Roxie's wrist with her small, heavily veined hand.

"I don't like you gettin' involved with the protesting. You can't bring your daddy back, or my health, and Blackburn's family is a lot to go up against." She coughed; it became a deep-throated fight for breath. Roxie held her till the attack passed, smoothed her damp hair back from her forehead, and mopped her pale skin with a damp washcloth. Her mother's face creased in a smile.

"I'm sorry I'm such a tie, sweet pea. You need to get on with your life. Find yourself a nice young man to settle down with. Don't waste your time lookin' out for me. We had our time, me and your pa, and they was good times, until . . ."

Roxie dabbed her mom's lips with the facecloth. "I'll be okay, Ma. You need to rest now. I'll be back later to make you some of your favorite: gumbo."

Her mother smiled. "That would be nice. Not too spicy." She trailed off, her eyes moist with tears.

Roxie kissed her cheek, gave her a hug. There was steel in her eyes.

"Don't you worry about me, Ma. I'm living my life, getting things done. Things that need to be done."

TWENTY-THREE

BUTTE LA ROSE, LOUISIANA – Present day

DUKE AND CHANDLER stood behind Phaedon and looked at the screen.

"What sort of equipment would give you more accurate data?" Duke asked.

Phaedon flexed his long, slim fingers, as if he was itching to tap into fresh data.

"Well, I don't think any of the local hospitals would like a corpse in their nice sterile CAT scanner. But there might be another way."

"What?" Duke asked.

"A Lidar unit—but that takes some serious coin," Phaedon replied.

Chandler looked blank. "Lidar?"

"Light detection and ranging," he said. "It uses lasers to measure and map land contours, then creates a 3-D picture of the terrain—or in this case, a skull."

Duke frowned. "I don't think we can spring for that. Maybe Roxie can come up with something."

Chandler looked at the women in the picture again. A combination of too much coffee and lingering jet lag had turned his brain into an image version of predictive text. It kept insisting these women were exactly who he thought they were. He remembered a line from the Sherlock Holmes story *The Sign of the Four*: "When you have eliminated the impossible, whatever remains, however improbable, must be the truth." The only problem was, they hadn't been able to eliminate the impossible. Not yet anyway.

He remembered when he and Claire had first joined Netflix and they'd binged on police procedurals. By the end of the weekend, all the shows had merged into a kind of plot soup. The detectives always had a drinking, drug, or gambling problem; were separated or had lost children; and were constantly embarking on doomed love affairs. Now, he felt this investigation was starting to blur between reality and his imaginings, like in a TV detective series. He needed to see something that wasn't in cyberspace. Something real.

He'd spent his time on the force analyzing crime scenes and studying physical evidence. Without having seen the clues in person, he felt he didn't yet have the empathy that would help him solve this case.

"Can I see the site where you found the carriage?" Chandler asked.

Duke shrugged. "Sure. I got a friend who runs one of them swamp tours. His son Zeke can take you out there this evening. I'll get Freddy to run you out to the marina. You can text him when you're on your way back, and he'll pick you up."

"Freddy?" Chandler said.

"You saw him at the airport—the protestor in the gator suit."

Chandler nodded, remembering the freckle-faced protestor. "Right." He looked at his watch; it was already late afternoon. He wondered how fast it got dark out in the swamps. He suddenly felt a long way from the familiar streets of London.

"He's okay, is he? I mean, I don't want to end up as alligator bait."

Duke laughed. "Nah—no chance of that. Zeke knows the swamps like the back of his hand.

TWENTY-FOUR

SPIRIT'S SWAMP, LOUISIANA – Present day

CHANDLER STARED AT Zeke's arm resting against the tiller of the six-seater airboat as it hummed across the surface of the swamp. Where a hand should have been, there was just a calloused stump—the result of an accident or maybe even a birth defect. Either way, Chandler couldn't take his eyes off it.

Freddy had picked up Chandler from the refrigeration warehouse and they'd headed across country to the I-10. Freddy was happy to extol on all kinds of trivia during the journey. The I-10, or as they referred to it over there, the Interstate, stretched across the country all the way from Santa Monica, California to Jacksonville, Florida. Chandler also learned that in Palm Springs it was known as the Sonny Bono Memorial Freeway as a tribute to the late entertainer, mayor, and congressman. When Freddy had told him this fact, he couldn't get Sonny and Cher's track "Bang Bang" out of his head. Numerous artists had covered the song, and Chandler had once made a point of listening to all the different versions. Lady Gaga, Polkaholix, and the Ukulele Orchestra of Great Britain's versions were among his favorites.

They left the I-10 and followed highway 22 into Livingston Parish and on through Maurepas. The town consisted of a post office, a dollar general, a school, and a Baptist church. Shortly after leaving the town, they headed over a bridge spanning the Tickfaw River and doubled back before peeling off into the quaintly named Make 'Em Wet Marina, where Zeke's father's swamp tour business was based. Freddy had dropped him off quayside, where Zeke sat waiting, chewing Perique, a local tobacco. Freddy texted Chandler his cell phone number before leaving so he could let him know when he needed picking up. Once Chandler joined Zeke on board his airboat, they headed down the Tickfaw River and through a series of twisting bayous that led away from the main tributary.

Chandler looked over at Zeke, who was still chewing on the pungent wad of tobacco, occasionally spitting some out over the side of the boat with consummate skill. He pushed aside a greasy hank of blond hair that hung down over his hooked nose, his dark eyes scanning the surface of the water for hidden obstacles. Chandler sat beside him on a pair of raised seats in the middle of the camouflaged craft. The boat was specifically designed for the terrain, powered by a mixture of water-jet drive and fan-propulsion systems. Zeke eased the throttle back, and the boat slid past the twisted roots of mangroves and under the hanging fronds of the ancient cypress trees that lined the banks. Chandler flicked another look at Zeke's stump. It was mesmerizing. Before he could stop himself he blurted out, "So, do you see many alligators? Duke said there were around two million out here."

Zeke looked at him, his dark eyes sizing Chandler up. Was he aware of his fixation? He spat over the side, and again Chandler marveled at how he knew which way the wind would carry the pungent juice.

"Maybe more. Some of them are pretty good at keeping out of sight," Zeke said.

"That's a lot, isn't it?" he said, his eyes drawn to the stump. He dragged them back up to find Zeke looking right at him, an amused smile turning up the corners of his mouth.

"I was born like this—didn't lose it to no gator—so you can settle down and relax, okay?"

Chandler mentally kicked himself. "Sure, great—I mean not great, obviously—er . . ." He trailed off, wishing he were dead. Zeke grinned.

"Don't sweat it; I get that a lot. Man on a boat spends his time traveling through a gator-infested swamp . . . but to tell you the truth, it gets me a shitload of tips."

Chandler relaxed. At least that was out of the way. Now, all he had to do was remember to tip big. Zeke steered the boat past more rows of ancient cypress trees, like giant wooden skirted dolls.

"You been out in the swamps before?"

Chandler shook his head. "Er, no."

Zeke handed him an aerosol can. "You might want to use some of this. There are some bugs out here that'll carry off small children."

He smiled at Chandler's expression. "I'm yankin' your chain! There's only a few skeets, you'll be fine. Just don't go trailing your fingers in the water."

Chandler felt his eyes being drawn toward the stump again. "Okay, I think I can resist that."

Something big slid down from a muddy bank and splashed into the water. Chandler thought he saw a long gray snout slide beneath the surface, but he couldn't really be sure. In fact, the longer he was out in the swamp, the less he could be sure about anything.

The light was beginning to go out of the sky as the airboat drifted through some of the smaller tributaries with names like Lost Bayou and Blood Bayou. Whatever else, Chandler thought, Louisianans didn't do humor when it came to naming their waterways.

As they went deeper into the swamp, the vegetation crowded in. Zeke told Chandler that some of the bald cypress trees with their buttressed bases were over a thousand years old. Chandler wondered what they had seen—watching over the swamps for all those years. Water snakes slithered away as the boat approached, and alligators stared at them from the banks as they passed. There seemed to be more of them the darker it got. Zeke cut the throttle, and the engine noise became a low growl.

In the distance Chandler could see points of light from some kind of industrial plant. Concrete stacks sent thin trails of gray smoke into the clouds above, and flames soared into the sky from a flare stack. Zeke cut the motor completely, and the prow of the boat nudged against a rotting wooden jetty. An area of the swamp had been cordoned off with police tape fixed onto small buoys that floated in the murky water. A muddy track stretched off into the distance. Zeke waved a hand around, encompassing the wilderness surrounding them.

"Welcome to Spirit's Swamp."

"Where exactly are we?" Chandler asked. Zeke busied himself tying the boat to a rusty shackle that hung from the edge of the jetty before answering. When he did, Chandler felt what he said was part of a tourist spiel Zeke had probably given a hundred times before.

"We're on the edge of the Maurepas Swamp Wildlife Management Area, twenty-five miles west of New Orleans and fifty miles from Baton Rouge. The management area covers two tracts, which together total over 63,000 acres. Most of it consists of flooded cypress tupelo swamp." He paused for dramatic effect. "All of which is ideal real estate for the millions of gators that live round here."

"I guess Spirit's swamp is a little off the beaten track?" Chandler said.

Zeke nodded. "Yup. Apart from the yearly swamp buggy race and the odd fisherman, most folk don't bother coming out this far."

Chandler remembered Duke telling him that the water was so toxic, contestants had to have a whole series of shots in case they swallowed any of it.

Zeke went on. "There's still a lot of wildlife around the area to be seen if you're lucky. White-tailed deer, squirrels, rabbits, and raccoons, even the odd bald eagle."

Chandler looked out across the darkening swamp. He doubted he would see herds of deer or flocks of bald eagles anytime soon. "What do the fishermen catch out here?" he asked.

"On a good day, largemouth bass, perch, maybe some crappie. A poor man can always get enough food to eat out of the water."

Chandler looked around and wondered what a patient alligator could get.

Zeke had handed him a tourist map when he first boarded the boat that showed how Lake Maurepas fed into the six hundred square miles of Lake Pontchartrain, which linked, via the Rigolets strait, into Lake Borgne and the Gulf of Mexico. Together, the three bodies of water formed one of the largest estuaries in the Gulf Coast region.

Chandler nodded at the rough track that ran past the jetty. "Where does that lead to?"

"It's a natural levee formed by the annual floods," Zeke said. "Way back when, it reached as far as Maurepas, back when it was known as Maurepas Island."

"So the women could have landed here by boat and had a carriage waiting?" Chandler said.

Zeke scratched at his stump before replying. "Maybe. Or they could have been making for the railway station."

"Station?" Chandler tried to imagine what a railway station would be like out in this wilderness.

"Yes. In 1887 the New Orleans and Gulf Coast Railway ran from Shell Beach to Poydras Junction in New Orleans, and then on as far as Baton Rouge. Back then the railway was booming. Investors were pouring money into railway stocks. There were hundreds of companies promising to make them millionaires."

"A bit like the dot-com boom," Chandler said.

Zeke smiled. "Pretty much. The railway companies used to build a few miles of track and then go broke. Someone else would come along and buy up their track for a song. The ones with the most track were usually the ones that survived."

"Leaving a lot of bankrupt investors behind in the dust," Chandler said.

Zeke nodded. "Yup. That's the way it was back then."

Chandler nodded at the distant lights and the flames from the flare stack. "What's over there?"

Zeke handed him some binoculars, and Chandler looked toward the lights.

"Blackburn's decontamination plant," Zeke said. "It used to be an oil refinery back when the oil field was still running, before the 1915 storm." Zeke spat some juice onto the bank. "The rigs were destroyed, oil pipes got ripped to hell, fouled up the whole area. Got into the water system 'n' everything. People started to get sick, kiddies turning out wrong."

Through the binoculars Chandler could make out the old refinery and a collection of industrial sheds. A separate shed sat next to the smokestacks. The flare stack belched flames into the night, throwing an orange glow over a parking area containing dump trucks and a row of chemical tankers. Chandler handed the binoculars back to Zeke. "Someone always pays the price for big business," he said.

Zeke looked out over the expanse of water. The silence hung in the air as they digested their thoughts.

Finally, Zeke turned to look at him. "Swamps hold a lot of secrets. Sometimes, when the big winds come, they stir stuff up that shouldn't be found." Chandler felt a chill run down his spine.

"You mean bodies?"

Zeke nodded. "Yeah. There's gotta be hundreds—hurricane victims, accidents, gangster hits. Hell, Jimmy Hoffa's probably under here somewhere!"

Chandler smiled. "Everybody loves a conspiracy theory."

Zeke leaned down to a big cooler, pulled out two beers. "You want a cold one?"

Chandler nodded and took the can from Zeke. He didn't like the idea of being out in the swamp as darkness fell, but his throat was parched, and he didn't want to upset Zeke by refusing his hospitality. He took a swig from the can and looked around. The sun was now a throbbing red blister between the sky and the swamp.

He looked at Zeke. "What do you think they were doing here?"

Zeke narrowed his eyes for a moment. "Maybe they was running from the storm—or something else."

TWENTY-FIVE

LONDON, ENGLAND – 1888

TRITON SAT IN the back of the carriage, the velvet curtains drawn tight across the windows. The man sitting opposite him was smartly dressed, in a dark topcoat and bow tie, his white shirt crisply ironed. Gold cufflinks adorned his sleeves. Though he was in his seventies, his eyes still bore a keen intelligence.

He leaned forward. "And you're sure of this?"

Triton nodded. "It's already happening. Once the extent of the threat becomes public, the situation will only escalate. Buying properties will be like picking apples off a tree. I'm giving you the opportunity to get in ahead of the crowd."

"It sounds like you've been listening to Baron Rothschild."

Triton smiled. "Not specifically, though maybe I should have. After all, he's probably the richest man in the world."

"Yes. Apparently he said, 'Buy when there's blood in the streets.'"

"I heard that," Triton said.

Philius smirked. "And you intend to take that quite literally, it would seem."

"The conditions in the East End are already appalling. You can only improve conditions by buying up and knocking down the slum dwellings. The houses you build will be more hygienic and far more habitable than those there now. You can transform London for the good of the people. At the end of the day it's the poor who will ultimately benefit. Once order has been restored and the perceived threat removed, they'll return."

Philius contemplated this. "That's a little like robbing Peter to pay Paul, isn't it?"

"Maybe. But in this case, Peter gets to live in a nice new home," Triton said.

Philius brushed an imperceptible piece of dust from his jacket. "And you make a tidy profit from the enterprise."

Triton smiled. "We make a tidy profit."

Philius nodded. "With every transaction there's always a winner and a loser."

"But in this case I'd like to think that everyone is a winner." Triton waited.

After a pause, Philius nodded. "You make a good point."

"I'm glad you think so," said Triton. "When Angela Burdett-Coutts supplied Florence Nightingale with the equipment she needed to treat injured soldiers, she turned a blind eye when it came to getting donations. All that counted was helping the poor and the suffering. She didn't care where the money came from." Triton produced two champagne glasses and an opened bottle. He filled the glasses and handed one to Philius. They clinked glasses, and Philius gave a wry smile, nodded at the champagne bottle.

"Looks like you were pretty confident I would support your grand endeavor."

Triton saluted him with his glass. "I was happy to risk a bottle of flat champagne for a deal worth thousands of pounds."

Philius took a sip of the drink, swallowed appreciatively. "How long do you think it will be before you can make a killing?"

Triton gave the smallest of smiles. "I'm starting tonight."

TWENTY-SIX

LONDON, ENGLAND – 1888

ANNIE CHAPMAN—OR DARK Annie, as her friends knew her—wasn't having the best of times. She'd gotten into a stupid fight over a bar of soap with Eliza Cooper and had come off much worse from the encounter; Eliza was a raw-boned Irish girl with fists like lumps of rock. Annie had been left with a black eye and a kaleidoscope of bruises on her face. She had a pounding headache and her body throbbed all over. She'd headed for The Black Swan pub on Hanbury Street and had consumed a large amount of cheap beer in an attempt to numb the pain. Three hours later, she was still in pain, and now had no money left for lodgings.

The problem she had with her lungs wasn't helped by the smoky atmosphere in the pub, and she could feel a coughing spasm building. She searched in her voluminous skirts for the envelope that held her pills and fumbled a couple out, then put the pills in her mouth and washed them down with the last dregs from her glass. It had been a bad week on the earnings front. She hadn't sold any of the antimacassars she'd crocheted, or the flowers she'd stolen from St. Mary's churchyard. The way she was feeling, the last thing she wanted was to have some slobbering oaf up in her drawers, but she didn't have a choice.

She remembered what Kelly had told her and her friends about "the club." The beautifully dressed women, gentlemen drinking champagne from crystal glasses sitting on gilded furniture—it was all a million miles away from her sordid existence.

She dragged herself upright and pushed through the crowded room toward the door. As she stepped out onto the street, a blast of cold, damp air sent her into a prolonged coughing fit. She leaned against the pub wall until it subsided. In the distance, she could see the dark shape of a carriage parked up at the junction with Commercial Street, the horse's breath smoking in the gaslight. She could tell from its shape that the cab was a Clarence, also known as a Growler because of the rumbling noise it made with its wheels on the cobbled streets.

Her husband, John, had been a carriageman working in Knightsbridge when they first met, and he'd taught her all about the different types of carriages. She'd had a ride in most of them, one way or another. But that was three children ago, before drink and tragedy had sucked the life out of them. Emily, their firstborn, had died of meningitis at the age of twelve, by which time their daughter Annie was working in a traveling circus in France. John, their third child, had been born disabled, shortly before Emily died. Neither Annie nor her husband could bear the terrible sadness, and they'd both started to drink heavily. Before too long, the bottomless pit of resentment caused them to separate. She'd managed to make do for a time on the money he'd sent her, but then suddenly it stopped coming. She learned later that the drink had finally killed him. The man she was living with moved out soon after that, and she was left alone with the darkness of her depression. Since then, her life had become a vicious circle of drink and prostitution; she drank to dull her senses so she could face the abuse to her body inflicted by strangers, and then drank more to make her forget it.

She headed toward where the carriage sat. She'd often made fast money off a toff wanting a bit of rough in his carriage. The fancy types seemed to get pleasure out of the act of depravity they put themselves through and usually favored a blowsie. She could be into his britches and done, with the money in her hand, in well under ten minutes—unless it was a cold night, in which case more attention might be needed.

As she drew nearer the carriage, a man stepped out into the light. She could tell by the way he walked he had served in a branch of the military. She'd been with enough soldiers to recognize the upright posture and easy movements of a man who'd gone through a period of training. Things were looking up. Maybe he'd seen her coming and wanted to let her know he was game for a bit of rough trade.

She was concentrating so hard on the man heading toward her that she didn't see the two step out of the shadows behind her until it was too late.

TWENTY-SEVEN

SPIRIT'S SWAMP, LOUISIANA – Present day

CHANDLER LOOKED AT the pile of crumpled beer cans that lay at his feet, along with his better judgment. The sound of the insects grew louder as the sun slipped below the horizon, and for a brief moment, the swamp was bathed in its pink afterglow. Zeke switched on one of the craft's spotlights, and an angry cloud of insects swarmed in the light. Chandler felt his skin crawl in anticipation.

"It must be difficult navigating round here in the dark," he said.

Zeke shook his head. "Nah." He flicked on a navigation system. The cool glow of its display gave his face a ghostly sheen. "We got GPS. Also got Bluetooth auto pairing, which I've cranked up to over a klick—see?" He pointed to a flashing red icon on the screen. "That's your cell. As long as it's on, we'll be able to find you—even in the belly of a gator."

Chandler gave a nervous laugh, and Zeke slapped him on the back. "Only joshing! Cell coverage is pretty patchy out here, but texts still get through."

Chandler looked out at the swamp. He didn't like the idea of not having communication. "Why's that?" he asked.

Zeke spat over the side. "Someone told me it was to do with bandwidth—kinda like a jammed freeway. Voice calls are like the cars in the jam, and texts are the motorcycles that can weave their way through. During 9/11, texts were one of the few things that still worked."

Zeke waved at the darkness. "This is the best part of the day. As the sun goes down, the swamp comes alive. The night critters come out—"

"Critters?" Chandler looked around.

Zeke chuckled. "Gators. A big one can grow to fifteen feet or more." Zeke produced a large machete from nowhere.

Chandler looked at it nervously. "Maybe we should head back?" he suggested.

The machete glinted in the moonlight as it flashed through the air in a high curving arc, before slamming into soft flesh.

Zeke handed Chandler one half of a large cantaloupe. Chandler took it gingerly, sucked at the sweet flesh of the fruit as Zeke started up the motor and headed back across the swamp.

Chandler saw some lights glimmering in the distance. Zeke saw his look, sucked at his teeth, and spat over the side.

"That's the old Raffeti place. 'S'bout the only house round these parts that survived the hurricane of '93. Built on limestone bedrock. It used to be some kinda orphanage." Zeke cleared a nostril with one finger and a brief snort. Chandler waited to see if the other nostril needed attention before turning to him.

"Strange place for an orphanage: the middle of a swamp."

Zeke nodded. "They weren't—" He paused as he searched for the right words, scratched at his stump. "They weren't all born right. A lot of them had problems."

Chandler looked at him. "Deformities, you mean?" He wondered if he was getting too near home with his questions.

Zeke caught his look. "Yeah. This was way before anybody knew about the effects of pollution or anything."

"Were they local children?"

Zeke spat. "No, these kiddies were brought to the orphanage from somewhere else."

Chandler struggled to understand. "From where?"

Zeke shrugged. "There's been a lot of stories over the years."

Chandler looked up from his cantaloupe. “You think they were brought out here from the cities? Unwanted babies?”

“Could be.”

Chandler watched the luminous wake pluming out behind them. Zeke turned to him and yelled above the roar of the engine. “Didn’t Mark Twain say ‘The swamp is a cruel mistress’?”

Chandler guessed this was a phrase he’d be hearing a lot.

TWENTY-EIGHT

LONDON, ENGLAND – 1888

EDWARD WROTE DOWN as much as he could while keeping one eye on the entrance to the Lamson terminal room. But every time someone sent a message around the building, the air pressure fluctuated, causing the sound level in the room to drop. He knew he was missing vital information, but there was nothing he could do. Once he'd consulted his notes, any holes in the story were going to have to be filled in by good old-fashioned investigation. As the men's meeting ended, he jammed the stopper back into the Lamson tube and fled. Somehow he managed to get out of the building unseen and make it home.

During his time working at the newspapers, one of the more experienced reporters had told him to look for the story behind the story. If there had been a ship lost at sea, the story wasn't why the ship sank but who went down with it. With the police, secret agents, royalty, and press all involved, his instincts told him they were all working to conceal the real story. To uncover that, he was going to have to track down the Irish girl, Kelly. He'd always planned to approach the *Pall Mall Gazette* with ideas for more sensational stories, but in a supreme irony, he'd stumbled onto a story that made the *Gazette* the last place on earth he could go.

It seemed Kelly had told four of her friends about something she'd seen outside the club on Cleveland Street one night. He'd also heard the agent referring to Eddy, the Duke of Clarence. What the duke's involvement was, he didn't know. But it was already well known that Eddy had an eye for the ladies and frequented brothels. Of course, that didn't merit the level of conspiracy he'd heard them discussing in Stead's office.

He looked at his notes. He'd had to write them so quickly, they barely made sense even though he'd been using shorthand. The agent had quoted Shakespeare at one point, a piece from *As You Like It*: "All the world's a stage, and all the men and women merely players; they have their exits and their entrances." The agent had made some comment about controlling their exits. Did he mean they were deciding on how they would be killed? Or was it just the illusion of their deaths? Perhaps they were planning to silence the girls permanently at a later date, once Victoria had died? She was quite old after all, and her health was failing.

Trying to find an Irish prostitute named Kelly was going to be hard. It was a common name, and there were thousands of Irish immigrants and as many prostitutes in the East End of London. His pen scratched at the paper as he scribbled his notes. He halted at a sound—but it was only the distant cackle of a woman's laughter on the wind. He thought back to the suggestions he'd heard Stead give to the agent for the killer's name, and then melded his prose . . .

They have fabricated a monster, a phantasm, and a butcher; a man with no soul, designed to terrify the fallen women and the poor of Whitechapel. A killer who is to be known as Jack the Ripper.

Annie sat in the back of the carriage, still shaking after being snatched off the streets. One of the men who'd put her in the carriage had given her a sip of brandy from a flask, and it was starting to calm her nerves. The man with the military bearing sat opposite her while the others kept watch outside. At first she'd thought she was going to be raped, or murdered. But now her breathing had settled, and the warmth of the carriage, in contrast to the chill outside, was as pleasant as she'd felt in a long time. She looked around the inside, noting the interior carriagework and the fittings.

"I've always preferred the Clarence to the Brougham. I catch me ankle on the low step getting into the Brougham." She felt the sides of the back seat and noted a folding seat along the side of the carriage.

"I see you've had a couple of extra seats fitted. Looks like you could have a real party in here." She pointed at the velvet curtains. "You could get dark quarter-lights if you wanted, give you a bit more privacy and style."

The man leaned forward. "I don't think that will be necessary."

On top of all the cheap beer, the brandy was making her light-headed.

"John used to say that the elliptical springs on the Clarence were far superior—I thinks that's the word, yes—far superior to the leaf springs on the Brougham, though I think he said that depended on the number of leaves . . ." She trailed off. Something glinted at her feet. She looked down and saw the brass hinges of a trapdoor set into the floor. She realized the man was looking at her and moved her eyes up to his face.

"Finished?" He looked at her with a half smile. "And who exactly was John?"

"Er, my late husband. He was a carriageman."

The man nodded. "That explains it."

Annie abruptly sat up straight. She remembered something that Mary had said about the man she'd seen in the carriage—a black carriage with blue velvet curtains and a man with a military bearing watching her. A man like the one sitting right opposite Annie now. She looked around desperately for a way out. The man seemed to sense her unease.

"Don't worry. No one is going to hurt you," he said.

"What do you want with me, Mr.—er?" Annie tried to sound as calm as she could, even though she felt like her heart would rip through her chest, it was beating so fast.

"My name isn't important. But what I have to tell you is." He paused until he had her full attention. "I believe you are acquainted with Mary Nichols, Elizabeth Stride, Catherine Eddowes, and Mary Kelly. Is that correct?"

Annie nodded. Her chest felt like a block of ice and she could hardly breathe.

"Good, then you probably know what this is about," said the stranger.

Her blood ran cold. She felt like her life was hanging by a thread. She had to tell this man what he wanted to hear, and she had to do it fast.

"We didn't tell no one else, I swear to God. I'll put me 'and on a hundred Bibles if you like—"

"That won't be necessary. We just need to discuss a few things."

"What?" Annie managed to get out.

He leaned over to her. "Where your body is to be found."

The cobbled streets glistened with moisture from the recent rain. Lightning flashed intermittently across the dark clouds that gathered above the gray waters of the Thames. In the distance, the night sky glowed a dull red as a vast fire raged across the docks. It had started in the South Quay warehouses and spread ferociously from building to building, fueled by the supplies of alcohol, coal, and wood that were stored there. The Connovia, a frigate in dry dock for maintenance, was on fire from stem to stern. Flames raced through her rigging, turning the ship into an incandescent wooden skeleton. Crowds stood transfixed while the firemen battled to bring the blaze under control.

Mary Ann "Polly" Nichols hurried past, her rapid flight standing out against the stationary crowds enthralled by the spectacle. She made eye contact with as many people as she could, as the government man had instructed. He'd said it was better if people saw her and remembered the time and the place. It would make things more plausible. (He'd had to explain what *plausible* meant to her.) The man from the government had told her what was going to happen later that evening, and why, not far from where she stood, her corpse was going to be discovered, identified, and photographed for the newspaper. Her body lying there, all slashed open with her guts thrown around. Her insides displayed like meat on a butcher's slab. She shivered as the gruesome images ran through her mind.

She headed through the back streets to an address she'd been given on Pelham Street, Whitechapel. She knew the other girls would have been given similar instructions to hers and wondered if she would see them before they all set sail for America. Polly had been drinking heavily and was half-rats when Kelly had told her about what happened that night outside the club on Cleveland Street. It had never occurred to her how dangerous the information would turn out to be. She'd soon sobered up when her door had been kicked in and she'd found herself up to her armpits in peelers. She wasn't frightened of the policemen; she'd been dealing with them for most of her working life, even slept with a few of them when it suited her. No, they held no fear for her. But the man that accompanied them, he was different. No one called him by his name, just sir, or guv'nor. He told her he was working for Queen Victoria, as some sort of secret agent.

She didn't care who he was working for. All she knew was that he had the look of a man who'd as soon kill you as stub out a cigarette. She'd spent enough time with the wrong kind of men to recognize who was dangerous and who wasn't, and this man was dangerous, very dangerous. The sort of man you'd listen to and do exactly what he said. He told her that because of what she'd learned about the Duke of Clarence, it was no longer safe for her to remain in the country, and that they would arrange for her to "disappear." She didn't like the sound of that, but he quickly put her mind at rest by describing exactly what *disappear* meant.

She reached the house on Pelham Street and knocked on the door in the special way she'd been told. Three knocks, a pause, and then three more. The door was opened by a large man with vast hands and a neck so thick it looked like his head grew directly out of his shoulders. As he closed the door behind her, she knew one thing was clear. No one was getting in or out unless he wanted them to.

TWENTY-NINE

LONDON, ENGLAND – 1888

SILHOUETTED AGAINST THE red glow of the dock fire, a man dressed in a long black cloak with a hat pulled low held the limp body of a woman in his arms. Blood trickled from her neck, forming a dark pool on the ground beneath him. A carriage stood waiting nearby. The man laid the body down on the cobbled street. He arranged her skirts and placed her legs in a lewd pose, then gave a low whistle. A man darted out of the carriage carrying a tripod supporting a wooden plate camera. He placed the tripod in front of the corpse and held up a flash tray. He ducked down under a cloth as the magnesium powder ignited in a crackling frenzy, its searing white light bleaching the dead face of Mary Ann "Polly" Nichols. The photographer slid the plate across as the light began to fade from the scene.

THIRTY

LONDON, ENGLAND – 1888

ROBERT FITCH HURRIED through the subterranean passageways of the Lyceum Theatre in London's West End, rushing past the faded and torn posters that adorned the walls, playbills of the many productions that had graced the stage over the years. He carried a small glass jar, half-filled with a pale viscous liquid, and was smartly dressed in a silk waistcoat and a dark evening jacket. He wore a mustache, and heavy sideburns framed his intense eyes. He could hear the sound of the orchestra rehearsing for the night's performance, the music drifting down through the passageways from the stage above. He knew he should be getting his makeup and brushes ready for the actors and actresses that evening, but something far more important was occupying his thoughts.

He'd been approached by a member of Queen Victoria's Secret Service. He only knew the man by his code name, Triton. He'd initially thought it was some kind of a joke being played on him by a member of the cast. They'd always said he'd make a perfect spy, as he could transform himself into whosoever he wanted just by using his stage makeup and collection of wigs. But as Triton explained what the service needed from him, he was swept along on a tide of fear and exhilaration.

He wasn't an adventurous man, and at any other time in his career he might have shown Triton the door. But he'd recently developed a new technique to produce lightweight facial molds that could transform anybody's face into that of a completely different person without needing large amounts of makeup. As Triton had outlined his plan, Fitch realized that not only would he have a hand in their clandestine operation, but a chance to field-test his new technique.

He increased his pace along the passageways, passing corridors that led off to the left and right, including one marked STAGE. He continued for a few more yards before taking a left-hand fork and coming to a door. It had his name on it and MAKE-UP DEPARTMENT in faded and cracked gilt paint. Fitch had worked at the Lyceum for many years and had always thought of it as his second home, but really he spent more time in his room at the theater than at his house. There was a poster for *Macbeth* fastened to the top of the door. Henry Irving and Ellen Terry were headlining the cast of the production. He elbowed the door handle down and pushed on through, taking care not to spill any of the liquid in the jar.

Inside were a dressing table and mirror. A collection of bowls half-filled with what looked like modeling clay of some sort sat on the top of the table. A pair of sturdy trestle tables occupied the middle of the room, on top of which lay two women. Their faces were covered with a thick layer of dark brown clay. Two drinking straws protruded from where their nostrils were obscured by the clay masks. Fitch carefully placed the jar of liquid onto another small table and reached over to feel the clay on the faces of the women.

"Good, I think I can safely say the consistency is now perfect. How do you feel?"

Both of the women raised two fingers in his direction in an obscene gesture. Fitch smiled.

"Oh, very droll. With your wit I dare say we could find a role for you in the next production of the Scottish play. Maybe around the cauldron."

He carefully removed the breathing straws from one of the women. Slipping a finger under the bottom edge of the clay, he peeled it off her face. The woman sat up and swung her legs off the edge of the table. She had dark brown hair worn in curls that framed pale gray eyes. She had on a black skirt and jacket, complete with a buttonhole containing a red rose and a white maidenhair fern, and a checked scarf. She was tall for a woman, standing at five foot ten, and all of her lower front teeth were missing. She also spoke with a stutter.

"J-Jesus, now I kn-know how it feels t-to b-be d-dead." She produced a small bag of cachous from her pocket and popped some into her mouth, chewing vigorously, like a horse; rolling them to her back molars to break them down before swallowing.

Fitch removed the straws from the other woman and prized the clay from her face. "Well, Lizzie, better to feel dead than be dead," he said.

Lizzie rubbed at her face. "That st-st-stuff smells l-l-like horseshit," she stammered.

The other woman, Kate, sat up, reached behind her, and produced a black straw bonnet trimmed with green and black velvet. She was shorter than Lizzie, with hazel eyes, dark auburn hair, and the letters *TC* tattooed on her left forearm. She wore a black cloth jacket trimmed with fur and a dark green chintz skirt patterned with Michaelmas daisies and golden lilies. She rubbed her face and smelled her fingers.

"Yer right, Lizzie. What is it?" She looked at Fitch as he carried both clay masks and placed them carefully on the dressing table, facedown.

"It's kaolin, china clay," Fitch said. "The purest form of clay available, not *horseshit*, as you so eloquently put it." He picked up the small jar of liquid and carefully poured it into the clay masks, then set the jar down and used a small paintbrush to apply an even coating to the inside of the clay molds.

"I need to keep this moving. It sets quickly." He cleaned the brush with some kind of liquid.

Kate wandered over to a shelf on which sat various stage props. She picked up a dagger and pushed the blade with a finger. It gave slightly against its concealed spring. Fitch came over and took it from her.

"Careful. I'll be needing that for *Hamlet* later." He put it back down on the shelf.

Kate put her bonnet on. "So what happens now?"

Fitch checked the consistency of the sap in the masks. "Well, Kate, we've been through this before—"

Kate nodded. "I know, but being stuck behind that mud has given me a headache and I can't remember nothin'."

Fitch sighed. "At eight o'clock this evening, you put on an act as if you're drunk, make a lot of commotion, so people get a good look at you," he said. "Maybe do your fire engine impersonation."

"Very funny, Mr. Mudpie. Then what 'appens?" Kate asked.

"You'll be taken into the cells and released at one in the morning. You make your way to the corner of Duke Street and Church Passage. A man wearing a red-knotted scarf will approach you. He'll show you this ring." Fitch showed them the hand on which he wore a silver ring with a twisted serpent design.

"Once you've made sure people coming out of the Imperial Club have seen you, make your way towards Mitre Square. A carriage will pick you up on the way."

Lizzie looked at him. "What about me?"

Fitch shook his head in exasperation. "You'll head to Fairclough Street to arrive at midnight. A man in a long black coat will approach you. He'll show you the same ring. You'll both remain there until somebody has seen you well enough to identify you later. When it's safe, you'll head to Dutfield's Yard, and a carriage will pick you up." He paused. "Are you both wearing your rings?"

Kate and Lizzie held up their hands to display the silver rings they wore.

"Good. You'll use them to identify yourselves if you are approached by anyone claiming to be from the government."

Fitch went over to the masks and touched the surface of the dried sap. He nodded, satisfied with the process. He carefully unpeeled one of the thin masks from inside its clay mold. It hung from his hand like a vestigial sack of wet skin.

He carried it toward Lizzie.

"Right, time for you to meet your maker."

Edward wrote his notes as the scrape of the lamplighter's ladder on the cobbles outside heralded nightfall.

And so it began. Hysteria and fear swept through London's East End, amongst the poor and the unfortunate. The papers had never been so popular. Those too poor to buy one would cluster around those that had, listening to the lurid details of the story being read out to the assembled crowd. From my window I could see a newsboy selling papers on the corner of the street, their headlines charting the spread of fear and forging history in their crucible of lies.

Edward put down his pen, stretched, and looked at the pile of pages stacked neatly in front of him. A thought crept into his mind and refused to go away. What if they were moving the women to another country to make it easier to dispose of them, when the time was right? His blood slowed to an icy crawl. If that was true, it made him an accomplice to their murder if he did nothing. He paced the room, aware of time running out. From the newspaper headlines and the body count, he knew there were only three more victims to be "discovered." It was too late to try and track down the other women, but if he found Kelly there was a chance he could at least save her and maybe find out more about the conspiracy and her part in it. He slipped on a worn overcoat and a hat to keep out the cold, and set off into the night.

The carriage stood in the shadows, the horses snorting vapor into the cold air, eyes rolling, hooves restless against the cobbles, as if they sensed what was taking place a few feet from them. Inside the carriage, Tumblety bent over the body that lay slumped on the seat, the flesh already stiffening under his touch. His knife was sharp and sure as he hacked through the pale body, his eyes black and dead. He paused, his hands stroking the dead flesh, caressing the wetness beneath his fingers like a lover. Then his knife went to work.

He reached into the cavity he had created, his mouth a grim slit. This was the part he loved the most. It brought a level of intimacy with another human he could never have while they were alive. He reached in and swiftly identified the organ by touch alone . . . cutting through the skeins of fibrous muscle that held it fast. He removed it and dropped it into a glass jar. It made a wet sucking sound as it slid inside. He sealed the lid shut. Now, he just needed to place the remains for maximum effect.

The carriage started to shake and the horses whinnied with fear. There was a sudden rushing noise, and smoke and steam enveloped the carriage. Tumblety heard the driver quiet the horses. The sound faded and the smoke cleared. Tumblety smiled to himself. They were stationed over a steam vent, or "blowhole" as it was called. The gratings set into the road gave access to the covered way through which the East London Railway ran.

When the railways had first been built, making the air breathable in the subsurface network had posed a problem. The smoke and steam belched out by the locomotives had to be dispersed. As a result, many openings originally designed to provide light were adapted as smoke vents. Blowholes were bored all along the route between King's Cross and Edgware Road, and this was adopted throughout the network. Triton had always insisted on having two carriages stationed over such blowhole gratings. That way, if they were ever compromised, he could lower the trapdoor in the carriage and be through the grating and into the underground tunnels in seconds. From there he could make his way unseen to the St. Mary's station vent in Whitechapel and up into the second waiting carriage.

Tumblety rapped twice on the roof and heard the carriageman crack the whip. The carriage lurched, wheels clattering against the cobbles as they headed off into the dark.

THIRTY-ONE

LONDON, ENGLAND – 1888

THE STREETS AROUND Dutfield's Yard were deserted. Even the most desperate of dolly-mops had long since given up plying their trade for the night. A blanket of dank gray fog rolled across the slick cobblestones, serving to cloak the carriage that stood waiting in the gloom. Tumblety moved quickly to the opposite side of the street and laid the corpse down against the brick wall of the house. He drew up her legs and arranged her skirts, exposing bloodied flesh. Pleased with his work, he gave a low whistle. A photographer jumped down from the carriage, set up his tripod, and held his flash tray above the corpse. The magnesium powder crackled and flared in the dark, throwing harsh shadows over the lifeless face of Elizabeth Stride before dimming.

He packed up his tripod and emptied the glowing powder onto the street. Tumblety headed back toward the carriage, the man atop it calling out to him.

"C'mon, get a move on! We still have one more to do and we're running out of night." He climbed back into the carriage, and the photographer jumped in behind him. The carriage driver snapped his whip, and the carriage clattered away through swirling curtains of fog before disappearing into the dark.

THIRTY-TWO

LONDON, ENGLAND – 1888

EDWARD HEADED DOWN Grafton Way and on into Fitzroy Square. The park was a favorite haunt for the local prostitutes, or dolly-mops, as his more down-to-earth colleagues called them. He'd learned a little of the slang that they used when he'd been taken along to question them as a wide-eyed young man. As he walked through the park, he was aware of shapes in the dark. The gleam of eyes as women sized him up, unsure whether he was a potential client or just someone unaware of the park's reputation.

They seemed far warier than he remembered. He wasn't sure if it was the recent crackdown by the peelers, or the lurid Ripper headlines in the papers. Either way they weren't taking any chances. Finally, a shape detached itself from the shadows and materialized beside him. Her features were coarse and her eyes dim. Her breath reeked of cheap gin, made worse by an attempt to cover the stench with peppermints. Edward stifled his gag reflex and raised his hat. She stared quizzically at him, straining to see him with her bloodshot eyes.

"Looking for company, love?" She smiled, her teeth like a row of black nails. He pressed a sixpence into her calloused hand and got straight to the point.

"I'm looking for a girl."

She smiled and once more the putrid stench enveloped him.

"Well, you've come to the right part of London for that, me old cock. Do you have lodgings, or are you going to be quick?"

He talked quickly, trying not to breathe in the stench. "I'm looking for a girl named Kelly. She's Irish. Maybe she hasn't been around recently . . . ?"

The woman looked at him slyly. "And why would you be wanting to see her, kind sir?"

Edward could feel more palm greasing was going to be needed.

"I just want to talk to her."

She looked him up and down, suspicion creeping into her expression. "Are you a peeler?"

He shook his head. "No, just a reporter after some background information."

She laughed, a hoarse cackle. "'Background information'—is that what they call it nowadays?"

He could see she was dragging out the exchange, and he pressed a thrupenny bit into her ready palm. She secreted it among the numerous layers of clothing that swaddled her squat body.

Edward nodded, realized he was probably wasting his time with this woman. Still, he had to at least give it one more try.

"Bloody cold this evening. You don't need that on top of this Ripper scare."

She was warming to him a little. "You're right," she said. "I'm old and ugly enough not to care—but the young 'uns, they don't want to end up cut. The peelers ain't doin' nothing to catch him, and more girls is getting sliced by the day."

Edward nodded. "Yes. The more publicity I can give the story, the more chance there is of the killer being caught. Somebody must have seen something."

She moved into the light. He could see that many years ago she'd probably been attractive, before life had taken its toll.

She lowered her voice to a husky whisper. "There was talk that one of the girls had seen this Ripper bastard—and that he'd seen her." She put her mouth so close to his ear that his eyes watered with the smell. "Word was she was keeping her head down in case he found her."

Edward knew Kelly hadn't seen the Ripper, because he didn't really exist. But maybe she was lying low for other reasons.

"You think she saw the Ripper?" he asked.

The woman shrugged.

"I don't know, but them girls is turnin' up dead with their insides spilled out, ain't they? Polly, Annie, Kate, and Long Liz, they was regulars round here. Then they just disappeared. And now they're turning up, gutted like fish."

Edward nodded. "So this other girl, the one you think saw the Ripper, can you remember her name?"

She smiled, made a pantomime of remembering. He produced another thruppeny piece and put it in her palm. The coin vanished in a flash.

"Well, now you mention it, her name could have been Kelly. Though they sometimes calls 'er Ginger or Fair Emma. She's Irish but sometimes speaks with a strange accent—someone said she could be Welsh. Has a right gigglemug."

"Do you know where I can find her?" Edward asked.

The woman nodded. "Miller's Court, off Dorset Street. I don't know the number, but when I was there a week ago, one of the downstairs windows was broken—ruddy draughty it was 'n' all."

Edward scribbled the details down in the small notebook he always carried.

"Thank you, you've been very helpful."

"Glad to help. If you need any more *background information*, I'm always available." She turned, lifted her skirts up, and shook her flaccid buttocks at him. She broke into a loud cackle, which ended in a wheezing cough that he could still hear long after he'd left the park.

Edward headed down toward Spitalfields through the chill of the night. A thick fog rolled off the river, and he cursed himself for not putting on a thicker jacket beneath his overcoat. He cut through the Christ Church graveyard and headed toward Dorset Street. By repute, it was the worst street in London. An area that the peelers would only police in pairs, with a murder rate of one or two a month. It boasted the cheapest lodgings in London, and after a few minutes of walking down the street, it was obvious why. The stench from excrement and rotting food was overwhelming, while the sound of babies crying, couples arguing, and drunken fights in the streets must have made sleep impossible. Miller's Court was one of the alleys off Dorset Street.

Once there, Edward began looking for a broken downstairs window. He came to number 13, and saw at once that two of the lower windowpanes were damaged. One was cracked and the other broken, with jagged spikes of glass protruding from the rotten wood of the frame. A candle guttered inside but did little to soften the squalor he glimpsed within. He knocked on the door. There was a shuffling sound and the door opened a crack.

"What do you want?" a woman asked in a low voice with an Irish accent. He saw a trace of blonde hair and cornflower-blue eyes in the gloom. He could see she was frightened.

"My name is Edward Travis. I'm a reporter. I'd like to talk to you."

There was a pause, then, "I got nothing to say."

Edward could see that she was shivering in the damp cold of the flat. Condensation dripped down the windows, and a few pieces of coal glowed a dull red in the grate.

"I know what happened outside the club on Cleveland Street," Edward said.

The door slammed shut. He went back to the broken window and, lowering his voice, tried again.

"Whatever the government agent told you—well, it might not be the whole truth." He waited.

There was the sound of the door opening and then a whisper, "Come in, quickly."

THIRTY-THREE

BATON ROUGE, LOUISIANA – Present day

CHANDLER AWOKE FROM a restless sleep in Duke's Airstream. His dreams fractured by faceless people wading through the swamp, their mouths stretched wide in soundless screams. For a moment, he thought he was still flying across the Atlantic, surrounded by the roar of jet engines. But the smell of fresh coffee, the cylindrical aluminum shell of Duke's Airstream home, and the whine of the coffee grinder had tricked his mind.

Duke had a classic limited-edition Airstream trailer. It was a magnificent piece of engineering: over thirty-four feet of polished aluminum, with a curved three-section panoramic window at the front and a slide-out section with an awning to one side. The inside was fitted with hickory cabinets. A king-sized bed filled one end while at the far end there was a sofa, which stretched across the eight-foot width of the trailer and provided a second bed. The slide-out section provided another seating area with a dining table and two sofas. There was also a toilet, shower, and kitchen complete with cooker, fridge, and pantry, and a television set had been mounted high above the dining table, taking advantage of the over six and a half feet of headroom.

If he had to think of a word to sum the trailer up, Chandler would have plumped for *palatial*. It certainly bore no resemblance to any of the cramped and damp caravans he'd spent time in on the windswept coasts of England. Chandler thought it would even comfortably accommodate the hunched figure of Harris Jenson, his dour boss.

He felt slightly guilty that Duke had given him the king-sized bed, but managed to assuage his guilt with the thought that Duke would have the benefit of its comfort for the rest of the year. He came out of his room and into the kitchen. He and Duke did a little shuffle past each other in the limited space and Duke handed him a mug of coffee.

"Sleep alright?" he asked.

"Like a baby," Chandler lied, in typical British fashion. "Thanks for putting me up, by the way."

Duke smiled. "I wanted you to have the real Airstream experience—that whole retro feel. Nothing to beat it."

Chandler nodded. "You're right there. I love it. But just let me know if I get under your feet. Okay?"

Duke grinned. "Sure. And speaking of things you'll love, Roxie's gonna be helping us with the reconstruction software today."

Chandler looked up. "What happened to Dr. Google?"

"He's at some gaming conference in St. Louis. He'll be back later this afternoon. Roxie's going to help us with the local history up at the library as well."

Chandler nodded, took a slug of coffee, and put the mug down.

"Okay, I'll just clean my teeth and I'm ready."

Duke gave him another wide grin. "No rush. Them bodies ain't going nowhere."

THIRTY-FOUR

BUTTE LA ROSE, LOUISIANA – Present day

AS HE AND Duke walked into the old warehouse, Chandler noticed some extra free-standing air-conditioning units around the working area. A girl stood with her back to them, setting up some more equipment. She turned and flashed a smile in their direction. With her blonde hair tied back, alert blue eyes, and tanned face, she was spectacular, and Chandler was sure he'd seen her before.

"This is Roxie," Duke said. "She's studying for a masters in forensic anthropology. Roxie, this is my friend Chandler."

She walked over to them and held out her hand. Chandler took it. For one crazy moment, he felt like bowing, as if he were in some period drama. She was having an effect on him that he hadn't felt since he was a teenager. He definitely needed some more coffee. He let go of her hand, aware that Duke was smiling, the knowing eyes in his jovial face twinkling.

Roxie smiled at him. "Chandler. You're a southpaw?"

He stood unmoving. "Er, am I?"

Duke shook his head. "She doesn't mean you're a boxer, just that you're left-handed."

Chandler smiled. "I guess it's genetic. My dad was left-handed," he said.

Roxie nodded. "Yes. Left-handed people are meant to be high achievers. The 'D' gene is for *dextral*, meaning right-handed, and the 'C' gene stands for *chance*, which means you have a fifty-percent chance of being right- or left-handed."

"I told you she was smart," said Duke.

Roxie smiled again. It was like the sun breaking through clouds. "Anyway, nice to meet you. I'll be picking up where Phaedon left off." She paused. "You're a Ripperologist, right?"

Chandler mentally shook himself. "Man and boy—it's a family tradition. I'm writing a book on the identity of the real Ripper. Well, I say *writing*, but in reality I spend most of my time staring at a blank screen, drinking coffee."

She kept a straight face. "Have you tried turning it on?"

Duke smiled behind his hand. Chandler grinned like an idiot.

"You should meet Zeke—he's the chucklemeister of the swamps," he said.

Roxie smiled. "Did he tell you about the millions of gators?" She read the answer in his face. "Ha! Don't worry; he uses that line on all his tours. You're more likely to see Jack the Ripper than an alligator, unless they want you to see them." She wrinkled her nose, managing to look even cuter than she already was.

"So, got yourself a bit of a mountain to climb," she said. "One of the greatest unsolved mysteries of all time."

Duke smiled, sensing the magnetic pull she was having on his friend. "Chandler thinks our find here might be kinda significant."

Roxie tilted her face and flicked a rogue curl behind her ear before speaking. "What is it about the Ripper that fascinates you?"

Chandler snapped out of his reverie. "It's the period of history that he carried out his crimes in that makes him—"

Roxie raised an eyebrow. Chandler shifted gears.

"Or *her*, so fascinating. Back then the Ripper would have been like Dahmer, Bundy, and Manson rolled into one in our day. They'd never seen anything like it: a sadistic serial killer without motive who left no clues." He paced around the area, putting distance between himself and Roxie, trying to get back some focus. "The violent deaths of the prostitutes, and the ritualistic way they were killed, had a huge effect on the population of Whitechapel at the time," he said, warming to his subject.

Roxie smiled at his enthusiasm. "Wow, you really dig this stuff."

Chandler paused. "I guess I can come across as a little obsessive."

Roxie shook her head. "*Obsession* is just another word for *focused*, and if that's what it takes to solve a crime, then obsess away, I say."

Chandler smiled. "That's a refreshing opinion."

Roxie shrugged. "My father used to tell me these great stories about the bodies in the Egyptian tombs, the Piltdown Man hoax. I was hooked. I knew then that I wanted to make the dead give up their secrets."

Duke coughed, and the other two looked at him like they'd just remembered he was there.

Roxie's cell beeped, breaking the spell further. She flicked it open, sighing.

"Sometimes I wish I'd never taught Mom how to text."

She replied to the message, her fingers flickering across the screen like a bird's wings. There was a soft whoosh as her message shot off into the ether. Chandler wandered over to one of the screens and she followed. It was filled with the faces of the women from the carriage.

"You got some more detail on the heads?" he asked. Roxie nodded. She tapped some keys on the computer keyboard. Five wire-frame heads appeared on another screen.

Roxie pointed to them.

"We digitized the five skulls from the swamp bodies. As you know, Phaedon matched the skulls' physiology to the photos from the carriage. But I wanted to get a more accurate depiction of how they might have really looked, rather than the crude photo overlay. I've rigged up a couple of old speedguns Chilly got me from the redundant stores down at the station. I connected them in parallel to make a Lidar unit."

Chandler looked at her. "You made a Lidar unit out of a couple of speedguns?"

Roxie tapped some more keys. "Budget restrictions are the mother of invention. I cross-referenced the data and fed the information into a facial-recognition program, so now we should be good to go."

Over on the other side of the room, the radar speedguns on the steel table pulsed with light, scanning the remains of one of the bodies shrouded in plastic, the head exposed. Reticulated laser beams played across the mummified skin stretched across the skull, bathing it in a ghostly green glow. Another screen filled with a black-and-white photograph of the five women. The computer cloaked the wire frames of the victims' skulls with the faces from the old sepia photographs. They rotated on the screen as the computer software coated them with digital flesh. Roxie pointed to the screen.

"Skull topography matches their features," she said.

"They're a definite match. Which confirms Phaedon's findings," said Duke.

Roxie glanced at the clock on her cell phone and got up.

"I've gotta go see my mom. She gets real cranky if I'm late with her food. You need anything, you let me know." She flashed another of her dazzling smiles at Chandler. "Nice to meet you."

Chandler fumbled for the right words. "Yes, er, you too. If I—we—need anything, I'll er . . ."

She tapped the screen of her cell.

"I've toothed you my contact details. I'm free later if you want me to show you the sights. Don't be a stranger. See ya."

She floated out of the lab. Chandler stared, her smile burnt onto his retinas like an eclipse of the sun. He mentally shook himself and turned to Duke.

"She's, er, nice."

Duke laughed, clapped him on the back.

"Nice? She *toothed* you for Chrissake. You're practically engaged."

THIRTY-FIVE

BATON ROUGE, LOUISIANA – Present day

CHANDLER SAT IN the passenger seat of Roxie's Jeep as they headed down the I-10. The air conditioner struggled to cope with the humidity and the heat outside. They were traveling down the hundred-mile route alongside the Mississippi River known as Plantation Alley. It was a strange mix of industrial complexes, trailer parks, upscale vacation homes, and cemeteries. Decaying plantations and ten-foot high cane filled the warm air with the smell of molasses and gave an illusion of how the surrounds must have looked in the nineteenth century. The great mansions along the river bends were still an impressive sight, despite their grandeur being diluted by the petrochemical refineries around them. Large steamers packed with tourists and with iconic paddle wheels churned the water of the great, winding river. The tinny sound of their prerecorded audio guides and cheesy organ music drifted across the water.

As she drove toward the Louisiana Capitol building, Roxie adopted the role of tour guide, filling Chandler in on the local history and points of interest.

"When the French claimed the area between the Bayougoula and Houma Indian hunting grounds in 1699, the boundary line was marked by a stripped tree reddened with the blood of slaughtered animals, so the area wound up with the name Baton Rouge."

Chandler smiled. "I guess they didn't bother much about image in those days."

"No, I guess not."

Roxie pulled up outside the Capitol building, and they climbed out of the Jeep and into a wall of humidity. Chandler stared up at the iconic thirty-three-story Art Deco edifice of Huey Long's obsession.

"Impressive," he said.

They walked up the steps, each one of them carved with the name of a different state. The looming statue of Long stared down at them from above. Roxie pointed at it.

"Long fought for this place and died in it. Killed by a doctor."

Chandler looked up at the statue. "They'll get you one way or another," he said.

Roxie gave a grim smile. "Yeah, usually with their charges."

They walked through the imposing entrance into the Memorial Hall, past the bronze relief of the state of Louisiana, surrounded by the names of the sixty-four parishes.

"This is the tallest capitol building in America," Roxie said.

Chandler looked around the imposing building. "How on earth did Long get this built during the Depression?"

"He did whatever it took," she answered. "He always saw the bigger picture."

"You mean the end justifying the means?" Chandler asked.

Roxie nodded. "He thought it was important to get things done, even if it meant bending a few rules."

They took the elevator up to the Observation Deck on the twenty-seventh floor. From there, they had a stunning view over Baton Rouge: the Mississippi, Louisiana University, and Huey Long's statue.

Chandler turned to Roxie. "How about you? Do you think the end justifies the means?"

Roxie shrugged. "Sometimes. The law protects those with the most money and power, and they're not always the people with the country's best interests at heart."

Suddenly Chandler remembered where he'd first seen her.

"You were protesting at the airport," he said.

She turned to him and smiled. “Yes. People like Governor Blackburn have the power and money to force through bills that work for their own benefit.”

“He seems to be in a helluva rush to clean the swamps up,” Chandler said. “Isn’t that a good thing?”

Roxie shook her head. “I’ve been out to the plant. With members of my group.”

Chandler looked at her. “Really? Don’t they shoot people for trespassing out here?”

“Only if you get caught,” Roxie said. “And we were lucky not to. They have more security than the White House.”

“Maybe it’s considered a terrorist target?”

Roxie shrugged.

“You don’t think that’s the reason?” Chandler asked.

She shook her head. “They have a biomass generator out there, and along with the decontamination operations they run, they manufacture HCFC-22, refrigeration coolant.”

Chandler looked at her. “I thought that stuff was banned—isn’t it a greenhouse gas?”

Roxie nodded. “Yes, but the byproduct of manufacturing it is HCFC-23, which is over fourteen thousand times more polluting than the coolant itself. And that’s what he’s paid big bucks to destroy.”

Chandler couldn’t believe what she was telling him. “Is it just me or does that sound crazy?”

Roxie smiled. “It’s not just you. It is nuts. A complete ban on them doesn’t come in until 2020.”

“So his operation is legitimate?”

Roxie sighed. “Unfortunately, yes. Blackburn doesn’t have a green bone in his body. With him it’s always about the money.”

“What makes you think he’s doing something illegal?” Chandler asked.

Roxie made a face. “When you interrogate a suspected criminal and you have no evidence, what makes you think he is guilty, or not guilty?”

Chandler smiled. “My instinct.”

"Exactly. Call it a hunch, animal instinct, or female intuition, whatever he's up to, I'm going to find out what it is."

Chandler looked at the slim, confident girl walking alongside him and felt a pang of fear. He turned to her.

"From what you've told me about Governor Blackburn, he has very few scruples."

Roxie stopped walking. "And?"

Chandler shrugged. "Maybe you should stay away from him and his plant?"

She shot him one of her knee-weakening smiles. "That's sweet. But I'm a big girl. I can take care of myself."

He shook his head. "I'm being serious. If they catch you—"

"I doubt Blackburn would want any negative publicity while he's running for the Senate."

Chandler nodded. But he wondered how far Blackburn would go to avoid it.

Roxie looked at her watch. "Okay. Are you still jet-lagged, or do you fancy seeing some more sights?"

Chandler wondered if she knew that whatever the sights were, they would just be a pale reflection alongside her own beauty. He found himself nodding animatedly like some lovesick schoolboy.

"Why not?"

THIRTY-SIX

SPIRIT'S SWAMP, LOUISIANA – Present day

ROXIE'S JEEP SAT to one side of the road. In the distance, the plant's smokestacks thrust concrete fingers into the darkening sky, the clouds above pink-bellied from the flames of the flare stack. Roxie and Chandler sat on the hood of the car and drank beer as they looked out over the swamp. Chandler took a slug from his bottle.

"When you said you wanted to show me the sights . . ."

He looked around at the dark wilderness that surrounded them. Roxie smiled, punched him in the arm.

"What, you don't like swamps?"

"Far from it," Chandler said. "The thing I find most irritating about London is its lack of swamps."

She laughed. "You Englishmen, you're so quaint. We've been here ten minutes, and I still have all my clothes on."

Chandler looked to see if she was being serious, before adopting a mock English gentleman's tone. "Oh, I'm sorry, how very rude of me."

She took another slug of beer. "Don't sweat it. A lot of men don't know they can use their mouth as a communication device."

"We're famous for our stiff upper lips," he said.

There was a long pause as she studied him. "You must think I'm pretty forward. I guess I've been around folks who didn't get a chance to live life as much as they wanted."

Chandler remembered the way she'd talked about her mother, the innate sadness that filled her eyes after she read her texts. "Your parents?"

She gave a sad smile. "Yeah, they had it tough."

Chandler looked over at her. Bathed in the moonlight, she looked like a Hollywood star from the age of the silver screen.

"I know what you mean. You only get one life, after all," he said.

She clinked her bottle against his. "To life."

Chandler looked across the swamp at the distant lights of Blackburn's plant.

"What happened between you and Blackburn?"

Roxie looked sad for a moment before answering. "My dad worked at one of Blackburn's refineries for most of his life, till he got sick. Leukemia."

"I'm sorry," Chandler said.

She shrugged. "He worked a lot with benzene. They said that's what caused it. Mom got sick as well—her lungs. We tried to get some compensation, to help her out. Blackburn's lawyers dragged the case out longer than my father could fight it. He died without getting a penny."

Chandler shook his head.

"That happens a lot." Roxie looked at him. "How about you? Are your folks still alive?"

"My mum is. But we lost my dad a while back. Cancer."

"I'm sorry," she said. "Were you close?"

"Yes. More so at the end. We were working on the book together."

"The Ripper book?"

"Yes. *Jack the Ripper: Monster or Myth?* Available in all good bookstores. If I ever finish it."

"I'm sure you will," Roxie said.

"I promised my father on his deathbed that I would. So, no going back on that one."

"Was he a policeman as well?"

Chandler nodded. "Yes. It's a family tradition. I caught the Ripper obsession from him."

"Why do you think he was so obsessed?"

"I don't know. He began to go through my great-great-grandfather's things, and he was hooked. When you're a policeman, you look for the things that aren't there rather than the clues that are."

"What do you mean?" Roxie said.

"Well, Edward—that's my great-great-grandfather—was a journalist all those years ago. He seems to have got a bee in his bonnet about the Ripper—"

"Not surprising considering what was going on back then," Roxie said.

"Yes. But we went through all of his papers and manuscripts and it's like there's a black hole where the real story should be."

Roxie smiled. "Well, now you've got Duke and all of us working with you. We might be able to fill that in."

"I hope so." Chandler paused. "It's just . . ."

"What?" Roxie asked.

"The day my dad passed. He was peaceful. The morphine was doing its job. He wasn't feeling any pain. I thought he'd gone, and then suddenly he sat up, opened his eyes, smiled, and looked right at me. He grabbed my arm. And then he said, 'What if I am the walrus?' And then he died."

"What do you think he meant?" Roxie asked.

Chandler shook his head. "I have no idea."

"It's a Beatles song, isn't it?"

"Yes. It was their psychedelic period. *Sergeant Pepper's Lonely Hearts Club Band.* The lyrics were wild. 'I am he as you are he as you are me and we are all together.'" Chandler continued, "'I am the eggman. They are the eggmen. I am the walrus. Goo goo g'joob.'"

"And you have no idea why he said that?" Roxie asked.

Chandler shook his head. "No. It might have just been the morphine. We always loved the same kind of music. Maybe he was just thinking of happier times."

Roxie nodded. "The mind can play strange tricks. Especially near the end," she said.

They stood there in silence for a moment. A mosquito circled Chandler with a low drone, and he swatted it away. Roxie laughed as he flailed around with his hand.

"We'd better get you back inside the Jeep—they can smell tourist flesh from miles away. Southpaws are a particular delicacy for them."

Chandler climbed down from the hood and held out a hand to help Roxie down. There was the roar of a powerful engine and headlights swept over them. A large dump truck sped past, throwing up dust as it thundered down the road. There was a bumper sticker on its rear fender: I DON'T HAVE ROAD RAGE. YOU'RE JUST AN IDIOT. Roxie took Chandler's hand and jumped down. She looked back at the truck.

"They're working twenty-four hours a day now."

They climbed back inside the Jeep and she put the radio on.

THIRTY-SEVEN

SPIRIT'S SWAMP, LOUISIANA – Present day

THE CATERPILLAR 773B dump truck was over thirty feet long, weighed one hundred tons, and had six huge wheels, driven by an engine producing over 650 brake horsepower. Khalid wound it up though the gears toward its maximum speed of thirty-five miles an hour. His instructions had been clear. One job, ten thousand dollars, and a chance to start a new life. But as he'd approached the Jeep, he'd seen that the girl and the English detective were outside the vehicle. He had no choice but to drive past. Unless they were inside the Jeep, there was no guarantee of success. He cursed his bad luck. He would have to come back.

Roxie selected a country and western station on the radio. The Jeep filled with a classic from George Jones: "He Stopped Loving Her Today."

"This is one of my mom's favorites," Roxie said. She cranked up the volume, first mouthing the words, then singing along. Chandler joined in.

"You know, she came to see him one last time. Oh, and we all wondered if she would. And it kept running through my mind. This time he's over her for good. He stopped loving her today. They placed a wreath

upon his door. And soon they'll carry him away. He stopped loving her today."

They shared a look as the song came to an end. Chandler tried to look away, but the pull was too strong. Roxie leaned forward, her lips inches from his. He hesitated for a fraction of a second—and the Jeep started to shake. A blinding light filled the interior, the noise deafening. The dump truck loomed in front of them, rammed them head-on. There was an explosion of sound. Metal on metal, glass shattering, airbags exploding. Chandler fought with the passenger door, but it was jammed shut.

"Get out!" Chandler screamed at Roxie. But the Jeep's chassis was twisted and her door was wedged in its buckled frame. Chandler stared through the shattered windscreen. The Jeep's hood was under the truck's massive front wheels, crushed by the other vehicle's sheer weight and momentum, and the truck's engine kept on revving, threatening to drive over them completely. Chandler looked frantically for something to smash the back window with, when the cacophony of noise overwhelmed his senses.

And then it happened. *His mind was jolted back to the smoking wreckage of the bomb-blasted bus—clawing at the red-hot metal, choking on the stench of burnt flesh. Searching for Claire. He heaved at the twisted metal fragments buckled around the smoking corpses trapped in the back. He could smell his own flesh burning.*

He heard someone screaming.

And then he was back in the Jeep, with Roxie's scream reverberating in his ears. He started to kick at the back window with his feet but couldn't get enough force to smash it. The roof was caving in. Then there was an explosion of noise and the back window shattered. He grabbed Roxie by the arm and dragged her through.

They landed clear of the truck's wheels and rolled to the side of the road. The truck careened on, crushing the Jeep, spitting out the remains like a beer can though a recycler. Something flew out from the back of it as it roared off into the night, a round, pale shape spinning through the air. It bounced on the track and skidded past them. Chandler looked at the sticker on the rear fender as the truck rumbled down the road. I DON'T HAVE ROAD RAGE. YOU'RE JUST AN

IDIOT. A surge of adrenaline flooded his bloodstream. He felt a red mist rising up behind his eyes. He savagely kicked the remains of a smashed light cluster, sent it spinning into the swamp, then jumped up and down, fists pumping the air. Screaming into the night.

"You fucking moron! Didn't you even see us? Jesus Christ on a fucking bike, what is wrong with you?"

He staggered, nearly collapsed. His forehead icy cold. And then he threw up. He wiped his mouth, shook himself, and went over to Roxie. He helped her up.

"You alright?"

She looked at him. "I'm okay. What just happened?"

"Er, I'm sorry about that. I sometimes have a bit of a mouth on me."

Roxie shook her head. "No. I can handle your docker's mouth," she said. "I meant one moment you're trying to get me out of the Jeep, the next second you're a zombie."

"It's why I'm not allowed on active duty," Chandler said.

"Post-traumatic stress?"

"Yes."

"Duke told me how you lost your wife."

He nodded. "Sometimes I get flashbacks, or just freeze. I haven't had an attack for years."

Roxie watched the glow of the truck's taillights disappearing into the distance, the sound of its engine still audible across the swamp.

"I don't suppose somebody's tried to kill you recently," she said, anger and fear in her eyes.

Chandler stared down the road. "When it happens there's no way I can tell between what's real and what isn't." He paused. "It's like I'm still connected to Claire even though she died years ago."

Roxie shrugged. "Some people would say it's spiritual."

"What about you?" he asked.

"I'd probably go with quantum entanglement."

"You would," said Chandler. "Now explain what it means."

Roxie smiled. "Einstein called it 'spooky action at a distance,' and considered it to be impossible. But most physicists believe two particles can be linked to each other even if they are separated by billions of light years of space, and that a change in one will affect the other."

Chandler nodded. "I agree with Einstein, that is definitely spooky. Do you believe it's possible?"

Roxie reached over and held his hand. "I guess it depends whether you go with Einstein or the crowd."

Chandler thought about it. "Or God. I guess one day we'll know which it is. And whether human beings work the same way as particles." He paused. "Is there any question you can't answer with science?"

Roxie smiled. "Love, I suppose—but then again, there's pheromones."

Chandler shook his head. "I'm sorry this has all got a bit deep," he said.

"That's not surprising," Roxie said. "Somebody just tried to put us six feet under."

Chandler nodded. "We'd better give Duke a call. That lunatic needs to be stopped before he kills someone."

Roxie pointed to the remains of her cell phone, crushed into the dirt. "Not with mine. How about yours?"

Chandler fished his phone out of his pocket and stared at the screen. "No network."

Roxie went over to an object lying among the swamp weed. Chandler followed her and looked down. He didn't have to look too closely to see what it was; he'd seen enough human skulls working as an officer in the Met.

"It came off the back of the truck," he said.

Roxie was already on her knees studying it. She indicated some faint marks on top of the skull.

"Looks like it's been mechanically stripped before being run through an acid bath. And the teeth have been removed."

Chandler bent down to look. "That's not normal, is it? Removing the teeth."

"Not unless you want to prevent identification. No teeth, no mitochondrial DNA."

"How long does DNA survive anyway?" he asked.

"I was on an archeological dig in a fifteenth-century graveyard on the island of Tenerife. We took some teeth and pulverized them between two metal plates, then we used a genetic analyzer and edited the sequences with software." She looked over at Chandler. "It's a numbers game. Like finding a heap of shell cases at a crime scene. Some of them might have striations on the casings and some of them could be damaged. You'd overlay the markings of each shell until you had a contiguous pattern that matched a particular gun barrel."

Chandler nodded. "Yes, that makes sense."

"The older the DNA samples are, the noisier the sequencing electropherograms. It makes editing the sequences more difficult."

"Yes, those eletropherograms can be really irksome," Chandler said.

"Irksome? You have no idea what an electropherogram even is, do you?"

Chandler gave a sheepish grin. "Not as such."

"That is such a British way of saying no."

"I do my best," Chandler said.

Roxie continued. "They're used to determine DNA sequence genotypes."

"You took the words right out of my mouth."

She smiled. "They've got more efficient ways to carry out DNA sequencing now."

"Maybe some human remains wound up in the machinery they use up at the plant. That might explain the damage," Chandler said.

Roxie shrugged. "They've never admitted to finding any, which in itself is a bit weird. There must have been quite a few people who ended up here over the years, what with the storms and such."

Chandler nodded. "Zeke seemed to think so. Unless that was another of his tip-attracting tales."

Roxie shrugged. "I think he's got a point." She looked around and found a plastic carrier bag from the mangled Jeep. She picked it up and carefully placed the skull inside.

Chandler straightened up. He felt a faint twinge in one of his knees. Roxie looked toward the plant.

"Blackburn has some sort of repeater mast to boost the cell phone coverage. If we head toward it, we'll get a signal sooner than if we head back toward Baton Rouge."

Chandler looked at her. "There's no way you're going near that plant without police backup. Seriously, if one of Blackburn's men really is trying to kill us, we should put some distance between us and the plant."

Roxie shook her head. "We'll still be miles from the plant by the time we get a signal. And besides, Duke will have officers out here fifteen minutes after we call."

Chandler nodded reluctantly. "Okay."

They walked down the road that led across the swamp, the lights in the distance and the flames from the flare stack getting closer. After some time, Chandler broke the silence.

"Tell me more about wy you decided to be a forensic anthropologist?" he asked.

"Apart from the glamour of spending so much time with maggots?"

"There is that," Chandler said.

They kept on walking, and Chandler listened as she filled him in on the anthropological path she'd chosen to follow and the obstacles she'd had to overcome. He had to admire her perseverance and stamina. Working two jobs while studying and doing voluntary work down at the morgue, along with looking after her mother, was no mean feat. As he watched her striding down the road, her blonde hair shining in the moonlight, he knew that among all the confusion of the case, there was one certainty in his life right now. He was falling in love.

They were a couple miles away from the plant when the signal bars on Chandler's cell flickered to life. He dialed Duke's number and put the phone on speaker.

"There you are!" Duke's cheery voice came out of the handset. "I was getting worried—thought you two might have gotten sucked into the Baton Rouge nightlife."

Chandler smiled. "Yes, well, we certainly got sucked into something."

"What happened?"

"We had a little contretemps with a twenty-ton dump truck."

"Contra what?" Duke asked, his confusion evident over the crackling line.

Roxie looked at Chandler. "That's your friend Chandler's way of saying some maniac in a truck from the plant tried to turn us into roadkill."

"Okay," Duke said. "Stay put. I'll get a team out there and have a paramedic check you both over."

"I really don't think we need a paramedic—"

Duke cut him off. "Don't be a wiseass, Chandler. You could have internal injuries you don't even know about. Your brain could be swelling up inside that dense head of yours while we're yacking. Before you know it, you could have an embolism and—*boom!*—you're gone."

"Well if you put it like that, maybe it wouldn't do any harm," Chandler said.

"Smart move," said Duke. "Once I've picked you up, we'll head out to the plant and find out what the hell's going on. See you soon."

Duke ended the call. Roxie shook her head.

"When people first started working in the oil fields, there were so many accidents they called the oil 'Louisiana blood'—the price you paid for the money made from it. But what happened tonight was no accident," she said.

Fifteen minutes after the call, blobs of light flickered in the dark behind them. They stuttered as they formed vague shapes, then a convoy of patrol cars and an ambulance. Wailing sirens accompanied the flashing red, white, and blue lights, and within minutes, Duke was pulling up alongside. He climbed out of the car.

"You guys alright? I can't believe you got out of that Jeep alive. My guys bagged up some of the wreckage. We'll probably get some paint transfer off the bodywork."

Roxie held up the old shopping bag. "Got some more evidence your guys might want to check out."

Duke peered inside. "Friend of yours?"

"It came from the truck that hit us," Roxie said.

Duke slipped on a pair of disposable gloves, reached into the bag, and held up the skull. "I guess you've already given it the once over."

Roxie nodded. "Someone's gone to a lot of trouble to prevent us from identifying it."

Duke nodded back.

"The teeth have been knocked out, which prevents us doing DNA testing." She pointed to marks on the jawbone. "You can see the fracture points here."

Duke studied the marks. Roxie pointed to a black smudge inside the eye socket.

"That's charring behind the orbital bone."

Duke peered at the eye socket in the skull. "From a fire of some kind?"

Roxie shrugged. "Maybe. Or an explosion." She sniffed at the skull. "There's a strong smell of oil."

"That's no surprise if it came from the swamp," Duke said.

"No argument there," Roxie replied. "We'll need to run lab tests to see what sort of contaminants or chemicals are present."

Two paramedics came over and joined them.

"You two need to let these guys check you over," Duke said.

The paramedics ran through the various checks with Roxie and Chandler while Duke reached into his car and lifted out a thermos flask and some plastic cups. He waited until the paramedics had finished. One of them came over.

"Nothing serious," he said. "Minor contusions and some cuts from the edges of the windscreen. They'll have some aches and pains for a few days, but there are no signs of any internal injuries."

Duke nodded. "Thanks."

The paramedic smiled at the thermos as he headed off. "That'll probably help."

Roxie walked over to Duke, and he handed her the flask. “Thought you might need a pick-me-up.”

Roxie smiled and unscrewed the top. She sniffed it. “Rum?”

Duke nodded. “I laced it with some coffee.”

He held the plastic cups while she filled them from the flask. Roxie took a sip.

“Wow, that coffee sure is weak. Still, I guess I’m not driving anywhere soon.”

Chandler came over from the ambulance, and Roxie handed him a cup of the coffee.

He gulped it down greedily.

“You really can’t have too much coffee,” Chandler said. Duke clapped him on the back.

“If you two are okay, we’ll head over to the plant. Maybe you can identify the driver if he’s one of Blackburn’s guys.”

Chandler shook his head. “He hit us head-on, so the lights were in our eyes. Couldn’t see a thing. But I’ll remember his bumper sticker.”

“Okay, I thought that might be the case. But if the driver is there, he’s not going to know that, is he? So when we get there just keep your eyes open and let’s see if we get a reaction from anybody.”

Chandler climbed into the passenger seat and Roxie slid into the back seat. They headed toward the distant lights of the plant, and for a few minutes there was silence. Duke turned to look at Chandler.

“I don’t want to pry, but what were you doing out in the swamps anyway? I thought you’d had enough of them while you were out with Zeke.”

Chandler shrugged. “A man who is tired of swamps is tired of life.”

Duke chuckled. “Sounds like something Chilly might say.”

“Yes, it must be catching. I think Roxie was planning to show me a different perspective on the swamp.”

Roxie kicked the back of Chandler’s seat. He looked round at her. “I didn’t mean—”

Duke smiled. “Easy with the department upholstery.”

Roxie fixed Chandler with a look. "I wanted to show you how busy the plant was at night, as well as a bit of sightseeing. I wasn't expecting to get such a close-up view of the truck."

"There it is," Duke said.

They saw the plant in the distance. Overhead sodium lights lit up the area, creating harsh shadows from the metal pipework that spidered around the plant. The police convoy came to a halt in front of the wire fence next to the security gates. A guard opened an electric barrier, and Duke drove through and parked next to a familiar black Escalade. They all climbed out as Blackburn and Kale left the building and headed toward them.

Blackburn stopped in front of them and smiled at Duke, extending a hand, all Southern charm. Kale stared on.

"Thank you for coming out, Deputy. I'm sure we can clear this up without too much trouble."

Duke ignored the outstretched hand and looked over at a compound where twenty or more heavy-duty dump trucks were parked.

"I didn't come out here because you invited me. I came out here because earlier this evening one of your men was involved in a hit-and-run."

Before Blackburn could reply Duke headed toward the compound, flanked by six of his fellow officers. Blackburn followed them, hurrying to keep up.

"I've already had my engineers inspect the trucks, so I can save you some time."

Duke flicked him a look.

"Well, that's very neighborly of you, I'm sure."

Blackburn ignored the slight and pressed on. He headed through the gate to the compound and toward a large Caterpillar dump truck that stood by itself.

Duke looked at it. "This it?"

Blackburn nodded. Chandler and Roxie joined Duke, who indicated the dump truck.

"Do you recognize it?"

Roxie went over to the truck, walked around the giant wheels. She reached into the gap between the massive axles on the rear wheels and pulled something out: the mangled remains of a colorful scarf. She folded it gently into a square.

"My mom gave me this." She went around to the rear fender, saw the memorable bumper sticker. "This is it," she said.

An officer went over to the chassis and scraped off a paint sample. "Looks like transference from the Jeep. We'll get it analyzed."

A man wearing overalls and a hard hat came up and handed Blackburn a clipboard.

Blackburn studied it before handing it over to Duke. "This is the personnel file of the driver of the truck," he said. "He joined on contract yesterday—he's from Somalia. We always run background checks, and his came up clean."

Duke looked at the sheet. "Of course. And this is his current address?"

Blackburn gave a shrug. "That's what he wrote."

Duke walked around the truck, studied the fresh gouges out of the frame along with the traces of red paint and pieces of broken windscreen embedded in its tires.

"So you hired him yesterday, and then this evening he drives his truck over a Jeep and vanishes into thin air?"

Before Blackburn could respond, Roxie was in his face, five feet and ten inches of blazing anger. "Wasn't it enough that you killed my father with your chemicals? Am I that much of a problem to you?"

Blackburn took a step backward, and Kale took one forward, reaching into his jacket.

"Really?" Roxie demanded. "What are you going to do, shoot me?"

Duke put a restraining hand on the agent's arm, clamping down with enormous force. Kale's expression showed he was in pain, but he said nothing.

"Drop it," Duke said. He released Kale's arm.

Kale withdrew his hand from inside his jacket and flexed his arm.

"You should keep your bitch on a leash, Duke," he said.

Roxie's hand whipped down and clamped between his legs, squeezing hard. "What did you call me?"

Kale started to buckle, the blood draining from his face.

Duke put a hand on Roxie's shoulder. "It's okay, Roxie. We'll handle this."

Roxie released Kale, who staggered back before pulling himself together.

"Jesus!" he said.

Roxie shook her head. "Nothing sticks to the Blackburns, and nothing ever will."

She turned away and strode back to Duke's patrol car. Duke watched her leave, before turning back to face Kale.

"Okay, here's what's going to happen: my men will search the area in case your man is still on the premises, and when we're satisfied that he's not, then we'll discuss the company liability situation."

Kale cocked his head to one side. "I think you'll probably need a warrant for that, Deputy."

Duke smiled. "You really want me to cite you the law?"

Kale shrugged. "I guess you're gonna have to."

Duke pushed past him, talking as he went. "Fresh pursuit of a dangerous suspect. If you're pursuing a suspect from a just-committed crime involving the infliction or threatened infliction of death or serious bodily injury, you may enter and search for the suspect in a residence into which he flees. In my opinion, the driver of that truck could well have fled into this establishment."

Blackburn snapped at Kale, "Go with him!"

Kale spun on his heel and managed a fast limp behind Duke. Blackburn watched him go, his lips pressed into a tight line. Chandler came over, held up the skull from the roadside in a clear plastic bag.

"Do you get many of these up at the plant?"

Blackburn shook his head. "What has that got to do with me?"

Chandler shrugged. "We're pretty sure it came from the load being carried by your truck. The one that nearly drove over my head, just to be clear."

Blackburn smiled. "This area has been hit by hundreds of storms over the centuries. All sorts of things turn up. If we'd found any human remains, we would inform the authorities as a matter of procedure."

Chandler looked at the governor, and Roxie's words came back to him: *animal instinct, female intuition.* Exactly what he was feeling listening to Blackburn. The man was lying.

"Really?" he said. "Considering how many storms you've had in these parts, it seems odd that you haven't turned up a single instance of human remains so far. And yet Duke managed to run into five while he was out for a Sunday drive."

Blackburn shrugged. "I guess we've just been lucky."

"Yes. Well, let's hope your luck lasts," Chandler said. "I imagine it would cost a lot of money to shut down production while the police investigate the area."

Blackburn said nothing. Chandler nodded.

"I've enjoyed our little chat. I'm sure we'll meet again."

Blackburn looked at him. "I'm sure we will. Drive safe."

Chandler walked over to Duke's car and climbed into the back with Roxie.

"They won't find anything," she muttered. "The driver will be on his way to the border by now, and any evidence will be in the furnace."

Blackburn watched as the last of the patrol cars left. He turned to Kale with a face like thunder.

"Where is he?"

Kale looked at him. He knew there was no point trying to calm his boss down. After Blackburn's confrontation with Roxie and Duke, and the failure of his driver to remove the English detective from the scene, he was way past reasonable discussion.

"He's over at the biomass furnace."

Blackburn nodded and strode away.

The biomass furnace sat in a large shed. Trucks dumped their loads by reversing up a long, sloped steel ramp. The biodegradable material ended up in a crusher unit and from there was taken by a wide conveyer belt and funneled into the mouth of the furnace. The area shook with the power of the combustion cycle, and conversation was difficult at the best of times. While the trucks were unloading, it was nigh impossible.

Blackburn looked around. Something moved in the shadows beneath the ramp leading up to the generator.

"Khalid? Get out here. Now."

There was a pause, and then a man stepped out into the harsh glare of the halogen arc lights. He was wiry, with dark eyes and a series of tribal scars on his cheeks. His body was always in motion, sometimes a hand twitching, sometimes a foot tapping. Blackburn wondered if it was a side effect of the chat leaves he chewed. Chat was a drug the Somalians favored that produced an unbeatable high, suppressed one's appetite, and prevented tiredness. He wouldn't have been surprised if Khalid had been out of his head when he drove the truck into Roxie's Jeep. Blackburn had made it quite clear that he didn't want anything leading back to him. A simple case of hit-and-run on a dark road. But the idiot had rammed them and then driven off without confirming the job was done. So instead of clearing up a couple of loose ends, Blackburn now had an extra one to deal with.

The man was jabbering, his eyes flicking around the shed as if it harbored hidden demons. "Sorry, boss, I screwed up. Give me another chance. I get the job done good next time."

Blackburn shook his head. "Too late for that, Khalid, I'm afraid. There are some things in life you don't get a second chance at. Come with me. I want to show you something."

He walked up the steel stairway that led to the biomass-processing hopper. Khalid followed him. They stood looking down into the huge metal container through which the raw material was processed. Rotating iron screws and sharp blades sliced and diced the cargo from the trucks into smaller and smaller pieces before it was all fed into the blazing maw of the furnace.

"Do you see what's going on here, Khalid?" Blackburn said, waving a hand over the top of the hopper.

Khalid shrugged. "Trash, yes?"

Blackburn nodded. "You see trash. But nowadays it's all about pollution and your carbon footprint. One way or another there's big bucks to be made from trash, and I intend to make them."

Khalid's eyes were blank, his understanding of the process minimal. Khalid twitched. Blackburn could tell that Khalid was struggling to understand what he was saying. "Big bucks, yes?"

Blackburn smiled. "Ah, well done, Khalid. Money really is the universal language. But the problem is, there are people out there who don't share my vision. They could mess up the whole deal. And I really need them to go away. Permanently. Which was what you were meant to arrange. Wasn't it?"

Khalid was staring at him now. Fear in his eyes. The sound of the truck reversing up the ramp grew louder, its hydraulic rams drowning out further conversation. But Khalid wasn't interested in conversation. He only had eyes for the snub-nosed revolver that Blackburn had pressed against his forehead. His head snapped back, a mist of red blood spraying behind him as the bullet ripped through his brain and sent him tumbling down into the whirling screws and blades. Blackburn dropped the gun into the hopper and headed back down the stairs.

They drove back to Duke's place in a somber mood. Duke's officers had gone through the plant and had come up with nothing. Roxie was sitting in the back of the patrol car, still fuming from her encounter with Kale.

"Whoever was driving that truck will be long gone by now," she said.

Duke tried to calm her. "It may not have had anything to do with Blackburn. I'm not saying he didn't know what his driver had done—I just don't think he set it up. He might have just been covering for him."

Roxie looked at the back of Duke's neck. He caught her eye in the rearview mirror.

"Maybe you haven't noticed, but it's become a bit of a thing to use a blunt instrument to get the job done these days," she said. "A truck has become the terrorists' weapon of choice."

"She's got a point," Chandler said. "Maybe Blackburn wanted to make it look like just an accident."

Duke shrugged. "We might still pick the driver up trying to get over the state line."

Chandler's cell rang. He fumbled it out of his jacket pocket. "Hi." He listened. "Okay, we're on our way."

He hung up, looked at Roxie. "That was Phaedon. He's found something."

THIRTY-EIGHT

BUTTE LA ROSE, LOUISIANA – Present day

TWITCHING BRANCHES DAPPLED the ground with shadows as Duke, Chandler, and Roxie pulled up outside the warehouse. They stepped out of the car and headed toward the entrance. Chandler felt something crawl up his spine beneath his shirt. He scratched his back and squashed whatever it was, felt fluid leak onto his flesh. The insects were one aspect of Louisiana he wasn't going to miss.

Roxie looked around. "Where is everybody?"

Duke shook his head. "I don't know. Chilly should be here with Phaedon."

They came to the door leading into the warehouse. Duke pushed it open. He gestured for Chandler and Roxie to stay behind him, unholstered his gun, and stepped inside. The warehouse was deserted. The carriage sat behind plastic sheeting in the middle of the room, where a fine mist of moisture intermittently drifted from spray heads above it, keeping it moist and preserved. Water dripped from it onto the plastic sheet beneath. The processing room pulsed with a blue glow accompanied by a low humming noise.

Duke pushed through the flaps in the plastic. The blue laser from the motion-capture machine flickered on the other side of the space. Duke edged closer to the machine while the scanner continued to sweep the area in front of it with a mesh of blue light. Duke saw someone sitting in a high-backed leather chair facing away from him. An arm with the sleeve of a police officer's uniform hung motionless over the side, and the back of a head lay stationary against the leather headrest. On a large screen, a wire frame was being digitally rendered with flesh. It looked like Chilly, his narrowed eyes unmistakable. His hand dangled from the chair, still clutching a Twinkie. Duke moved slowly toward the chair, then peered around the side. Chilly sat there, motionless. Duke reached out to touch him.

Phaedon crashed through the plastic doors behind him, Chandler and Roxie trailing in his wake. "Hey, Duke! Had to take a leak. Too much of the old java."

Chilly blinked in the chair. "Damn! Sorry, didn't mean to move."

Phaedon hit a key. "It's cool—we got the scan. It doesn't take that long."

Chilly took a bite of his Twinkie and grinned at Duke. Duke holstered his gun.

"I had to take the risk you wouldn't shoot me for possession of a Twinkie," Chilly joked

Duke shook his head "When we didn't see you out front—"

Chilly laughed. "You thought the Bayou Bogeyman had got me, huh?"

Duke smiled. "Well, when I saw an uneaten Twinkie in your hand, I assumed the worst."

Chilly snorted, shaking his head. "I could give 'em up, easy." He chomped into the pastry. "I never realized how difficult it is to keep still for a few minutes—no wonder that Mona Lisa chick never gave a proper smile." He got up and stretched his legs. "Boy, I'm all busted out of shape."

"You know, they think her name was Lisa Gherardini. She was a silk merchant's wife who was having an affair with da Vinci."

Chilly smiled. "The dog."

Roxie went on. "Some Italian researchers think they've found her skeleton beneath the remains of a convent in Florence. They haven't found a DNA match yet—or a skull."

Duke gave a grim smile. "Maybe we can help them with that."

Phaedon tapped the keyboard. "The development guys were pretty stoked with it at the games conference, but they say they want more layers."

"Well," said Duke. I'm guessing you didn't get us down here to talk about your game."

Phaedon grinned. "Nah. Look." He punched up the original photograph of the women and Tumblety on the screen. "I saw something in the back of one of the photos." Phaedon zoomed in, revealing a wooden hut on stilts. "I ran it through an image search machine and found this." He pulled up a site called Lost Louisiana. He clicked on a link, and the screen filled with a picture, a painting of a village composed of palmetto and cane-thatched houses on stilts in the water.

"Saint Malo," said Phaedon. "It was a fishing village on the shore of Lake Borgne, mainly populated by Filipino immigrants, hunters, trappers, and fisherman. It was totally destroyed in 1893 by a hurricane. I uploaded the Lidar scans that a certain little lady produced while my back was turned—"

Roxie smiled. "I used your original data."

Phaedon grinned. "The best kind. Then I did a reverse image search using the pictures of the women from the carriage. And, well . . ." A Jack the Ripper website flashed up on-screen. The page showed post-mortem pictures of the first five Ripper victims, arranged in order of their deaths: Mary Ann Nichols, Annie Chapman, Elizabeth Stride, Catherine Eddowes, and Mary Jane Kelly. On-screen, the five victims' faces from the Ripper website were matched to the five women in the photo from the carriage. The program flashed: 100% MATCH. Chandler stared at the screen. The impossible, far from being eliminated, had just been proved.

For a while they just stood in the warehouse, staring at the pictures on the screen. It was Chandler who finally broke the silence.

"Is this real?" he asked.

Phaedon grinned. "The computer doesn't lie."

Roxie stared at the pictures with a look of morbid fascination. "I didn't think there were any pictures of the Kelly girl apart from the post-mortem ones?"

Phaedon nodded. "There weren't. I ran her post-mortem press pictures through a 3-D modeling program along with the Lidar data and got a match with the skull physiology. Took about three hours and, believe me, I have more computing power here than NASA."

Duke rubbed his face and looked at the screen, his mind spinning like a roulette wheel. "You know what this reminds me of?" he asked.

"What?" Chandler said.

Duke smiled. "Witness relocation."

THIRTY-NINE

LONDON, ENGLAND – 1888

MARY MADE SOME hot tea to drive the chill from their bones while Edward told her what he'd overheard at the *Pall Mall Gazette*. Mary in turn told him about Fay's death, and who her companion had been—Eddy, the Duke of Clarence, heir to the throne. The reason behind the conspiracy was clear. A savage murder involving royalty outside a club of such ill repute could only spell disaster for the monarchy.

"Did you get a look at the attacker?" Edward asked.

Mary replied, her voice hesitant. "It all happened so quickly. He had a hat pulled low and wore a dark cloak."

"Did he have a mustache, or a beard?"

"A mustache and sideburns."

"And he came from the shadows behind the carriage?" Edward asked.

"Yes."

Edward looked her in the eyes. "You're sure?"

Mary nodded. "He must have. Why do you think—?" She stopped. Her eyes searching his face.

Edward spoke carefully. "It's just that from what you've told me, the carriage had been waiting there for some time, so anybody hiding behind it had to have been there all the time, or—"

Mary nodded. "Come from inside the carriage," she said. "I was half-asleep. Someone could have hidden behind the carriage once it was dark and I wouldn't have known."

He saw Mary shiver and realized the fire had died in the grate.

"I'll get some coal. Otherwise we'll freeze to death," he said.

Edward returned with a bag of coal he'd bought from one of the tinkers at the other end of Dorset Street along with a couple of hot potatoes. While they devoured the potatoes, Edward looked down at his notebook.

"Mary Ann Nichols, Annie Chapman, Elizabeth Stride, and Catherine Eddowes. Is that right?"

Mary nodded. Her eyes welling up with tears. "We didn't tell no one else. Just kept our heads down in case the man that saw me came looking."

"And he did," Edward said.

"Yes. He said he was a secret agent to Queen Victoria and we should do what we was told."

Edward listened. "What else?"

Mary hesitated. "That we should stay off the streets, and they would come for us when the time was right. He said we would be leaving the country, traveling by boat to America, where we would be protected. They gave us enough money to get food. But we weren't allowed to earn none. If you know what I mean."

Edward looked up. "Go on."

"He said that without his help, we would be in grave danger. And that if we did what he said, we would be safe."

Edward gave her a reassuring squeeze on her shoulder and handed her a handkerchief to wipe her eyes. Mary looked at him.

"But I'm not safe, am I? They're all dead. First Mary and Annie, and now Lizzie and Kate . . . the Ripper, he's sliced them up—"

Edward took her hand gently. "It's part of the conspiracy, Mary."

She looked at him. "I don't understand."

Edward flicked back through his notebook. He paused at a page. "Jack the Ripper is just a frightening name they made up to sell more newspapers."

He looked at Mary. She was struggling to take it all in.

"So we're all going to die so they can sell more newspapers?"

Edward shook his head. "No, Mary and Annie are still alive. The bodies found on the street were just made to look like them. They were probably from the hospital or the morgue.

"So they sliced them up just to make a spectacle for the newspapers," she said.

Edward nodded. "The *Gazette* was in dire financial straits. The agent threatened to reveal the editor's situation to his rivals if he didn't go along with their plan. Now, he gets the scoop of the century, his paper becomes successful, and his money problems disappear."

Mary nodded. "You said there were other people at the meeting. What do they get out of it?"

Edward replied. "Well, the assistant commissioner stands to get promoted, and because of all the publicity about the Ripper, the police get more funds and officers to protect the public. I expect they will somehow have to make believe they've caught the Ripper at some point, to regain public confidence. Maybe they'll have to fake his death as well. I really don't know."

Mary looked at him. "Couldn't we all have just promised to keep our mouths shut and start a new life outside London?"

Edward shook his head. "They didn't want to risk it. If one of you sold your story to a republican newspaper like the *Manchester Guardian*, the scandal could bring the monarchy down."

"So what are you going to do?" Mary said.

"When I have the whole story, the people responsible will have to face the consequences. But right now we have to get you away from here. Somewhere safe. I don't trust the government or its agents. That's why I'm here. You're only safe while Queen Victoria's alive. Her health isn't too good, and I think that if anything happened to her you'd all be in danger."

"What can we do?" Mary asked, her face pale in the flickering firelight.

Edward went on. "There's just you left now. Once your death has been orchestrated, you'll all be shipped out of the country."

"But why go to all this trouble?

Edward nodded. He had his own theory. "Have you ever been to one of those magic shows where the magician creates a puff of smoke and his assistant vanishes?"

Mary nodded, remembering her brief time in Paris. "Yes. I saw Herrmann the Great when I was in France. He put his assistant in a cabinet, and when the smoke cleared, she was at the back of the theater."

"Well, Edward said, I think all of this—the bodies, the newspaper stories, and the photographs—they're all just smoke."

FORTY

LONDON, ENGLAND – 1888

MARY LISTENED WHILE Edward explained his theory.

"While everybody is running scared, reading about the murders and terrified that they might be the next victim, no one is going to be listening to any rumors about what Eddy's been up to, even if somebody did try and tell them," he said.

Mary nodded. "They're hiding the real story behind a fake one, a killer they've invented and named Jack the Ripper."

"Exactly. I'll make a journalist out of you yet."

Mary gave a grim smile. "How long do you think I've got—before they come for me?"

Edward paused for a moment, marshaling his thoughts. "I imagine they'll want to space the murders out to make them more sensational for the newspaper. They want to make your death the most sensational and newsworthy. We may only have a few weeks to make plans."

Mary looked at him. "What sort of plans?"

"Do you have any family or friends in Ireland?" Edward asked.

Mary shook her head. "I don't get on with my family. But I have a brother, Henry. He's in the Scots Guards, stationed in Dublin."

"You could get to Ireland by boat. You'll be safe there."

Mary nodded. For the first time in a long while, she had some hope.

"I don't have any money, just enough for food."

"I'll lend you the money for your passage."

Mary smiled for the first time that evening. "I'll need some clothes," she said hesitantly.

"If you want I can stay the night, and then in the morning we can go to the market. If you don't mind me staying, that is?"

Mary took his hand in hers.

"Of course I don't. After what you've told me, I certainly don't feel safe by myself anymore.

They rose at first light and, after a cup of warm tea and some bread and jam, headed away from Whitechapel to one of the many markets near Seven Dials in Covent Garden. The streets were thronged with stalls selling all kinds of goods. There were the flower girls crying out for people to buy their bunches of violets, a small boy with his shoe-cleaning stand, a man selling bottles of ginger beer, and a street doctor peddling ointment. A watery sun cast its warmth over the market as Edward and Mary made their way down the street. Edward stopped to buy a bag of whelks and a bag of mussels from a fish stall next to some Italian street musicians.

He tucked into the whelks before offering the bag to Mary. "Want to trade?" She nodded and held out her bag of mussels, then looked around.

"I think there are some clothes stalls farther down."

They walked among the jostling crowds and found a row of carts selling fancy wares. Mary picked up a shawl decorated with small birds and draped it over her head, striking a pose.

"What do you think?"

"I think it suits you very well," Edward said.

A craggy Scotsman with a long, ratty beard picked up another shawl and held it out.

"I'll no cheat ye. Buy that one for a shilling and I'll throw in this one for half the cost," he said in his deep Scottish burr.

Edward reached into his pocket and produced a coin. "Why don't we say a shilling for the pair?"

The burly Scotsman mimed a look of offense. "Ye wouldn't want the young lady to think ye was cheap, would ye?" he said.

Mary smiled. "The more he saves on shawls, the more he can spend on food for me."

Edward produced a thruppeny bit. "How about we split the difference?"

The Scotsman shook his head and held out his hand. "It's a deal." He nodded at Mary. "You've a smart wee lassie there."

Edward looked at Mary as she tried the second shawl on.

"Oh, I'm sure of that." He dropped the coins into the man's hand.

The Scotsman winked. "Youse have a good day, and take care. We live in strange times."

Edward nodded to him, and they set off along the street past people hurrying through the market clutching their wares.

"What did he mean, we live in strange times?" Mary asked.

Edward looked around. "Poor people in the East End have been running scared since they started reading about the Ripper. Families are starting to sell up and move out. They're desperate to leave."

Mary nodded. "Do you think that's part of the plan?"

Edward thought about this. She had a point. While the area was gripped with fear, property prices had plummeted in Whitechapel. No one wanted Jack the Ripper as a neighbor.

"It's possible," Edward said.

Mary looked around the teeming market. The grubby urchins selling ragged clothes and knickknacks, the world-weary faces of the stallholders eking out a living, paupers begging, stealing, or selling everything they had, including their bodies, just to survive. Maybe this was a chance for her to start her life again.

"I'd just like to know if my friends are safe," Mary said.

Edward nodded. He knew how she felt. He didn't know the women, but already he was burdened by the guilt he felt about their situation and his inability to influence it. He decided that the best course of action was to try and keep Mary's spirits up.

"From what you've told me about them, I have a feeling they're more than capable of looking after themselves."

FORTY-ONE

LONDON, ENGLAND – 1888

THE NAKED BODY of a woman lay on the mortuary slab. Triton stood looking down at her. Fitch watched him from the corner of the room, chewing nervously on a fingernail and trying to gauge what was going through the other man's mind.

Triton leaned forward, staring intently at the corpse's face. "It's incredible. I've never seen anything like it." He turned toward Robert. "And they're made from opium sap, you say?"

Fitch nodded. Triton touched the face of the woman with his finger. He drew it back quickly, as if he'd been stung.

"It feels . . . so real."

"Yes, it behaves like real skin," Fitch said. "We used pig's blood to make the wounds more authentic. The membrane is so thin, it molds to the face perfectly."

Triton peered into the corpse's eyes. "The eyes, how did you—?"

"Colored contact lenses," Fitch said.

Triton looked at him. "Contact lenses. What are they?"

Fitch produced a small wooden box no more than three inches square. He opened it to reveal a velvet-lined interior with small slots in which sat spherical lenses.

"Adolf Fick and August Müller independently developed corneal lenses last year," he said.

"Like miniature spectacles?" Triton said.

Fitch nodded. "Yes, but they sit on the actual eye. This woman had grey eyes, so I had to add green-tinted lenses."

Triton looked at the eyes more closely. "They're incredibly realistic," Triton said. "I'm glad you agreed to join the operation. You're a good man. It was all a bit of a rush. I'm not sure anyone else could have pulled it off at such short notice."

"Coming from you, that really means something," said Fitch.

Triton looked at the face again, fascinated by its realism.

"And you add the cuts and other, er, embellishments before they're put in place and photographed?"

"Yes," Fitch said.

"Where did you learn how to do this?"

"In Paris. Jules Baretta taught me the art of Moulage while I was a student over there. This is a natural extension of the art. The materials I'm using haven't been employed in this way before. Death masks have been around since the ancient Egyptians of course."

Triton nodded. "Yes, though a solid gold mask might prove a little unwieldy in this case."

Fitch gave a tight smile. "I like to think of my work as living masks."

"Well, your time in Paris certainly wasn't wasted." He pulled out a fob watch and checked the time. "You need to get moving. With the coverage the murders are getting in the papers, things are moving faster than we anticipated. Copycat killings, letters to the police from people claiming to be the killer."

Fitch scratched an itch behind his ear. "Yes, I'm sure everybody wants to climb onto the bandwagon. Pretty soon half the criminals in London will be claiming they're the Ripper."

"Yes. But they aren't, are they?" Triton said. "Because he doesn't exist."

Mary lay in Edward's arms. For the first time in a long while, she felt safe. The past week had been one of the happiest times she'd had in her short life, and she felt no shame at the apparent speed of their relationship. In the atmosphere that hung over the city, and the danger she was in, time was too short to worry about social niceties. At any moment her life could change forever. Wasn't she allowed some joy in it, even if it was just for a fleeting moment? She thought so, and had surrendered herself to him without a moment's hesitation. She couldn't say at what point she fell in love with him; it just happened. Later, in the dark, she asked him if he had known when his feelings for her changed from savior to lover and was surprised to learn he couldn't tell her either.

She'd been with many men, some of them kind, a lot of them cruel, and some of them so foul in their demands she'd felt she would never be able to wash herself clean again. But lying there in the dark, naked and enveloped in Edward's gentle arms, she realized the love she'd been missing.

The next morning, Edward had gone down to the port and booked her passage to Cork. They hurriedly packed some things, and he gave her a lingering kiss.

"I won't be long," he said. "I just need to get my things and lock up. We'll be on the boat by tonight."

Edward opened the door and gave her a last look before he left. She watched him go. In her hand she held the silver hunter-case pocket watch that he'd given her so she would know when to expect him back. She ran her finger over the initials E. R. T. engraved into the back of the watch, before sitting down on the edge of the bed to await his return.

He'd been gone for about an hour when they came. Mary's hand rested on the small, battered case she had packed for the journey. There was a noise outside. The sound of footsteps. She stood up, thinking Edward had returned, but then came the sound of splintering wood as the door was kicked in and a group of men forced their way into the room. A stout man with a shock of ginger hair clamped his hand over her mouth. She could smell the whiskey on his breath as he leaned over her.

"Just keep quiet and don't struggle." He looked at her case. "Looks like you was planning on leavin' without us," he said. "Young girl stepped into the path of a Growler up at Spitalfields. No point in wasting an opportunity like that—the doctors likes 'em fresh."

Two more men carried a woman's body in and placed it on the bed. They opened their leather doctor's bags and took out rolled-up tool pouches containing surgical instruments.

A man with a walrus mustache drove a razor-sharp knife into the woman's abdomen. Blood oozed around the incision. Mary was dragged onto the street and bundled into a waiting carriage. As the carriage raced through the night, she struggled to accept what she'd seen. It was something she'd remember for the rest of her life: a corpse with her face.

Cream and Tumblety hacked at the corpse on the bed. No longer human, it now resembled an anatomical specimen. Cream looked down at Tumblety's handiwork. The candlelight reflected blood splatters gleaming on the wall. The bloody organs strewn around the bed glistened in the light. Cream covered his mouth, dry retching before regaining control. He turned to Tumblety, who was raising his knife again.

"Jesus! Isn't this enough?"

Tumblety stared at him, eyes devoid of expression.

"This is the last one. It has to be spectacular."

He leaned forward and sliced deliberately, his tongue licking at his dry lips, his eyes reptilian in the light from the fire.

Edward sat in the cab as it moved cautiously through the swirling fog that rolled toward them from the docks. He leaned out the window and looked up at the carriageman,

"For God's sake, man, can't you go any faster?"

The carriageman spat into the thick fog. "Can't see a thing, sir. But we must be getting near now—it's thicker coming off the water."

Edward had raced back to Miller's Court in time to see a carriage clattering away from Mary's lodgings. He'd ordered his cab driver to pull up in an alleyway before he jumped down to the street. He'd waited until the other carriage had sped past him before entering the lodgings. What he saw on the blood-soaked bed would live with him forever. If he hadn't known that the grotesquely arranged corpse was part of the conspiracy, and not his beloved Mary, the shock would probably have killed him.

Something had altered the conspirators' schedule. He'd heard talk that there had been copycat killings. Whatever the reason, they'd stepped up their arrangements to spirit the women out of London and transport them to America. He'd left a safety margin of a week, but it hadn't been enough, and now it seemed he was about to lose the only woman he cared about.

Barely visible in the gloom beside the docks, a group of five women, accompanied by peelers, disembarked from a carriage standing next to the gangplank of a frigate. Fog swirled past the name on her stern, *Elysian*. Mary looked desperately around as a man guided her onto the gangplank. His military bearing set him apart from the others. Mary had heard someone call him Triton. He guided her aboard, walked back down to the dock, and signaled to a deckhand. The gangplank was drawn up, and the crew cast off the ropes. The peelers and Triton climbed into two waiting carriages and sped off into the night.

Moments later, Edward's carriage clattered to a halt dockside. He jumped down in time to see the name on the stern of the ship as it disappeared from view. He stared out over the Thames, his eyes full of sadness. He swore to himself that he would find Mary, no matter how long it took.

FORTY-TWO

BATON ROUGE, LOUISIANA – Present day

THE MORNING SUN glinted off the aluminum skin of the Airstream from below a bank of low cloud. Duke had risen early and was sitting outside on an old chair, strumming a Muddy Waters tune on a battered steel guitar. Chandler swung open the door to the Airstream and stood blinking in the morning light. He'd spent another restless night, his dreams punctuated by fragments of the ongoing case. It was like a jigsaw puzzle with all the wrong pieces. Duke finished off his strumming with a squealing slide wail. Chandler rubbed sleep out of his eyes and looked at the gleaming instrument in Duke's hands.

"I love that guitar."

"It's an old National Style O. It was my pa's." He nodded toward the Airstream. "There's some coffee on the go if you want."

"Thanks, I'll get some." Chandler had gotten used to his early-morning fix of the brain-jolting brew that Duke always had on the go and promised himself he would make a note of the brand before he left. He went back inside and headed for the jug. Black-and-white pictures of Duke in various smoky jazz clubs covered the walls, reflecting the full and colorful life Duke had previously led.

He saw a photograph of Duke standing in front of an armored personnel carrier somewhere hot. The vehicle bore the ensign of the UN peacekeeping force. It was a part of his life that Duke hadn't mentioned, and Chandler wondered why. Looking around, he realized how small he'd let his own life become since Claire's death. He'd buried himself in the family obsession. Whether that was to shut out the pain of losing her and his job, or because he needed to solve the mystery, he didn't know, but since landing in Louisiana, things had changed. He no longer wanted his life to be defined by the mystery of the Ripper.

He didn't have to think too hard to explain the change. It was Roxie. She was a force of nature he'd been totally unprepared for.

Chandler went over to the coffee machine and filled two mugs. He looked out across the lake. It was a magnificent view. The university the trailer looked onto consisted of hundreds of buildings spread over two thousand acres, bounded by the Mississippi River on one side and University Lake on the other. Duke's Airstream faced the lake, and Chandler could see a group of joggers in the distance. The boundaries of the water formed a natural five-kilometer run that was popular with the students.

He took the mugs and headed back outside and over to where Duke sat on a piece of grass that sloped down to the lake.

"Nice spot you have here," Chandler said as he placed Duke's mug on the small table beside him.

Duke nodded. "Sure is."

He plucked a few more wailing chords. Chandler watched as Duke's fingers danced across the bridge of the old guitar.

"Do you still play in your band? I saw some photos inside."

Duke put the guitar down, took a slug of coffee. "I jam with some of the guys down at Gumbo's Club," he said.

"You know, one of our groups took their name from a Muddy Waters song."

"Which one?" Duke asked.

"'Rollin' Stone,'" Chandler replied.

Duke chuckled. "I should have known that."

Chandler took a sip of his coffee. "I saw a picture back in the Airstream of you in an APC. When was that taken?"

Duke looked out across the lake, took a sip of coffee before putting the mug down. Chandler saw a look of resignation flicker behind his eyes.

"Another life, my friend. Before I was a deputy," Duke said.

"Somewhere in Africa?" Chandler asked.

Duke nodded. "Rwanda, about fifty miles outside Kigali. Some unpronounceable village in the middle of nowhere. We were on a reconnaissance mission in a T72 tank, the one with the Dolly Parton armor. It was a cramped son of a bitch, but fast. Had a hundred-twenty-five-millimeter main gun that was pretty damn effective."

"What happened?"

Duke took a deep breath. "There was a ceasefire in the civil war between the Rwandan patriotic front, who were mainly Tutsi refugees, and the government of President Habyarimana. When the president's plane was shot down near Kigali Airport, all hell broke loose."

Chandler remembered. "The Rwandan genocide," he said.

"Yes, but back then we had no idea what was about to happen. First thing we knew of it was when a load of pickup trucks turned up packed with Hutu tribesmen armed with machetes and guns. Our mandate was to only use force if we were under attack."

"What did you do?"

"We got in their faces. At first we stayed on the edge of the village. But when they started hacking the hands off the men and raping the women, we couldn't just stand by. We drove the tank right into the village. They knew we had orders, but when I pointed our gun at them, they didn't know whether or not we would follow them. We let them have a dose of machine gun rounds over their heads and cranked the main gun barrel down so it was in their faces."

"Did that stop them?" Chandler asked.

Duke sat silently for a moment, staring into the distance as a flock of white ibis flew across the lake, their wings flaring gold in the sunlight as they wheeled across the sky. "Yes. They decided not to risk it. We went in and did what we could for the injured. Within three months they'd slaughtered nearly a million people."

Chandler nodded. "While the West stood by."

Duke took another sip of coffee. "That was when I decided the peacekeeping force wasn't for me," he said at last. "Over here I can make a difference."

The sound of an approaching engine interrupted their conversation. A brand-new Jeep Cherokee pulled up alongside the Airstream with Roxie at the wheel. She opened the door, jumped out, and headed toward them.

Chandler stared. In the morning sun, she was even more beautiful than he remembered. He ran a hand through his hair in an attempt to smarten himself up.

He grinned at her. "You look very . . ." He paused, lost for words. Then he decided on, . . .j aunty."

Roxie smiled. "Jaunty? I love the way you keep the ancient languages alive."

Duke looked back at the Jeep with a smile. "If that's your old Jeep, I want the name of your body shop."

Roxie shook her head. "It was delivered by one of Blackburn's flunkies first thing this morning. They had some paperwork. As a gesture of goodwill, and without admitting any responsibility blah blah blah."

Duke shook his head. "Did you sign it?"

Roxie smiled. "No way."

"Sounds to me like damage control," Duke said.

Roxie nodded, shot a knowing look at Chandler, then waved an envelope at Duke.

"I got some stuff for you."

"Thanks, Roxie. You want coffee?"

"Sure."

Duke ducked back inside the Airstream.

Roxie looked around, nodded at some distant joggers.

"Perfect weather for a run." She turned to Chandler. "You should go for a jog around the lake. It's beautiful."

Chandler gave a shrug. "The lake might be beautiful, but Lycra is a cruel mistress. And besides, I'm not really built for speed, whereas you . . ." He waved his hand over her like an assistant on a game show.

Roxie smiled. "That sounds like something Chilly might say."

"I agree. I also doubt we'll be seeing him jogging round the lake anytime soon."

Roxie beamed at Chandler. He bathed in her radiance.

"I went through the newspaper archives up at Iberville Parish Library," she said. "I reckoned that if there had been any English women staying out here back in the day, it might have hit the local papers. Maybe some sort of local interest piece."

Duke came out with a mug of coffee and handed it to Roxie. He took the envelope she offered and opened it. He pulled out some scanned copies of *The Times-Picayune* newspaper and a sepia photograph. He glanced at the photograph before handing it to Chandler. The picture was of the same five women pictured with Tumblety in the photo from the carriage. They wore scarves and rough skirts and bore the sort of stilted expressions that came with the photography of the time. They looked more like a gang of outlaws than anything else. In the background was a house on stilts. Chandler looked at a scan of the back of the photo and read the inscription.

"'The Bloods'?"

Roxie nodded. "They all wore red scarves apparently. Most of the coverage focuses on the storm, but there was a small side article inside about some huts being set on fire in Saint Malo."

Duke flicked through the scanned pages of the newspaper and found the article headline. He tapped it with his finger. *ARSON ATTACK IN SAINT MALO.* The same picture of the women from the photograph was printed there. "Says the article was written by a Louie de Chiel," he said.

Roxie nodded. "There's a Miss Blanche de Chiel who lives out in the bayous. I checked the records. Louie was her father, and his trade is listed as journalist. She's a bit flaky, though."

Chandler looked at Roxie. "How flaky?"

Roxie wrinkled her nose. "Well, if she was in your country she'd be looking forward to a telegram from the queen pretty damn soon. She's got a touch of dementia—has good days and bad days. Takes photographs of butterflies out at old man Ryker's field behind her house. My mom says she was a real tomboy in her youth—lost an eye covering a civil rights demonstration—but she's in a wheelchair now. Got a big guy that pushes her around, name of Jesse. She's still feisty, though. Her husband died a while back. She likes to be known by her maiden name."

Chandler looked at the photograph. "I think we need to pay Ms. de Chiel a visit."

They headed down Florida Boulevard, running parallel to the Amite River, then through Denham Springs and past a clutch of boarded-up antique shops that lined the main street, before leaving the town and picking up the old river road. Roxie drove, and Duke sat in the back.

Roxie waved her hand at the surrounding fields. "Ninety percent of the homes in this town were flooded a few years back. They're still getting back on their feet."

They followed a track past a collection of abandoned old properties that would have been magnificent back in their prime; back then trees festooned with Spanish moss and wild bougainvillea. Even in decay, the area had a haunted beauty.

Roxie's new Jeep provided a more comfortable ride than Duke's ratty Skylark or the spongy suspension of his patrol car.

"Great car," Chandler said. "Though I can think of easier ways to get one than what we had to go through."

Duke chuckled in the back seat. "That's for sure."

Roxie smiled at Chandler. "Well, I can't think of a more memorable first date."

Chandler smiled back. It was good to hear she had considered it a date. It left the future wide open for him to improve on—or mess up.

"You obviously haven't dated many Englishmen."

Roxie laughed. "Well, I'm looking forward to seeing what you come up with next."

She slowed as they headed past a broken-down sign and brought the Jeep to a halt at the end of a track overgrown with weeds and tall grass. What once must have been a beautiful garden at the front of Blanche de Chiel's house was now rampant with wild flowers and weeds in equal measure.

Roxie switched off the engine. "Old man Ryker's field is up ahead."

Chandler climbed out and looked into the distance. He could make out the rusty smokestacks of old steam locomotives and some derelict rail carriages. Roxie headed through the grass, and the men followed behind. Admiral butterflies danced around them as they walked, the light reflecting off their iridescent wings in a spectacular blaze of color.

Roxie turned to Chandler. "She likes to take pictures in the afternoon when the butterflies are feeding."

They pushed aside the tall grass and continued down the track. Chandler saw a lady in a faded straw hat sitting in a wheelchair. A tall African American man in his seventies, but still with a powerful physique, stood next to her. As the three of them got closer, Chandler could see she wore an eye patch and was cradling an old Leica M3 camera like a baby.

They reached the end of the track, and Jesse came to meet them. Chandler wiped the sweat off his forehead with a sodden handkerchief. He could feel his shirt sticking to his back in the heat of the afternoon.

Duke held up his badge. "Duke Lanoix. If we could, we'd like a few words with Ms. de Chiel."

The old lady nodded to Jesse, who moved aside. She looked at Duke, sucked her teeth, and spoke with an old-style Southern lilt. "I don't believe we need to stand on ceremony out here. Blanche will suffice." She nodded to Jesse again. "Give the lady and gentlemen a drink, please, Jesse. I do believe they might expire without it."

Duke held up a palm. "I'm fine, thanks."

Jesse opened a hamper that lay on the ground, produced a thermos jug, and filled two glasses.

Jesse handed a glass to Chandler, who accepted it gratefully and took a sip.

"Mmm, packs quite a punch."

Roxie sipped hers appreciatively and turned to Chandler. "Mint Julep—it's mainly bourbon and syrup over mint leaves."

Chandler took another sip. "Looks like you're the designated driver, Duke."

Blanche gave him a stern look. "I'd ask you to keep your voices down—I'm expecting some *Vanessa atalanta* about now."

Chandler smiled. "Red admirals."

Blanche raised an eyebrow. "You know about butterflies, Mr. . . . ?

"Chandler—Chandler Travis."

"Travis?" She paused, grasping at the vestigial memories floating like gossamer through her mind.

"Travis, you look familiar. You're from London. I knew a man from London once . . ."

Her look became distant for a moment. Chandler waited until she came out of her reverie. She looked up at him, seemed to shake off the past.

"Butterflies start their life real ugly, as caterpillars, then hang in that itty-bitty sack, and then one day they're beautiful and free, flying through the air like God's tiny rainbows . . ." She pointed the Leica M3 toward the old locomotive, almost submerged under the weight of the swamp cottonwood that snaked around its rusted smokestack. Chandler watched her smile as she squinted through the old camera's viewfinder with her good eye.

"They like the heat of the sun on the old iron—here, look."

Chandler took the camera from her carefully. He looked through the viewfinder at the locomotive. Half a dozen butterflies spread their wings along the gentle curve of the engine's rusted boiler. Red admirals in shades of orange and brown, ranked like soldiers bathing in the sunlight. "They're beautiful."

Blanche looked up at Jesse. "Jesse got me a more powerful lens when I started getting interested in the butterflies—he's too good to me, Lord knows what it cost him." She reached over and squeezed the big man's hand.

He smiled down at her. "You're worth it. Besides, they practically give 'em away. Nobody likes to admit they use anything other than the fifty millimeter, but there are some things you can't get close to, and them critters are skittish."

Chandler handed the camera back to Jesse, who slipped it into a canvas bag that hung from his shoulder.

"They always best in the afternoon sun—makes 'em drowsy, easier to follow through the lens," Jesse said in a deep Southern drawl, his voice like rich molasses.

Blanche nodded. "Yes. Their life cycle is the reverse of humans. We start out beautiful, and then, mostly, we get ugly." She gave a sad smile.

Duke looked at her, spoke softly. "They say that beauty comes from within, Blanche."

She smiled at him. Chandler saw a faint trace of the strikingly beautiful young woman she must have been.

"Well then, Mr. Lanoix, I could do with being turned inside out."

Duke smiled. "You can call me Duke."

She fixed him with her steely eye. "We're all like butterflies, Duke. If you were one, which would it be?"

Duke shrugged. "A big one, I guess."

She looked thoughtful. "You'd be a *Graphium sarpedon*—a bluebottle. That's what they call the police in your country isn't it, Mr. Travis—boys in blue?"

Chandler nodded. "That's right. But I think the Latin is a nicer name. Bluebottle, that has other connotations . . ."

Blanche nodded. "Yes, death and beauty often go together."

She looked around the beautiful field, a sadness in her face.

"Well, Duke, you didn't come all the way out here just to perspire with me, so what exactly is it you want to discuss?" Duke handed her the photograph of the Bloods and the newspaper article.

"Oh my," she said.

Duke spoke carefully, as if Blanche herself were a butterfly he didn't want to disturb. "We just wondered if you could help us with some historical background."

Blanche touched the picture with a frail finger twisted by arthritis. Jesse put a comforting hand on her shoulder. Chandler saw a tenderness there, with deep roots.

She took a breath, her lungs wheezing in the humid air.

"I wanted to be a photographer—like Martha Gellhorn, striding down the beach at Omaha. I had some fire in my belly then. Got myself burnt 'cos of it. That's how I met Jesse. He saved me."

Duke nodded, waited patiently. Blanche looked at the picture.

"The Bloods. Of course this was all before I was born. I heard my grandfather talking to my mother about them when I was just a kid. She didn't know I was listening. He thought they were running a business."

Duke nodded. "A brothel?"

"That's what people said."

"Can you remember what your grandfather said about them?" asked Duke.

Blanche shook her head. The picture shook as her hand trembled. They listened to her quiet voice as she struggled to remember what they'd talked about all those years ago.

FORTY-THREE

SAINT MALO, LOUISIANA – October 1, 1893

MOONLIGHT SILVERED THE waters surrounding the village. It was built in the typical Manila style: houses on stilts with immense hat-shaped eaves and wooden balconies. The dull glow of the fishermen's oil lamps spilled through the windows, and the haunting rhythm of Cajun accordion and fiddle music drifted across the water. Distant lightning flickered in the sky, and thunder rumbled overhead as rain began to fall.

A boat rowed toward the jetty. Men wearing hats, their faces covered by scarves, rowed, while others carried burning torches, sheltering the flames from the sheeting rain. A heavyset man with a vicious scar beneath one eye stood at the prow. He held a rope and had a pistol jammed into the leather belt that held his ragged pants in place. He squinted through the sweeping rain, searching for a suitable place to tie up.

"Aim for the big hut. Once it's on fire, we head out. Anyone gets in our way, I'll take care of them. Understood?"

The men nodded with muffled grunts as the boat nosed alongside the landing. The man with the scar secured the boat to a post, then took his torch, stood up, and hurled it onto the roof of the largest hut. His men followed suit, their torches arcing through the night, exploding in sparks and flames. The roof was soon ablaze. The night filled with women's screams as smoke obscured everything.

FORTY-FOUR

RYKER'S FIELD, LOUISIANA – Present day

THE PHOTO SLIPPED from the old lady's hands. Chandler picked it up. She looked down at the newspaper article. Duke spoke softly, keeping her in the moment.

"What happened to the women, the Bloods, after the attack?"

Blanche looked up. Her eye was misty, her mind drifting between the past and the present. "They just disappeared," she said.

Jesse nodded. "Saint Malo was one of the villages in the path of the storm."

Chandler shook his head. "It doesn't make sense, running a brothel in Saint Malo. It was so far off the grid, there wouldn't have been any customers."

Duke nodded. "The arson attack could have been for all sorts of reasons. They were still foreigners in a foreign land back then."

Chandler said, "Zeke said it had been an orphanage way back when. Maybe that was what was going on, and people jumped to the wrong conclusion."

Blanche cleared her throat. "Back in those days there was no real adoption process. Children born out of wedlock were sometimes taken in by friendly neighbors, or adopted from hostels for unmarried mothers." She paused, wiped her face with a handkerchief and took another sip of the mint julep before continuing. "My apologies, this heat makes me parched. Have you heard of the term *änglamakerska*?"

Roxie and the others shook their heads.

Blanche continued, "It's Swedish for *angel maker*. It was a euphemism for the practice of baby farming."

Roxie looked at Blanche. "You think the women were acting as surrogates?"

Blanche shrugged. "It makes more sense than a brothel, doesn't it? The children would be sold to rich, childless couples in the cities."

"Local girls must have been involved," Chandler said. "Apart from Mary, who was in her twenties, the others were all in their forties. Too old to be reliable surrogates."

Chandler swatted at a persistent mosquito. "Back then, unmarried mothers were stigmatized by society," he continued. "In Victorian times, unwanted children were just abandoned, so orphanages were set up to prevent infant mortality. There were so few places that orphaned children were placed in prisons or workhouses, or left to fend for themselves on the streets." Chandler held up the photograph. "What was the date on that newspaper?"

Blanche handed the newspaper clipping back to Duke. Her face, for the briefest of moments, held the innocence of a small child.

"I can't see so good on small stuff, 'cept through a lens."

Duke looked at the paper clipping. "October fifth, 1893."

Jesse cleared his throat. "The Evil Wind hit on October second, 1893. A lot of my ancestors died in that storm."

Chandler stared at the photo. "They could have left the village before the fire."

Roxie gave a sad smile. "And sailed right into one of the worst storms ever to hit Louisiana."

FORTY-FIVE

SAINT MALO, LOUISIANA – 1889

FISHING BOATS WITH ragged sails bobbed in the waters alongside the landing stages that linked the group of fifteen or more huts that formed the main village. The sound of pigs grunting drifted across the water from patches of land surrounded by fencing. Mary sat with the rest of the women playing cards in the large back room of the hut. It was cooler back there, and had a small verandah netted off at the back that allowed a slight breeze to cool the sweltering heat of the day. The hut had been furnished with expensive antiques shipped over from New Orleans. Tumblety wanted to make sure that his visitors were given the right impression when they arrived. The women had initially been given a cold reception by the rough fishermen in the village, but gradually they'd managed to pick up some of the local Cajun dialect and been accepted.

Mary Ann Nichols, known as Polly, was dozing in a large cane chair. She'd loosened her corset, and her pendulous breasts threatened to spill out of her blouse every time she shifted in her sleep. Next to her sat Annie Chapman. Her pale complexion and breathing difficulties had improved slightly in the warmer climate, but she wasn't a well woman. Elizabeth Stride, known as Long Liz back in London, was teaching her friend Kate Eddowes how to play Bourré, a local card game. With the constant rain and humidity, the heat could be unbearable. But as the months passed, they gradually got used to it.

Tumblety and Cream had taken to satisfying their own base desires with the women whenever the mood took them. It had started on the voyage over. Tumblety had taken particular pleasure satisfying his needs with Mary, as she was the youngest and the prettiest. Night after night she'd had to endure his violent and perverse abuse. The smell of his cigars and the alcohol on his breath had made her feel ill. The contrast between his violence and the tender lovemaking she'd enjoyed with Edward was too hard to bear, and she was relieved when he'd abruptly tired of her. The reason was plain to see: she was with child.

When they realized she was pregnant, the men had taken her to a house out in Spirit's Swamp near Maurepas Island, outside Baton Rouge. There they had given her a medical procedure called a blood transfusion. She was connected to glass vials of blood with tubes and needles. Her blood was taken from one vial while she received blood from another. They told her it would make her baby stronger. She didn't like the procedure and neither did she trust them. She'd always felt weaker after the sessions and was glad when they were over. The other women had rallied around to try and comfort her during the lonely nights, as she grew heavy and tearful. She'd been pregnant before, but the babies had been stillborn.

She reflected on the irony of her situation. The miracle of birth should have been shared with Edward, her true love—but now Tumblety's evil spawn had poisoned that experience.

After six months out in the swamps of Saint Malo, the doctors had begun their new venture. They'd been to New Orleans and Baton Rouge and returned with young girls, who they'd moved into the hut. Tumblety started to entertain rich men and their wives. The young local girls were dressed in the finest of clothes and taught how to serve drinks and food to the guests. Sometimes a man would retire to one of the bedrooms with the girl of his choice. Mary and her friends were spared this and relegated to behind-the-scenes activities, like preparing food and cleaning the rooms. Within a few months it was obvious that some of the girls were with child.

One morning, while Tumblety was away visiting New Orleans and Cream was out fishing, Mary and her friends had managed to speak with Emilita, a half-caste Filipino girl with unusually light skin and lustrous raven hair. She was one of the local girls who spoke reasonable English. They listened as she told them her story in faltering speech. She was already with child when Tumblety had brought her to Saint Malo. Tumblety had then taken her to a rich man's house in the French quarter of New Orleans, and they had gone inside and met the man and his wife. Emilita had been told to leave the room while the men talked business. When Tumblety came out, she'd seen him putting a roll of bills into his pocket. Emilita was devastated when she realized he'd promised them her baby. Tumblety had told her that there were a lot of rich people who were more than happy to pay for a child, and that she should consider herself lucky. She would get paid, and the child would have a far better upbringing than she could have provided. He'd told her that sometimes the man couldn't father a child, but rather than admit it, the couple would fake a pregnancy and bring up a surrogate's child as their own.

The women had heard rumors that babies born to "women of ill repute" were handed over to an orphanage in the swamps outside Baton Rouge. It was now clear that Tumblety and Cream had been operating out of the house in Spirit's Swamp before moving their business to Saint Malo. After Emilita left, Lizzie shook her head in disgust. It was difficult to understand her at the best of times with her stuttering speech, but now, with her emotions running high, her excitable gabble was virtually impossible to decipher.

"W-w-what are we g-g-going to do about them? They c-c-can't d-d-do this to them g-g-girls." Lizzie's hands twisted a damp handkerchief like it was someone's neck. Mary placed a comforting hand on her shoulder.

"We have to be careful, Lizzie. Edward said we would be safe while Queen Victoria was alive," she said, "but her health isn't good. What if something happens to her?" Mary held her swollen belly with her hands. The baby's kicking had grown stronger, and she knew her time was near.

Kate nodded at her stomach. "You're fit to pop. You'd best hope nothing 'appens to Queenie until after you've dropped the little one."

"But what if it's not a boy?" Mary asked. "I fear for what he'll do to it if it's a girl."

Polly touched Mary's stomach. "From the size of you, it looks like you might 'ave two peas in that pod."

Mary looked down.

And then her waters broke.

She looked at the spreading puddle on the floor beneath her feet and felt a mixture of relief and fear.

"We need to get the midwife," Polly said and raced from the room.

Cream was just back from his fishing trip and hurriedly organized one of the fishermen to take him to Shell Beach. Tumblety was still in New Orleans, and they didn't know when he would return. Cream promised to send the midwife back to Saint Malo and, once he'd been located, bring Tumblety back with him. The birth was early, and he felt sure that Tumblety would have wanted to be there for it.

The women made Mary comfortable as Cream prepared to leave. He came into the room carrying a small doctor's bag, opened it, and produced a bottle labeled *Dr. J Collis Browne's Chlorodyne.*

"If the baby starts to come before the midwife gets here, give her a small dose of this. It will ease the pain." He handed the bottle over to Polly, who sat holding Mary's hand.

Polly opened the bottle and sniffed it. "Smells like laudanum," she said.

Cream nodded. "That is one of its components, along with chloroform and cannabis."

Polly put the cork stopper back into the bottle.

Cream looked at his pocket watch. "With luck, I'll be in New Orleans by midday and the midwife should be here by early evening. Once I've found Francis, we'll both return with as much haste as we can muster."

Mary looked at Cream. He and Tumblety didn't always see eye to eye, and she thought it might be possible to sway him in a certain direction.

"Dr. Cream," she said.

Cream looked over at her. "What is it? I must leave quickly if I am to catch the New Orleans train."

Mary nodded, forced a smile. "I'll be very grateful for you to dispatch the midwife, but if you have any trouble finding Dr. Tumblety, please don't feel you have to exert yourself too much if it becomes a problem. Do you understand?"

Cream nodded. "I believe I do, Mary. I, too, have been of the opinion that Francis can be—if I might speak plainly—overly forceful in his attentions. While his past in some ways influences his mistrust and resentment of the female species, I can understand that his presence during the birth might be an unnecessary burden. So if I am unable to locate Francis before the last train, well then, so be it." Cream turned and went out through the door.

Polly turned to Mary. "What's your game, my love?"

Mary held her hand up, signaling Polly to keep quiet. She listened to the fisherman talking to Cream before casting off from the jetty outside. They heard the snap of the sail as the wind filled it.

She turned back to Polly. "I think you may be right. It feels like I have more than one kicking inside of me."

Polly nodded. "But how is not having that monster here going to help those poor souls?"

Mary looked at her, a glimmer of hope in her world-weary eyes. "The only witness to the number of babies will be us and the midwife. I'd like to believe that I can give one of them the chance to escape this vile place."

Polly smiled. "You're a smart one, Mary Kelly. I always knowed it." She reached over to the chlorodyne, uncorked it, and took a swig. "May as well start the party early; we've got a long night ahead of us and lots to be done."

FORTY-SIX

BATON ROUGE, LOUISIANA – Present day

GOVERNOR BLACKBURN'S HOUSE was built with old money, a mansion in the style of a French château on Augusta Drive, the country club area of Baton Rouge. He much preferred to stay in his own home rather than the official governor's residence overlooking Capital Lake. Inside, crystal decanters sat on silver trays next to sculptures by Degas, while a purple and gold Louis XIV chaise longue fought for attention with a Van Eyck diptych. Every room in the house dripped with antiques and expensive works of art. The governor's two white hounds lay stretched out on a Persian rug in the middle of the living room. Bookshelves lined with Victorian medical books covered one wall, while on another, a large oil painting showed a man who looked like an older version of Dr. Tumblety, standing in a characteristic hunting pose with two white carriage dogs at his feet.

Blackburn poured himself a drink from one of the decanters while Kale stood uncomfortably in the middle of the room holding a half-empty glass in his hand. Kale always felt uneasy at Blackburn's house, intimidated by the man's ostentatious display of wealth and afraid that he'd knock something priceless off a shelf. He watched as Xavier, a silver-haired Puerto Rican tailor, tried to adjust the suit jacket that Blackburn wore while he moved around the room. At last, Blackburn paused for a moment while Xavier fiddled with some pins.

Kale regarded the dogs with suspicion—as they did him. He was convinced that they were sizing him up. One of them had started to dribble foam-flecked saliva from its huge jaws. Kale took a step back, placing an ornate writing desk between himself and the drooling beast.

Xavier straightened up from his task, looked at Kale, then back to Blackburn. "One more fitting, and it will be finished. When would you like me to come back?" he said.

Blackburn handed him the jacket. "Come back tomorrow, at eleven thirty."

Xavier took the jacket and retreated from the room, closing the door quietly behind him. Blackburn watched him go.

"You'd think fifteen thousand bucks would get you something pretty damn quick. Five months! Helluva suit, though."

Kale put his glass down on the mirror finish of a massive Steinway grand piano that sat in the corner of the room. Blackburn glowered at him, his eyes black pits in his reddening face.

"What the hell are you doing?"

He snatched up the glass and thrust it back into Kale's hand, slopping some of the drink over him. He wiped a tiny speck of moisture from the lid of the piano and glared at Kale.

"This is a limited-edition grand piano signed by Henry Z. Steinway. Cost a hundred and twenty thousand dollars. It's made from the finest ebony, walnut, and mahogany. Does it look like a damn drinks coaster to you?"

Kale took a deep breath and ground down on his anger. Working for Blackburn had its advantages, but the downside was that sometimes he could be an obnoxious prick. Today was quite clearly one of those times.

Blackburn took another slug of his drink.

"We've been pussyfooting around for too long now. After yesterday's events, it's obvious we need to go in hard."

Kale ran his fingers through his hair. "Lucky you managed to get the driver out of the way before Duke turned up."

Blackburn shrugged. "Did you see what was left of the Jeep? There's no way they should have survived that!" he snarled.

Kale looked for somewhere to put his glass down and ended up just holding it. "Well, maybe if you'd run the plan past me first, things would have worked out better," he said.

Blackburn made a conciliatory gesture with his hands. "Well, you're here now."

Kale shook his head. "Yes, now there's a mess to clear up."

"It's what I pay you for. Just get your men ready."

"We need to wait," Kale said. "Right now they're still looking for the driver of the truck. When they don't find him, they'll start winding down the investigation, then we can decide what to do."

Blackburn nodded. "One of my contacts approached me with some information. He does some gardening up at the de Chiel place—although from what I hear, he pretty much just rearranges the weeds. Anyway, he overheard Blanche talking to her companion, Jesse. She mentioned some documents, seemed worried about them."

Kale looked longingly at his now empty glass. "And why does that concern you?" he said.

Blackburn continued, "A few weeks ago, Blanche came to Marsha for advice. She didn't think she had much time left and was looking for guidance on tidying up her affairs."

Kale had met Marsha on several occasions and had been transfixed by her catlike eyes. He knew Blackburn called on her judgment before he made any big decisions, and guessed he hadn't consulted her about the truck driver.

Blackburn continued. "Blanche was conflicted about a pledge she'd made a long time ago."

Kale straightened up. This was of interest.

"Who did she make the pledge to?" he asked.

Blackburn shook his head. "She didn't say. Marsha sensed it was something that happened when she was a young girl, and that the person who entrusted her with the information had died. But one thing she did know for sure: it involved the English detective."

Kale leaned forward. "Chandler Travis, Duke's friend?"

Blackburn nodded.

Kale continued. "And you think this information she's got is about you?"

Blackburn nodded again.

"Okay, well, your family made its fortune during the oil boom," Kale said, "so I'm guessing there's some kind of illegality in your past—am I right?"

Blackburn's lips compressed into a hard line.

"I'll take that as a yes. So, she has some information about one of your ancestor's crooked deals that could torpedo your campaign."

"I can't afford to take the risk if she has." Blackburn said.

Kale went over to the drinks cabinet, poured himself a shot of J&B, and downed the whiskey. "Go on," he said.

Blackburn stood up again, paced the room like a caged animal.

"My ancestors falsified some documents. There may be some evidence that could be embarrassing. No big deal."

Kale nodded. "Unless of course you're running for the Senate."

"Yes," Blackburn replied. "Take some men and go out to the de Chiel place. Blanche and Jesse both go to a snooker club that he's a member of in the afternoons. That means they'll be out of the house for at least two to three hours. The information has got to be in there somewhere."

Blackburn finished his drink and stood up. "And organize a raid on the warehouse where Duke is conducting his investigation."

Kale frowned. "On what grounds?"

Blackburn shrugged. "Suspected contamination, dangerous toxins, endangerment to the health and safety of the community—that should be enough to get you through the door."

Kale sighed. "Are you really sure you want that much noise?"

Blackburn stood there, his face like stone.

Kale tried again. "I don't understand. Why is Duke's investigation a problem to you?"

Blackburn walked toward the door. Clearly, the meeting was over: Kale had been given his orders, and Blackburn wanted him gone. But Kale sensed there was something else going on that he needed to know about. Even if he only got a half-truth out of the man, it was more than he had right now.

"What is this about? I need to know what I'm dealing with here."

Blackburn turned toward him. The words came out reluctantly.

"The document my grandfather had falsified—it was a geological survey."

Kale nodded. "So you made a killing on the value of the land. It happens. Of course, there are always loose ends that need tidying up. The surveyor?"

Blackburn dropped his eyes to avoid Kale's searching look. Kale nodded. It was obvious that the surveyor had gotten greedy, come back for second helpings, and had to be bought off, or worse. He waited until Blackburn looked up again.

"And?" Kale said. He could see Blackburn's hand balled into a fist by his side, fingernails digging into the palm of his hand.

"As a result of the report . . . there were consequences." He paused. Kale saw his jaw clench.

Finally Blackburn took a breath and came out with it: "People died."

Kale stared at him. It was worse than he thought. "How many are we talking about?"

Blackburn closed his eyes as if reliving it. "Over two hundred."

Kale felt like he was caught in a living nightmare, and he was the one being asked to make it go away.

"Jesus! Most people have skeletons in their closets, just not that many." He shook his head before continuing. "Where are the bodies?"

But even as the words left his mouth he knew the answer.

Spirit's Swamp.

FORTY-SEVEN

SAINT MALO, LOUISIANA – 1889

BY THE TIME the midwife arrived, late in the afternoon, Mary's contractions were coming every four or five minutes. The midwife's name was Evelyn Stocker. Originally a nurse from England, she had come over to New Orleans to help during the "Saffron Scourge," an outbreak of yellow fever that had killed over 150,000 people, devastating the state of Mississippi. Evelyn, who was pregnant at the time, lost her husband to the disease. And if that hadn't been enough tragedy, her child had been stillborn following a difficult birth with an inexperienced midwife. She'd promised herself that she wouldn't let that happen to other mothers, and had stayed in New Orleans and retrained as a midwife.

Mary told her that she and the other women had fled London to escape abusive relationships and wound up in Saint Malo. Once they were settled, they became used to the solitude and had been joined by two men who looked after them in exchange for various services. Evelyn didn't ask what these services might be; she was there to deliver children, not sermons, so whatever was going on with them was their business. She told the women to fetch boiling water and clean towels for the birth while she prepared for the delivery.

"We need to shut out any mosquitoes during the birth. An infection from a bite could prove fatal to a newborn baby. Get some material to seal around the windows and doors."

Polly and Lizzie went away and came back with some old curtains that they cut up and used to seal off any gaps around the room. Mary had started to feel familiar sensations as the baby began to shift within her. Evelyn probed and felt her.

The midwife nodded to herself. "I'm pretty certain that you have more than one. I can tell you have had a child before, maybe several."

Mary nodded, her teeth clenched against the pain. "Yes, both were stillborn."

"I'm sorry to hear that. It happens more than it should. But everything seems to be fine at the moment. She turned back to her task.

Mary gestured to the bottle that sat on the table, next to a glass. "I was told that might ease the pain."

Evelyn flicked a look at it. "It might, but it will also increase the time you spend in labor. Who told you to use it?"

Polly replied, "One of the men who looks after us. He's a doctor."

Evelyn palpitated Mary's stomach. "Well, luckily he's not claiming to be a midwife." She moved Mary's shift clear of her belly, picked up a glass, placed it on Mary's stomach, and put her ear to it. She held up her hand for quiet before announcing, "Two hearts, both strong."

Mary felt Evelyn's hands gently probing.

"You're almost fully dilated. It won't be long now."

Mary went rigid as a violent pain lanced through her. She heard a strange keening noise—and realized it was coming from within her. Her legs started to shudder. Her body went into spasms. The pain burnt deep inside of her, a pain she remembered.

Evelyn reached over for the bottle. She uncorked it and offered it to Mary.

"You can have a sip of this. We don't have to worry about slowing down the birth now. I can see a baby's head."

Mary eagerly drank from the bottle. Anything that took the pain away was a mercy. "Thank you." She put the bottle down.

Polly wiped the cold sweat from her forehead and squeezed her arm. "Give them a good push, love. Better to get them out before they starts to muck you about."

Another spasm set Mary to screaming. Evelyn reached down and checked the baby's progress. A shiny bluish dome was starting to emerge, a tuft of dark brown hair visible through the glutinous covering that dripped from the baby's head.

"Push!" Evelyn said. "The faster we get this one out, the better chance the other one will have."

Mary strained, pushing down with her backbone against the rough mattress, trying to force the alien being inside her out into the world.

"That's it, one more," Evelyn said.

Mary strained, her back arched as she tried to deliver. There was a thick sucking noise, and something shiny and blue slid out into Evelyn's waiting hands.

"You have a daughter," she said, then quickly wiped the blood and waxy matter from the child's face and gently rubbed her feet. Soon the baby gasped and then began to cry. Evelyn wrapped her in a blanket before handing her over to Polly, who held her gingerly as if she were afraid of breaking her.

Polly looked down at her. "What about the cord?" she asked.

Evelyn shook her head. "Give it a moment: I believe there's still some goodness from the mother to come."

Polly shrugged. "I never heard that before."

Evelyn smiled. "You won't have. It's just something I learned while I was working in England. The later you cut the umbilical, the smarter and healthier the babies seem to grow up. You'd never really notice unless you went back to the family over a period of years, and that doesn't always happen. It seems the umbilical cord is full of special blood that benefits the baby."

Polly rocked the little baby girl, who was beginning to quiet, her skin becoming pink in places.

"Like some sort of super blood," Polly said.

"Exactly. Keep an eye on this one while I get the other one in the right position."

Evelyn moved nearer Mary, taking care not to snag the first umbilical. Mary looked over at the baby.

Evelyn saw her look and smiled. "She's healthy, and she's going to have a brother or sister very soon, so let's focus on the next little soldier, shall we?"

Mary nodded.

"Good. One more big push like before. The next one will have more room to move about, so it should be easier."

"Do you have any of your own?" Polly asked.

Evelyn shook her head. "No. I'd have to find a man I could put up with for that to happen."

Polly nodded. "That's always a problem. Ain't that right, Mary?"

But Mary was too busy trying to catch her breath to answer. Sweat dripped off her face, and it was taking all her strength to keep herself from screaming with the pain. She felt something shift and heard the afterbirth land in the small pail that had been placed under her. Evelyn scooped up a small pair of scissors and deftly snipped the umbilical of the baby girl, before turning back to Mary.

"Nearly there, one last push!"

Mary pressed her back down hard on the bed, tensing her muscles, trying to ease the baby out.

Fear was starting to creep into her head. She remembered back to when she'd lost her first baby. She'd been in labor throughout the night and had been bleeding before her waters broke. The midwife had told her not to worry, that it was perfectly normal to have a small amount of bloody discharge. But the bleeding had become heavier, and the movements inside her had started to grow weaker. She knew that something was wrong.

The midwife had tried to help. The umbilical cord, the baby's lifeline, had become twisted around its neck. By the time she gave birth, the baby was still and lifeless.

"PUSH!"

Evelyn's voice cut into her thoughts like a knife. She could feel something tearing inside her. And then there was a warm, wet rush and Evelyn was holding another purple-headed baby dripping with fluid. She wiped the baby's face and gently rubbed its hands and feet until it began to wail. Lizzie held out a small blanket to wrap the baby in and gently cradled it as Evelyn turned back to Mary. She wiped Mary's face with a damp cloth.

"Just a little housekeeping now, love. One more push—we just need the second placenta to come out, and you're done."

"It's a boy," Lizzie said, holding him up so Mary could see.

Mary arched her back and felt something shift as the placenta spilled out and into the pail.

"Well done. Now I'll just cut him free," Evelyn said as she cut through his umbilical cord.

Mary straightened up in the bed as Polly and Lizzie handed her the babies to hold. Mary looked from one baby to the other. They were both beautiful, that was for sure. But there was something odd about them: they didn't look like twins.

She turned to Evelyn. "Are they both alright?" she asked.

Evelyn smiled. "Of course. You have a beautiful, healthy son and daughter."

Mary nodded. "Yes, but, it's just they don't look . . ." She trailed off, unsure what to say.

Mary spoke sympathetically.

"All babies tend to change a lot as they grow. Their hair color, the eyes . . ." She stroked the cheek of the baby girl, whose mouth was forming a small O shape.

Evelyn turned to the women. "We need to clean up here. Take all the towels and cloths we've used and get rid of them, then empty the bucket and wash your hands. We can't have anything that might spread disease to the babies."

The women busied themselves with their tasks as Evelyn moved nearer to Mary.

"There may be something I can tell you about your babies, but I need to ask you some questions that might seem very personal to you. Do you understand?"

Mary nodded. "Of course," she said. Evelyn waited until the women had left the room with the bucket and cloths before continuing.

"In the week before you arrived here, and the week after, how many men were you intimate with?"

Mary looked at Evelyn, her face a picture of confusion. "I only slept with one man by choice before I arrived here," she said.

Evelyn gave her a look. "Someone else raped you?"

Mary nodded. "During the crossing."

Evelyn looked down at the baby girl. "They may have different fathers."

"So you've seen this before?" Mary asked.

Evelyn nodded and stroked the baby girl's cheek. "I have. Just not in humans."

Mary sat with her friends and Evelyn as the dawn drew near. Cream had been true to his word and had not tried too hard to find Tumblety. Maybe he really didn't know where he was, or maybe he did, and had deliberately concealed Mary's condition. Either way, neither of them had returned. Mary and Evelyn spent the night talking. Mary had taken the risk and told her the real reason they were hiding in Saint Malo and the part she and her friends had played in the conspiracy. Evelyn listened wide-eyed as she took in the full implications of the conspiracy. Mary detailed the privations the women had endured under Cream and Tumblety while Evelyn sat grim faced. As dawn approached, Evelyn started to work out how she could change Mary's situation. With Mary having no family or parental ties, Evelyn was determined to help her. Having delivered the babies, the midwife already felt a bond with the infants second in depth only to their biological mother's. Evelyn had wanted to help but had to wait for Mary to make the first move. The emotional strain Mary was under having just given birth made it a delicate situation. To Evelyn's relief, Mary did ask her for help. The words came tumbling out in a rush, like she knew that time was running out, and together they worked out a plan. Mary could feel the tears welling up inside her at the selfless support she was being shown from a woman she'd only just met.

Evelyn smiled, as relieved as Mary at her decision.

"It's bad enough what he did to you; you can't allow him to ruin your daughter's life as well," Evelyn said.

Mary reached across to stroke the cheek of one of the tiny babies on the bed. "I'll try and see her as much as I can. Tumblety won't know I've had twins. And she'll have a better life with you than she could ever have with me out here."

Evelyn nodded. "I'll call her Evelyn Mary Travis. That way she'll never forget us." She held Mary's hand. "Is there any chance you might be able to leave here—go back to England?"

Mary shook her head. "Not at the moment. I'm not even sure we're safe here."

"Maybe now that he has a son, he'll leave you alone," Evelyn said.

"He's under orders to make sure no one finds out who we are or where we are," Mary said. "You would be in great danger if he knew I'd confided in you, never mind given you this child."

Evelyn nodded and squeezed Mary's hand. "Maybe it could be possible to get word to your friend?"

Mary smiled. "Edward? I don't know where he is now. In fact I wouldn't even remember where he used to live. We planned to go to Ireland. But the night we were due to leave, well . . ." She halted as the horrific memories flooded back.

"It would be a shame if Edward never got to see his daughter," Evelyn said, looking at the baby girl as she wriggled and gurgled contentedly in Mary's arms. "I have friends in England. Maybe if I go back there to visit them, I could track him down. You might at least be able to write to him, perhaps even find a way to escape from here and be together again?"

Evelyn saw a spark of hope flicker in Mary's eyes, then dim again.

"I won't put much faith in that—it would hurt too much. But my heart would be eternally grateful if that should ever happen."

Evelyn looked at her watch. "I must be going. It wouldn't do us any good to still be here when that monster returns."

Mary nodded. "I understand. But you need to make sure he never learns the truth. And if anything happens to me, promise me you will disappear. Leave this place. Leave the evil behind."

Evelyn nodded. "I promise."

Mary looked at her tiny daughter. "Well, I'd better say goodbye to little Evelyn." She kissed the baby girl on the cheek. The infant's eyes opened and fixed her with a look of total love and innocence. Mary was suddenly swamped by a numbing emptiness that reminded her of the desolation she'd felt when her babies were stillborn. She watched as Evelyn carried the child carefully out of the hut and climbed into the small fishing boat that would take her to Shell Beach Railway Station for first light and the early train back to New Orleans. She continued to stare out across the water until the boat was nothing but a speck in the distance.

Tumblety returned with Cream the next morning. He claimed to be sorry to have missed the birth and made a big fuss of the baby, commenting on how much it already resembled him. To Mary's relief, he had no suspicions of the twin she'd sent away. Over the months that followed, Mary suckled the child until he could be weaned off her milk, and by the time the boy was two, Tumblety had taken over the job of looking after him. He'd also filed the birth certificate using his new identity, Francis Blackburn, and named his son Adam Blackburn.

Tumblety had mellowed slightly under the effect of fatherhood and allowed Mary to accompany him on his monthly supply runs to New Orleans. She told him there had been complications with the birth and that the midwife had recommended that she be examined at regular intervals to monitor her condition. Like most men, he neither knew nor cared what her condition was, and so Mary was able to visit Evelyn without suspicion. Tumblety assumed that the young Evelyn was the midwife's daughter, and Mary was relieved to see she was growing up into a beautiful and self-assured little girl.

Months turned into years and still the midwife had found no trace of Edward. It was as if he had vanished off the face of the earth. After four years passed, Mary had all but given up hope. She was still isolated in Saint Malo, with limited access to her daughter, and Edward was becoming a distant memory. But as the summer's heat turned cooler and they headed through September that year, everything changed.

FORTY-EIGHT

LONDON, ENGLAND – September 1893

EDWARD HAD CONTINUED his search for Mary through the years. He'd written to all his contacts in the newspaper business, and to every harbor master on the American coast. But every inquiry had proved fruitless and every lead had reached a dead end. Edward was beginning to think that Mary and her friends had been murdered at sea and their bodies thrown overboard. It was a conclusion he didn't want to accept, but as the years went by, he was starting to believe that it was the only explanation.

By September 1893, he had run out of direction and hope. But even though he'd spent many sleepless nights plagued by dark thoughts, he had still managed to achieve a measure of success in his career as a journalist in London. He'd been offered a job with *The Times* as a reporter, and had been taken under the wing of its new managing director, Moberly Bell. Moberly had been brought in to turn the financially shaky newspaper around and believed in hiring enthusiastic young reporters to give a more modern feel to the paper's editorial content. The two of them had gotten on well, and Edward was now writing a popular column on American politics through the eyes of an Englishman. The column had been a big hit in England and was being reprinted in the *New York Times*.

As Edward put the finishing touches to his latest column, his copy editor dropped a letter onto the desk in front of him. "Here's something that might cheer you up," he said.

Edward picked up the envelope. It had an American stamp and postmark.

"What is it?" he asked.

"Could be your first piece of fan mail from America," the editor replied with a smile, then turned and headed back across the room, past the clatter of typewriters and into his office.

Edward looked at the address on the back of the envelope. It was from the US Marine Hospital in Algiers, New Orleans. He ripped open the letter and started to read. And his heart stopped.

Dear Mr. Travis,

I hope this reaches you, and that you are in good health. My name is Evelyn Stocker. I am a nurse and midwife working at the US Marine Hospital in Algiers, New Orleans. I am writing on behalf of Mary Jane Kelly, whom I believe you are acquainted with?

Edward slumped back in his seat as he read through the letter. Mary was alive! His heart leaped with joy, but then, as he read on, he grew angry as he learned of the treatment Mary and her friends had suffered at the hands of their captors. When he read the names of the men that were meant to be protecting the women, his blood turned to ice. Dr. Francis Tumblety and Dr. Thomas Neill Cream, both of them suspected murderers. Now it all made sense. Who better to orchestrate the bogus murders of the Ripper conspiracy than men who had no choice but to do what they were told—or face the consequences for their real crimes? When he read that Mary had given birth to twins, a girl and a boy, it made him even more determined to find her. The midwife had implored him to get in contact with her by return mail. She was deeply concerned for the safety of Mary and her friends, and laid out a timetable of events, which between them might help the women break free.

Evelyn promised to send more details but had thought it imperative to plan their escape before wasting any further time. Evelyn had been in the hospital and had seen a man reading a copy of the *New York Times*. She had glanced at it and caught sight of Edward's name on his column. She hadn't wanted to write until she had met with Mary and they had discussed a possible plan.

Edward had been intending to approach *The Times* with his story once he was sure Mary was safe. Now it looked like that might finally happen. He went immediately to his editor and told him he had an important story out in New Orleans, a story that would make headlines. The editor took some convincing and had to run it past Moberly before he would sign off on it. Moberly gave the go-ahead and advanced Edward enough funds for his travel and a month's expenses. He told Edward in no uncertain terms that if he came back empty handed then the advances would come out of his wages. Edward thanked him and raced out of the office to organize things. He had already written a reply to Evelyn in great haste and posted it. If he made speed, he knew he could be on a ship bound for America that very night and make land within ten days, less if the wind was with them. He raced home and began hurriedly throwing some things into a small bag. Within the hour, he was headed for the railway station to buy a ticket to the Southampton docks.

FORTY-NINE

SAINT MALO, LOUISIANA – October 1, 1893

IT WAS LATE on a bright Sunday afternoon, and the sun was a golden ball rolling beneath the low clouds above the lake. Cream and Tumblety weren't due back from New Orleans until late evening.

Mary and her friends were starting to accept that they might finally have a chance to break free from their captors with Edward's help. Though Tumblety had mellowed over the years, Cream had recently become more violent, and his mood swings were unpredictable. They all knew why. He'd sailed to England the previous year and hadn't returned for several months. While he was gone, Tumblety had shown them a newspaper he'd brought back from New Orleans. The headlines reported that Cream had been hanged and confessed to being Jack the Ripper as he plunged to his death. Tumblety explained that the public needed to believe that the Ripper had been caught and that London was safe once again.

Sure enough, Cream returned. But something had gone wrong with the fake hanging. He now wore a leather collar to support his neck and was in constant pain. His vocal cords had been badly bruised, and he still had a rasping quality to his voice.

Mary spent the rest of the afternoon praying that Edward's ship would soon arrive and that she would finally be reunited with her daughter. But then her heart sank. She heard the sound of a boat hitting the wooden jetty outside. Cream and Tumblety were back, and they were early. Much too early.

The men burst into the hut, their faces like thunder. Tumblety had upset some rich man in town who'd been promised a baby. Something had gone wrong, and the girl he had been with hadn't conceived. It seemed he wasn't prepared to accept Tumblety's suggestion that maybe he was the problem. His manhood had been insulted and he was out for revenge. The man had a lot of friends in low places, and they were more than happy to settle a score with the foreigners out in the swamps. Tumblety made it quite clear: they had to leave, and quickly. Mary ran to her room and snatched up her old carpetbag. She opened the drawers of a small cabinet by her bed and collected her meager possessions, wrapping up her diary in a piece of oilskin one of the fishermen had given her. She grabbed Edward's silver hunter-case pocket watch and kissed it before dropping it into her bag. Her plans were in ruins. If she left the village now, Edward would never find her.

A shout from Cream outside interrupted her thoughts.

"Come on, we have to go. Now!"

Mary pulled a shawl from the drawer and tied it to the bedstead before running out of the hut and onto the jetty. Her hands were shaking, and there were tears in her eyes. Outside, the sun was now obscured by dull gray clouds, and rain swept across the swamp, blurring the surface of the water. The women huddled in the boat while Long Liz loaded the last of their bags. Cream and Tumblety waited impatiently on the dock.

"Come on!" Cream shouted angrily and grabbed Mary's arm, his fingers digging into her flesh. She slapped him hard. He reeled back in pain and surprise, rubbing at the red mark that glowed on his cheek.

"You bitch!"

His eyes blazed, and he lunged toward her, his hands rigid talons. Long Liz stepped between them, planted herself firmly on the ground and swung her foot up with colossal force. Cream screamed with pain as her boot connected with his groin, lifting him clear off the ground. He crashed to the floor, his face ashen.

"I ain't f-f-forgot my d-d-dancing steps!" Liz stuttered.

But Cream wasn't listening. He lay like a sack of coal on the jetty, his mouth trembling, eyes bloodshot, drool trailing from his open mouth as he gasped for air. Tumblety shoved Liz out of the way, pulled a pistol out of his jacket, and swung his aim between Mary and Liz.

"There are men in boats coming to kill us and burn this place to the ground. We haven't got time for hysterics. Now get into the damn boat."

Long Liz grabbed Mary by the shoulders. "It's not safe to stay here," she said.

Mary nodded. Polly, Annie, and Kate helped her into the boat. Tumblety went over to Cream, who lay twitching on the jetty.

"Pull yourself together and get into the boat or I'll leave you here with the rest of them. Come on!"

He grabbed Cream under one arm and motioned for Long Liz to take the other. Together they dragged him over to the boat, before dropping him unceremoniously into the hull. Mary looked back to see the local girls standing fearfully by the door to the hut.

"What about them?" she asked.

Tumblety shoved her into the boat and jumped in before pushing off into the darkness. "They'll just have to take their chances."

Moments after they left the village behind and headed across the lake, Mary heard the screams of the remaining women and the coarse shouts of the attacking men. And as she looked back she saw a lurid red glow lighting up the sky. The village was on fire.

FIFTY

RYKER'S FIELD, LOUISIANA – Present day

DUKE LOOKED AROUND the sun-dappled swamp, feeling drowsy in the heat.

"Man, were they in the wrong place at the wrong time," he said.

Blanche turned to Chandler. "Why do you want to know about these women?"

Chandler looked out across the swamp, trying to make sense of it all before he spoke.

"It's just, well, the evidence we've found shows that these women drowned during the great storm of 1893."

Blanche nodded. "So what's the problem?" she asked.

Chandler smiled at her. "The problem is, they'd already been murdered by Jack the Ripper in England five years earlier."

They journeyed back in Roxie's Jeep, each of them deep in their own thoughts. Roxie broke the silence.

"Did you get the feeling that Blanche was worried about something?"

"Yes," Chandler said. He'd sensed that, tough though she was, the old lady had something on her mind that was upsetting her. "Jesse told me that over the last few years she's started to show signs of dementia, so it could be that she couldn't even remember what was worrying her. Jesse said that some days she remembered back seventy years like it was yesterday, and other days he wasn't sure if she knew who he was."

"She liked you," Roxie said. "That English accent is a big hit with the mature broads." She smirked.

Duke gave Roxie a meaningful look.

"Looks like it doesn't go down too badly with the younger set, either."

Roxie blushed, and Chandler shifted uncomfortably in his seat.

Duke changed the subject. "When you introduced yourself, she said she knew someone in London. Who do you think that was?"

Chandler shrugged. "I don't know. Depending on how well her memory was working, it might not even have been a real person."

Roxie nodded. "Well, she's given us some things to think about. Tumblety and Cream running a baby-making operation out in Saint Malo makes as much sense as anything."

"I'd love to get some answers from the diary, but I just don't see how, considering the extent of its water damage," Chandler said.

Roxie replied, "Once they've dried it out, I might know a way to read the pages without destroying them."

Chandler looked at her. "Is that possible? I thought the pages were meshed together."

"They are, but this is a new kind of technology. It potentially allows you to read the book without having to open it."

Chandler smiled. "That would be good news. Water seems to have been responsible for nearly everything bad in this investigation. It would be nice if we could beat it for once."

FIFTY-ONE

SHELL BEACH, LOUISIANA – October 2, 1893

DAWN SILVERED THE sky as the fisherman guided the boat onto the shore of Shell Beach. Cream had recovered slightly, and though bent over and wincing, he managed to drag himself out of the boat and up the beach as they made their way to the railway station. The sky was clearer here, but they could hear the distant rumble of thunder from across the lake. A train whistle sounded as they drew near the platform, three short blasts. It was getting ready to leave.

"C'mon," Tumblety said. "If we miss this one it'll be another three hours before the next."

The women increased their pace, but Cream could only manage a slow hobble.

"M-m-move yerself, or I'll k-k-kick you up the arse," Liz threatened, and Cream sped up.

Tumblety bought tickets, and they all scrambled aboard as the train gave one last blast of its whistle and the pistons thrust, jerking the engine and causing the cars to bang together as the buffers and coupling chains took the strain. The train clattered along the track and headed toward Poydras Junction. The women sat silently, their stress and fear replaced by exhaustion.

A man and his wife sat with their daughter opposite Cream and Tumblety. Cream winced as he changed position, trying to get comfortable and failing.

"You folks from round here?" the man asked.

The doctors shook their heads, not wanting to get involved in a conversation.

"Your pardner looks like he's been too many miles in the saddle," the man said, nodding at Cream.

On the other side of the carriage the women stifled their smiles.

"My friend had a nasty fall. His pride was hurt more than anything," Tumblety said.

Cream looked across at him, his eyes speaking volumes.

The man nodded. "That happens," he said. "You plannin' on gettin' out ahead of the storm?"

Tumblety looked at him. "What storm?"

"They reckon it's gonna hit the southeast. We're hopin' to get farther upcountry and miss the worst of it."

Mary leaned toward the man.

"How long do you think it will be before it hits?"

The man shrugged. "Hard to tell. Sometimes these winds have a habit of sneakin' up and kicking you in the toolbox."

"Jimmy, the child," his wife scolded.

"Hush, woman. Ain't nothin' she ain't heard back at the farm."

"We're headed for Maurepas Island." Mary said.

The man shrugged. "Then you'd best trust in the Lord."

They arrived at Poydras Junction just over an hour later. The train whistle blew, the brakes screeched, and then, with a clank of the couplings, the locomotive ground to a halt. They retrieved their luggage and climbed down from the carriage. The platform was full of passengers hurrying to get onto the next train into the city. They joined the queue of jostling people and climbed on board the waiting train. The New Orleans train had more carriages, but they were fuller, and Cream and Tumblety had to stand, while the women managed to get seats. The journey from Poydras Junction to New Orleans was around eighteen miles, and within the hour they were climbing down from the carriages once more and heading across the platform of New Orleans Union Station.

Apart from Mary, the women hadn't left Saint Malo since they'd come to America; they were astonished at the station's size and grandeur. It was a three-story hip-roofed structure with a cupola, a broad portico, central columns, and arched entryways at each end of the entrance. It was an impressive sight, and the women stood entranced. Mary could see through the arched entrance onto the street outside, where carriages stood waiting. The passengers all seemed to be in a hurry to get somewhere. She wondered if the storm the man had told them about was getting near.

The women had been told to stay with the luggage while Cream and Tumblety organized tickets for the final leg of the journey to Maurepas Island, from where they would all go by carriage out to Spirit's Swamp and on to the orphanage. Mary could see Cream and Tumblety in the ticket office, talking and gesticulating. Cream kept flicking nervous looks toward them. She knew that if they tried to escape they wouldn't get far. Exhausted from the journey, and without food or money, they would soon be found.

In the ticket office, Tumblety and Cream were deep in conversation.

"Are you sure you're up to the journey?" Tumblety asked.

Cream nodded. "I'll be okay. I could kill that bitch, though."

Tumblety looked at him. "Just get to the orphanage ahead of the storm. I have to stay here to look after Adam." He handed Cream a sheaf of tickets. "We'll have to see whether we can continue operations as usual once things have settled down."

Cream took the tickets and headed back out into the station.

Mary watched as Cream limped toward them. "You must have caught him a right blow," she said to Lizzie.

"No more than he d-d-deserves," Lizzie replied.

Kate looked over at the ticket office. "Looks like Tumblety isn't coming with us," she said.

Mary looked at her anxiously. "That means we're alone with Cream."

FIFTY-TWO

MAUREPAS ISLAND, LOUISIANA – October 2, 1893

THE LOCAL TRAIN was more worn and noisy than the mainline one, its seats stained and scratched and the floors littered with discarded papers, pieces of food, and animal droppings. The journey was slow and tedious, with many stops on the way. Eventually the locomotive ground to a halt and Mary heard the guard shout out, "Maurepas Island, last stop!"

The women stood up and started to gather their belongings. They followed Cream down onto the platform and out onto the street, where a carriage stood waiting. The few passengers who were left to disembark stared curiously at the driver as he sat holding the reins.

The women began loading their possessions into the empty steamer trunk that had been roped to the back. The carriageman jumped down. Cream held some money out to the man. The man looked at the money in his hand and at the sky above.

"Begging your pardon, sir, but I'm not heading out tonight. You'd best make for safe lodgings as soon as you can. This storm ain't gettin' any kinder."

Cream gave a hard smile and added some more money to the pile in the driver's hand. "How about you rent me the carriage and I return it to you back here tomorrow at midday?"

The man rubbed at his chin before coming to a decision. "How about you add some more as a deposit . . . in case you don't make it."

Cream added some more bills, and the man nodded before pocketing the cash, tipping his hat and heading back into town.

Cream held the carriage horses steady as they shifted nervously, their eyes wide with fear. The wind was getting stronger, and the women leaned into it as they walked around the cab and climbed in. Once everyone was safely on board, Cream cracked the whip and the horses galloped away.

Mary looked at the women's tired faces. They were all exhausted, tired, and hungry from the journey. She imagined Edward making his own way across the Atlantic, headed for the port of New Orleans. She wondered what he would think if he made it to Saint Malo and found her shawl, if it was still there. For all she knew it could have been burnt in the fire. In which case, he would probably think she was dead and give up his search. She needed to let him know she was still alive. But how? And then it came to her. Cream was on his own. She turned to Polly.

"I was worried about being left with Cream—especially after what happened back at the village—but now I think it might be a good thing."

Polly looked at her. "What do you mean?" she asked.

Mary leaned forward. "Well, there's five of us, and only one of him."

Polly nodded. "But he's got a gun," she said.

"He won't get a ch-ch-chance to use it. I'll see to that," Liz said with a smile. "He won't risk anything with me—not if he wants to wa-wa-walk straight again."

"Right," said Mary, "we'll pretend to be asleep, and then when he tries to wake us, we'll jump him. Everyone agreed?"

They all nodded.

"I'd rather die trying than be stuck out here for the rest of my life," Liz said.

Mary squeezed her arm. "We'll be there soon," she said. "Let's get ready."

FIFTY-THREE

ATLANTIC OCEAN – October 1893

EDWARD HAD MADE his way to the docks in time to get a last-minute seat in steerage and board the *SS City of New York*. The ship, which weighed seventeen thousand tons and was nearly six hundred feet in length, was one of the first express liners to use twin screws and boasted a top speed of over twenty knots. As he'd looked toward the receding docks of Southampton, Edward wanted every one of those knots to move him nearer to Mary.

He'd planned to spend as much time as possible on deck to avoid the claustrophobic conditions in steerage, but the sea had a heavy swell as they cast off, and the weather hadn't gotten any better as they journeyed across the Atlantic. After ten days of rough seas, they ran into a storm approaching the Gulf of Mexico. Silver veins of lightning laced the dark skies overhead, and the liner needed all its power to keep on course through the mountainous waves surrounding it. Edward, long ago forced to abandon his plans to stay on deck, had to endure the hot and fetid conditions below, surrounded by the wailing of children and the moaning of the seasick. He soon learned that the captain had decided it was too dangerous to head directly to New Orleans and was planning an alternative route.

Edward cursed his bad luck. Ever since the day he had watched the *Elysian* disappear into the fog, he'd been dreaming of this moment.

It had been five years since he'd last seen his beloved Mary, and he still remembered every detail of the night she'd left.

After watching the Elysian *disappear into the fog, he'd gone directly down to the Royal Albert Dock port office to check the passenger lists. America was a vast country, and the ship could have been headed for anywhere.*

With space for around five hundred vessels to moor in the dock's upper pool, and about three times as many occupying it, the port office was always in chaos. Edward had visited it on many occasions while researching for stories to submit to the papers. There was always information to be gleaned from the port. Because of the overcrowding, precious cargo would spend weeks at a time in lighters before it could be dealt with. This left them exposed to river thieves who worked in the port, running well-organized criminal trade in which revenue officers connived on many an occasion, pointing out the more lucrative targets. There were various factions within the criminal classes—river pirates, night plunderers, light horsemen, heavy horsemen, scuffle-hunters, and mudlarks—and they all had tales to tell. Edward had made the acquaintance of the chief port officer, George Lumsden, while doing his research and was glad when he waved him over. He pushed open the half-glazed door into the office.

"Edward!" he exclaimed. "What brings you to this pit of confusion? Nothing fit to print?" George clasped Edward's hand in a firm shake.

"Quite the opposite, I'm afraid," Edward said.

George waved him into a scuffed leather chair that sat in front of his crowded desk overflowing with files and manifests. Edward leaned forward.

"I need to know where a ship that recently left the pool was headed."

George smiled, raised his hands in the air. "I'm hoping you have more clues for me to go on than that."

Edward nodded. "I have indeed. The Elysian*. A frigate. It left earlier this evening, around six. I remember hearing the church bells strike."*

George slid a thick leather-bound ledger across his desk. His nicotine-stained fingers traced down the spidery columns of names, figures, and times that filled the page. He flicked backward and forward through the book, shaking his head.

"Six o' clock, you say? There's no record of any ship named the Elysian *leaving today, or entering the docks anytime in the last few weeks."*

"That's not possible—I saw it with my own eyes," Edward said.

George pursed his lips. "Could you be mistaken?"

Edward sank back in his seat. "I remember every detail, and I could swear that the ship was so named."

"Then something is afoot, my dear Edward."

"Would it be possible for a ship to moor up under one name and leave under another?" Edward asked.

George shrugged. "It's possible, but to what purpose?"

"I'm working on a story where nothing is what it appears. This might just be another act of subterfuge." Edward stood up and leaned over the ledger. "Do you have a record of any frigates that left at around six this evening?"

George ran his finger down the list. He paused.

"There's only one. The Cherbourg, *a sailing frigate, private charter."*

"When did the Cherbourg *moor up?" Edward asked.*

George ran a finger down the ledger again and came to a halt.

"The day before, and here's something odd. She was empty. No passengers, no cargo. That makes no sense. Any master worth his salt would make sure he had paying cargo or passengers in both directions."

Edward nodded. "Unless they didn't care about the money, but only their privacy," he said. "I don't understand."

George explained. "Shipmasters are not required to record the names of unassisted passengers who pay their own fares or are privately sponsored."

Edward leaned forward. "So if the Cherbourg *left under the name the* Elysium, *there's no way of knowing where her final destination might be?"*

George shook his head. "Whoever's running this operation certainly doesn't want to draw attention to themselves. Have you any idea where they're bound for?"

"Only that they're headed for America."

"That's a big country."

Edward looked out over the Thames at the myriad ships bobbing on the water. He only knew one thing for certain: with every second, Mary was getting farther away from him.

FIFTY-FOUR

SPIRIT'S SWAMP, LOUISIANA – October 2, 1893

MARY LOOKED THROUGH the window at the featureless landscape as the carriage jolted along the muddy track bordering the swamp. It was getting darker, and she could see flickers of lightning in the distance. She remembered the journey from before. The orphanage was about five miles from Maurepas, and it had taken just over an hour to get there the last time she'd been. As they headed deeper into the swamp, it started to rain. Not the soft, warm rain they were used to, but silver bullets of water drumming against the roof of the carriage. Outside was just a desolate expanse of waterlogged vegetation and rotting cypress trees.

The carriage came to a sudden halt. She heard Cream climb down from his seat and then a metallic click. The women's eyes grew wide and Mary gave them a nod. They all feigned sleep. The horses snorted with fear. The wind suddenly dropped, and the sky became dark. It felt like they were in the eye of the storm. Mary lowered the window and looked out. A sudden gust of wind ripped the scarf from her neck, sending it floating up into the sky, a blood-red wound against the darkness. She saw Cream with a gun in his hand and then something looming up behind him. She heard a roaring noise and started to scream. Then everything went black.

FIFTY-FIVE

ATLANTIC OCEAN – October 1893

THE LINER BATTLED against the fierce headwinds, the sea foaming against its hull as it pitched and yawed through the mountainous waves surrounding it on all sides. Edward had decided to brave the howling wind and the rain and stood on deck clutching on to the railings. He could see the island of Puerto Rico in the distance. They were headed for the safe harbor of San Juan and would soon be docking.

Once they were in the lee of the island, the wind dropped and the towering waves reduced to a heavy swell. The rain subsided into a light drizzle, and Edward could see the sun trying to burn through the layer of gray cloud that hung above the town. Edward looked down at the water as the liner nosed into the port. San Juan was one of the busiest ports in the Caribbean, and with so many other ships seeking refuge from the storm, it was even more chaotic than usual. Edward watched as a flotilla of steam tugs battled to orchestrate the liner's safe docking. With the blast of steam whistles and much shouting, the vast liner was finally positioned and safely docked alongside the quay.

As soon as the gangplank was lowered, the crew swarmed down it, shouting and gesticulating to the group of local dockworkers that had helped secure the ship. It was now late afternoon, and the storm could be seen heading away toward the west, while a weak sun had clawed its way past the clouds, bathing the port in warm sunshine.

Edward stood on the top deck and looked out over San Juan, with its cobbled streets and crowds of people bustling past. The passing of the storm and the reappearance of the sun had energized the city, and people were making up for their enforced stay inside. He watched as a steam-powered tram loaded with sugarcane headed out of the port along the tracks that hugged the coast.

The weather continued to improve, and soon stevedores were clambering up the gangplank, loading fresh supplies of coal and food. At midday, the ship slipped its moorings and headed back out to sea. They made good time, and the seas were calm in the wake of the storm. By the third day they had passed the shores of Cuba and Florida, and were crossing the Gulf of Mexico. New Orleans was only a few hours away.

They navigated across Lake Borgne, down the Rigolets, and past the desolate walls of Fort Pike. The ship continued on and entered Lake Pontchartrain. With the sun a misty yellow blur above them, they moored at the quayside in the port of New Orleans. Only then was Edward able to take in the level of devastation surrounding him.

The powerful hurricane had destroyed many of the buildings in the port and along the shoreline as far as he could see. Edward looked around for a boat to take him from the port to Saint Malo, but the harbor was littered with evidence of the storm's passage. Many smaller craft were overturned, half-submerged, or with their masts broken and their sails torn. The only method of transport that hadn't been destroyed was the railway line that ran from Poydras Junction to Shell Beach. But Poydras Junction was over twenty miles away.

Edward looked around desperately, every fiber of his being wanting to keep moving, to find Mary. Suddenly, he heard a man speaking in French.

"Monsieur."

Edward looked down to see the wizened face of an old fisherman staring up at him from the deck of a small lugger. It was tied to an iron ring that was set into the stone jetty. The boat was relatively unscathed, though the nets that lay on the deck were ripped and tangled.

Edward shook his head. He knew some French, but not enough to converse with a local fisherman in his own dialect. "English?" he asked.

The man nodded. "You want passage?" He gestured at his torn nets. "I lose my catch."

Edward reached into his pockets and pulled out a dollar bill. He held it out to the man. The man took the note, smiled, and then tucked it into his pocket.

"Where?" he asked.

"Poydras Junction, the railway station," Edward replied.

The fisherman nodded and helped him climb into the boat. They set off down the Mississippi, the wind tugging at the small, ragged sail as they headed past Algiers Point across the river from the French Quarter, and then the great railway yards that stretched back for twenty-two blocks. The fisherman nodded toward an impressive old building.

Its windows were smashed and part of its brickwork had fallen in.

"Hospital," he muttered.

Edward stared in horror. It was the US Marine Hospital, where Evelyn the midwife worked. If it weren't for the storm, she would have been inside, and she could have taken him to his daughter, the daughter his heart ached to see. But where would they have gone to avoid the storm? He desperately wanted to go into the hospital to see if anybody knew of their whereabouts. But he and Evelyn had made their plans, and he had to stick to them.

Evelyn had promised him she would send more news of Mary and her circumstances, but he hadn't waited for her mail to arrive before deciding to make his way to Saint Malo. He was determined to free Mary and her friends from the men who had held them captive for all these years. Only then could he and Mary start their life again, as a family.

But as Edward and the Frenchman made their way down the river, his worry grew with every mile. Everywhere he looked, there was evidence of the storm's power. The bloated bodies of cattle and dogs—and even worse, the bodies of men, women, and children who had been caught in the floods—floated past.

After two hours, they came to a bend in the river at Poydras Junction. The fisherman pointed. "Station," he said.

They pulled up next to some slimy green wooden steps. Edward thanked the fisherman, heaved his small bag onto the side of the jetty, and hauled himself up the steps and onto the slippery wooden planks. In the distance he could see the squat shape of the railway station and the line stretching away into the distance. A locomotive waited at the platform, a small group of people standing alongside. Edward could see coal being shoveled into the tender and clouds of steam beginning to rise from the smokestack. The driver gave three sharp blasts on the whistle. Edward hurried toward the station and managed to get a ticket before scrambling aboard the train. It gave a last blast from its whistle and headed off.

As the carriages shook and rattled their way down the tracks, Edward stared out of the window. They passed row after row of ramshackle buildings, all in disrepair. He saw the broad expanse of Lake Borgne stretching to the horizon. Everywhere he looked, there was evidence of yet more destruction.

A passenger sat opposite Edward, his face burnt by the sun, his large hands calloused by farmwork. He saw the fear in Edward's eyes, leaned toward him, and said, "A lot of folk left the villages for higher ground before the storm hit."

Edward nodded, grateful for the slim hope the man offered.

It took over two hours for them to reach Shell Beach. The train was forced to slow down on numerous occasions because parts of the line were still underwater. Edward saw the remains of some villages in the distance. Even the largest of the houses were missing a roof, or had had their windows blown out by the force of the storm. He saw people carrying everything they owned on their backs, people whose whole lives had been destroyed within the span of a few hours.

The locomotive shuddered to a halt at its final destination. The station had miraculously survived and, though it was surrounded by debris, still had a roof and a few intact windows. Edward studied a rudimentary map he'd brought with him and saw that Saint Malo was five miles along the coast from Shell Beach. He jumped down from the train and made his way onto the beach. He looked out over the waters of Lake Borgne. The shoreline was littered with debris; pieces of wood and clumps of palmetto thatch floated on the surface of the water. He heard footfalls behind him and turned to see the man from the train standing next to him. The man cleared his throat before speaking.

"I'm guessin' you're after finding somebody?"

Edward nodded. The man swept his hand across the lake.

"Maybe you should wait until the waters have dropped. It'll be safer. Big storms have a habit of coming back and biting you on the ass."

Edward shook his head. "I have to find out if she's safe or . . ." He stopped, fear holding him in its icy grip.

The man nodded. "A woman. Now I understand."

"I need to get a boat," Edward said.

The man looked around him. "Plenty of boats along the beach. You just need to find one that isn't holed and some oars. Where are you trying to get to?"

"Saint Malo," Edward said.

The man shook his head. "That's farther down the coast. Can't say there'll be much left of it. Just a few fishermen there to begin with, as far as I know. Likely left before the storm hit." He looked at Edward. "If you want a hand, I've done some rowing."

Edward nodded. "Yes, if we can find a boat, I'd be very grateful."

After a short walk, they managed to spot an intact boat that had been turned on its back next to the remains of an old jetty damaged in the storm. Farther down the beach, they collected some oars. They floated the boat and climbed in. They took it in turns to row across the muddy lake toward Saint Malo. After more than an hour of rowing, they halted to rest their hands. Edward's were already covered in blisters. Then they saw something in the distance: the remains of a large hut, its roof badly burnt. It had been torn apart by the storm and was lying sideways, one half of the roof submerged, the stilts that used to support it sheared off. There were other, smaller huts, but they were badly damaged too and most of them were partially submerged, with only the tops of their wooden roofs showing. Edward knew that the hut the girls lived in was the biggest one in the village, and from what he could see, he was looking at it. The small jetty alongside had survived the storm and was level with the water. Edward tied the boat to a post and stepped out onto the flooded jetty.

"I'll stay here and mind the boat. You be careful," the man said.

Edward nodded. The water sloshed around his ankles as he trudged toward the gaping hole in the side of the hut. Pieces of broken cane furniture floated inside what was left of one of the rooms. Edward stepped off the jetty and waded into the hut. He heaved a door open against the weight of the water behind it and made his way into a smaller room. There was a bed, a wooden chest with draws half-open, and an upturned chair. He feared that no one could have survived the force of the storm, or the fire that seemed to have swept through the hut.

He saw something tied to a brass bed frame: a brightly colored shawl patterned with a design of small birds. With a start he realized it was the same one he'd bought for Mary at the market. He untied the shawl and held the sodden fabric against his cheek. Maybe it was his imagination, but he thought he could still smell her. He knew the mind could play tricks, but he felt sure this had once been Mary's room. Maybe she'd left the scarf there deliberately to let him know she was safe? But where had they gone? A few short weeks ago he had been given hope. But that was before the storm.

He carefully tucked the shawl into one of his coat pockets and made his way back out onto the jetty. The man waiting saw the look in his eyes, nodded, and said nothing. They rowed back in silence. By the time they arrived at Shell Beach and climbed wearily out of the boat, the sun was setting. Edward thanked the man warmly for his help and bid him farewell before boarding the train back to Poydras Junction.

It was dark by the time the train pulled into the station, and Edward disembarked and set off to find lodgings for the night. He planned to contact the newspaper as soon as the telegram office was working again. Moberly was a reasonable man. Edward felt sure he could convince him to let him stay out there as their foreign correspondent, and allow him to earn a living while he tried to locate Mary and the women.

It was several weeks before the telegram office was up and running and Edward was able to contact Moberly. Moberly was an astute businessman and realized that a series of articles from an Englishman's perspective showing the human tragedy in New Orleans would sell papers. And so, Edward could keep up his search. But with hundreds of people drowned or missing throughout the city, Edward was just one more person who had lost someone. For weeks after the storm, survivors were pulling the rotting corpses of their family members out of the marsh and beach surf. Without food or water, exhausted and emotionally drained, they had no option but to dig mass graves and even build funeral pyres out of lumber washing ashore, such was the devastation.

Edward had gone over the midwife's letter time and time again, hoping to find some clue that might help him in his search. She had mentioned that one of the men holding the women and Mary captive had adopted the baby boy and christened him Adam Blackburn. Edward had hoped the letter she had promised to send would arrive in London and be forwarded to him out in New Orleans, but in the months that followed, nothing arrived. The postal system in Louisiana had been catastrophically disrupted by the storm, and thousands of postal deliveries had been lost when the city's post office was destroyed.

Edward found no trace of anybody called Blackburn, but again, records and details had been destroyed by fire and the terrible floods. As the years rolled by, though he never stopped looking, a part of him gradually let Mary and his daughter go. He decided that if anybody he cared for was still alive, then chance would decree whether or not they found him, or he found them. And so it was.

He lived his life as best he could, working as a journalist for *The Times* and local papers until in 1915, a massive hurricane once again swept across the Gulf of Mexico and tore into the city of New Orleans. Colossal winds ripped the roofs off many of the buildings in the city and caused the St. Louis Cathedral clock to stop at 5:50 p.m., the height of the storm.

Edward was in the *Times-Picayune* building when the storm hit and witnessed its effects firsthand. Windows shattered, the walls cracked and shuddered, and the wind shrieked like a banshee outside the building for hours before finally abating. The printworks were badly damaged, and the paper's production was halted. When it was finally up and running again, Edward helped the editorial staff to catch up on the many reports coming in from the other cities and surrounding areas. As he hurried down to the print room, his eye was caught by two stories. One bore the headline BLACKBURN OIL AND GAS FIELD DESTROYED BY STORM. HUNDREDS DEAD AND MISSING! He quickly read the details.

Adam Blackburn, the owner of the oil field, was missing, along with hundreds of investors, oil workers, and their families. They'd been in the middle of a celebration when the storm hit. Edward looked at the story and was stunned. His son Adam was alive, or had been. But now he was missing, or worse.

The second story concerned a young boy called Randal Faucheux living out at Laplace, near Maurepas Island. He claimed to have seen a fire in the same area as the oil field out at Spirit's Swamp, before the storm hit, and talked about seeing fireworks and hearing explosions. Reading through the article, Edward saw that the prevailing opinion was that this was probably just an outbreak of ignited marsh gas—known locally as will-o'-the-wisp—or the flames from the oil field flare stack. But as he skimmed through the stories, his journalist's intuition began to twitch. Something else was going on here.

He made his way down to the station and was soon on his way from New Orleans to the Maurepas Island station. If he was to get to the oil field before dark, he would have to hurry.

Edward stood among the desolation of the oil field out at Spirit's Swamp. Tendrils of smoke writhed across the ground, swirling past his feet as he moved cautiously toward the mangled remains of an oil derrick that lay on its side in front of him. He'd gotten a ride out from the station to the site from a farmer on a horse-drawn cart. The farmer had promised to pick him up if he was still there when he went past on his return trip. Edward had thanked him and walked the last few hundred yards to the oil field. As he looked around, he saw a broken sign lying on the ground. He bent to pick it up and turned it over. It read Blackburn Oil and Gas. He dropped it back down and watched in horror as the sign slowly sank from view; the ground was scattered with patches of quicksand.

He heard a cough. Somebody else was out there. The smoke cleared, and no more than a hundred feet in front of him stood an African American woman. She wore a beaded necklace and colorful clothes and carried a rough hemp basket. As she turned to look at him, he was transfixed by her eyes. They gleamed with a yellow fire like those of some exquisite jungle cat. And then the smoke shifted in the wind and she was gone. It was so quick Edward wondered if he'd imagined it.

He moved carefully across the devastated field, avoiding the numerous patches of oily quicksand that were spread around the site. Jagged rocks had been thrust up into the air and were still warm to the touch. The ground was riven with deep fissures, as if there had been an earthquake. The acrid smell of gas filled the air, and he could see fires smoldering in the earth's cracks. He picked his way around pools of oil and the remnants of once colorful bunting, now burnt and stained with oil.

It was if the war that raged in Europe had arrived in the swamp for one night, and then moved on. He saw a child's teddy bear lying in the dirt, and the twisted remains of a pram. Since arriving in New Orleans he'd become used to the practices of voodoo, and the folk spirituality of hoodoo, and the mythological differences between the American and British cultures. And the more he learned, the more he was starting to believe that there were certain areas inhabited by negative spirits. He was beginning to wonder if Spirit's Swamp might be one such place. Two ferocious storms had swept across Louisiana during his stay, and it felt as if the area was destined to have a history that kept repeating itself.

Since that first fateful storm back in 1893, his life had been full of missing people and dead ends. But now he had enough information to bring down the government and maybe even the monarchy, not to mention a national newspaper and the police force. But what good would it do for him to publish the truth if it resulted in the deaths of those he loved? Now, because of another storm, hundreds of people were dead or missing, including his son, and still his mind was seeing conspiracies.

In the rough proofs of the oil field story, he'd read that a prominent local photojournalist, Louie de Chiel, had been covering the event, and Edward wondered if he had left ahead of the storm. Louie had told a few friends in the newsroom that he planned on arriving in his new Pierce-Arrow car. The manufacturers had sold it to him at a steep discount provided he use it to get them some good publicity. They wanted shots of the car with Adam Blackburn standing next to it. Edward guessed there was some tie-in there with the fact that a person didn't need to own an oil company to afford to run it.

The wind had picked up by then, and the smoke was thinning as Edward approached the twisted metal remains of several more oil derricks. They had been toppled to the ground and lay like jousting knights unhorsed. Edward saw an old oil drum, half-buried. To one side of it something in the dirt reflected the light. Edward looked closer. It was a camera flash unit. He looked at the lid of the oil drum. It was skewed, like it had been put on in a hurry. Edward prized it off and looked inside. There was something lying at the bottom. He reached down as far as he could, touched cold metal. His fingers closed around a square object, a Graflex 3A press camera, the favorite choice of photojournalists everywhere. Edward looked at it and saw some initials engraved on the body. *LDC.* Louie de Chiel. Like a lady and her handbag, a photographer and his camera were never separated. There could only be one explanation as far as Edward was concerned. De Chiel knew he was going to die, and wanted his photographs to survive.

Edward heard a mechanical clattering sound, like the rattle of an industrial sewing machine, punctuated by the staccato crack of a backfire. The sound could only be one thing: a Ford Model T. He looked in the direction of the approaching sound. The vehicle was heading toward him. Its lights glimmered weakly through the drifting smoke. As it got nearer, he saw the word SHERIFF painted down one side. Two men sat up front.

Edward had recently written a story about the mechanization of the New Orleans police force. He knew that they only had two police cars, ten motorcycles, and around thirty horse-drawn wagons. He'd been at the oil field for only two hours, and New Orleans was over an hour away, which meant if they were here on his behalf then someone had tipped them off almost as soon as he'd arrived. That being said, someone had also authorized the use of one of only two motor vehicles on the force to head straight out to the swamp. Generally a motor vehicle would only be used in situations of extreme danger, where a life depended on swift action and speed was essential.

The clattering grew louder. The Ford lurched out of the smoke and braked to a halt. Its lights dimmed as the engine shuddered to a stop. Edward stood with his back to the oil drum, his hands behind him. The two officers watched him through the windshield. They must have decided he was no immediate threat because they climbed out of the car, popped the clips on their pistol holsters, and stood there.

Edward's editor, a man of few words and many quotes, had once told him there was no such thing as a coincidence. To have one of the only two police motor vehicles in New Orleans turn up in the middle of nowhere at exactly the same time as him gave credence to that saying.

Edward nodded to the older of the two officers, a florid-faced individual with a ragged mustache and rolls of fat spilling over a too-tight belt, the tarnished buckle digging into his stomach.

"Good evening, Officer. You look a little lost. How can I help?" Edward said, trying for humor to test the waters. He watched both men for a reaction. It wasn't long in coming.

The florid-faced officer's hand strayed toward his holster, but his whip-thin partner laid a calming hand on the big man's arm.

"I'll take this, Clyde," he said, and moved a little nearer to Edward. He forced a smile. "We heard there was somebody out here and thought we'd take a look-see. Thought there might have been a survivor from the storm." He paused, cocked his head in a quizzical manner before continuing. "But I'm guessing you're not from round here."

"I imagine my accent gave me away?" Edward said.

Clyde leaned forward, his mouth a museum of stained and cracked teeth.

"You're British, right?"

Edward nodded. "I'm a journalist, doing a piece about the oil field."

Clyde's head drew back, like that of a tortoise retreating into its shell, and his eyes narrowed.

"Ain't no oil field to do a story on, so far as I can see."

Edward nodded. "Yes, looks like the storm did a pretty good job of cleaning up here after the main event."

The whip-thin officer flicked a look at Clyde. Whatever the look meant, they were both in agreement.

"Main event?" Clyde's partner rested his hand on the top of his holster.

"Yes. Whatever happened before the storm," Edward said.

Now they were both paying very close attention to what he was saying. The thin one nodded.

"You mean the celebrations?"

Edward shook his head. "No, I mean the explosions, the fire. Look at the state of this place. There are fires burning fifty feet below the surface. Something else happened out here. Something big. That's the story I'm writing." He pulled his hand from behind his back and held the Graflex camera up. "And I have the pictures to go with it."

As one, the officers pulled their pistols out and leveled them at him.

"Be best for you if you handed that over to us. For safe-keeping. We might be able to reduce the charge from a felony to plain old looting."

Edward smiled. "Looting? I think that's a little bit of an exaggeration, Officer," he said. "It's just investigative journalism. If you play your cards right, I might be able to work you into the story. You know the kind of thing: 'Local police officers solve the mystery of Blackburn Oil and Gas Field tragedy.'" He pointed the Graflex at them. "How about a smile for the camera?"

Whip-thin cocked his gun. "How about you give us the camera and we give you a lift back into town?"

Edward shrugged. "How very gentlemanly of you. Here, catch."

He hurled the camera into the air toward them. Like two of the world's worst catchers, they both dived for it. Edward whipped his other hand from behind him and triggered the flashgun in their faces. They reeled back, blinded, letting the camera hit the ground in front of them.

Edward snatched it up and darted away into the smoke and darkness. The officers staggered after him, firing blindly into the night. Moments later he heard them yelling. They'd blundered into quicksand.

Edward stood next to the Ford. He reached down and cranked the starter handle. It spluttered into life. Edward reached into his pocket and checked that the roll of film was still there before putting the Ford into gear and pulling away.

He headed back toward Maurepas and abandoned the vehicle in some dense scrubland before heading into the station. He took the train back to New Orleans and tried to catch up on some sleep as the carriage clattered through the dark, but he couldn't. A thought kept pushing its way to the front of his mind: What if someone had been shadowing him since he left the newspaper office? Someone with instructions to make sure he didn't uncover what really happened out at the oil field?

How long would it be before someone found the police vehicle and went looking for the missing officers? Maybe they would never be found. How far down does quicksand go? Whatever was going on, he had a problem. His guess was the officers had been there specifically to find out what he knew, and if they decided he knew too much, then that was something they could solve with a bullet. Now, someone out there knew that two police officers had gone out to the oil field to find a journalist. And not just any journalist, but one Edward Richard Travis, formerly of London, formerly of no interest to anybody whatsoever. Until now. Only Mary knew what he'd overheard at the *Pall Mall Gazette* building, and no one knew what he'd found at the oil field. But pretty soon someone would start to put things together, and if they found him—well then that would be that.

He was going to have to disappear.

FIFTY-SIX

RYKER'S FIELD, LOUISIANA – Present day

BLANCHE SAT IN her wheelchair on the back porch and watched the cars approach through the lens of her Leica. One of the first things Jesse had done when he started fixing things up was build a sweeping ramp up from the garden around to the end of the porch. Now she could choose to work in the garden or read outside without having to climb any steps. She'd had a headache when she woke up that morning, and had decided to forgo her afternoon trip to watch Jesse play pool at his club. Blanche could see anybody approaching for miles, and she knew whoever these visitors were wouldn't be arriving for at least a quarter of an hour. The last mile to the house was along a rough track, and city folk were always cautious with their low-slung vehicles and bumpers, frightened of bottoming out on the stone-filled ruts that always formed after a heavy rain.

The antebellum plantation house had been passed down through the generations. With its first-floor balcony supported by Roman-style colonnades, it had once been a grand sight, before Blanche's husband died and it fell into disrepair. Jesse did his best to keep things straight, but they had little money coming in and more going out each month.

In the past, when the place had been a working plantation, it had been a good idea to have a large field of view from the house.

There had been a growing number of slave uprisings, and a prudent owner would be wise to see one coming and take steps to protect himself. But the men headed her way now weren't slaves.

It had been over seventy years since she'd been given the information she felt sure they were coming for. In a moment of weakness, with her mind starting to become more confused, she had gone to someone for advice. She was sure the men in the cars were the result of that visit, and she cursed her stupidity. But she was sure they would never find the information they sought. After all, she'd had more than enough time to hide it over the years, back when her mind was still as sharp as a razor. No, the problem had been to make sure that it reached the right people. When the deputy and the nice English detective had arrived and talked to her about the old days and her father, she'd immediately felt that it was the right time to guide them to the secret she had kept for so long.

They were both bright men, well educated and already highly focused on the trail of a mystery that stretched across two countries and a hundred years of history. The mint julep had blown away the cobwebs, given her mind enough of a jolt to set up the chain of events necessary to point them in the right direction. The Englishman had given her the opening she needed. Butterflies. She just hoped they were as smart as she thought they were. She only had time to leave a couple of clues; they would have to piece the rest of it together themselves. Once they had worked it out, then the promise that she'd made to Edward all those years ago would be fulfilled.

She wheeled herself back into the house, and by the time she made it back out and into the garden again, she could hear the cars grinding up the overgrown track. Satisfied that everything was in place, she turned her wheelchair around and headed back toward the house. But something caught in one of the wheels, and before she knew it, the chair was on its side and she on the ground. She struggled to get up and felt something tear inside her chest. A sharp, numbing pain spread down one side of her body. She managed a brief thought before the darkness swept over her: no one would be able to hurt her anymore. By the time the cars came to a halt on the track by the house, she was dead.

Roxie parked outside the new digital media center, the flagship technical resource of Louisiana State University. She had come to see Drew Evans, a professor of electronic systems technology she'd met while she was doing her anthropology undergrad. He was sitting on the steps in the sunshine as she walked toward the building and waved a hand in greeting. He finished the can of juice he was drinking and threw it with unnerving accuracy into the trash can that sat over twenty feet away.

"He shoots, he scores," he said, before grabbing her in a bear hug and whirling her around. He put her down and they both laughed.

"That's student harassment, you know," she said.

He shrugged. "What are you gonna do? You look great."

They headed up the steps and into a large room packed with test equipment, screens, and computers. A few students were tinkering with a drone in the corner.

Roxie looked around. "This is amazing. How long has it been up and running?"

"About a month," Drew said. "There was a helluva lot of cables and conduit to go in considering we live in the wireless age."

Drew headed for a piece of equipment that resembled a small black box with a domed receptor on one end. Roxie joined him. Drew tapped a computer tablet, and the screen filled with icons and readouts.

"It's a terahertz camera. The guys up at MIT have been playing around with the algorithms that make sense of the images it can produce."

Roxie looked at the display, fascinated. "And it really can read a book through its cover?"

"Yup," Drew said and tapped some symbols. Gears whirred, and the camera hummed down toward an ancient manuscript sitting on a base plate below it, its cover formed from a blackened piece of animal hide.

"This manuscript is over a thousand years old," Drew said. "It was found in a genizah, in a cave in the Bamyan Valley, Afghanistan."

"What's a genizah?" Roxie asked.

Drew tapped some more icons on the tablet, concentrating as his fingers swiped, pinched, and tapped the screen.

"A storage area in a Jewish synagogue or cemetery for old Hebrew-language books and papers on religious topics until they can be given a proper burial."

"Wow, I didn't know books got a proper burial," Roxie said.

"Yeah, it's one of their customs. We've been using the manuscript as an experiment to fine-tune the algorithm that translates the signals from the camera. It analyzes materials organized in thin layers."

"Like a book," Roxie said.

"Yes. It can distinguish between ink and paper because they bend light to a different degree, which helps the system tell them apart," he explained. "The air pockets differentiate the pages."

"Like a visual echo?" Roxie said.

"You got it. Femto-photography captures images at a trillion frames a second. Most of the radiation is either absorbed or reflected by the book, and some of it bounces between the pages."

"So, the algorithms filter out errors?" Roxie said, starting to grasp the complexity of the system.

"Yes," Drew said. "Some planet brains up at MIT and Georgia Tech came up with the algorithms needed to detect false signals and interpret distorted or incomplete images." He paused and adjusted something on the tablet. "There—we've got something."

Roxie stared at the screen as a mosaic of letters swam across it. Shadowy black squiggles floating in an electronic sea of distortion.

"Is that it?" Roxie looked disappointed.

"Hold on. Let the algorithms do their stuff."

Drew tapped some icons, and the sea of words gradually untangled themselves from the background. Now, they were distinguishable letters lying on their sides like collapsed bricks.

"Wow, that is amazing. What am I looking at here?" Roxie said, squinting at the screen.

"Ancient Aramaic, a thousand years old," Drew replied.

"And this is without even opening the book."

"Yes, and look."

Drew adjusted a control on the tablet. Up on the screen, pages of the book shifted backward like a digital accordion as the computer process probed deeper into the manuscript.

Roxie's face lit up with excitement. "So the system is like a sophisticated visual sonar, only it detects individual letters, not submarines," she said.

Drew nodded. "That's pretty much it. Only difference is the speed of the reflections. With a standard sonar system, the acoustic reflections are measured in seconds. The speed of terahertz radiation is millions of times faster. It's between infrared radiation and microwave in the electromagnetic spectrum. That's why it can pass through clothing, paper, cardboard, wood, masonry, plastic, and ceramics. It's the same technology they use at airport security." Drew paused. "So, are you going to let me in on the big secret, or do I have to buy you dinner?" he asked with a smile.

Roxie smiled back. "It'll be me buying the dinner if you lend me this equipment. As to the secret, how would you like to solve one of the greatest conspiracies of all time?"

"Okay, now you've got me hooked. Let's do dinner and then I'll try and wrangle a way of lending you the kit for a few days without anybody noticing."

Duke and Chandler stood watching with the students as Roxie and Phaedon set up the equipment. Roxie adjusted the position of the diary on the motorized platform beneath the terahertz camera.

"This is pretty damn impressive, Roxie," Duke said.

"Yes, but we've only got it for a few days."

Duke laughed. "No, I was meaning the way you're able to make a man hand over thousands of dollars' worth of kit for the price of a meal."

A ripple of laughter came from the students.

Roxie laughed and said, "Hey, Drew and I go way back. And I have a receipt for that meal for you, by the way."

"Ouch!" Duke said. "Just kidding."

Phaedon continued tinkering with cables and launching software on the computer.

Roxie turned to him. "I'd like to say it sounded simple when Drew explained it to me, but to be honest, I got him to make up an idiot sheet."

Phaedon smiled. "You had me at time-gated spectral kurtosis."

"Really?" Roxie smiled. "So no love for my quantum cascade laser and microbolometric array?" she shot back.

Phaedon shrugged. "Maybe a little."

Duke smiled. "In English, guys."

"Okay," Roxie said. "Once we've uploaded the images into the university cloud, we'll be able to run the algorithms and process them."

"How long do you think the system will take to scan the diary?" Duke asked.

Phaedon gathered his thoughts. "As you know, the system works like a high-speed sonar, only it uses pulses of terabyte radiation instead of sound. The pages and the letters can be imaged by recording the pulses reflected back using something called time-of-flight measurements."

Phaedon looked around, checking to see if everyone was following. Duke nodded for him to continue.

"Collecting the data is the fast part of the process. After that, the algorithms go to work sorting out the false reflections and filtering out distorted or incomplete images. Trillions of computations are carried out one letter at a time."

Chandler looked worried. "How long are we talking? Days, weeks, months?"

Phaedon smiled. "The university has a supercomputer called Hypergator that runs at five hundred teraflops. Once the data's in the cloud, I can link it up to other university computers and run them in parallel. That way we can use their processing downtime. It'll triple our computing speed. We could be looking at as little as twenty-four hours."

Chandler's face lit up. "That's fantastic. I thought it was going to take forever."

Phaedon patted him on the shoulder. "That's because you still live in the Bakelite era, dude."

FIFTY-SEVEN

THE SOMME, FRANCE – 1915

AFTER THE EVENTS out at the oil field, Edward contacted one of the less savory characters he had come across in New Orleans while working on the local paper. Within a few days he had secured fresh papers and a new identity as Edward Stocker, and he'd made the decision to join the war effort back in England. Whoever had him followed out in Spirit's Swamp would never be able to track him down in the chaos of war.

He'd wound up in France as one of only five journalists covering the advance at the battle of the Somme and producing copy and pictures to boost morale back home. The advance began just before 7:30 a.m., July 1, 1916, when a huge mine containing 66,000 pounds of ammonal exploded fifty-five feet beneath Swabian Height, a German field fortification south of the village of Boisselle. One of the other journalists later told Edward it was the loudest man-made sound in history and could be heard as far away as London. Edward could believe it. His ears had still been ringing when the artillery barrage started up moments later.

General Haig had believed that the huge mines beneath the German positions, combined with the creeping barrage, meant that the British troops would meet little resistance from any surviving

German soldiers and the battle would soon be won. He was utterly wrong. The advance was a catastrophic failure.

As the reports came back to the journalists on the front line, it became obvious that the Germans had hunkered down in deep bunkers and well-constructed trenches. Eighteen British divisions had walked into a hail of lead, massacred by entrenched German machine-gun posts and rifle fire. Then their own Z Company's secret weapon, the fearsome flame thrower, was employed to terrifying effect as British troops went over the top on that fateful day. For years after the war, Edward would still have nightmares from what he witnessed that morning—German soldiers staggering out of their trenches like human torches, their flesh burning and the sound of their screams drifting across the battlefield. Edward wrote what he saw, which was carnage, and filed his report along with some gut-wrenching pictures.

He later discovered that truth was the first casualty of war when it became obvious that high command didn't want unbiased or truthful coverage, but only what suited their propaganda and kept morale up back home.

He stumbled back to the trench and met up with two of the other journalists, Philip Gibbs and Basil Clarke. Edward had seen enough. It was time to take a stand. He took a sip of warm, weak coffee from a battered tin cup and started into his piece.

"Do you really want to look back in a month, or a year, or five years, knowing that a million people died while back home everybody thought we were winning the war?"

Basil put his mug down. "What do you think we should do? Print our own newspaper?"

Edward shrugged. "If that's what it takes. Even if we get only one story printed and enough people see it and think twice about signing up, we could save thousands of lives. Wouldn't that be worth it?"

Gibbs gave a wry smile. "Outlaw journalists?"

"Like the Three Musketeers," Edward volunteered.

Gibbs mulled this over before replying.

"I'm good friends with Howell Gwynne, the editor of *The Morning Post.* If I could convince him to post the reports under a pseudonym—"

"Like Edward suggested, the Three Musketeers," Basil said.

They looked at each other, nodded, and shook hands. And that was the start of their life away from the scrutiny of the war cabinet, the army censors, and their masters. For months they traveled behind enemy lines, avoiding capture by the French, the Germans, and their own side to report the real truth of the war. *The Morning Post* risked its reputation and readership by publishing their heartbreaking stories to public and government condemnation. But soon the reality of the letters from the front and the firsthand accounts from the casualties returning home made it obvious where the truth lay.

Gradually an uneasy truce between the government and the tabloids was established and more of what was actually happening made it to the front page. By the end of the Somme campaign, over a million men had died and Edward and his fellow journalists had been shocked to the core by the sights they had witnessed. Edward was suffering from what the doctors called shellshock. Countless hours crouched beneath a constant barrage of artillery shells screaming overhead or exploding nearby had reduced them all to nervous wrecks. It would be many years before the effects would subside and they could return to anything approaching a normal state of mind.

The ground shook as the artillery continued its relentless bombardment. Deep behind the enemy lines, Edward pressed his face into the dank mud at the bottom of the shell hole he was crouched in. He had thrown himself into it as the first salvo of massive shells blistered the air above his head.

Something twitched in his peripheral vision. He turned his head to see what it was: a hand, slowly unfurling like some grotesque gray plant. The arm ended in a bloody fragment of bone and tissue just behind the elbow.

He heard a low moan behind him. He stared into the mist and smoke that cloaked the wide depression with its drifting tendrils of gray smoke. He saw a German soldier, or what remained of him. The man was just a legless torso with one arm stretched out, dragging himself toward the remains of his other shattered limb, his eyes wide with shock and pain. Edward's eyes met his, and they shared a look that said more about the pointlessness of war than any of the words he'd written. Edward wondered what the soldier thought he could achieve with the blood pooling beneath him and his life ebbing away. But a human being's innate determination to survive overrides all sense and pain. Edward watched as the man grabbed the bloody remnant of his other arm and slumped down into the dirt. His last mission over, the light faded from his eyes. And then the earth started to shake once more.

FIFTY-EIGHT

NEW YORK CITY, NEW YORK – 1936

EDWARD SNAPPED AWAKE. The bed was still shaking, but he was no longer under artillery fire in the Somme. He sat up and took a deep breath. It was 1936, and he was in the small brownstone building on East 22nd Street where he rented a tiny one-room tenement apartment. Too cold in winter and too hot in summer, it had been all he could afford when he'd made the voyage over from England after the end of the First World War. The streetcars rumbling past outside had woken him. Though it had been twenty years since the nightmare of the Somme, the shadow of those days still haunted his dreams.

He climbed out of bed and went over to the tiny bathroom. He reached into the cubicle and ran the shower and waited until the ancient heating system brought the water up to a decent temperature. The warm water pounded his back, massaging the aches and pains away from his shoulders and neck as it ran across the jagged network of scars that patterned his legs, a reminder of the trench mortar that exploded next to a farmhouse he was hiding in outside the village of Bazentin. He padded out into the bedroom and dried himself off before dropping the towel onto the large iron radiator that rattled and wheezed in the corner of the room. He waited for his morning cough to subside before dressing and putting the coffee percolator onto the cooker ring. He dried his hair and got dressed quickly. It didn't do to hang around too long without anything on unless it was the height of summer. He slipped his shoes on and went over to the bubbling percolator, lifted the pot off the stove, and poured himself a mug of steaming coffee. He was just finishing the last dregs from the mug when he heard the newsie calling out from the street below.

He went down one flight of stairs and out onto the street. The newsie handed him a copy of the *New York Times* from the pile in his satchel. Edward handed him three cents.

"Thanks, Jimmy."

The boy saluted him. "See you tomorrow, Mr. Stocker."

The boy had learned that Edward had been in the war and since then had always given him a mock salute. Edward didn't want to disappoint him by telling him he was just a journalist and not a real soldier—though on reflection, part of winning the war was getting the truth out.

Edward unfolded the paper as he went up the stairs and back into his room. Then he stopped, stared at the front page and felt the blood drain from his face. There was a photograph of Adam Blackburn shaking hands with another man.

The headline read BLACKBURN OIL AND GAS SEALS DEAL WITH PHOENIX OIL. There was a second picture of Huntington Beach in California. Hundreds of oil derricks filled the shoreline along the beach, stretching as far as the eye could see, devastating the natural beauty of the beach. Two men stood on the sand, incongruous in suits and hats with their trousers rolled up and their shoes on the ground next to them. Blackburn was using the other man's back to rest the paper of a contract on as he signed. Edward read the article.

Blackburn claimed to have been delayed getting to the oil field on the night of the storm in 1915, and was later taken ill with a rare blood disease. He had been flown to a hospital in Brussels where a specialist had managed to save his life, control the infection, and, after a long period of isolation and pioneering blood transfusions, succeed in curing him. He'd been hospitalized for over twenty years.

The agreement was for Phoenix Oil to buy the land in Spirit's Swamp from Blackburn under the condition that the swamp would be decontaminated before any drilling could take place. Edward reached the end of the article and stared at the headlines in front of him. He should have been happy that his own flesh and blood had survived such a catastrophic event, and that he appeared to be a morally sound environmental pioneer. Edward peered at the photograph on the front page. Adam Blackburn looked exactly like he had all those years ago. And that was the problem. Whoever this man was, he couldn't be Edward's son.

He poured another coffee and flicked through the paper as he drank it. His eye was caught by an article in the arts section. There was an exhibition being held by a new group of artists called the Photo League. Composed of stills photographers, the collective included many names that Edward recognized from his years in journalism, but one name stood out. Blanche de Chiel.

The name was too unusual to be a coincidence. Whoever it was had to be related to Louie de Chiel, the photojournalist who had photographed what happened that horrific night in 1915 out at Blackburn's oil field.

The exhibition was being held in the penthouse artist's studios on the top floor of the Flatiron Building, right across the street from the brownstone where Edward had his apartment. He walked across the room and pulled out a small battered suitcase from under his bed, flicked the catches open, and took out a dusty Graflex 3A camera. He slipped it into a small black duffel bag and headed out.

The Flatiron Building was a twenty-two-story skyscraper and one of the tallest buildings in the city. Its iconic design, reminiscent of a classical Greek column, had divided public opinion since its completion back in 1902. The penthouse at the top of the building was a late addition and was built to house rental studios for artists. Many of the artists, who included Louis Fancher, contributed work to the pulp magazines that occupied the offices below. The building cast a long shadow across the street in the evening sun as Edward made his way round to the front entrance.

The Flatiron formed a triangular footprint edged by Fifth Avenue, Broadway, and East 22nd Street, and anchored downtown Madison Square and the uptown end of the Ladies' Mile. As Edward walked along the crowded streets in the sunshine, he felt a million miles away from the war in Europe that he'd left behind. Once back in England, he'd slowly recovered from his experiences and the effects of shellshock before returning to America and to journalism. The public had been clamoring for news after the war, and the newspapers were rushing to fill the need. He'd begun to pick up the pieces of his life and restart his search for Mary and his children. But he wasn't a young man anymore, and nowadays his health was failing. He had to take steps to protect what he knew and find a way to bring justice to the guilty. When he'd seen the article in the arts section of the paper, the germ of an idea had taken root. A way to finally reveal where the bodies were buried.

FIFTY-NINE

BATON ROUGE, LOUISIANA – Present day

DOWN IN THE city morgue, Jonas Kern, a spry salt-and-pepper-haired man with a long, mournful face, studied a headless male torso that lay on the steel table in front of him. At the other end of the room, disentangled from each other, their mummified skin tight on their faces, the five female corpses from the swamp lay on separate tables. Duke and Chandler stood next to Jonas as he inspected some puncture marks on the inside of the male torso's thigh.

"How's it going?" Duke asked.

Jonas grunted. "Pretty much nowhere."

Duke turned to Chandler. "Jonas has been getting headless torsos turning up in the swamp over the years—what the gators leave of them, anyway."

Jonas straightened up from the torso. "The only common distinguishing feature are these." He indicated the puncture wounds on the inside of the leg stumps with a scalpel.

Chandler leaned forward to get a closer look. "What are they?"

Jonas shrugged. "They all lead into the common iliac arteries. On each body, they're all partially healed, so whatever caused them remained in place until death."

"That's weird," Duke said.

Jonas smiled. "No more weird than a headless torso, I guess. Anyway, you're not interested in my torso." He moved over to the five corpses from the swamp.

Duke followed him. "Nothing personal—you're just not my type."

"I'm crushed. Anyway, I believe you think you know the identity of these fine specimens?"

Duke nodded. "The computer has an opinion."

Jonas looked at the corpses, polished his glasses. "Ah, yes. It usually does," he said. "Pretty soon it'll be like luggage on a carousel: bodies in one end, ID and cause of death out the other."

Chandler shook his head. "We're a long way from that in this case."

Jonas looked closely at one of the bodies. His Southern accent became more pronounced as he concentrated.

"I thank you for your perspicacity. So, despite their attractive appearance, these ladies are over a hundred years old."

Duke nodded. "The latest timeline we can substantiate from articles found with the bodies is 1893."

Jonas shot him a quick look. "That would fit with my initial findings. The women were in their forties when they died, apart from this young lady." He pointed to one of the corpses. "She was the youngest, approximately midtwenties, and examination of the pelvic area shows she had given birth." He walked around the steel table. "Preliminary findings indicate that they all drowned. If they were out on the night of the hurricane, it would have been preceded by a storm surge of colossal force. They wouldn't have known what hit them."

He moved over to a small kidney dish and picked out a couple of rings. Both were of a distinctive design in silver: a pair of twisted snakes around a dagger. "They were all wearing these." He handed them over to Chandler.

"It's the sign of healing, isn't it?"

Jonas nodded. "It's called the caduceus. The symbol was originally used by the Greeks to signify commerce and was associated with the god Hermes. It's also very similar to DNA's double helix.

It's considered a symbol of rebirth because of the way a snake sheds its skin." He looked to Chandler. "You say they were from London, possibly prostitutes?"

"Yes."

Jonas wandered over to a washbasin and ran some water. He soaped up, rinsed, and dried his hands on some paper towels, still deep in thought.

"Around the time these women were alive, it was estimated that as many as sixty thousand prostitutes were operating in the city of London, some as young as thirteen. These women here all show signs of scarring consistent with sex work."

He cocked his head at them. Chandler thought it made him look like an inquisitive cockerel.

"An acquaintance of mine says you have some kind of a conspiracy theory?"

Duke turned to Chandler and shrugged. "Phaedon's his nephew."

"Ah," Chandler said.

Jonas grinned. "Big swamp, small town."

Chandler smiled and answered his question. "If these victims are who we think they are, then that would mean—"

Jonas interrupted, "Rewriting history?"

"Yes," Chandler said. "And as a result, the chronology of one of the most infamous serial killers in recent history."

Jonas moved around the corpses.

"It's what we do: establish the victim's true history, shine a light into the dark and expose the person or event that cut short the writing of their particular story."

Chandler looked at the ring and then back at Jonas. "Do you have an opinion?" he asked.

Jonas snorted. "Opinions are like assholes—everybody has one."

Duke smiled. "And yours is?"

Jonas took his glasses off, polished them again. Chandler suspected it was going to be a long theory, and that it was directly related to how long the polishing took. At last, the coroner slipped his glasses back on.

"There was always something wrong with the Ripper case. Too many suspects, too few facts—it was almost as if the police and the press were working together to produce some sort of social effect rather than trying to solve the case."

Chandler studied the youngest corpse before speaking.

"What if Jack the Ripper was a creation rather than a reality?"

Jonas cocked his head again, his scalpel-sharp mind running through a myriad of possibilities.

"It would take organization, power, and money. Some female corpses, a makeover to make them resemble the supposed victims. A slice-and-dice number on the bodies to sensationalize the murders by somebody who enjoyed their work, someone with no choice but to follow orders," Jonas said.

"Our old friend Francis J. Tumblety?" Chandler suggested. "He had the necessary skills."

Jonas paused. "But he couldn't have acted alone. Placing the bodies, organizing the tabloid pictures, controlling who found them and where. There's no limit to what he could have orchestrated if the government was behind him." Duke and Chandler listened as Jonas stalked around the mortuary spinning his tale, eyes shining as he warmed to the task.

"It would be like a nineteenth-century *Mission Impossible*."

Chandler rubbed his eyes, tried to imagine the scope of the conspiracy. "Who would go to all that trouble? Making it look like a killer was murdering prostitutes in such a violent manner, and then, after faking their deaths, spiriting them out of the country?"

Duke grunted. "Same as always: somebody with something to hide."

Chandler stared at the youngest corpse. "Somebody rich and powerful?"

Jonas looked at him. "It doesn't have to be a person," he said.

"You really think it was the government?" Chandler asked.

Jonas smacked his hands together, the sound reverberating around the tiled walls of the room.

"Why stop there? Why don't we throw the monarchy into the mix? Then you would have the mother of all conspiracy theories. And what's the best way to hide a conspiracy?"

Duke smiled. "Same way you hide a tree—in a forest."

Chandler looked around the white-tiled walls of the morgue, shook his head to clear it.

"So they created their own conspiracy theory to hide the real one? But what was the real one?"

"That's what we're all here to find out," said Duke. "We need to identify these women for certain, and then trace their lives prior to them ending up in the swamp."

Jonas looked at the youngest corpse.

"I'm hoping to get some mitochondrial DNA from the dental pulp of this young lady."

"How will that help us?" Chandler asked. "She's not likely to be in any database."

Jonas nodded. "No, but we're looking for familial DNA. If she has any relatives still alive that are in the database, we might be able trace their family tree back far enough to get a positive identification. I'll do the extraction and Roxie can do the sequencing up at the university lab. She's the expert at that."

The sound of a cell phone ringing interrupted them. Jonas fished his cell out and answered it. He listened for a second, his face grim.

"Where? Okay, we'll be there." He looked over at them. "They've found another body in Spirit's Swamp."

Chandler looked out across the scene of controlled chaos at Spirit's Swamp. Crime scene investigators swarmed around the site, and a dive team was busy in the water. A body lay on a tarpaulin by the side of the dive team's pickup truck. Jonas was crouched down next to it. Chandler watched the dive team as they worked. He didn't envy them their task. Working in the oily water, thick with sinewy roots just waiting to snag the unwary, was the stuff of nightmares. One of the dive team had told him they had to work by feel most of the time.

Chandler covered his nose as marsh gas bubbled up from below the water. He was clearing his throat when Duke appeared next to him.

"You need to come and see this."

He followed Duke over to where Jonas was working on the body. Chandler looked at the well-preserved corpse spread out on the tarpaulin in front of them. The man had a large mustache, and his eyes stared sightlessly upward. One of them was strange, off-center.

Jonas pointed to a silver twisted-serpent ring on the corpse's finger. "Same ring as the women from the carriage." He produced an evidence bag. Inside was a rusty revolver. "Whatever happened, it was fast. The pistol was cocked but hadn't been fired."

Jonas bent over the corpse, pointing out features.

"Ligature marks around the neck—healed scars—from sudden pressure. Looks like a hanging."

Chandler shot him a confused look. "A hanging?"

Jonas nodded. He held up a loop of leather, indicated the corroded buckles used to fasten it.

"This was around his neck. Looks like some sort of support."

Duke studied the corpse. "You're saying he died from a hanging?"

Jonas stood up. "No. I'd say he died from an immediate sustained laryngeal spasm caused by an inrush of water into the nasopharynx or larynx."

Jonas used his fingers to prize open the man's throat and shone a torch inside.

"There's evidence of a thick mucus plug in the back of the throat that would be consistent with that analysis. I'd say he was hit by a massive body of water."

Chandler looked at him. "Like a tidal surge."

Jonas nodded. "Exactly. I'm guessing he was caught in the same storm as the women. He's wearing the same kind of ring, and he was found in the same location. I'll do a full autopsy later, but that's my opinion for now."

Chandler pulled his computer tablet out of his pocket and flicked through some pictures of Ripper suspects. Two of them flashed up side by side: Dr. Francis J. Tumblety and Dr. Thomas Neill Cream.

He angled the screen to Jonas. "Look at his eyes." Jonas studied Cream's eyes, noting the one that was turned inward.

Chandler tapped the tablet screen. "Cream had exotropia. He would have made an ideal buddy for Tumblety. The only thing wrong with that theory is that he was hanged in 1892 for poisoning a prostitute called Matilda Clover—"

A gurgling noise cut him short as bubbles exploded to the surface of the swamp. Something large and black foamed out of the muddy depths. In a moment of eerie silence, a horse's head rose into the air, both grotesque and comical. There was laughter from the group of watching crime scene investigators. One of the dive team held the head in front of his masked face. He waded to the shore and dumped it on the ground.

Pulling his mouthpiece off, he did a bad Marlon Brando impression: "Youse come to my swamp, insult my family . . ."

Duke looked over, cracked a smile at the gallows humor.

"Okay, Wade, this is a crime scene, not a circus."

One of the other divers high-fived Wade as they both headed back into the water. Moments later, another diver surfaced from out of the swamp and gave a thumbs-up to the officer manning the winch. The motor whined as the slack was taken up. Two wooden carriage shafts emerged from the dark waters, and the winch dragged them slowly onto the bank.

Jonas handed Chandler a corroded hunter-case pocket watch in a transparent evidence bag. "One of the divers found this in the remains of a carpetbag: again, another set of initials."

Chandler looked at the back of the watch and its engraved letters. "'E. R. T.,'" he read aloud.

"Mean something?" Duke asked.

Chandler touched the watch through the plastic, hardly daring to believe his eyes. Duke clapped a hand on his shoulder, snapping him back into reality. "Hey, we got enough mysteries without you holding back on us. Spill it."

Chandler held up the watch.

"I think this belonged to my great-great-grandfather, Edward Richard Travis."

SIXTY

NEW YORK CITY, NEW YORK – 1936

EDWARD PULLED OUT his pocket watch and looked at the time. The birdcage frame of the elevator bounced and lumbered its way upward toward the penthouse floor. He checked the time a lot. It reminded him that his original pocket watch was out in the world somewhere with Mary. It made him feel good to imagine her checking the time and thinking of him. The other passengers looked nervously at the floor indicator as the hand shakily informed them of the lift's progress. The hydraulic mechanism was notoriously unreliable. One office worker had joked that his commute was thirty minutes even though he lived opposite the building. To everyone's relief, they reached the top floor. The elevator shuddered to a halt and the doors rumbled open.

Edward walked down a corridor and into the spacious exhibition. Music was playing and a table was stacked with cold food and drink. There was a list on one wall of the artists taking part in the exhibition, accompanied by a picture and a small bio. He read Blanche de Chiel's name. Born in Louisiana, she was twenty-one years old and a photojournalist who specialized in taking pictures of the poor and homeless. She had also set up a charity to help feed the homeless in New York, and cited her photographer father Louie de Chiel as her inspiration. Edward's hunch was right.

He scanned the crowd of people clustered around the food table and the photographic displays that adorned the walls. Weegee was exhibiting, and the walls were hung with stark black-and-white photos of crime scenes captured in unflinching detail. There were pictures of shooting victims lying in pools of blood on the pavement, car crashes, and poverty-stricken families sleeping ten to a room. Edward turned suddenly and bumped into somebody. He found himself face-to-face with a striking blonde girl, made even more memorable by the searing blue of her eyes.

"Easy, stranger!" she said.

Edward smiled at her. "Sorry, I was miles away."

The girl nodded. "His stuff's pretty brutal, isn't it?"

"I guess that's what makes him Weegee." Edward thrust out a hand. "Edward Stoker," he said.

The young woman transferred the Leica she held to her left hand and shook his hand with her right.

"Blanche de Chiel. My stuff's a little less bloody."

She waved her hand at the wall of photos behind her. They were beautifully framed pictures of New York's homeless and destitute. Families huddled in doorways. A small boy curled up with a mangy dog on the sidewalk. Farther down, there were pictures of the 1935 Harlem riots. Smashed shopfront windows, looters running across the streets carrying stolen goods.

"You took these?" Edward said.

Blanche nodded. "Somebody has to cover reality to compensate for all the glamour stuff that's clogging up the newsstands."

Edward shook his head. "And you still found time to start a charity for the homeless."

Blanche shrugged. "My father left me some money. I've seen enough misery on the streets since I've lived here to last me a lifetime. If I can do something to help them, why not?"

Edward looked at her. If she was as tough as she appeared, then he could trust her to handle anything he threw at her.

"Your father was a photographer," Edward said.

"Yes. He died before I was born." She tapped a picture of a man sitting in the driver's seat of a Pierce-Arrow car. The passenger was a heavily pregnant woman. She was smiling.

"That's him; and that's Mom when she was carrying me. I bought a car just like it to deliver food to the soup kitchens. I'd like to think my father would have taken me on picnics if he had lived."

"I'm sure he would have," Edward said. He looked around at the room teeming with people, dropped his voice.

"Can we go somewhere a little more private?"

"Why?"

She looked at him suspiciously. *And why not?* he thought. After all, why would you go somewhere with an old man you'd just met for the first time?

He reached into his duffel bag and pulled out the dusty Graflex 3A.

"This belonged to your father," he said.

Blanche took the camera and held it in her hands tenderly. Her finger traced the engraved initials.

"I've seen pictures of him with this camera."

Edward reached back into the duffel and drew out a small package of postcard-sized photographic prints.

"And these are the pictures he took out at the Blackburn Oil and Gas field the night he died."

SIXTY-ONE

BATON ROUGE, LOUISIANA – Present day

BACK AT THE Airstream, Duke and Chandler fortified themselves with more coffee. Duke had set up some corkboards to one side of the living room area, on which were pinned an assortment of photos and printouts. A sort of small-scale incident room. Chandler was still trying to work out how the pocket watch had ended up in the carriage. He was logged into his Dropbox account and was sifting through the various scanned papers and photographs stored there. One was of a heavy sideboard with a set of drinks decanters on it. Alongside the tray sitting on top of the sideboard was a fob watch. Chandler zoomed in on it, the grainy photograph filling the screen.

"I'm sure it's the same one."

"Okay," Duke said. "Say it is your great-great-grandpa's watch. How come it wound up in the carriage?"

"Maybe he was interviewing one of the prostitutes and traded his watch for information?"

"Information?" Duke said. "Is that what they called it back then?"

Chandler smiled. "Touché! He was very young at the time."

Duke tapped each of the photos for emphasis as he talked. "We've got five women, prostitutes working in London supposedly murdered by Jack the Ripper in 1888. Only somehow they end up drowning in the middle of a Louisiana swamp five years later."

Duke moved over to a picture of Dr. Tumblety on the wall. "We find letters from Francis J. Tumblety, a prime Ripper suspect, on the same carriage as the dead women, and photographic evidence that he was in Saint Malo with them. Then there's our carriage driver, possibly Dr. Neill Cream, who by all accounts was hanged in 1892. And yet here he is in a Louisiana swamp, on the same carriage as the dead women, a year after his supposed death."

Chandler went over to his bag and pulled out a book. He flicked to a page, tapped a picture of Dr. Cream. "Say agents of the government did set up the execution of Dr. Cream. There are witnesses to this, so it has to be convincing. They pretend to hang him. Maybe they have some sort of concealed wire that runs through the rope to a harness?"

Duke nodded. "But something goes wrong."

Chandler closed the book. "They get him to cry out, 'I'm Jack the Ripper' as he falls to his death. The support wire snaps, and he nearly dies. He has to wear a support brace because of the injury to his neck muscles."

Duke looked at the pictures on the corkboard. "So they have him make a fake confession as he goes to his death, which allows them to bring an end to the murders and the investigation?"

Chandler nodded. "The police get their man and everybody's happy. They get more money and men, and London becomes safer," he went on. "And if we go along with Jonas's opinion, the police and the coroners fake the five women's deaths, using Doctors Cream and Tumblety, who have no other choice but to go along with their plan."

Duke paced the Airstream, his mind putting the century-old jigsaw puzzle together. "They both had the skills needed to sensationalize the style and method of the supposed killings . . ."

Chandler stared at the pictures of the five women. "Only things start to get out of control. Copycat killers, nutcases wanting to claim credit for the crimes . . ." He poured another mug of coffee and looked at Duke, who nodded. Chandler filled Duke's mug.

"Maybe Tumblety did a little freelancing for himself," he continued. "There were other victims that turned up around the canonical five. Annie Milwood, Ada Wilson, Emma Smith, and half a dozen others, not to mention the female torso they found at the site of the original Scotland Yard."

"So you're saying it might even have been Tumblety who carried out the copycat murders once he'd had a taste of playacting it?"

Chandler nodded.

Duke shook his head. "He was one sick mother."

Chandler took the picture of Tumblety off the corkboard. "No doubt about that. Either way, the agents of the government decided to get Cream and Tumblety out of the country."

Duke nodded. "Yeah, and maybe part of their agreement was for the docs to protect the women while they were out there with them."

Chandler stared at the picture in his hand. "But instead, they exploited them for their own ends." He put the photo down on top of a newspaper on a small shelf to one side of the Airstream.

Duke rubbed his chin. "Maybe it was always part of the plan to make the women disappear for good, once things had died down. It could be that's what the carriage driver, or Dr. Cream if it was him, was planning to do, but then the storm surge took them all out."

Chandler touched the digitally reconstructed picture of Mary Kelly on the corkboard. "Which is when the conspirators got lucky. No more witnesses."

Duke nodded. "If you can call the biggest natural disaster to hit Louisiana for a hundred years luck."

Chandler sat down. He suddenly felt very tired. "And all the evidence of their conspiracy ends up buried in the swamp—until now." He looked over at Duke. "Do you really think the government was behind all of this?"

Duke shrugged. "Who else could control things at this level? It's huge."

Chandler went over to the small table and picked up the picture of Tumblety. He looked down at the newspaper it had been lying on.

The tight-lipped smile of Governor Roman Blackburn stared up at him from beneath a headline: NEXT STOP, SENATE? He picked up a black marker pen, drew a large walrus mustache on Blackburn's face.

Duke looked at it, cracked a grin. "Shouldn't you be over that sort of thing, at your age?"

Chandler put the picture of Dr. Tumblety alongside the picture in the newspaper. "Look familiar?"

Duke stared down at the two pictures. "Well I'll be damned. Two peas in a pod."

"It's probably just a weird coincidence," Chandler said. He went over to the corkboard and tapped the picture of Tumblety with the Bloods and the two white carriage dogs. "Although, he does have the same taste in dogs."

Duke chuckled. "I think we've been looking at so many facial reconstructions on this case, we can't tell shit from Shinola anymore."

Chandler went to his bag and pulled out a Jack the Ripper reference book. He flicked through the index, opened the relevant page.

"One of the aliases adopted by Dr. Francis Tumblety was J. H. Blackburn, a poor choice of name that got him arrested in the eighteen sixties in connection with the Lincoln assassination. After he was released, he decided it would be wise to leave America."

Duke looked over at the book. "When did Tumblety arrive in London?"

Chandler looked down at the page. "He started traveling between New York and Europe from around 1860. He turned up in Liverpool in 1888, where he was arrested on charges of gross indecency and indecent assault—euphemisms for homosexuality. He was charged on suspicion of the Whitechapel murders on the twelfth of November, 1888, and bailed on the sixteenth, after which he fled to France and then took a steamer back to New York."

Duke thought about this. "But Mary Kelly's body was found on November ninth, and Tumblety and Cream were on their way to America by boat with the women the same evening."

Chandler shrugged. "Misdirection again. They stick a walrus mustache on some guy and run a story in the press. Meanwhile, the real Tumblety is on his way to the middle of nowhere in Saint Malo, Louisiana. The Victorians were already using fake news back then."

Duke looked at the pictures again, rubbed his eyes. "Hell, I don't know anymore. You draw a mustache on a pig and I'll see Jack the Ripper."

Chandler closed the book. "I know how you feel."

Duke's cell rang. He scooped it up and hit "Answer."

Chandler could hear an air of panic from the voice leaking out of the speaker.

"Take it easy—when?" He nodded. "Okay, we're on our way." He cut the cell off and headed for the door.

Chandler followed him. Duke ran to his car and climbed behind the wheel. The starter motor churned until the engine finally caught.

Chandler scrambled into the passenger seat. "What's going on?"

"That was Chilly," Duke said. "The Feds are at the warehouse, talking about hazardous waste and shit. They're trying to take the evidence."

Chandler finally managed to get his seat belt fastened.

"How many people do we have up at the warehouse?"

"Just Chilly and Phaedon," Duke shouted over the roar of the engine. "I stood the rest of them down while the terahertz camera was doing its thing."

Chandler was relieved to hear that. He didn't like the thought of Roxie being anywhere near Kale after the incident up at Blackburn's plant.

"It feels like they're trying to scare us into shutting the investigation down," Chandler said.

Duke nodded. "Well, they're shit out of luck."

SIXTY-TWO

BUTTE LA ROSE, LOUISIANA – Present day

FBI AGENTS STOOD outside the old warehouse, some sheltering themselves from the sun beneath the branches of a large tree, others standing by their cars working their cell phones or radios. Men in hazmat suits with their helmets off talked in groups, smoking and drinking coffee from insulated flasks. Inside the warehouse, Agent Kale stood inches from Chilly's face, spitting out his words through clenched teeth.

"Do you have any idea how much money you're costing the US government having me and my men sitting here watching you pick your nose?"

Chilly looked from Kale to the officers behind him, then reached into his pocket and pulled out an empty Twinkie wrapper. He tried to keep his one and only vice under control, but some days he needed the extra buzz of sugar that a Twinkie could give him. This was fast turning into one of those days.

He'd been at home with his wife, Myleen, when the call came in. They were preparing for a barbecue for some of his swamp buggy friends. Chilly had picked up a selection of ribs, burgers, and steaks from Ritchie's Deli and enough beer to get them through the evening, and Myleen had promised to bake one of her famous Doberge cakes. It was an old recipe passed down from her grandma and was his favorite. An original Louisiana specialty, the Doberge cake was made by alternating multiple thin layers of cake with dessert pudding. Myleen used half chocolate pudding and half lemon pudding, then covered the cake in a thin layer of buttercream and a fondant shell. Chilly had been sampling the mix straight from the bowl when his cell phone rang. Phaedon was on the line, and panicking. The warehouse was surrounded by patrol cars, and Agent Kale was demanding to be let in. Chilly knew that without a search warrant, Kale's only way in was by threats and cajoling. He told Phaedon to stay cool, and hotfooted it down to the warehouse. By the time he got there, Kale had talked his way inside, and a scared-looking Phaedon stood at the back of the warehouse, flicking at his smartphone screen as if it were a digital worry bead. Chilly had laid out the legal situation and Kale had ordered his men out, and they'd been engaged in a pissing contest ever since.

Kale's angry voice snapped him back into the present. "Well?" he spat.

Chilly looked up at Kale and swallowed. "You know the procedure. I can't hand over the situation to you until Deputy Lanoix authorizes it—unless you have a warrant. Do you have one?"

Kale ran his fingers through his hair. He knew there was no way he would have been granted a warrant on such tenuous grounds, and his only chance had been to bluff his way in. Time was running out and if he was to find anything, he needed to act fast. He moved toward Chilly, his face a mask of insincerity.

"How's Myleen doing, Chilly? Still as pretty as ever?" He put his arm around the deputy, moving him away from the door of the warehouse. "Got a couple of kids, don't ya? Emma and Joey. I hear they're real cute. You wouldn't want them sucking in any pollutants, would you? We're just trying to help the neighborhood here, Chilly, prevent a toxic incident—"

The roar of a badly maintained engine filled the warehouse as Duke's Skylark slammed to a halt outside. The driver's door was flung open and Duke climbed out. He pushed past some officers and was in Kale's face within a few strides. He had a couple of inches on the agent and moved close enough to make Kale crick his neck.

"What exactly do you think you're doing here?" Duke growled. "Besides riding roughshod over police protocol and being a downright pain in the ass?"

Kale snapped his sunglasses on. "Just looking for a little interdepartmental cooperation."

Duke tilted his head down the necessary three inches to bring his eyes level with Kale's shades and snarled.

"Well, I'm sorry, but what I'm seeing here is some jumped-up Federal Bureau of Incompetence lightweight waving his dick around in my backyard. Tell me I'm wrong."

Kale took his glasses off, wiped the lenses, put them back on, and gave Duke his best tight smile. "As you know, the government has seen fit to give us wide-reaching powers—"

Duke laughed. "Which, if I'm not mistaken, you are busy abusing! This isn't a homicide. There are no wanted criminals here, no illegal drugs, no suspected terrorist activities—in short, no reasons for you to be here. And since when did the FBI decide to get involved in alleged 'environmental issues'?"

A familiar black Escalade slid to a halt in the background, sending dust spiraling into the moist air and drawing irritated glances from the agents as it enveloped them. Its tinted window slid down a few inches. From inside, Governor Blackburn motioned his head at Kale, who reacted instantly.

"Okay—looks like we're done here for today. We'll be back tomorrow morning; you can count on it." Kale waved a *wind it up* sign to his men.

Duke looked down at him. "I look forward to it."

Kale turned on his heel and headed toward the Escalade. The rest of the Feds gradually dispersed and climbed into their cars before driving off. Duke watched as the convoy followed Blackburn's car down the road. Silence returned to the warehouse.

Phaedon slipped his cell back into his pocket and shrugged at Duke. "Sorry, man. Violence ain't my bag."

Duke waved a hand. "Forget it. The guy's all talk."

"Yeah, I know. But he has a gun, and he does look pretty unstable. Guy's a left swipe for sure," Phaedon said.

"Yeah, I won't argue that point," Duke said before turning to Chilly. "You okay, big boy?"

Chilly wiped sweat off his forehead. "I need a shitload of Twinkies, and I need them now!"

Chandler came over to Duke. "What's his story?"

Duke stared at the disappearing vehicles. "Agent Joshua Kale. I first met him when I was investigating a fatal traffic accident a few years back. When I got to the scene it just didn't look right. Evidence turned up linking Blackburn's car to the scene, and there were prints on a bottle of alcohol that didn't match the victim's. Before we got to trial, vital evidence went missing and the DA dismissed the case."

"I'm guessing Kale was the officer in charge of the case?" Chandler said.

Duke nodded. "He was the only other officer with access to the evidence. Since then, he's been in Blackburn's pocket."

Duke's cell rang. He listened. "Okay, thanks for letting me know. I'll be right there."

Chandler looked at his friend. Duke's expression was grim.

"What's happened?"

Duke shook his head. "It's Blanche."

SIXTY-THREE

NEW YORK CITY, NEW YORK – 1936

THEY SAT AT an old, dusty table in the large cellar beneath the Flatiron Building, a copy of the *New York Times* open in front of them. The cellar extended into the vaults that stretched more than twenty feet below the streets outside. It had once been home to a fashionable French restaurant, the Taverne Louis, with over four hundred seats. But now all that was left were a few sad-looking gilt-edged chairs, some old menus, and half a dozen abandoned tables.

Blanche quietly looked through the pictures as Edward told her everything. Adam Blackburn's complicity in the oil field disaster and the role his foster father Dr. Francis Tumblety had played in the Ripper conspiracy. He thought she took it pretty well, all things considered.

"So Blackburn got lucky," Blanche said.

"Yes. The storm destroyed all the evidence," he said, "apart from the photographs and what I've been able to find out."

She looked at the photo of Adam Blackburn standing in front of a crowd of oil workers and investors before turning to Edward. "But you don't believe this is your son?"

Edward shook his head. "You saw the picture of him at the oil field. He looked the same back then as he does in the newspaper photo today, twenty years later. It doesn't make sense."

She glanced at the newspaper. "It says he underwent a revolutionary new medical procedure to clean his blood. They could have put him into a deep sleep, like a coma, which slowed down the aging process."

"Like Rip Van Winkle," Edward said.

Blanche shook her head. "It does sound a bit *Loony Tunes*, doesn't it?" She looked at the front page of the paper. "But if that isn't Adam Blackburn, who is it?"

"I don't know. I just have the feeling that if I approached him I would be putting myself in danger."

Blanche nodded. "Because of what happened when you went out to the oil field?"

"Yes," Edward replied. "I never found out who was following me, or how the police knew to go out there. That's why I had to disappear."

Blanche nodded. "And why you took so long to contact me."

Edward looked at her. "I only realized Louie had a daughter when you started to be recognized for your photography." He took a deep breath. "I didn't know if I should tell you. Rake up the past. But when I saw the story in the paper, and your name in the exhibition . . ." He paused. "I'm not getting any younger. And then I met you, well—"

"You thought I was tough enough to handle it." Blanche nodded.

Edward looked at her. "Sometimes it's best to leave history alone, but sometimes it needs to be rewritten."

"I understand," said Blanche. "But the Blackburns need to be brought down. And the real story of the Ripper has to be told."

Edward nodded. "That's the other reason I came to see you," he said. "There'll come a time when you can reveal everything I've told you. But you have to wait."

Blanche looked at him, suddenly realizing what he meant.

"Until after your death," she said. "That's it, isn't it?"

Edward looked at her. "When I'm gone, they'll have nobody to threaten or hurt."

"What about me?" Blanche asked. "The people I care about?"

"That's why you have to wait until the time is right," Edward answered.

Blanche touched the stack of photos. "Will these be enough?"

Edward nodded. "Yes, along with my notes, which I'll send you." He slipped the stack of photos into the bag with the camera and put it on the table in front of her. "I want you to keep these safe. I'm running out of time. My lungs are shot."

Blanche squeezed his hand. "I'm sorry. The war?"

Edward nodded. "Yes. Mustard gas. We were in Cambrai, attacking the Germans with tanks. We shelled them ahead of the advance. The wind changed direction and we walked straight into it. Bloody ironic."

"How long?" Blanche said softly.

"I don't know," he said.

She looked at him, trying to understand.

"So let's get this straight. You don't know whether Mary or your daughter are still alive, and you think the man claiming to be Adam Blackburn is an imposter—or a freak of nature."

Edward nodded. "I must come across as some kind of fruitcake."

Blanche smiled. "English fruitcake, the best kind."

She looked around the dusty cellar. "I have to go now. But I'll make sure whatever you send me gets into the right hands when it's time."

Edward smiled. "Thank you. I know it sounds unbelievable, but it's real."

Blanche nodded. "If what you say about Blackburn is true, he deserves to pay sooner rather than later." She paused, thinking. "Couldn't you just tell the police and let them deal with it?"

Edward shook his head. "After what happened out at the oil field, I'm not sure I trust the police."

"I can understand that," Blanche replied. She stood up from the table. "I have to deliver some food to the soup kitchens, so take this." She pulled out a card. "Send your notes and get back to me if you need my help bringing that bastard Blackburn down."

Edward nodded and took the card. "Thank you," he said. "You take care."

Blanche lifted her camera up and took a picture of Edward.

"So I remember."

She gave him a quick hug, headed across the cellar, jogged up the stairs and was gone.

SIXTY-FOUR

RYKER'S FIELD, LOUISIANA – Present day

DUKE PULLED UP at the end of the drive leading to Blanche's house and climbed out into the hot, sticky afternoon air. He looked around and remembered Blanche and the conversation they'd had. He couldn't imagine more fitting surroundings for her to live in. The de Chiel place was an old neoclassical plantation house, once grand but now run down, its paintwork faded and flaking. An old moss-draped tree hung over the garden, and pink bougainvillea lined the winding path leading toward the front porch. In the middle of the overgrown lawn was the dead stump of an old tree. Bottles of varying sizes hung from its cut-down branches.

CSIs worked the area. Jesse sat on the porch, staring out into space, his face drawn. Jonas was crouched down by Blanche's body, making notes as he worked. She lay on the ground next to her overturned wheelchair. Duke looked at the dejected figure of Jesse and braced himself for the emotional outpouring he knew was sure to come. In all his years as a deputy, he'd never gotten used to this part of the job.

He went over to Jesse. The big man looked up, his eyes misty. He shook his head, tried to come to terms with the loss of the woman he'd known for so many years. Duke put a comforting hand on his shoulder. Tears welled up in Jesse's eyes at the simple gesture.

"I should have been here, but I went out to shoot some pool," he said. "Normally she comes with me. The doc seems to think it was a heart attack."

Duke nodded, spoke carefully. "She was probably in the garden when they broke in."

Jesse looked toward where Blanche's body lay. "You think she tried to stop them? That they . . ." His face crumpled. "Who would want to hurt her?"

Duke shook his head. "I don't think anybody hurt her, Jesse. Like you said, it seems like she had a heart attack."

Duke waited as Jesse stared out over the ramshackle garden. He gave a half smile as some butterflies rose from the pink and purple irises among the weeds. Duke wondered if this was nature giving Blanche a colorful wave goodbye. Jesse watched as the butterflies swirled around their heads before settling onto a patch of bright yellow flowers farther down the garden.

"She was a brave woman," Jesse said. "Followed the race riots with her camera—she wanted to show the truth. That day, when they saw her, they stopped beating on me, turned on her. They didn't want the truth told. That's when she lost her eye. She had it to the camera when they hit her. So I got her to a hospital."

Duke nodded. He could imagine what a feisty woman Blanche must have been back then.

"She was different. She had her own values." Jesse smiled through his grief, remembering. "She took me on when she married, to help with the house. When her husband died, well . . ." He trailed off as an officer came over to them. He held a small wooden-framed glass-fronted box in a plastic evidence bag.

He showed it to Duke. "This was on the ground next to her. Along with her camera."

Duke took the bag. Inside the box was a butterfly, pinned in a frame, iridescent blue wings glinting in the light. The mounting card on the back of the box was torn and coming away from the frame, probably damaged when it fell. He remembered his conversation with Blanche, out in the field as she photographed her precious butterflies. He heard her soft voice, tinged with sadness: *You'd be a* Graphium sarpedon*—a bluebottle.*

He turned to Jesse. "What do you think she was doing with it?"

Jesse shook his head. He took the box from Duke and turned slowly away while he studied the butterfly in the box. He touched the glass, like he was stroking its wings.

"I don't know. She has a collection in the house, but she never took them out in the sunshine. She was afraid the color would fade from their wings." He handed the box back to Duke. "Does it mean anything to you?"

Duke had been thinking about that while Jesse had been studying the box. The butterfly was the very one she'd compared him to out of all the others. After many years in the force, he'd learned that coincidences were rare.

"Remember when we were out in Ryker's field? She said if I were a butterfly, I'd be a *Graphium sarpedon*. A bluebottle. This butterfly." Duke tapped the case. "This means something."

Jesse looked over at Jonas as he knelt next to Blanche's body. His face grew hard.

"Back in the day, her mind was as sharp as a razor. She'd do the *New York Times* crossword in fifteen minutes. And she loved her sudoku. If she was trying to tell you something, she'd do it in a way that only made sense to you."

Duke looked around the garden, trying to put it all together: butterflies, bluebottle, *Graphium sarpedon* . . . Jesse was right; Blanche was smart, and in this case, smarter than he was.

He looked over at an old wooden garage that sat by the side of the house. "Did Blanche have a car?"

Jesse nodded. "Kinda. I used to drive her in mine. She got an old one in the garage, though—ain't been used for years. Her father had the same model."

"She was born after her father died, wasn't she?" Duke said.

"Yes. Her mother used to travel around with Mr. de Chiel while she was carrying Blanche. He left Blanche money in trust, and she used some of it to buy the same model of car. Recently it's been playing up. Every time we took it for a long run, it would cut out. Never did find out what the problem was—something to do with the fuel pump, maybe? I tried to get her to sell it, but she wouldn't hear of it."

"Can I see it?" Duke asked.

Jesse got up, ambled toward the garage. He seemed to have shrunk in size, like he'd become older without Blanche beside him. They reached the garage. Jesse tugged at the warped door with the peeling paint. The door finally yielded and swung open. Dust motes sparkled in the sunlight that filtered through the murky glass of the garage windows. Duke eased back the shutters that covered one of the windows to let in more light. The car was a dark red color. Its muted brass fittings gleamed in the shadows. Jesse touched the hood, leaving a tramline of dust as he trailed his fingers across the lustrous red paintwork.

"It's a 1915 Pierce-Arrow," he said softly. Duke looked at the car, and something started to take shape in his mind: a memory that refused to reveal itself completely. But from his experience, he knew that it would. Eventually.

He left the garage and walked over to the house. The CSIs were finishing up. Duke nodded to an officer, slipped some protective covers over his shoes.

"Find anything?"

The officer shook his head. "We'll have to process the prints back at the lab, but there are a lot of smudged traces, so they were probably wearing gloves. From what I can see, they searched the whole house from top to bottom, so whatever they were looking for I'm guessing they didn't find it."

Duke nodded. "They didn't look in the garage, so maybe they were disturbed before they could finish."

"A UPS man delivering a package saw Blanche lying in the garden and called 911," the officer said.

"Maybe they saw the delivery truck and hightailed it," Duke said.

"Looks like it. Jonas may have some more thoughts."

"He usually does," Duke said. He had a feeling that the answer to whatever Blanche was trying to tell him was somewhere in the garden.

Blanche's body had been removed and Jonas and the CSI team had left the scene. Jonas had some preliminary findings and told Duke he would get back to him with a more detailed report in the morning. It looked like Blanche's heart had given out. The CSI team found traces showing two vehicles had been present, and at least three or four people were involved in the break-in. It seemed likely that Blanche had been out in the garden taking photographs when they'd arrived and that she'd panicked and toppled from her chair trying to reach the house.

Duke had asked Jonas if he could shed any light on why she would leave the butterfly box. Jonas looked at the butterfly case and studied the scene carefully. There were wheelchair tracks around the garden, some near the front porch, and some near the old tree stump festooned with hanging bottles. But for once, Jonas didn't have any opinions. They both agreed that if Blanche had been trying to tell him something, it must be very well hidden.

Duke held the butterfly frame in his hand as he stood in the garden. The bougainvillea glowed purple in the rays of the setting sun. The windshields of passing cars on the distant road threw flashes of sunlight across the garden.

For a brief moment, like a photographic flash, Duke caught a glimpse of something blue flickering on a tree. But it was gone before he could make it out—an illusion? He looked at the ground beside the wheelchair. As Jonas had noted, tire tracks from the wheelchair led toward the bottle-laden tree trunk and then returned. Duke frowned. There was another flash. A blue-and-white image appeared on the path, and then it was gone.

Duke blinked, rubbed his eyes and shook himself. "I've gotta get some sleep," he muttered as a cab pulled up at the end of the drive.

Chandler climbed out and paid the driver. He walked up the drive, crossed the yard to Duke, and put a hand on his friend's shoulder.

"I'm sorry. She was a good lady."

Duke looked up. "Yeah, I know."

Chandler pointed at the tree stump festooned with different-colored bottles. "What's that?"

Duke looked toward the tree. "It's a hoodoo tree. They're spirit bottles. Some people believe that when an evil spirit sees the sunlight bouncing off the glass, it's enticed by the light and enters the bottle, then prefers to remain in its colorful prison rather than trouble the world of the living."

Duke reached into his pocket and pulled out a business card. "They found this inside the house beside the phone."

Chandler read the card. "'Future Information Corporation: Marsha Brochell, corporate futurist. Let us plan your future.' Seems like Blanche was looking for some sort of guidance," he said.

Duke wandered over to the hoodoo tree. Chandler followed, intrigued by the bottles that tinkled in the night breeze. Duke touched the bottles with his fingers, thoughtful as he studied them. Something blue and white flared across the tree branches. Chandler looked at the tree more closely.

"What was that?"

Duke looked around, trying to pinpoint the source. "I don't know. It happened earlier. I thought I was seeing things, but that's the third time now."

Chandler looked at the butterfly case in Duke's hand. "And that?" he asked.

Duke held it up. "It was next to her on the ground."

Chandler reached out and took it gently from Duke. "*Graphium sarpedon*, a bluebottle. That's you as a butterfly, according to Blanche, right?"

The sun sank lower in the sky. A fuzzy blue-and-white image trembled on the garage wall. Duke waved his hand in front of the hoodoo tree, and the image vanished. Chandler headed toward the tree.

"There's something in one of the bottles."

He followed the source of the reflected light as the sun hit one of the upended bottles on the tree. A blue bottle. He carefully removed the bottle from the tree and reached inside, pulled out a piece of film negative. It was a frame from a large-format still-camera and was the size of a postcard. He held it up to the light.

Duke stared at it. "She wanted me to find this." He produced a small flashlight and shone it through the negative, then held both up so that a clear picture appeared on the white wall of the garage: some workers standing in front of an old oil derrick.

There was a name on the side of the structure: BLACKBURN OIL AND GAS. In the background, a man leaned against a familiar car. A Pierce-Arrow.

Chandler looked at the negative on the wall. "That's Blanche's father's car. What does it mean?"

Duke scratched his stubble. "Feds trying to shut us down, you and Roxie nearly killed by a truck, and now Blanche—this has Blackburn's fingerprints all over it." He switched the flashlight off, and the picture winked out.

Chandler looked back at the garden. Everything seemed as muted as the photo negative, all the life and color drained with Blanche's passing. He patted his friend on the shoulder.

"Why do you think she left the picture for us to find?"

Duke headed for the car, a big man casting a long shadow in the light from the setting sun.

"I don't know. But I'm sure as hell gonna find out."

Duke and Chandler sat next to Roxie on a couple of the worn plastic chairs in the library at Iberville. Roxie wound a microfiche through the lens of the small projector and studied the black and white images on the screen. A laptop was open and printed photos were spread across the table. The library was deserted. Roxie slowed the machine and adjusted the focus. Chandler looked around at the empty room.

"Are you allowed in here this late?" he said.

"I spend more time up here than most of the students. And leave it tidier. They trust me to lock up," Roxie said.

"What did you find?" Duke said.

"I was looking into Marsha Brochell's background. I did a search through local photo archives online and then the microfiche."

Chandler looked at the photo of Marsha on the laptop screen. It was a headshot of an impressive-looking African American woman with auburn hair flowing over her shoulders. "Powerful-looking woman."

Roxie looked at him. "You better believe it." She held up a printout of a black-and-white photo. It showed a congregation standing in front of a church. A striking woman of color with a distinctive beaded necklace stood to one side of the group. "This was taken outside the Baptist church at False River here in Louisiana. Most of the congregation are from the Alma plantation." Roxie tapped the woman in the necklace. "Recognize her?"

Chandler looked at the picture. "I recognize that necklace. Marsha's wearing it in her headshot. He nodded to the laptop.

Roxie said, "Well, she must be a relation, because this was taken in 1861. The plantation belonged to John Palmer Sturridge. On April fifth, he sold the plantation and his entire holding to a land baron in England. This was at a point when over a quarter of a million tons of sugar was being produced in a year."

"Why do you think he did that?" Duke asked.

"Nobody knows, but if someone advised him, they knew what they were doing. The Civil War broke out a week later, and by the end of the war, sugar production was less than six thousand tons a year."

Roxie slid another picture across the table. "Here she is again, this time in a car on Wall Street with Jesse Livermore."

The photograph showed a youthful-looking man with slicked-back silver hair and horn-rimmed glasses. The woman in the passenger seat was smartly dressed, identical to the woman in the congregation, and wore the same beaded necklace.

Roxie tapped the photo. "Jesse Livermore was a stockbroker. One of the most successful in America, for a while. In 1906, just ahead of the San Francisco earthquake, and on a hunch, he shorted Union Pacific Railroad stock and made a fortune. Then during the 1907 stock market panic, he shorted the market and made over three million dollars. He did the same again, and after the 1929 crash, he was worth over a hundred million dollars. In today's money that equates to over a billion dollars. So either he was a genius, amazingly lucky, or—"

"He was getting good advice," Duke said.

Roxie picked up a copy of a newspaper front page with a headline: BLACKBURN OIL AND GAS SEALS DEAL WITH PHOENIX OIL. There was a photograph of Adam Blackburn shaking hands with another man on a beach. Roxie pointed to a woman in the crowd at the side of the picture.

"There she is again," Roxie said. "Or someone related to her."

"What's the connection?" Duke asked.

"A few years later, Phoenix Oil went bankrupt and Blackburn bought the same land back for peanuts," Roxie explained.

"A colleague of mine in the Met always used to say there's no such thing as coincidence," Chandler said.

"Well, that's good to know," Roxie said, "because . . ."

She slid another photograph across the table. It looked like an older version of Roman Blackburn accompanying Marsha Brochell into the Metropolitan Opera House in New York.

Roxie tapped the picture. "In September 1992, the British pound was forced out of the European Exchange Rate Mechanism. George Blackburn had built up a large short position in the market, and when the value of the pound fell, he made over a billion dollars."

Chandler nodded. "Along with George Soros."

"So if we listen to your friend in the Met and rule out these very profitable coincidences, what does that leave us with?" Roxie said.

Chandler replied, "Marsha Brochell, CEO of the Future Information Corporation."

Duke said, "We've looked into her past, now let's go find out what she has planned for the future."

SIXTY-FIVE

NEW ORLEANS, LOUISIANA – present day

THE OFFICES OF the Future Information Corporation were in a mirrored wedge that soared thirty-six stories into the sky above New Orleans. In contrast to the old French Quarter, this was the financial part of the city and in a different league to the tourist traps downtown. Chandler took the elevator up to the thirty-fifth floor and headed through the glass doors into a cool and very corporate Zen-style atrium that formed the reception area. Glass cases mounted on the walls contained ancient voodoo masks, bottles of potions, and relics of the old school of astrology. He headed over to the reception desk. A young eastern European girl with the cheekbones of a supermodel gave him an expensive-looking smile.

"Can I help you?"

Chandler smiled back, sure his smile wouldn't have the same effect on her.

"I have an appointment with Marsha Brochell?"

The receptionist pointed to a touch screen in front of the desk. The outline of a hand glowed on it.

"Just put your hand on that. I'll do the rest."

Chandler put his hand on the screen, which changed color, mapping his hand. Some writing appeared on the screen: an astrological chart and some directions.

Room 7, 36th Floor.

A magnetic security card slid out of a slot. He picked it up, and some new text filled the screen.

Mars and Saturn in conflict—challenging times ahead. Have a nice day.

Chandler stood there holding the card. He fumbled in one of his pockets and pulled out a small oblong package wrapped in colorful birthday paper. He turned back to the girl at reception.

"Can I leave this here? It's a necklace, a present for my wife, and I'm terrified of dropping it somewhere."

The girl nodded. "I'll put it here on the desk so I can keep an eye on it."

Chandler smiled. "You'd better remind me to pick it up when I leave."

"Sure."

Chandler headed toward the elevator and the doors pinged open, anticipating his arrival. The powerful elevator whisked him upward. Within seconds, it announced his arrival at the thirty-sixth floor with another prediction about how his life was going. Chandler was already bored with it.

"Get back to me when you have the lottery numbers," he said.

He walked out into the corridor past a sign that read, THE FUTURE OF YOUR BUSINESS IS THIS WAY . . . The walls were tastefully decorated with modern art, and a small fountain trickled into a bed of lilies and red flowers. Soft music played. It was all very hypnotic.

A woman appeared next to him as though by magic. Glossy auburn hair and eyes that resembled those of a jungle cat, she exuded an animal magnetism. She wore a beaded necklace around her neck. It was probably the only piece of jewelry or furniture there that didn't have a designer label on it. He tried not to stare at it.

"Mr. Travis? I'm Marsha." She saw his eyes flick to her necklace. "It's Masai."

He blinked. "Er, right. It's very . . . colorful."

Marsha touched the beads as she talked. They seemed to glow as her fingers caressed them. "Each color represents something. Red—bravery, strength, and unity. Blue—the color of the sky, energy, and sustenance. Green represents the land; orange, friendship; yellow, fertility and growth. White stands for purity and health, and black for harmony and solidarity."

Chandler looked back up at her face. He felt like a moth headed for a flame. He snapped out of it. "I didn't know that. Thank you."

She gestured to an open office door and walked in. Chandler followed. It was all very high tech, with large monitors and computer terminals everywhere.

"Nice place you have here."

Marsha caught his look. "Not what you were expecting?"

Chandler looked around. "Well, I wasn't expecting chicken bones."

Marsha smiled at him. Her teeth were dazzling white, and he felt another wave of inadequacy.

"We prefer a more . . . contemporary approach. Rather like your profiling department, we do a thorough search of publicly available information, from which we can build up a picture of our client's position and public image. We then ask for more in-depth details."

Chandler nodded. "So you don't really claim to see into the future then?"

"I believe that in many cases you can see into the future," Marsha replied. "It's just that some people choose not to."

"What do you mean?" he asked.

"There are many examples where the future is clear but people chose not to see it," she said. "Smith Corona's mechanical calculator division was wiped out in the seventies by cheap electronic calculators, and again in the mid-eighties, their typewriter division collapsed due to PC-based word processing. Then there was Kodak and digital imaging, the Swiss watch industry and cheap Japanese quartz timepieces . . ."

Chandler smiled. "I'm sure there's something apposite I could say about crystal balls, but I take your point. Some people are able to see where things are going more readily than others," he said.

Marsha nodded. "Exactly. Sometimes it's just as simple as being in the right place at the right time. Astrology is big business, Mr. Travis. Companies are looking for an edge. Even an educated guess that gains them one percent of a billion-dollar deal is worth having."

Chandler stared at her. "What sort of edge did Ms. de Chiel need?"

There was an almost imperceptible pause as Marsha thought about this. And then, like a computer that had located the correct information, she replied, "The de Chiel family have been clients in the past. During her husband's illness, Mrs. de Chiel came to us for support. She recently had some issues that she wanted personal guidance on."

"What sort of issues?"

Chandler waited. Had he seen a flicker of concern in those strange, catlike eyes?

Marsha wandered over to the window and looked out across the city. Her hands stroked the beaded necklace that rested against her neck.

"The information that passes through here is always of a confidential nature—it has to be that way, when so much money hinges on tiny pieces of information."

"Yes, well, we believe Ms. de Chiel may have been murdered because of some information she had," said Chandler.

Marsha paused. Once again Chandler was reminded of a computer sifting through data for the most appropriate reply.

"I'm sorry to hear that. But her consultation with me was really just one of reassurance. She was old, and her health was failing. She wanted to know if there was anything in her future she needed to take care of, before the end."

Chandler leaned forward. "Right. And was there?"

Marsha smoothed her hair back over an ear adorned with an azure stone. "Nothing that I could see."

Chandler stared at her. She was too perfect—like her answers. He wasn't going to get anything from her she didn't want to give him. He was going to have to try a different approach.

"Okay, well, if you think of anything in the future that might be of use to our investigation, please give me a ring. I'll write my number down for you." He fumbled in his jacket, came up empty handed. "I don't seem to have a pen."

Marsha smiled, handed him one of her cards and a pen. Chandler took the card, wrote his cell number on the back, and handed it to her. He tried to give her the pen back, but she waved it away.

"In case your pen doesn't turn up in the near future."

The pen was embossed with her firm's name. Chandler slid it into his jacket pocket.

"Thank you."

Marsha watched him leave the office, her mouth a tight line.

Chandler got out at the atrium floor and walked over to the receptionist, who was busy on the phone. She handed him the package he'd left and gave him a nod. He mouthed a "thank you" and headed out through the mirrored doors onto the street, then pulled out his cell phone and tapped in Duke's number.

"Duke? Yeah, I just got out. Trust me, if I had two guts, both of them would be saying the same thing. Something stinks here."

Marsha looked down from her window as Chandler climbed into Duke's car on the street below. She paid a lot of money for an office on the top floor of the First Bank and Trust Tower, but it was worth it. Her abilities were at their greatest when combined with a wide physical viewpoint.

She knew from the moment the English detective had entered the building that there was a problem. One of the many gifts that had been passed down through her bloodline was the ability to sense a threat to the natural order that surrounded her. She'd inherited this ability from her great-grandmother Leatrice Brochell, one of the first voodoo queens to practice in the city of New Orleans.

As a young girl of fourteen, Leatrice had worked on a sugar plantation, taking drinking water around to the other slaves cutting the cane down and helping transport the crop to the sugarhouse for grinding. One day she'd been passing the boiling room when the plantation owner's son, Jeremiah, had cornered her. He was a muscular and arrogant brute and had clamped his hand around her mouth to silence her protests. He took his belt off and fastened it across her open mouth to silence her scream. She was helpless against his strength, and he had backhanded her into submission. Over the next hour, he raped her savagely and repeatedly until blood ran from her and he grew tired. She must have passed out, because when she came to, she was lying on a blood-soaked bed looking up at the voodoo queen Marie Laveau.

One of the women at the plantation had found Leatrice lying unconscious outside the boiling room and had gotten her into New Orleans on the back of a farmer's cart. She'd been taken to Marie's house and been given some bitter-tasting medicine. Leatrice drifted in and out of consciousness as Marie uttered incantations over her, never sure if she was awake or asleep. After a week had passed Leatrice was well enough to return to the plantation.

Jeremiah had told his father that she had run away to cover up his violent act. The day she returned to the plantation, his father was away on business. There, the word had spread among the slaves, and together with Leatrice they planned their revenge. They waited until the day they were due to burn off the sugarcane trash, the process of setting fire to the cane to remove the leaves before harvesting. Leatrice saw Jeremiah watching her during the day and had smiled at him as she walked into the cane field. Such was his arrogance that he actually thought she had enjoyed the traumatic experience he'd put her through, and he followed her into the cane field. By the time he realized his error it was too late.

He was tied to a stake and gagged with his own belt. Leatrice was given a jug of molasses to pour over his head, then she and the other slaves walked away. The fire swept through the sugarcane, and a thick pall of smoke hung over the fields. For a few moments Leatrice thought she could hear Jeremiah screaming. Maybe the ferocious fire of the molasses had burnt through his belt and he was able to make some hideous noise before he died. Leatrice's voodoo powers began to grow stronger from that day onward, and were eventually passed down through the generations to Marsha.

As a stunningly attractive teenager, Marsha quickly learned that sex and information would give you power, and that both could be sold for money. She'd grown up surrounded by Louisiana voodoo practices, and her mother had taught her the four phases of a voodoo ritual: preparation, invocation, possession, and the farewell. Her mother had explained to her how the songs were used to open the gate between the deities and the world of humans. Marsha had no desire to end up as a high-class hooker, but neither did she wish to be a token wife on the arm of a rich businessman.

She'd seen the stalls and shops selling voodoo spells and trinkets on the streets of New Orleans and Baton Rouge and saw no future in them. Then she'd met Francis Tumblety, in his alter ego as Francis Blackburn, in New Orleans and seen into his dark past. She'd seduced his heir, Adam Blackburn, on his eighteenth birthday and helped him with her powers during the dark days when his mortality had been threatened. And now Roman, too, would soon need her restorative powers. Though Marsha herself could achieve a form of longevity through her own spiritual strength, Roman had to rely on science and her support to achieve the same ends. Over the years, the process had become less onerous and achievable on a far shorter timescale. Working with the Blackburn dynasty, Marsha soon realized that the way forward in big business was through information. Clients would pay for her astrological guidance to make their decisions, and by telling Marsha their plans, they supplied her with valuable intel. In turn, like part of a data Ponzi scheme, she was able to provide the correct decision for one corporation based on the knowledge supplied to her by another. As long as more companies benefited from her services than suffered, her business continued to grow.

And then the English detective had arrived and put the whole operation under threat.

She looked out across the city. The vehicles on the streets below glittered like diamond-coated bugs as the sun reflected off their windshields. She let her mind drift away, and her view became replaced by flickering mirrors filled with a myriad of possible futures that gradually became darker, and then opaque, as the possibilities ran their course. In the end it was all too clear that the English detective's history and their future were fatally entwined. She picked up her cell phone and hit speed dial.

SIXTY-SIX

BATON ROUGE, LOUISIANA – Present day

JAZZ BURBLED FROM the radio as Duke and Chandler headed down the I-10 and back toward the warehouse out at Butte La Rose. Duke accelerated the Buick up the gradient and onto the Horace Wilkinson Bridge, which would take them across the Mississippi and out of Baton Rouge. The sun sparkled off the river below, and the blue sky above them was peppered with white clouds. But Chandler wasn't looking at the view. He'd been watching data stream across the computer tablet he held in his lap ever since they'd left New Orleans. Discarded gift wrapping littered the floor by his feet. He had an oblong box connected to his computer tablet. A red LED light winked as the solid-state drive transferred information.

Duke looked over. "How the hell does that thing work anyway?"

Chandler shrugged. "No idea. Phaedon set it up. He told me I just had to put it within a few feet of one of their computers and it would do the rest. He said it was a remote-access scanner."

Chandler looked at the data on the screen. Client details scrolled past. "Looks like they're hand in glove with pretty much every big corporation in Louisiana, including Blackburn Industries."

Duke nodded. "So if Blanche had information that could be damaging to Blackburn—"

"Marsha could have tipped him off," Chandler finished.

Duke gave a grim smile. "And Blanche ends up dead." He paused. "There's gotta be a link between Marsha and whatever Blackburn's doing up at the plant. I'm sure of it. We just need to find out what it is."

Chandler nodded. "Roxie was convinced of that as well. I think that's why we nearly ended up as roadkill."

"That's for sure," Duke said. "From what Roxie found, if Marsha's involved there'll likely be a pile of money riding on the outcome of whatever they're planning."

"If that's the case, we just need to follow the money."

Governor Blackburn's Escalade sat at the side of the road, its engine idling, the whine of its air-conditioning barely audible. Tinted windows filtered out the sunlight. Inside, it was cool and dark, a high-tech cave. Marsha sat opposite Blackburn, a palpable sexuality in her stillness. He sipped on a drink from a cut-glass tumbler. His black eyes stared at her with an unnatural intensity—a controlled passion.

"How much do they know?" he asked.

Marsha stared into space, as if seeing across an infinite distance.

"The locals are still fishing, but the Englishman will find out—it's in his nature, and his future."

Blackburn gave a tight smile. "Can his future be changed?"

"You tried to derail them before," Marsha replied, "out in the swamp. All you did was make them more suspicious." She weighed her words carefully. "It's time for you to move on. The English detective is a threat to you because in some way he is a part of you."

Confusion flickered like storm clouds across Blackburn's dark eyes. "What are you saying?"

Marsha tried to soothe him, her voice gentle. "I don't always get the whole picture—sometimes it's just a feeling deep inside—but whether I understand what it means or not, we must heed the signs. You have to back away from him and the destruction he brings."

Marsha leaned forward, her body pressing against him. "If you move quickly you can save yourself, but you must do it now, before it's too late. You can come back. You always do."

Blackburn shook his head. "We're so near. We've been working on this for generations—"

Marsha nodded. "I know. It used to take years, but now it will feel like the blink of an eye. The sisters have done good work. We're reaching a point where we will no longer need them."

Blackburn looked into her catlike almond eyes. "You have the power within you," he said, "but I still have to live through the process." He looked troubled as he remembered. "The darkness, the cold, the emptiness in my mind . . . every nerve tingling as it finds its way—"

Marsha cut him off with a look. "I know that, and I hope that one day we can be as one. But for now, you need to be protected. We need to make sure you survive and continue your work."

Blackburn placed his hand beneath her chin and then stroked her cheek, like a collector caressing a piece of sculpture. She stared deep into his eyes, as if probing for some kind of information that would make her task easier. Blackburn's face tensed as she took control of his mind, then relaxed as she left him.

She kissed him, pulled back to study his reaction. "Different versions of the future have already been decided. We have to align ourselves to the version we desire."

Blackburn gave a cold smile. "Then so be it."

Marsha smiled back at him, her look full of passion, and then straddled him. Blackburn groaned as she slammed down onto him.

He cupped her face. "There'll never be anybody else like you, will there?"

She bent down and whispered into his ear, "Not in your lifetime."

Blackburn gripped her hard as she bucked on top of him, his expression a mixture of pleasure and fear.

SIXTY-SEVEN

BUTTE LA ROSE, LOUISIANA – Present day

WHEN THEY ARRIVED back at the warehouse Duke immediately checked that nothing had been taken before ringing the morgue. Jonas told him that the bodies were still safely under his control and everything was secure.

Duke nodded. "Good. Kale and the Feds have been sniffing around the warehouse trying to find out what we've uncovered. I guess we're rattling someone's cage."

Jonas replied, "I'm guessing it's Blackburn's cage."

Duke smiled. "That's your opinion. Catch up with you later."

He hung up and moved across the room to where Chandler was staring at the large screen above the terahertz camera. It was a polarized sea of flickering colors constantly updating as the algorithms streamed their data into the digital cloud.

"How's it going?" Duke asked.

Chandler tore his eyes from the screen. "Phaedon rang me from the university. He thinks we should be getting the first page pretty soon. Apparently the algorithms can distinguish a hard cover much faster than they can a normal page."

"So the normal pages will be slower coming?" Duke said.

"Seems so," Chandler replied. On the screen above them, the data coalesced like a digital mountain range in a coded desert.

Shadowy letters were forming, becoming clearer as trillions of computations added more detail to them.

"Look!" Chandler pointed to the screen, hardly believing his eyes. A final blaze of color flared across the screen before becoming a pulsing background to the rows of text that shimmered on the monitor. "The first page!"

Duke looked at it. "What language is that?"

Before Chandler could answer, his cell phone rang. He looked down at the ID. "It's Phaedon." Chandler accepted the call.

"Hello?" He listened. "Yes, we're looking at it now. Yes, that would be great. We'll catch up with you later."

He hung up and turned to Duke. "Phaedon's running it through Google Translate—we should get it soon."

Chandler looked up at the screen. "There," he said. The page became English, and some words flashed up at the corner of the screen: *Welsh to English.*

"Welsh?" Duke said before reading the words on the screen aloud. "'I am now in a new land—a land where the people are as foreign to me as I am to them. I hope this can be the start of a new life, away from the hell I left behind . . .'"

Chandler looked at Duke. "Mary Kelly was originally from Ireland, but she spoke Welsh."

Duke saw the excitement burning in his friend's eyes. "You think this is Mary's diary?"

Chandler nodded. "It looks that way."

"This is big, huh?" Duke said.

Chandler turned to Duke. "This could affect everything that's been written about the Ripper over the last hundred years."

Duke clapped him on the back. "How's the team doing with the letters?"

Chandler hit some keys. Faint, handwritten words swam into focus on the screen.

"They got some words from the letters addressed to Cream from Tumblety. A lot of the information was lost due to water damage and couldn't be deciphered. But look at this." He handed Duke a printout from part of a letter.

Duke studied it. “When was this sent?”

Chandler held up a scan of the front of an envelope. He tapped the stamp. “This stamp and the information in the letter show it was posted from England in 1893.”

Duke read aloud the few words that had survived. “‘We may well be looking at winding up our business and clearing up any loose ends. I will be coming over soon, and we can discuss it then.’” Duke put the paper down. “Well, if they wanted to get rid of the women, taking them out into the swamp and shooting them would be a pretty easy way of doing it.”

Chandler nodded. “We found Cream’s body near the carriage. So if we assume he was driving, and he had a gun with him . . .” He left it hanging.

“Only, the storm got to them first,” Duke said.

Chandler looked at the screen. “We’ll just have to wait while Hypergator does its thing to see the other documents.”

Duke produced a sepia photograph. “I got a print made from the negative we found in Blanche’s garden. The woman up at the Oil and Gas Museum might be able to shed some light on the history behind it. I’m going up there now. We’ll meet up later, okay?”

Chandler nodded, already engrossed in Mary’s diary. “Sure,” he said and turned back to the screen.

SIXTY-EIGHT

INNISWOLD, LOUISIANA – Present day

AN HOUR AFTER leaving the warehouse at Butte La Rose, Duke drove past a sign for the Oil and Gas Museum and entered the outskirts of Inniswold. He saw the building ahead, pulled up alongside the squat white barn that housed the museum, and got out.

The wind had dropped, and he could hear the engine block ticking and the exhaust pipe crackling as it cooled. The museum was more or less a hobby of the woman who ran it, and had been set up in a converted barn behind her house. Her father had made a lot of money in oil, and she had wanted to preserve some of the local history from the boom years. Duke pushed through the doors and stepped inside. The walls were lined with old black-and-white photographs of Oil City in the early days. He saw pictures of Bonnie and Clyde and Diamond Jim, as well as other famous visitors.

He called out, "Hello? Anybody here?" His voice echoed round the room. A door at the far end of the hall creaked open and a spry gray-haired old lady appeared. She looked suspiciously at Duke. He smiled and extended a hand. "Deputy Duke Lanoix. Mrs. Jones? We spoke on the phone."

The old lady smiled broadly. "Yes, I remember now. But it's Ms. Jones these days. Floyd got his head caught up in some machinery in '86."

Duke shifted uncomfortably. "Sorry to hear that."

The old lady shrugged. "Don't be. Man was a damn fool. What can I do for you, Deputy?"

Duke pulled out the photo of the oil field. "I was wondering if you could tell me anything about this."

She took the photo and studied it. "Well, I can tell you about the car. It's a Pierce-Arrow, I'd say probably 1915. Next to the Packards, the Pierces were the cars the rich folks would go for. Most reliable car ever built. Wouldn't stop till you ran out of gas." She leaned toward him. "I was a bit of a fast lady in my day. Loved anything mechanical." She looked back at the picture. That's Blanche de Chiel's father, Louie de Chiel, standing next to it. He didn't get much of a chance to use it, though."

Duke looked at her. "What do you mean?"

Ms. Jones shrugged. "He got caught up in the great storm that hit Louisiana in September 1915, the same year he bought it. Over two hundred and seventy-five people died. Their bodies were never found."

Duke pointed to the sign in the background of the photo. "What about Blackburn Oil and Gas—what do you know about them?"

The old lady put the photo down on the table and went into a back room. She reappeared with some ledgers and papers in a box. She started to root through them, talking as she pulled papers out.

"A lot of wells sprang up in the early twentieth century—it was like the Klondike gold rush all over again."

Duke smiled. "Except this time it was black gold, huh?"

The old lady fixed him with a beady eye. "Sure was. Round here, we called it Louisiana Blood. It pumped life into the area, but it also brought its share of troubles—and scoundrels. Men who'd as soon kill you for an acre of land as take a piss, 'scuse my French. Bonnie and Clyde, Diamond Jim—all sorts holed up in Oil City."

"I knew Bonnie and Clyde were shot in Louisiana," Duke said.

The old lady sucked her teeth in agreement. "Yup. They go on about pollution now, but in those days we used to dump our trash in the swamps—and I ain't talking about refrigerators and junk, if you get my drift."

Duke nodded. "Sure I do. It's kind of why I'm here."

Miss Jones spotted something in the box and pulled it out. "Blackburn Oil and Gas, here we are. Seems the company was set up in a hurry by young Adam Blackburn in 1915. He claimed to have found oil out in Spirit's Swamp." She handed Duke a newspaper article. "Looks like he'd been left some money and the land in Spirit's Swamp by a rich benefactor. Before the boom, that land would've only been worth around five cents an acre, and it was more like five hundred dollars during the boom."

Duke gave a low whistle. "Says here Adam Blackburn sold shares in the company before they'd even started drilling."

"Yes," Ms. Jones said. "It was a buying frenzy, rather like the dot-com bubble at the end of the nineties—people would've been biting his hand off to get a piece of the action."

Duke looked at the box full of old papers. "So what happened?"

Ms. Jones pulled out another newspaper article, blew the dust off it, and held it up to the light. "This is a newspaper from 1915." She tapped a headline.

Blackburn Oil Field Destroyed In The Great Storm—No Survivors!

"And what happened to the investors?" Duke asked.

The old lady clicked her teeth together. "Adam Blackburn had organized a big celebration for them. They'd struck oil within the first few weeks of drilling, and he wanted to make a big thing of it, impress the investors he already had and maybe hook a few more. He had marquees put up, hired caterers, and erected tents to house everybody. He even booked a five-piece band. The festivities were meant to start on Monday and run through the week, no expense spared. Blackburn was supposed to turn up and make a big speech."

"But?" Duke asked.

Ms. Jones shrugged. "The hurricane was already headed toward the Gulf Coast on Monday the twenty-fifth of September. I guess they didn't know how bad it was going to be," she said. "There hadn't been a hurricane that destructive since the Evil Wind of 1893."

Duke shook his head, imagining the carnage. "What happened to Adam Blackburn?" he asked.

"People assumed he died in the storm," she said, smiling tightly. "Turns out reports of his death were exaggerated."

"What do you mean?" Duke said.

"Next time Adam surfaced was in the thirties. He sold a majority share in the Spirit's Swamp land to Phoenix Oil—"

"Phoenix Oil?" Duke remembered the link Roxie had unearthed between Marsha Brochell's ancestor and Adam Blackburn.

Ms. Jones nodded. "Yes, he made millions, by all accounts, paid back the investors' original stakes, plus interest to the families of those who died during the storm. It was a lot of money, so nobody was complaining." She pulled a newspaper out of the file box dated 1936, traced her finger down the column of newsprint. "He claimed to have taken ill on his way to the celebrations."

Duke scratched his chin. "What, and then twenty years later he pops up right as rain?"

Ms. Jones nodded. "He said he'd been treated for a rare blood disease in some private hospital in Brussels. She circled back around to the picture, picked it up, and reached for a small magnifying glass.

Duke saw her studying the crowd of people in the picture. He leaned over. "Something wrong?" he said.

She handed him the magnifying glass. "Depends when this picture was taken,"

Duke focused the lens over the crowd in the photo. "What am I looking for?"

She leaned forward and tapped a man in the picture who stood apart and in front of the crowd, as if addressing them.

"Do you recognize him?"

Duke squinted through the lens again. "It looks like Governor Blackburn."

She nodded. "All the Blackburns do. That's Adam Blackburn."

Duke felt the hairs on the back of his neck twitch. He put the magnifying glass down carefully. "The Adam Blackburn that claimed he never made it to the celebrations?"

The old lady nodded. She tapped another man in the picture standing by the Pierce-Arrow car. "That's Louie de Chiel, Blanche de Chiel's pa. He was covering the story for the local paper.

Duke shook his head. "This doesn't make sense."

The old lady shrugged. "Everyone in that picture died."

Duke looked at the picture again. "Except Adam Blackburn," he said.

In his years as a deputy, he'd had to look at numerous pictures of murder victims provided by relatives or friends, and they always came with their own particular brand of poignancy. No matter how young or beautiful they were in the picture, once you knew they were dead, they never looked the same.

He shook his head to clear it of ghosts, and pressed on. "So how come Phoenix Oil never drilled on the land?"

The old lady closed the back-room door before turning to him. "Talk was, the contract prevented them drilling for oil until certain conditions were met."

Duke paused. The hairs on the back of his neck twitched again. "What conditions?"

The old lady shrugged. "You'd have to check the company records for that. Didn't make much difference, though, 'cos Phoenix Oil went bankrupt soon after Blackburn did the deal, and he bought the land back for cents on the dollar."

Duke nodded. "That family makes a killing whatever they do. So Governor Blackburn still owns the land?"

The old lady smiled. "Yes. And as far as I know, he's still bound by the conditions of the original contract."

Duke nodded. "But the land has been declared a protected wild-life area, hasn't it? So he can't drill there."

She gave a lopsided grin. "Maybe, but I wouldn't be surprised if that don't get changed real quick, if he winds up in the Senate."

Duke rubbed his eyes. He'd never been good with paperwork, and the ins and outs of big corporations always gave him a headache.

He stared at the old black-and-white picture. Blanche had left him a trail of bread crumbs, and he was just too dumb to follow them.

He turned back to Ms. Jones. "Thank you, you've been very helpful," he said.

The old lady nodded. "My pleasure." She paused. "Seems to me that an awful lot of things about the Spirit's Swamp oil field don't add up."

Duke looked at her keenly. "Go on," he said.

"My grandpa and my pa were oilmen. Part of the reason I set the museum up was because I knew so much about the industry from listening to them talk. I remember my pa telling me something my grandfather had told him. He'd been playing cards with some of his oil buddies and they got to talking about the Blackburn oil field."

Duke leaned in. "How long ago was that?"

The old lady thought about that for a moment.

"Same year as the storm, 1915. One of the old-timers told my grandpa that the land Adam Blackburn bought had been surveyed before and the buyers had backed out for some reason."

"What sort of reason?" Duke asked.

Ms. Jones shrugged. "He didn't know. Maybe they did some test drillings and didn't find anything, or the ground was too unstable—"

"Unstable?" Duke asked.

Ms. Jones nodded. "Yes. Drilling for oil is a bit like coal mining. Sometimes the risk outweighs the returns," she said.

Duke thought about this. "So who would have known why the other buyers pulled out of the deal?" he asked.

Ms. Jones smiled tightly. "I guess that would be Adam Blackburn and his surveyor, and they're both dead.

SIXTY-NINE

SPIRIT'S SWAMP, LOUISIANA – 1915

ADAM BLACKBURN STOOD looking out across the oil field. The oil derricks were silent, and the plant was deserted ahead of the celebrations he'd planned. Construction of more wells would continue once fresh investors had come on board.

His father had died when he was twelve and left him a large amount of cash and shares in trust until he was twenty-one. The sisters in the orphanage out in Spirit's Swamp had brought him up between them until he was old enough to travel to New Orleans to finish his schooling. He remembered his father being there in the early years, and the many blood transfusions he'd had to endure in the dank vaults beneath the sisters' house. His father had explained to him that he had a rare blood disorder and that the transfusions would make him stronger and smarter than most boys his age. As they were hooked up to the transfusion tubes by the sisters, his father would tell him about his own childhood, and his many ideas. It was a way of distracting Adam from the throbbing pain of the blood coursing between them. By the time his father died, Adam no longer needed the transfusions. His friends often remarked that he had an old head on young shoulders, something he took as a compliment.

Along with his inheritance, he had been left a large tract of land out in Spirit's Swamp. His father had bought the land several years before he died when it was cheap, ahead of the oil boom. By 1915, the value of the land had skyrocketed, and Adam had no problem forming a company and floating it on the stock market. The investors had piled in without a moment's hesitation, especially after they'd seen the potential in the surveys. By the time the first rig had struck oil, Adam was twenty-six and already a millionaire.

But there had been a problem. A week before the planned celebrations at the site for the investors and the inaugural oil strike, the surveyor had confronted him. Adam had hired Lloyd McPherson to survey the land, and paid him a lot of money to ensure the results gave the right impression to his would-be investors. McPherson was happy to take the money, and the results were on record for any investor to check before parting with their hard-earned cash. But when Adam had struck oil, the surveyor soon realized how much money was involved and had his nose back in the trough. Adam remembered their exchange out in the swamp one night as the sun began to set. McPherson had stood there, his face red with anger as Adam shook his head.

"That's not going to happen," Adam said. "I paid you what we agreed, and that's that."

McPherson had laughed. "I produced a survey showing it was oil-rich land, which it wasn't. And worse than that, with the methane pockets, it's highly unstable. You're lucky you managed to drill without blowing yourself to hell. You want my advice, you'll pay me what I want and I'll produce another report that will show things have changed and get you off the hook. That way, no one gets hurt and you don't have to pay back a dime."

Adam felt a red mist rising in front of his eyes. He'd discovered while he was growing up that he sometimes had no control over the anger that rose unbidden up inside him. He remembered how his father had been—the terrifying rages that seemed to engulf him for no reason. Adam had taken to slaking his carnal needs with the many prostitutes that inhabited New Orleans; the things they let him do to them helped to quell his violent temper. They were hardened to the ways of men, and for the right amount of cash would take whatever he dealt out.

A sudden explosion of noise jerked Adam out of his stupor. McPherson was staring at him, a look of disbelief on his face. The surveyor looked down and touched his chest with a hand that came away dripping blood. His eyelids fluttered as he crumpled to the ground, blood bubbled from his mouth as he tried to speak. He fell sideways and rolled down a small incline into the swamp. Adam watched as his body floated off into the gloom. Within seconds, the alligators appeared, their teeth clamping down into his flesh, tails churning the muddy water into pink foam as they dragged his body below the surface.

Adam looked at the gun in his hand. Smoke was curling up from the hot barrel, and his finger was still clenched around the trigger. He shoved the pistol back into his pocket and looked around. McPherson's beaten-up Mack Junior truck sat at the side of the track, the keys still in the ignition. Adam started it up. The engine spluttered but soon settled to a regular beat. He looked around. In the distance, he could make out the silhouette of a pump jack. The sound of its dull thud carried across the silence of the swamp. He reached over and slammed the truck into gear. It lurched forward, picking up speed before splashing into the water. Its engine struggled as it sank below the surface until it finally stalled.

Adam stared at the dark swamp water and the ripples spreading across its oily surface. Like his father, it was moments like these that he felt the need to seek help from her. The woman who'd always been there for them over the years. She'd met his father in New Orleans in the years leading up to his death and had been instrumental in implementing the life-saving transfusions between them. McPherson's appearance had been unfortunate. But she would know what effect it might have on their future—she always did.

Colorful bunting was strung between the oil derricks, and men and their families ate and drank the plentiful food and drink that had been laid out on tables in front of the large tents around the site. Louie de Chiel, a journalist from the local paper, came up to Adam Blackburn.

"Can I get a shot of you with the car?" he asked. "I promised the garage I'd get some pictures." Adam nodded and went over to pose beside the Pierce-Arrow as Louie took his picture. They then swapped positions, and Blackburn took a picture of Louie alongside the car.

"Thanks, Mr. Blackburn," he said. "Doesn't look like the weather's going to hold for the ceremony. I'd better get some pictures of you and the celebrations while I still have enough light."

Blackburn gave him an insincere smile. "Okay, just make sure you get my best side." Blackburn posed in front of a large tent where a family was busy eating lunch. They raised their glasses when they recognized him.

The father of a small boy nodded to Blackburn. "Great day and wonderful food, sir," he said.

Blackburn turned and smiled. "My pleasure. If it wasn't for all of you, none of this would have been possible."

De Chiel took some photographs of Blackburn posing with the family, crouching down with the children and generally playing the munificent host.

Blackburn stood up. "I'd better get ready to do my speech. You all enjoy yourselves," he said as he pulled a fob watch from his pocket and studied it. His expression clouded. He didn't have much time. She had told him what lay ahead, and that his future was preordained. She'd explained to him that his father had made sacrifices in his life that would enable the Blackburn bloodline to endure. She wouldn't be drawn on the manner of his death, only that it would be a brief pause in an extended lifetime.

De Chiel took some more photos of the crowd and the celebrations. He looked up at the sky. It had become a sheet of lead. He was on the edge of his exposure limits with the film he had loaded, and cursed himself for not loading faster stock.

He was setting up to take a picture of a family standing next to an oil derrick when the earth shifted. He stumbled, nearly dropping the camera.

"Did you feel that?" he asked. "Felt like a tremor."

"Maybe someone's doing some blasting," the father said. "Come on, take one more."

De Chiel raised his camera, tried to focus a shot. But before he could click the release, there was a shrieking roar, and oil gushed out of the top of one of the derricks.

Louie stumbled backward. "What the hell!" And then he was shooting pictures as fast as he could, as chaos enveloped the gas field.

The line of oil derricks began to tremble. People ran for their lives as the earth around them began to crumble. An oil derrick collapsed, sinking into the ground as the earth beneath it liquefied, swallowing it up like some giant mouth. A jet of superheated gas burst out of the ground in a screaming spume, enveloping a running man in its lethal heat, stripping the flesh from his body. Another man ran past him screaming in agony, flesh hanging in strips from a skeletal hand. Louie kept on snapping, winding on, snapping, and then he started running for his life.

Oil storage tanks buckled and burst open. A wall of black liquid surged over the running men and their families, knocking them off their feet. They struggled to keep their heads above the black tide, choking as they tried to breathe through oil-filled lungs. Louie had run out of film. A wall of oil thundered toward him. He was going to die. He saw an empty oil drum, dropped the camera inside, and slammed the lid on it as the black wave came at him.

The derricks were gone, swallowed up by the unstable ground. Men clinging to debris were sucked beneath the earth's surface as it liquefied. Colossal forces ripped through the unstable rocks deep below. A few desperate men ran for higher ground. Pools of oil beneath a rig ignited, sending tongues of flame into the sky. The surrounding swamp water became a blazing hell. Black smoke belched into the air. The ground split open in an explosion of flaming gas. Women and children, their clothes on fire, were sucked below the surface of the burning oil as they tried to escape.

Louie raced to his car and threw himself inside. He fired up the motor and hit the gas. The car lurched forward, its wheels spinning in the oil. Louie frantically tried to get traction, but it was too late. A wall of oil smashed into the car, turning it onto its side. He tried to open the door above him. But as he fought to get a grip, he felt the earth beneath the car fall away, and he plunged into blackness.

SEVENTY

BUTTE LA ROSE, LOUISIANA – Present day

WHILE THE DIARY was being deciphered, Chandler studied the manuscripts that Phaedon had finished stabilizing. The more Chandler read, the more it became obvious that Tumblety was either way ahead of his time or insane. He picked up a letter from the editor of *The Lancet*.

We find your paper both unbelievable and a travesty of the medical profession. The possibility of artificial gestation within external uteri is frankly preposterous, let alone the question of its ethics. Kindly desist from your groundless claims and tasteless suppositions . . .

Chandler turned away from the screen. He felt like he needed to wash the images from his brain. He tapped a number on his cell phone.

Duke answered immediately. "Hi, Chandler, what's up?" He was headed to the Iberville Parish Library to meet up with Roxie and, from the sounds of it, had Chandler on speakerphone.

"I'm going over some of the stabilized papers and documents now. Dr. Tumblety was one messed-up quack."

Duke laughed. "Tell me something I don't know."

Chandler continued, "Seems he had delusions of grandeur when it came to the act of procreation—"

"You talking about his collecting habits?"

"I read about that, but no. I've got some letters here from the editor of *The Lancet.* Seems he was doing research on ectogenesis."

Duke shouted into the microphone, the car engine noise threatening to drown out his voice. "Ecto-what?"

Chandler looked at a crude drawing on the screen: pictures of tubes leading to a glass specimen jar containing a uterus linked to some kind of pump.

"It means growing a fetus in an artificial womb."

"Sounds like this cat Tumblety was way ahead of his time—and out of his gourd," Duke said.

"Yes," Chandler replied. "No doubt about his mental state. From his notes, it looks like he thought he could grow a fetus within the female reproductive system, only the female didn't figure in his plans."

"So his uterus collection wasn't just about some sick revenge gig," Duke said.

"Seems not."

"Okay, that all sounds pretty freaky: I'll swing by later and check it out once I've met up with Roxie. I need her to track down some company records."

"Okay, I'll catch up with you later."

The line went dead.

Duke was approaching the outskirts of Plaquemine. A crowd of people stood on the street listening to a man talking from a raised platform. A familiar black Escalade was parked nearby. Agent Kale leaned against the hood.

Duke slowed the car, pulled over to the side of the road, and wound his window down. He listened to Blackburn's rhetoric as it crackled through the PA system.

"So I'm telling you that the legislation in this country is sucking the life out of you people—hell, it's sucking the life out of me! We all understand that the earth's resources aren't going to last forever. We know we have to be responsible with the whole issue of pollution . . ."

Kale looked in Duke's direction and spoke into a walkie-talkie. Blackburn's speech reached a crescendo.

". . . but I think the whole perspective of the environment versus the people has gotten out of hand. I believe that it's time to open up the swampland, to use its natural resources for the good of the people. I mean, hell, I understand the critters need to be protected, but what's more important, a few gators, or the people who need to earn enough money to send their children to school, to put food on the table, to have a better life?"

Kale headed toward Duke's car. He had two agents with him, and neither of them looked pleased to see the deputy. Meanwhile, Blackburn certainly looked like he had the people on his side. He wound up his speech, pointing at the cheering crowds.

"With your votes, I can turn this thing around! We can bring prosperity to this area again, open up a new wave of industry and jobs for the people that matter most: YOU! YOU! And YOU!"

He stabbed his finger like a rapier at the rapt crowd. Duke accelerated past Kale and the agents, leaving them in a cloud of swirling dust. Kale took off his sunglasses and wiped them clean. He stared after Duke's car and pulled out his cell.

Duke stood next to Roxie in the library. Some old ledgers and black-and-white pictures of oil fields were spread across the desk. She had her laptop open and was busy searching online databases. Duke looked around the library with a sense of nostalgia. He'd spent a lot of his early days there, before it had been modernized, thumbing through detective novels as a boy and reference books later on. He half expected to see old Ma Bradlington, the white-haired lady who had ruled the library when he was a student with a stern look and her clicking teeth. But she'd been dead for many years.

Roxie studied the screen. "It seems that Francis Tumblety adopted a child and brought him up as Adam Blackburn. Apparently he took pity on a woman from London who he met over here—"

Duke looked up. "I'd say he did more than take pity on her given the obvious physical resemblance between Tumblety and the Blackburns," he said. "Chandler was right on the money with that one."

Roxie shook her head. "But that doesn't make sense. By all accounts, he loathed women."

Duke shrugged. "Maybe he needed a son and heir, and she fitted in with his plans."

"But what happened to her?" Roxie said.

"We'd need her name to find that out," Duke said.

Roxie said, "Adam was only twelve years old when Tumblety died. In 1915, when he was twenty-six, he set up Blackburn Oil and Gas in Spirit's Swamp."

Roxie picked up a sheet of paper from the stack of old records and started a search on her laptop. Duke watched her fingers dance over the keys. She continued talking as information scrolled past on the screen.

"The great storm hit in 1915, by which time he'd already made a fortune from the shares he sold in the company."

Duke studied the papers. "So the deal he did with Phoenix Oil in the thirties?"

Roxie flicked through some records on her screen. "Company records should show up something . . ."

A scan of an old contract flashed up. "Here we are. Seems Phoenix Oil wanted the land for future drilling. They'd seen other sites dry up, and wanted something for their land bank. So it looks like, in exchange for half a million shares in Phoenix Oil, Adam Blackburn ceded the land in and around Spirit's Swamp, to be assigned in perpetuity until such time as drilling commenced, at which point, a fifty percent split would be deemed payable to the surviving members of the Blackburn line—provided the agreed level of geological and structural clearances had been fulfilled."

Duke rubbed his eyes. The information was piling up too fast for him to unscramble. "Which means what, exactly?"

Roxie smiled; she was just hitting her stride. "Well, it seems Adam Blackburn was pretty advanced back then when it came to taking care of the environment."

"Come again?" Duke said.

"The contract specified a certain level of reclamation take place in the swamp. The clearance of polluted land, importation of sterile soil, draining and filtering of toxic materials." Roxie looked up. "Doing that would cost a fortune even today. Back then, with their limited equipment and technology, it would have been unsustainable."

Duke nodded, "So that's why Blackburn is so hell-bent on cleaning up the swamp. Because once he's fulfilled the contract—"

"Exactly. Once he gets elected, he can change the designation of the swamp from a protected wildlife area to one he can drill in and start to open up the wetlands to commercialization," she said.

"And his family goes back to doing what they do best, earning a fortune." Duke thought this through. "But there's something else going on out at the plant. There must be."

Roxie looked at him, spoke carefully. "What do you mean?"

Duke went on. "The bodies we found in the swamp, we found them by accident. But all of a sudden the Feds are all over us, along with Agent Kale, who's in the pocket of Governor Blackburn. Why would someone who wants to exploit a protected area of natural beauty be so worried just because we dig up some century-old bodies?"

They looked at each other.

Roxie spoke first. "I'd say there's something in the swamp he doesn't want us to find."

SEVENTY-ONE

BATON ROUGE, LOUISIANA – Present day

ROXIE SAT IN a small laboratory off from the main science building. It was more of a storeroom now. It had been the original lab before the new facility had been enlarged around it. There were racks of test tubes and retorts lining the walls, and stacks of broken equipment piled up awaiting disposal. In the corner of the room wheezed an ancient fridge containing soft drinks, rather than the spores and bacteria that it had previously housed. Windows ran down one side of the room overlooking a car park in front of University Lake. An old wooden bench in the center of the room was cluttered with filing trays and a centrifuge.

Roxie sat in front of it and worked at her laptop. She was using a MinION sequencer to analyze the sample Jonas had given her. The device was only four inches long and an inch wide and was plugged into the USB socket of her laptop. Networked with the university's supercomputer, it could process data incredibly fast, and within two hours she was looking at the results from the mitochondrial sample that Jonas had provided from the youngest of the women found in the swamp.

She called Chandler, who was at the old refrigeration warehouse. The terahertz camera was starting to uncover the pages of the diary from the carriage, and he was engrossed in the century-old information that was being thrown up. She told him he needed to come out to the lab, and promised him that his trip would be worthwhile. She smiled at his bad attempt at innuendo before ending the call.

She uploaded the DNA sequence to NDNAD, the National DNA Database in the UK, and CODIS, the Combined DNA Index System in the USA, hoping to get a familial hit. Now all she had to do was wait.

An hour after her call, she heard a tap on the frosted-glass porthole in the wooden door leading into the lab and saw Chandler's shadow. She opened the door and let him in.

Chandler looked at her as she stood against the light from the windows behind, her blonde hair gleaming like spun gold. The white linen blouse she wore set off her tan, the dark outline of her bra strap curving over her toned shoulders. Her jeans clung to her hips and her eyes shone above a wide smile.

She gave him a hug and a kiss. "You look tired."

"Too much time staring at screens and faded manuscripts," he said. He waved an arm around the room. "Nice apartment you have here."

"It's one up from the warehouse," Roxie said. "At least I can see daylight."

She moved over to the laptop, sat in the chair, and tapped some keys. He could smell her perfume as she passed and hoped it had been applied for his visit.

"You were very mysterious on the phone," he said.

She flicked him a smile. "Not really. This is just something you need to see."

Chandler nodded at the sequencer plugged into her laptop. "Is that it?" he said. "They used to be the size of a fridge."

"Not anymore," Roxie replied. "This uses nanopores. It's fourth-generation DNA sequencing."

She smiled at his puzzled expression.

"Remember out in the swamp, when I talked about smashing up mitochondrial DNA, and using software to match up the overlap within the fragments?"

Chandler nodded. "Something about electropherograms," he said.

"Yes," she said. "This uses a tiny protein, a nanopore, with a hollow tube at its core, just a few billionths of a meter wide. It can decipher the sequence of a DNA strand as it threads through the pore, like a piece of ticker tape." She paused and looked at him for a response.

"Right." He nodded. "So, this does the job in one go?"

"That's right," Roxie replied, moving over to a large monitor connected to her laptop. "Look at this."

Chandler stared at the screen. It looked like a digital silhouette of a city skyline, but with some echoes overlapping parts of the readout.

Roxie tapped the display. "This is the DNA from the sample Jonas sent me. Let's call it Mary Jane Kelly's for argument's sake."

"It's looking that way," Chandler said. He looked back at the screen. "What are those echoes?"

"Have you heard of chimerism?" Roxie asked.

"Is that when somebody has two kinds of DNA in their body?"

Roxie nodded. "Yes. You're looking at evidence of it in Mary's DNA. But there's something else in her sequence that I'll get to in a minute," she said. "Chimerism can happen for a variety of reasons. One is superfecundation, when separate ova are fertilized by sperm from two different fathers. The woman has to have slept with a second partner within days of her initial fertilization. It's a common occurrence among animals, like dogs and cats. If one of the fetuses doesn't go to full term, they merge in the womb, and the surviving fetus becomes an organism with intermingled DNA.

Chandler looked puzzled. "So Mary could have had twins?"

Roxie nodded. "Yes. But as I said, that's only one way chimerism can occur."

She clicked on a file. Another DNA sequence appeared next to the Mary Jane Kelly sample.

"This is what a normal chimeric sequence looks like." She pointed to a part of the screen. "You can see there are two unique DNA profiles." She pointed at Mary Jane Kelly's DNA sequence. "Whereas here, see these echoes in her sequence?"

Chandler stared at the screen. "Multiple DNA?" he asked.

Roxie nodded. "Yes."

Chandler shook his head. "And how does that happen?"

Roxie shrugged. "In some cases, our cells mutate and take on a different DNA. They're called genetic mosaics. But the ability to genetically engineer something like that certainly wasn't around when Mary was alive."

Roxie's laptop gave a soft chime.

"Something up?" Chandler asked.

Roxie nodded. "I uploaded her DNA into the NDNAD and CODIS databases. Looks like I've got a hit from the UK database."

She clicked on the attachment. Chandler watched her. She just sat there staring at the contents. He put a hand on her shoulder. Her perfume enveloped him in an intoxicating cloud. He could feel the warmth of her skin through the thin cloth, the back of her neck taut with bronzed muscle. She looked spectacular. He snapped back into focus, and read the name on the screen. It was a name he was very familiar with.

Chandler Travis.

They sat among the whir of the air conditioner, the shudder of the fridge compressor, and the distant sounds of the campus, trying to take in what they'd just read.

Chandler cleared his throat. "This puts a whole new complexion on things, doesn't it?"

Roxie nodded. "It means you're related to the woman we believe to be Mary Jane Kelly."

"Are you thinking what I'm thinking?" Chandler asked.

"That Edward Travis could be the father?" Roxie said. "He was around during that period, and involved in the case. His pocket watch turned up in the carriage, and the family history says he met someone and she had twins," she went on. "Maybe Edward managed to track these women down, followed them out here, and got involved with Mary in the process."

Roxie watched the screen as Chandler's DNA sequence downloaded on her laptop.

"I wasn't expecting to find you in the database," she said.

Chandler thought about that.

"They took blood from me back in 2005."

"After the terrorist attack?" Roxie asked.

Chandler nodded.

"They wanted to eliminate your DNA from the other victims," she said.

The screen filled with a DNA sequence. Roxie adjusted the brightness on the screen as it fought with the sun coming through the windows. She overlaid the two DNA sequences, her slim brown fingers flickering across the keys. The similarities between the two were obvious. Digital echoes reverberating back over a century.

She looked at Chandler. "It's a match. If this really is Mary Jane Kelly's DNA, then you're related. No doubt about it." She paused for a moment and looked closer at the screen, then said, "And you're also chimeric."

Chandler stared at the display, fascinated. "Really? So why don't I have different-colored eyes, or striped patterns on my skin?"

"You're thinking of Blaschko's lines," Roxie said. "Everybody has those, but you'd need to be under a UV light to see them. Chimeras sometimes have far more visible patterns as each DNA instructs the skin to be darker or lighter." She smiled at him. "I don't know if you have any interesting patterns on your body"—she paused—"yet. Besides, chimeric DNA can manifest anywhere in the body. It can even be in an internal organ."

He watched as she bent over the keyboard, his eyes drawn to the way her breasts crushed against the thin fabric of her blouse, and imagined her pressed against him. He looked back to the digital hills and valleys stretching across the screen.

"My family tree only goes back as far as Edward Travis and his daughter Evelyn Mary Travis. So if Mary Kelly gave birth to twins from two different fathers . . ."

Roxie nodded. "There could be someone out there with a familial link to the other twin."

"So we might get a hit from a descendant of the other twin. If they're on the database."

Roxie nodded. "They'd also have to be chimeric, so the other part of their DNA matched yours," she said.

"That's like looking for a sperm in a haystack," Chandler replied.

Roxie swiveled around on the chair and gave him a hug. He felt as if he were in the center of an electrical storm.

"This must be weird," she said, releasing him and looking at his face.

"It's not something that happens every day, I'll give you that," he said, his skin still tingling from her touch.

"Could your father have known you were chimeric?" Roxie asked. "It might have come up when they carried out the original tests for cancer. Maybe they told him, or it was in his notes?"

Chandler thought back to those last few days. It had been a maelstrom of hospital visits and phone calls, consultants and specialists.

"They did ask me for a second blood sample when there was a possibility he might need a transfusion."

He remembered his father playing the Beatles song over and over again and his final words. Roxie looked at him. They both said it together.

"I am the eggman."

He looked at the screen as the words echoed through his head.

I am he as you are he as you are me and we are all together . . .

"Maybe that's what he meant. He was trying to tell me I was a chimera like him. He would have had the results back from the hospital from both of our DNA, but with all the drugs he was on, he couldn't get it straight in his head."

He looked at Roxie. "So how did we end up with chimerism? It isn't hereditary, is it?"

Roxie shook her head. "No. And we don't know why Mary Jane Kelly has multiple DNA. It's possible that somewhere among the noncoding, junk, or dark DNA, something caused a mutation. There's a school of thought that says that the DNA we think of as junk is there to protect us from mutations, to switch off and lock up any rogue DNA that could corrupt our genetic blueprint."

Chandler smiled. "Like genetic jailers?"

"Yes," Roxie said. "Scientists have discovered a molecular gate that embraces DNA during cell division. Once it's protected, the double helix starts to unwind and begins the copying process. It could allow chimeric DNA to pass down through the generations, only unlocking the gate when it was triggered by a specific biological event: in this case, fertilization."

Chandler looked at her. "A molecular gate? That's a stab in the dark."

Roxie shrugged. "Maybe. But if you do have a twin out there who shares your DNA, I can load your sequence into the database and see if it throws anything up."

Chandler nodded. Roxie looked at him, concerned by how distant he seemed.

"What is it?" she asked.

He shook his head. "I don't know. Molecular gates, the superthing?

Roxie smiled. "Superfecundation."

"Yes, that. Chimerism, dark DNA, mosaics, dead twins being absorbed! It's like a bad horror movie."

Roxie shrugged. "It's man and nature, red in tooth and claw. In times of desperation, animals eat their young. Absorbing a dead twin at the cellular level is just an efficient use of resources as far as the human body is concerned."

"Maybe," Chandler said.

Roxie reached out and squeezed his shoulder. "Let's look at what we do know," she said. "Nowadays we genetically engineer the DNA from three parents or more to produce a healthy baby. We use recombinant DNA, blood transfusions, stem cell injections . . . All of these situations can cause microchimerism. Multiple DNA."

Chandler looked at her. "But there wasn't any genetic engineering back then, so what does that leave? Blood transfusions? Could that be how she ended up with multiple DNA?" he asked.

Roxie said nothing. Chandler went on.

"What about stem cells?"

Roxie nodded. "Yes, in the field of regenerative medicine they believe they can use them to regrow almost any cell in the human body."

"Immortality?" Chandler said.

"That's where the big bucks are," Roxie said. "But as usual, nature's ahead of us."

"What do you mean?" Chandler asked.

Roxie looked at him with a smile. "Back in your country, scientists at Nottingham University have discovered that planarians, flatworms, are able to regenerate indefinitely. You cut them in half, and they regenerate new organs. They've been cutting worms in half for years and have cloned over two thousand worms from one individual," she said.

"I don't think I'm ready to be cut in half just yet," Chandler said. "But I'll give immortality a trial run." He rubbed his tired eyes. "Blanche talked about the änglamakerska," he said.

Roxie nodded. "Yes, 'angel makers.' She thought they could have been running a baby farm out in Saint Malo."

Something was gnawing away in the back of Chandler's mind. Then it came to him.

"Babies! Aren't umbilical cords rich in stem cells?" he said.

"You think Tumblety could have been using blood from the umbilical cords?" Roxie asked.

"I don't know."

"Taking or giving blood was pretty risky back then," Roxie said. "They had no idea about blood typing. I suppose they could have gotten lucky. If none of them were RH and some of them were type O, they might not have had problems. It would at the very least have resulted in microchimerism."

Chandler rubbed his temples, tried to massage away the headache he could feel building. He said, "Until the database or the diary throws up something, we've reached a dead end."

He looked at Roxie. She looked incredible, staring back at him frankly. It was now or never. He touched her face, leaned forward, and kissed her softly on the lips before pulling back.

Roxie smiled, moved over to the door and slid the lock across before coming back over to him. She gently held the back of his neck and kissed him. Deeply.

Chandler felt the heat of her flesh through the thin blouse that clung to her breasts. Her hands moved over him. He heard the soft swish of his belt as she pulled it through the loops of his jeans. She pushed her chair out of the way with her foot, slid out of her jeans like a snake shedding its skin, and revealed her amazing legs.

She laughed. "Time to check out those Blaschko's lines."

He unbuttoned her blouse, and the fabric floated off her shoulders. She pulled his shirt over his head and tossed it onto the bench. He reached behind her and unclipped her bra. Her breasts spilled into him. She was beaming, and his headache had vanished. They both slid to the floor in a naked heap. She straddled him and he cupped her breasts. They were every bit as magnificent as he'd imagined. The heat grew between them and he smiled so wide he felt his head would split in half. And then it was over and they lay nestled against each other on the floor as the sunlight blazed through the windows above.

SEVENTY-TWO

BUTTE LA ROSE, LOUISIANA – Present day

DUKE PULLED UP at an old gas station a few miles outside Butte La Rose and the refrigeration warehouse. The faded wooden sign hung on rusted chains, its cream and red paint bubbled and flakey. The remnants of the name were barely readable: just an *S* and an *A* were visible.

A grizzled old African American man headed out of the small office to serve him. His worn baseball cap confirmed the name of the station: *SAMMY'S*. The man's face was deeply etched with lines, evidence of a hard life. The station must have been packed with customers on their way to the oil fields at one time, but that was many years ago, and the old diner next to the gas station looked like it had been boarded up for centuries.

The man nodded to him. "Fill her up?"

Duke hopped out of the car and stretched his neck. "Sure."

The old man unhooked the nozzle and went toward the filler cap. Duke popped it open. The man put the nozzle in and spat.

"You gonna need your own oil well to fill this sucker up."

Duke smiled. "Tell me about it."

The sound of a distant phone ringing came from the office. The old man shot an irritated look at the sound.

"Damn. Don't she ever give up?"

Duke nodded to the office. "You get it—I got this."

The old man smiled gratefully, revealing a flash of gold-capped teeth.

"Thanks. My sister's going through some kinda crisis. Man trouble . . ."

He went into the office. Duke watched the numbers go around as his car swallowed the fuel like a hungry horse. His mind drifted back to his conversation with Jesse about Blanche's old car.

Every time we took it out for a run, it would cut out. Never did find out what the problem was. Something to do with the fuel, maybe . . .

The gas continued to slosh into the car, making an echoing sound as the tank filled.

Next to the Packards, the Pierces were the ones the rich folk would go for. Most reliable car ever built. Wouldn't stop till you ran out of gas . . .

Duke snapped back to the present as fuel overflowed from the tank onto his shoes.

He jumped back. "Damn!"

They lay on the floor for what seemed like a lifetime. But it only felt that way because of how fast things had happened between them. Chandler had thrown a pile of lab coats from the back of the door onto the floor to make a comfortable place to lie. When the frenzy of their lovemaking had cooled, he'd realized it had been merely postponed from that night out in the swamp. He hadn't been that close to a woman for over a decade, and now he felt like he'd washed himself clean. All the angst, the blame, and the fear had been cauterized by the white heat of their lovemaking. Whether it was the kind of love that endured, he neither knew nor cared at that moment.

She nestled against his shoulder. A strand of damp blonde hair clung to her temple. He moved it gently with his finger. Her eyelids fluttered. She yawned, put her hand over her mouth.

"Pardon me. Where are my manners?"

He looked over at her. "I would imagine they're with your clothes on the bench."

They each wore a lab coat as an impromptu dressing gown.

She smiled up at him. "Well, I don't know which sequence of your DNA you pulled that performance from, but I'm glad you did."

He grinned like a goofy teenager. "I don't know myself. But you certainly managed to open whatever molecular gate you needed to. It's been a while."

She laughed. "I think I kinda knew that when you kept asking me how I was doing."

"Well, you know how polite us Brits are," he said.

She uncurled herself from him and stood up. The lab coat gaped, revealing her tan body against the white material. Even wearing a drab lab coat, she was spectacular.

She saw him staring. "See something you like?"

He reached up. Flicked the coat off her shoulder like a politician unveiling a statue at an opening ceremony. The coat puddled around her ankles as he pulled her down to him.

"Again?" she asked.

He smiled. "Of course."

She squirmed onto him. Her slender arms wrapped themselves around his neck, and she gave a low moan as they connected for the second time in an hour.

Duke pulled up outside the old de Chiel place, fished in the glove box, and pulled out his Maglite. He walked toward the garage, ducking under the crime scene tape that fluttered in the breeze, and pried the door open, the hinges squealing in protest. He peered into the gloom, flicked the Maglite on, and shone it around the dusty interior. Cobwebs hung in ghostly shrouds from the wooden supports, and a film of dust clung to every surface. The beam illuminated the brass gas cap of the Pierce-Arrow sitting hunched in the shadows. Duke moved over to it, and after a struggle, managed to unscrew the heavy metal fuel cap. He shone the flashlight down into the hole. Its beam reflected off the surface of the fuel, sending circles of yellow light dancing across his face as he gently rocked the car. Something was floating inside the tank.

He looked around the garage and saw a rusty coat hanger lying on top of the rough workbench that sat to one side of the garage. He grabbed it and straightened it out, forming a small hook on one end. He poked it into the tank and fished around. The hook snagged on something, and he began to pull it out, but it caught on the edge of the tank opening and plopped back down into the fuel with a soft splash.

Duke shook his head and tried again, muttering to himself, "You been there a long time—I can wait a few more seconds."

He hooked it again and carefully eased it out into the light. It was a cylindrical shape wrapped tightly in oilskin and tied with kitchen twine. He went over to a toolbox and rummaged around inside. He found an old knife, oily and still sharp. He sawed through the twine, put the knife down on the workbench, and unwrapped the oilskin. Inside were some rolled-up notes and some letters. Duke started to read through them. The letters were addressed to Blanche.

SEVENTY-THREE

LONDON, ENGLAND – 1894

THE LIGHT FLASHED off the sharp blade as it sliced through the air before plunging up to its hilt in the stiff black bodice. There was a moment's silence, then a slightly breathless but firm voice spoke.

"That's very realistic, I must say. And the blood, where does that come from?"

Queen Victoria's eyes sparkled with excitement. Though she was in her seventies, Fitch could see the zest for life and the childish enthusiasm for innovation she had embraced during her reign.

"It has a concealed syringe in the hilt that ejects the blood when needed," he said.

Victoria took the knife from him and studied it with an innate curiosity.

Fitch continued, "I thought it best not to cover you with pig's blood. It is the devil to wash out." He looked around the impressive white drawing room at Buckingham Palace. With the architect John Nash's molded plaster ceiling, the vast chandelier, exquisite green silk hangings, and the Axminster carpet of russet and gold, it looked more like a stage set than a real room.

"I can imagine," Victoria replied, chuckling to herself. She handed the knife back to Fitch and settled into her chair, then gestured to the two people who hovered in the background.

"For goodness' sake, you two, will you just sit down? I'm not going to eat you. This is just an informal meeting. You have carried out a most extraordinary operation under extremely difficult and dangerous circumstances, Mr. Fitch here in particular."

Fitch shook his head. "Not at all, Your Majesty. We all had a part to play."

"Don't be modest, Mr. Fitch. It was crucial that Eddy believed his mistress had been murdered. I'm only sorry there wasn't another way to rein him in." She paused, her face suddenly sad with the thought of Eddy's suffering. "But he was a difficult young man."

She turned to Triton. "We were lucky you were able to extend the original plan to encompass a far grander scheme to divert the public's attention."

Triton said, "There really was no other option, Your Majesty. Sooner or later Eddy would have been exposed and the fabric of the monarchy and our nation compromised. He could have handed the Fenians a political opportunity that would have brought the government down. I know what happened hit him hard, but in the long run it acted as a curb to his more . . . dangerous habits. After all, both myself and Your Majesty had his best interests at heart."

Queen Victoria nodded. "Yes, he was a strange boy, but we loved him for all that. And now he's dead."

She turned to address Triton's companion. "But you, my dear—I know one expects sacrifices for queen and country, but yours was above and beyond."

The woman known as Fay leaned forward. Her chestnut hair tumbled like a waterfall across her shoulders. She took Triton's hand and squeezed it. "We both made sacrifices."

Triton nodded. "Queen and country, Your Majesty."

The queen smiled. "Well, you all did an incredible job. Do go on."

Triton steepled his fingers together. "As you know, we lost the women in the storm that hit Louisiana, along with one of the men we had out there with them."

Victoria nodded. "I'm sorry to hear that, but forces of nature are outside even my control. And what about the other man—Tumblety? I believe they both had quite a sordid history."

Triton nodded. "Yes, but sometimes you have to deal with the devil to get to heaven, Your Majesty."

"Quite. I believe they used the situation for their own ends?"

"Yes," Triton said, "that was an unfortunate state of affairs."

Victoria nodded. "Go on."

Triton paused before replying. He hated loose ends, but in an operation of that size and complexity, they were inevitable. You could anticipate most of the possibilities, keep a balance of control using a mixture of loyalty, fear, and money, but there was always a random element that could complicate even the best of plans—and in this case it was love. They could never have anticipated the tenacity of the young reporter who traveled halfway across the world in search of the woman he loved. The storm had done them a favor. Without knowing whether Mary was dead or alive, Travis didn't dare risk exposing their operation for fear of jeopardizing her safety.

Victoria listened while he told her of the advantages alongside national security that had occurred as a result of the Ripper conspiracy. The growth of the press, the improvements to the police force, and the increased safety on the streets of London, along with the progress made in the slum tenements. He skipped over the land deals that he had personally benefited from. After all, some sacrifices needed to be rewarded with something more substantial than the glow of national pride.

Despite her age, the queen didn't miss a trick and honed in on the only real threat to their continued stability.

"Are you sure that the journalist . . . Edward Travis?" she asked.

Triton nodded.

"Yes, Travis—will remain silent? After all, the information would be worth a fortune," she said.

Triton had a ready reply. "He's not interested in money, Your Majesty; otherwise, we could have bought his silence. He was in love with one of the women, Mary Jane Kelly. Without knowing her fate, he will do nothing to jeopardize her safety."

Victoria looked sad for a moment. She, more than anybody, knew what it was like to lose someone you loved more than life itself. It had taken her decades to get over the loss of her beloved Albert.

"And if he finds out she's dead?" Victoria asked.

Triton spoke gently. "There can be no proof without a body, and there is none. Over two thousand people died in that storm. The fate of six people, who had already been presumed dead, thousands of miles from home in the middle of a storm will never be discovered—trust me, Your Majesty."

Victoria shifted in her chair. Her body was stiffening with age, and as the days rolled past it became more difficult to get comfortable or have a good night's sleep.

She fixed Triton with a steely look. "Very well. You will continue to monitor the situation and ensure nothing untoward happens to him while I am alive." She leaned forward and smiled. "And I intend to live forever."

Triton answered, "I wouldn't wish it any other way, Your Majesty."

The trio stood up, bowed, and took their leave from the magnificent room, leaving the most powerful woman in England looking after them as they walked through the ornate doors and out of the palace.

Triton was glad to get out into the crisp morning air. He never felt comfortable under Victoria's unswerving gaze. Out in the real world there was still a journalist, along with his daughter and the midwife that delivered her. He wasn't worried about the journalist, or Tumblety; they were both more or less under his control. But he had no means of knowing where the daughter and midwife were, or even if they were still alive. That was a situation he shared with Travis.

He waved goodbye to Fitch. "We'll see you at the theater this evening for *Becket*. I hear Henry and Ellen are tremendous."

Fitch nodded as he headed off. "They always are."

Triton took Fay's hand, leaned over, and kissed her.

"Why don't we go straight home? I could do with a drink," he said.

She gave a throaty laugh and dragged him down the street. "I think we'll be having more than drinks, my love."

SEVENTY-FOUR

NEW ORLEANS, LOUISIANA – 1946

EDWARD LOOKED ACROSS the ward of LaGarde General Hospital. Most of the men surrounding him were casualties of the war. Some had missing limbs, others disfigured faces and horrific burns. Sometimes their screams made sleep impossible. He was now in his seventies and his lungs had finally given up on him, his breathing more difficult with each passing day. The morphine kept the pain at bay, and the nurses were ministering angels to him and the many patients they had to deal with. But the hospital was soon going to close, and he knew his time was also running out.

The hospital had a checkered history. The Orleans Levee Board had begun a project in the twenties to reclaim land from Lake Pontchartrain. They built a weir out into the lake and pumped sand behind it, then constructed Lakeshore Drive and its seawall. But just as it was ready for residential development, the Federal government had stepped in and leased the whole area for wartime bases. A vast military complex was built, including a hospital with 1,650 beds in anticipation of casualties, along with a POW camp. But now the war was over and people needed houses, not beds. Things were changing.

Edward still enjoyed reading the newspapers. They reminded him of happier days, when he'd been a part of the journalistic process.

He'd been admitted into the hospital under his own name. If he was going to die, it was going to be as Edward Richard Travis.

He touched the package by his bedside and smiled at Blanche's name and address. It was a kind of ritual for him. He'd followed her progress in the papers and seen her photos along with the stories she wrote, following the sick and the homeless around America. Since the war had ended, many veterans had fallen on hard times, unable either to find work due to their injuries or to cope with civilian life after the horrors they'd witnessed. What was referred to as shellshock back in the day was now being looked at as a separate psychological problem that affected thousands of ex-soldiers.

Catching a flicker of color, Edward looked up. Somebody had entered the other end of the ward. She was probably in her fifties, with blonde hair and wearing a bright scarf. She stood talking to the matron, who pointed down the ward in his direction. The woman nodded and smiled. She walked toward him, her steps light, her back straight.

Edward stared at her. There was something about the way she moved that jolted his memory back over fifty years in the blink of an eye, to another pretty blonde woman. She came up to the end of the bed and read his name on the clipboard that hung there.

"Edward Travis?" she asked, and smiled at him.

He coughed into a handkerchief. His eyes watered with the pain.

"Yes," he managed to say, his voice weak.

She came closer to look at him. "My name is Evelyn—Evelyn Travis. I'm your daughter."

The result of his love for Mary was standing in front of him. And then she was wrapping her arms around him, tears streaming down her cheeks.

She pulled back and studied his face. "I didn't think we would ever meet. Mary told me about you when she visited, when I was little. She told me it was a big secret, all very hush hush. She made it into a game. And then when she stopped coming and I grew, Evelyn—my mother, I mean—she told me a different story. About how Mary was my real mother. About what you'd found out, and why Mary and her friends had to leave England."

She gestured to a chair next to the bed. "May I?"

Edward nodded. She sat down.

"I expect you have a lot of questions?"

He looked at her. He had only one that mattered. If she really was his daughter, then one of them was answered. The others were important, but not as much as meeting a daughter you'd never seen.

"Ms. Stocker—Evelyn?" he asked.

Evelyn gave him a sad look, squeezed his hand. "The woman who raised me? She joined the Red Cross and went out to serve in Egypt during the First World War. She sent me a picture of her sitting on a camel. She looked happy."

"What happened?" Edward asked.

"She got some dreadful disease. From mosquitoes."

Edward nodded. He'd read about malaria and its devastating effects. He summoned up as much courage as he could muster, then asked, "And Mary . . . your mother?"

Evelyn sighed. "She stopped coming after the storm. Ms. Stocker and I left New Orleans ahead of it—we couldn't risk staying. We were meant to hear from Mary and meet up with you both. But when we didn't hear anything . . ." She trailed off.

Edward nodded. "By the time I got to where Mary was staying, there wasn't much left. I didn't know whether she was dead or alive." He looked at her, imagined what Mary would have looked like at her age.

"Ms. Stocker told me that it was important that we weren't found. She thought you'd find us, or we'd find you. But with the chaos, and then the war . . . I met someone and fell pregnant. He joined up and didn't come back. I had his son, John."

"The war changed a lot of lives," Edward said, sadly.

Evelyn nodded. "Yes, but I kept the Travis name, passed it on to John. He's married now and living in England. They've just had a baby boy. Peter."

Edward smiled. "I'm glad. But how did you find me?"

Evelyn gave a sad smile. "Pure chance. I was visiting one of Mary's old friends on the ward. I saw your name on the board. Travis isn't that common a surname. And here you are."

She leaned over and gave him a kiss on the cheek. "I'm sorry it took so long."

Edward smiled weakly. "Better late than never." He reached over and picked up the parcel. "If it's not too much trouble, I'd like you to post this for me."

She weighed it in her hand, raised her eyebrows, fixed him with her blue eyes.

"I imagine there's a story behind this?" she asked.

He squeezed her hand. "I think we both have a lot to talk about."

And so it was. While the sun washed through the dusty windows of the ward, they sat and talked. And when they'd heard everything there was to hear, she leaned down and gave him a kiss, picked up the package, and walked down the length of the ward and out of his life.

SEVENTY-FIVE

NEW ORLEANS, LOUISIANA – Present day

MARSHA STARED OUT of the office window across the New Orleans skyline. The heat of the sun was waning, and the headlights of the cars below started to flicker on. Everything she had predicted was starting to fall into place. The dark mirrors of the future whirled in front of her. The fate lines of Roman and Chandler were aligned on a course that was inevitable. She had tried to guide Roman on a path that would save him, but he was intractable. Marsha could do nothing more than prepare for what was to come.

She had driven out to the Raffeti house that afternoon. The sisters had met her at the door. The blind one stayed in the shadows, as if hiding from the light, her tongue trilling. Marsha followed them down through the foundations of the house to the place where they did their work.

For well over a century, they had carried out the procedures that Dr. Tumblety had put in place. Originally, they had worked with the unwanted babies and the stillborn fetuses from the brothels of Baton Rouge and New Orleans. There had been countless setbacks, and they had come near to giving up on many occasions. But gradually, the victims they harnessed for their experiments had lived longer, and the results became more predictable. Things had reached a turning point. Marsha had been phoned that morning with news of a breakthrough.

The sister with the twisted face had bombarded her with science over the phone. Marsha told her to slow down and listened as she explained. Something they'd been trying to achieve for over a century was now a reality. All those years ago, Dr. Tumblety had been derided for believing he could produce a fetus outside of the womb. It had seemed impossible at the time, and his methods of experimentation, had he been caught, would have earned him the noose. But fate took a hand, and the government had offered him a way out that allowed him to continue with his experiments. And now the process had exceeded their wildest expectations.

Marsha went down to the dank catacombs. The glass troughs containing the biological growth cells were stacked beneath the low ceiling. She picked up an insulated container and filled it with the cells and nutrients necessary for their needs. The insulated container was essential for safe transportation. The sisters were already preparing to remove anything that might implicate them, or Roman. She loaded the container into her car and drove back to New Orleans. She used the private express elevator from the underground parking lot up to her office. She put the container in the refrigerator in the small kitchen to one side of her room, poured herself a drink, and went over to the panoramic glass wall that looked out over the city.

She let her mind float free, and was pleased to see that some of the obsidian mirrors that whirled around her had become a flickering bronze color. The sisters' latest development had already managed to control the impact of Roman's obstinacy. No matter what happened during the final confrontation between Roman and Chandler, they could begin again.

The whirling mirrors started to align across her mental horizon. Each glittering facet flickered with an alternative future. By channeling her will, she could meld their possibilities to the least destructive outcome for them all. One thing still weighed on her mind, though. When she had talked with Roman, she'd held back information she knew about the English detective. With each successor in the Blackburn dynasty, the chain of memory was dislocated. In Roman's history, the truth about his ancestry had become blurred, a situation she had no intention of correcting. She picked up the phone and dialed his number. He picked up at once.

She spoke urgently. "You need to be ready." She listened as he spoke.

"I knew you would call. I take it you've seen something?" he said.

Marsha closed her eyes. This was always difficult, especially with someone as powerful as Roman.

"Yes. You should make preparations."

Another pause.

"And if I don't want to go?"

She opened her eyes. She had done as much as she could; the fates would overrule any further interference. Her power had limits, after all.

"Then you have tonight to do what you will."

When he spoke, his voice seemed drained of its power. Resigned to his fate.

"I understand. I look forward to seeing you again—in another place, if it has to be that way."

The line went dead, and Marsha's heart lurched inside her chest. She'd felt the hollowness of knowing before, and it never got any easier. She looked around the office for what she knew would be the last time, and started to make some calls.

SEVENTY-SIX

BATON ROUGE, LOUISIANA – Present day

ROXIE'S CELL PHONE rang. She scooped it up.

"Hi, Phaedon. What's up?" She listened. "The whole thing? That's amazing. Can you email it to me? I can print it out in the lab. I'm with Chandler now. Thanks. Good work."

She put the cell back on the desk and tapped into her email. She hit "Print," and the machine across the room started to spit paper into its tray.

Roxie smiled. "The rest of the diary has been deciphered. I'm printing it out now. Duke's waiting for us up at the university library. He's found some documents that Blanche had hidden in her garage. They're from Edward Travis."

Roxie and Chandler left the lab together, but as they headed toward the entrance to the library, she got a call on her cell phone. Her expression was tense as she listened. She killed the call and turned to Chandler.

"It's my mom. I have to go see her."

Chandler nodded. "Of course. Is it serious?"

"No," she said, unconvincingly.

They walked over to her Jeep and she climbed in. She leaned out of the window and gave him a kiss before driving off.

Roxie looked in the rearview mirror and saw Chandler standing outside the university as she drove away. He didn't look happy. He was a detective, after all; his senses were highly attuned to the signs of deception. She hated lying to him.

It hadn't been her mother that had called her on the cell, but Freddy. They were planning to go out to the Blackburn plant that night. It was shut down for routine maintenance, which meant that there would be no staff in the control room and only two security guards on site. It was a window of opportunity that Freddy and Amy were keen to exploit.

Amy was a cute kid with an obsessive eye for detail. They'd met while Roxie worked part-time at Hooters and found they shared a common goal in protecting the environment. Amy introduced her to Freddy, and Roxie soon became part of a larger group of environmental activists.

Roxie felt sure that Chandler would be worried if he found out what she was planning. He might even get Duke to prevent her from going.

Roxie arranged to meet them outside the plant so they could go in together. She intended to return within a few hours and head back to the university library to catch up with Duke and Chandler. That way no one would be any the wiser. Unless she and the others found something at the plant. In which case all bets were off. It was obvious to her that Blackburn wanted to derail their investigation and was prepared to go to any lengths to stop them. This usually meant that there was a lot of money at stake, or he was covering something up. Something from his past that might spoil his run for the Senate. A skeleton in the closet—or the swamp.

Chandler and Duke sat in the library at Louisiana State University. The manuscript of Mary's diary and the papers from the car lay on the table in front of them. Duke looked at Chandler.

"So you really had no idea your DNA was so messed up?"

Chandler shrugged. "According to Roxie, it's far more common than you might expect. People who have organ transplants, blood transfusions, or IVF treatment can all end up with some form of microchimerism. So, no, what is"—Chandler made air quotes—"*messed up,* as you call it, is where the other DNA came from. Obviously I knew I was related to Edward Travis, but I had no idea about the identity of the woman Edward had been involved with."

Duke shook his head. "Yup. It makes your relationship to the case pretty damn personal."

"That would be an understatement," Chandler said. "All of those wild conspiracy theories—the newspapers, the government, the police and the monarchy's involvement—between Mary's diary and Edward's notes and letters, it's all in here," he said.

Duke nodded. "He worked out what really happened at the oil field before the storm destroyed all the evidence."

"But he didn't want to expose Adam Blackburn, because he thought he was his son," Chandler said.

"Blood's thicker than water," Duke replied.

Chandler nodded. "But then, when he's dying in a hospital in New Orleans, his daughter tracks him down and he finally learns the truth."

"That Adam wasn't his biological son but a fraternal twin spawned by Tumblety. So he had no reason to continue covering for him," Duke said.

"But it was all too late by then," Chandler said. "In the letters he wrote to Blanche, he told her that Adam Blackburn had gone to a hospital in Europe, apparently for more treatment. And then he upped and disappeared."

"Maybe he felt so guilty, he topped himself," Duke said.

Chandler rubbed his arm, his scar nagging him in the heat. "It's not likely," he said. "One thing we do know about mass murderers is they don't usually feel guilt. It's more likely he decided things might get a little awkward if the truth about what he did came out."

Duke smiled. "You're probably right. But now you know Dr. Tumblety, alias Francis Blackburn, isn't one of your ancestors, that lets you off the hook. You could have wound up being related to—"

Chandler jumped in, "Jack the Ripper? That would be ironic. And impossible as he never existed."

"Try telling that to his fan base," Duke said. He looked at the photo from the oil field. "Adam Blackburn's story about missing the celebrations because of the storm and holing up in some hospital in Europe doesn't hold water. Because here he is alive and well at the investors' party."

Chandler looked at the newspaper picture of Adam Blackburn signing the contract at Huntington Beach. "And here he is twenty years later, and he doesn't look a day older."

Duke opened a folder. "Jesse showed Roxie some photos from an old portfolio of Blanche's. Found one that might interest you."

Duke held up a black-and-white photo. It was of a man in his sixties sitting at a table in an old cellar. Behind him, reflected in a mirror, was Blanche holding the camera.

"That's Edward Travis, my great-great-grandfather!"

Duke nodded. "When Blanche said you reminded her of someone from London, she was thinking of Edward," Duke said. "He must have found out Louie de Chiel had a daughter. He told her what happened to her father in the oil field, and about the Ripper conspiracy."

Chandler said, "In the letters to Blanche, he kept referring to the photos her father took at the oil field before the storm."

Duke nodded. "Yes. He kept telling her that when the time was right, she could use the photos and the notes he'd sent her to bring the Blackburns to justice and expose the Ripper conspiracy. But where are they?"

Chandler shrugged. "Maybe she hid them a long time ago and forgot where they were." He looked at the notes and the letters. "If the negative she left on the hoodoo tree for you to find was from the roll Louie shot that night, then Blanche must have hidden the rest of them somewhere."

Duke nodded. "She left us clues telling us where they are, but we're too dumb to work it out." He flicked through an old letter of Blanche's. "All these years, Blanche was waiting for the right time."

Chandler shook his head. "That's why Blanche went to see Marsha. She wanted to know if it was the right time. And now none of it matters. She's gone, and all of the guilty are dead."

Duke gave him a look. "Guilt like this never dies; it's just passed down through the generations. It's why Edward sent the documents to Blanche. He knew there would come a time when Tumblety's ancestors would try and cash in."

Chandler said, "If this comes out, his political career is over."

Duke nodded. "Amen to that."

Chandler looked through the library window. The sun was a dark orange smudge on the horizon. Duke stood up and stretched his back. "I don't know about you, but my brain's fried—I need to chill."

Chandler looked at him. "Really? You're going to walk away from this when we're so near the end?"

Duke gave a tired smile. "Did you know that if you want to reset your sense of smell, you need to run up and down some stairs? It reboots the olfactory mechanism. It's the same when I play music. It reboots my problem-solving abilities. Besides, isn't it about time you took Roxie out on another date? Drinks are cheap at Gumbo's, and I know how you Brits love a bargain."

Chandler shrugged. "I guess we could both do with a break. I'll give her a ring, tell her to meet us at the club."

SEVENTY-SEVEN

SPIRIT'S SWAMP, LOUISIANA – Present day

MOONLIGHT SILVERED THE filtration pools surrounding the decontamination plant, silhouetting its towering smokestacks. Concrete silos sat in the ground like giant eye sockets next to rotating paddles, slowly combing the dark water inside large circular tanks.

Three figures wearing camo suits and woolen ski masks crouched behind a clump of bald cypress trees festooned with Spanish moss on the outskirts of the plant. One of them looked through night-vision binoculars, eased up his mask, and scratched a freckled face. Freddy, the teenager in the gator suit from the airport. Two girls stood next to him: Amy, dark haired with a snaggle-toothed smile, and Roxie. Freddy put the binoculars down before speaking.

"There are four liquid gas trucks parked up in the compound. We made a note of their license plates. They use the same trucks in rotation. These pictures are from the last two weeks. They deliver in the morning and then at the end of the week they leave to refill. They all came back in this morning," Freddy said. "But look." he showed Roxie two pictures. One of a truck waiting outside the security barrier to come in, another of the same truck waiting to leave.

"What am I looking for?" Roxie said.

Freddy pointed to the tires. "The space between the tire and the wheel arch."

Roxie nodded. "There's no difference between empty and fully loaded."

Freddy smiled. "It was Amy who spotted it."

Amy gave a small smile and blushed. "I'm a bit of a minutia freak," she said.

"Nothing wrong with that," Roxie replied. "We need to check the tankers."

"There's a shift change soon," Freddy said. "They usually have a smoke and something to drink. We'll have about fifteen minutes."

Roxie nodded. "Okay. Freddy, you cut the wire and follow me. Amy, you keep watch."

Freddy looked through the binoculars. "There they are."

Two security guards came out from inside the low concrete security hut next to the swing-up barrier. They headed toward a utility vehicle in a parking space on the opposite side of the compound to the four liquid gas tankers. The guards pulled some beers out of the cab, opened them, and lit up a couple of cigarettes.

Freddy ran over to the fence, cut the wire at the bottom, and held it up. Roxie and Amy slipped through, and Freddy followed. They jogged around and crouched behind the tankers. The sound of the security guards' voices carried across to them. Amy squirmed out of a small rucksack and lowered it to the floor. She handed some aerosols to Freddy and Roxie.

"Freezing kit," she said.

What are these for?" Roxie asked.

Amy smiled. "Watch and learn." She crept alongside one of the tankers, sprayed the side of the metal down low with a blast of CO2. A graduated line appeared across the metal side of the tanker.

Amy pointed to the line. "The temperature differential shows how much liquid is still in the tank. This is practically empty," she said.

Roxie went over to the second tanker and sprayed, while Freddy leapfrogged to the next one and mimicked her actions. Amy went along to the final truck and did the same.

"All empty," Roxie said.

Freddy grinned. "They're just eye candy. Coming and going, logging in and logging out."

Roxie looked over to where the guards were sitting. "We need to get access to the plant's computer and check the inventory."

Amy nodded. "These trucks should be bringing in liquid methane, butane, ethane, and propane for the coolant manufacturing process. So why are they empty?"

Roxie shook her head. "They're meant to be making HCFC-22 refrigerant, and burning off the HCFC-23 by-product."

Freddy nodded. "Which they make millions from via the carbon credits system."

Roxie smiled. "But to get that money, you actually have to manufacture the coolant."

Freddy did a silent fist pump into the air. "Gotcha! Blackburn's going through the motions, claiming the carbon credits without spending a dime on the process apart from running some empty trucks around."

"We need to get moving," Roxie said. "They're not going to sit out here all night."

Amy shrugged on her rucksack, and they jogged back around to the security building, hugging the wall. They headed toward a door that led into the plant.

Roxie turned to Amy. "You keep watch. If you see them move, you bang on the door and get the hell out of here. Okay?"

Amy nodded. Freddy opened the door and they slipped inside. There was a corridor crowded with pipes and electrical conduits that led to a door marked CONTROL ROOM.

Inside, the room was dimly lit. There was only the glow of computer screens displaying the flow rates and pressures of the various processes still running in the plant. A bank of security camera feeds provided views of the plant from various angles inside and out. There were some desks and computers down one end of the room.

Roxie and Freddy shone flashlights around. Roxie pointed to the filing cabinets and nodded to Freddy.

"Check them."

Freddy went over to the cabinets and started to flick through folders. Roxie jogged over to a computer and pulled her cell phone out. She tapped an app on the screen. A graphic flicked up, followed by an icon: *Dataflood. ACCESS ALL AREAS.*

Roxie smiled. "Go fetch."

She hit a key. Passwords raced across the screen. Separate windows began to open as the hack took hold of the system. She looked at the figures that swirled before her, saw something.

She tapped the screen. "Bingo!"

"What?" Freddy looked over. "What have you found?"

Roxie tapped an icon on her cell. "I'm backing this up to the cloud, but there's no record in their inventory of any deliveries of methane, ethane, propane, or butane,"

she said. "The whole thing's a fake. The tankers come and go, and the furnace processes swamp trash and feeds the flare stack to make it look like they're burning off the HCFC-23."

"No wonder he doesn't want us snooping around," Freddy said. "But surely there's an inspection before the government signs off on this sort of operation?"

"Maybe there is," Roxie said. "But he only needs to show the process for real initially. Once he's signed off, he keeps on making false claims. He may not even bother doing that."

Freddy nodded. "Right. He just pays the inspector off. This scam is worth billions. He wouldn't even feel a million-dollar payoff."

Freddy's eyes flicked to one of the security monitors in time to see one of the guards grabbing Amy. "Shit! They've got Amy. We have to get out of here. Now!"

Roxie snagged her cell phone, and they ran toward the exit. A meaty-faced guard burst through the door, leveled his gun at them. The other guard came in holding a struggling Amy.

"Well, lookie here," the second one said. "We got ourselves a regular party, don't we? Get 'em cuffed, Dwayne."

The first guard moved toward Freddy. "Sure thing, Billy. Now, son, let's do this without any fuss, okay?"

Dwayne pulled some cuffs from his belt and headed for Freddy. Amy sank her teeth into Billy's wrist, drawing blood.

He yelped in pain. "Goddamnit!"

Amy broke free and ran for the door. Freddy dodged Dwayne, who, caught off guard, involuntarily fired his gun, hitting Freddy in the shoulder and knocking him to the floor. The sound of the shot echoed round the room, and everybody froze.

Roxie had been good at sport all her life. But speed wasn't always the important thing. A girl had been raped and nearly killed on the LSU campus one year. They never found the culprit, but there had been a big move toward self-defense among the girls. The university had brought in a United States army sergeant called Aubrey. She was over six foot three and a combat medic, and there wasn't a bone she didn't know how to break or fix. She went through the many ways to incapacitate or kill someone if you believed your life was in danger. It was pretty damn obvious that if you snapped someone's shinbone, he wasn't going to come running after you. The same applied if you broke both of their wrists. Aubrey had run through many other non-lethal defense tactics. Some were not for the squeamish—eye gouging, nose breaking, knee fractures, and head butts to name a few. But she made one thing abundantly clear: you had to strike the first blow. At the end of the day, Roxie could outrun most men. But in a confined space with guns, there really was only one surefire tactic. Aubrey had called it "going for the brains."

Roxie ran at Dwayne. Her foot swung upward in a sweeping arc between his legs, with her entire body weight behind it, as if she was kicking a football.

Dwayne went white and hit the floor with a dull thud, like someone had dropped a bag of potatoes. Roxie sprinted toward Billy, who was trying to pick up his gun from the floor. She stamped on his wrist, hard, and the sound of his bone shattering filled the room. He gave a high-pitched scream. Roxie slammed him on the side of the head with a metal trash can, knocking him to the floor. Game over. She checked both men were down, then ran over to Freddy. He was holding his arm, putting pressure on the wound. Roxie bent down.

He looked at her. "Leave me. Go. You need to tell people what's happening. I'll be alright. They won't do anything to me now you've seen what's really going on up here."

Roxie looked at him. "I can't just leave you here," she said.

"You can't carry me across the swamp either. Get after Amy. Go!"

Roxie nodded, stood up, and sprinted through the door, down the corridor and out into the night. She slithered under the fence, picked herself up, and ran. In the distance she could make out the dark silhouette of Amy running past the silos. Roxie sprinted after her, legs pumping.

Headlights swept across the plant, and Blackburn's Escalade slammed to a halt outside the security hut. Kale and Blackburn jumped out. Blackburn opened the back of the Escalade and pulled out his rifle, looked across the plant, and saw Amy. He looked through the telescopic sight, adjusted the crosshairs on Amy's running figure.

"There you are," he said.

Amy came to a halt alongside the concrete silos, her face sickly white. Her hand flew to her mouth as she started to gag.

Blackburn adjusted his sights and squeezed the trigger. The hard crack of the gun's report echoed through the night. Amy jerked backward and tumbled into the silo. She lay crumpled in the dirt, bleeding out, staring at something in front of her. Bodies. Skeletal remains mixed in with bloated cadavers. She was in a charnel pit. She looked up, hearing someone running toward her, shuddered once, and was still.

Roxie came to a halt by the side of the silo and looked down.

"Amy! Oh my God, no!"

She dropped to her knees. A bullet whined off the steel guardrail beside her, the flat report of the gun following it. She spun around and took off, running like the wind, weaving between the silos, racing toward the filtration fields.

Blackburn tried to get a sight on her but was blocked by machinery. He glimpsed her for a second, and then she was gone.

"She's headed for the filtration fields," he said.

Kale stared at him. "What the hell are you doing? This isn't the Wild West. You can't just gun people down—there are guards at the plant."

Blackburn shot him a cold smile. "I pay their wages. They don't give a shit."

Kale shook his head. "This is madness. You're just digging a hole for yourself."

Blackburn shrugged. "They shouldn't have broken into the plant. It's dangerous. Everybody knows that. She won't get far. Take the boy to the sisters. I'll clear up here." He opened the side door of the Escalade. Two white shapes stared out at him, their eyes bright. Jaws slavering with excitement. He waved his hand at the darkness.

"Go fetch!"

The hounds hurtled off into the swamp.

Roxie ran across the concrete walkways between the filtration pools. She halted, tried to catch her breath. Two white shapes raced toward her through the darkness. She scrambled over the walkway, dropped down into the filtration beds. Moonlight sparkled off her wake as she sprinted through the shallow water. The hounds were gaining on her.

She vaulted over a low wall and was out of the gravel beds and into the open swamp in a heartbeat. But now the going was a lot slower. Submerged roots clawed at her legs, and her feet slid in the treacherous mud. She saw the silhouette of a house in the distance. She scrambled up a muddy bank and pulled her cell out. The hounds were almost on top of her, howling in anticipation.

She yelled at the phone, "Call Chandler!" Voice activation kicked in. Chandler's number flashed up on her screen, then went to voice mail.

She screamed at the phone. "Chandler! It's Roxie. Blackburn shot Amy, and Freddy's wounded. He's insane. I'm in Spirit's Swamp, headed for the old Raffeti place.

He's been destroying human remains, hundreds of them, up at the plant. That's why he wanted your investigation shut down . . ."

She looked down at the screen. *No signal.*

"Shit!"

She ran toward the house. A faded wooden sign hung above the door: RAFFETI. Behind her, the hounds howled, their eyes glistening in the dark. She wrenched the front door open and slammed it behind her. The hounds hurled themselves against the door in frustration, snuffling against the glass, smearing it with drool. Roxie slid to the floor, exhausted, her lungs burning, heart pounding.

The hallway was pitch black. The old house settled, its wooden frame creaking in the wind. Outside, the hounds clawed at the front door. She was trapped. She could hear the dogs padding around outside, looking for a way in. She made her way down the dark hallway, reached a door at the end of it, and opened it. Steps led down into a dark corridor. She heard the front door opening. Someone was coming.

She took a firm hold of a metal rail on the wall, and slowly made her way down the steps, feeling for the edge of each one as she went. She reached the final step and felt the cool tiles of the corridor wall beneath her fingers. She could make out the dim shapes of old gas lamps along the walls. She heard some kind of trilling noise, like a distant bird or an insect of some kind. Then another noise, something scuttling along the passageway ahead of her. Rats?

She turned around and faced back the way she'd come. Her cell signaled a text with a muted ping. It was her mother. The screen sent a pulse of blue light up the steps toward the door.

Which is when she saw three faces from hell staring down at her.

SEVENTY-EIGHT

BATON ROUGE, LOUSIANA – Present day

GUMBO'S WAS A small jazz club, dimly lit and jam packed with people. The walls were covered with yellowing sepia photos of musicians from a bygone era. Louis Armstrong, Fats Domino, Scott Joplin, and Jelly Roll Morton were just a few of the ones Chandler recognized. He'd secured himself a seat at the bar, which gave him a good view of the stage and the audience. His career in the force had given him a lifetime habit of people watching, and looking at the varied clientele in the club was all part of the show for him.

A saxophone soared from the stage as a tall musician wearing a dreadlock top knot played a jazzy version of the classic "A Whiter Shade of Pale." Duke accompanied him with his wailing steel guitar. As the song reached its climax, the crowd went wild, clapping and cheering. The crowd clearly loved it. Chandler looked at Duke's smiling face. He had to admit, Duke had been right: the whole olfactory thing, taking a break. Duke was glowing with energy. Chandler was reminded of the old saying about all work and no play making Jack a dull boy. He'd been Jack for too long. But then he remembered Roxie and their time together in the lab. And now Jack wasn't quite so dull anymore.

There was a pause as the musicians took a break, and then a ripple of clapping washed across the room as a beautiful Creole singer stepped up to the mic. The room fell silent. She launched into a spellbinding rendition of Hoagy Carmichael's "Georgia on My Mind." The atmosphere was electric. Her voice was rich and powerful, filling the room with its deep resonance. Chandler checked his cell phone again. There was still nothing from Roxie. He'd left her a voice mail and a text and now worried about coming across as needy. Since he'd seen her George Clooney lookalike professor dropping off the equipment, he'd been nursing pangs of jealousy and suspicion.

She'd skipped going to the library to go and see her mom. Or so she'd said. He'd seen a flicker in her eyes as she'd driven off. Just the slightest look, but it was enough. All those years at the Met conducting interrogations had honed his instincts. He could read a lie in a look, and he'd never been wrong. Whatever Roxie was doing, she wasn't visiting her mother.

A waitress went over to one of the corner booths carrying a tray with two half-filled glasses. In the shadow of the booth, Agent Kale handed her a folded bill. He pointed at Duke onstage and Chandler at the bar. The waitress looked toward the small stage where Duke and the musicians were whipping up a storm. Her attention was distracted for a second, just long enough for Kale to do what was needed. The waitress turned back and smiled.

She went over to the stage and put one of the glasses on a small stool next to Duke. He mouthed a "thank you." Despite the perceived wisdom concerning musicians and drink, he never mixed liquor with his music. He would take a drink after the set.

The waitress went back to the bar and put the second glass down next to Chandler. She nodded toward the back of the room. "You have an admirer."

Chandler shrugged. "Nothing ventured, nothing gained." He toasted toward the booth and took a swig of the drink.

"Ouch—what is that?"

The waitress smiled, picked the glass up, and sniffed it.

"Just some Southern Comfort."

Chandler took a slug of his orange juice from the bar.

"Well, let's just pretend I downed it in one go. I'm meant to be driving Duke home anyway."

The waitress smiled. "How long have you known Duke?"

"A few years now," Chandler said. "He was over in London on a lecture tour. We talked a lot, drank a lot, and listened to a lot of jazz."

The waitress polished some glasses. "Sounds like Duke. He loves his jazz. My name's Maya by the way. You're Chandler, right?"

Chandler smiled. "Yes. My parents were big fans of American pulp fiction and old movies."

Maya nodded. "*The Big Sleep*, *The Long Goodbye* . . . I've seen them movies. That's a cool name."

The band began to play again, and Maya went off to serve some drinks. Chandler took another sip of the Southern Comfort. It still tasted horrible. He drank some more orange juice to chase the taste away. Whether it was his feelings of inadequacy or a bruised ego, he wasn't sure, but he was becoming increasingly enamored with Maya. With her golden skin and mesmerizing eyes, she was looking more attractive by the second, and as the night wore on and Roxie failed to show, he couldn't stop wondering where she was, and more importantly, who she was with. He pulled out his cell phone. His finger hovered over the "Redial" button.

Roxie was in a white-tiled room. Gas lanterns hissed on the wall. She looked down at her naked belly and strained against the straps that held her to the cold steel operating table. The room was laid out like a Victorian operating theater. Three of the Raffeti sisters, dressed in old-style white nurses' uniforms, stared down at her. Their faces were expressionless. For a moment, Roxie thought it had to be a nightmare. But it wasn't.

Sergeant Aubrey's voice jumped into her head: "Worst-case scenario: if some motherfucker does get ahold of you—never, ever, let them see you're scared."

Roxie wondered if that applied to the three motherfuckers that were staring down at her at that moment. After they'd strapped her to the table, she thought she'd heard Freddy's voice coming from somewhere outside the room. Then it had been suddenly cut off, as if he'd been hit. She needed to play for time.

"Why are you doing this?" she asked, trying to hide the fear in her voice.

The sister with one milky eye picked up a crude anesthetist's mask and poured liquid from a bottle onto its pad. She turned the tap on a cylinder next to the table. Gas hissed from the mask. The sister with the twisted face picked up a large surgical knife.

A pop song suddenly blasted out from Roxie's cell phone on a table in the corner of the room. The sister with a stump for a hand went over and tried to switch it off, knocking it off the table and onto the floor. Chandler's voice crackled through the speaker.

"Hello?" Roxie shouted out. "Chandler!"

The milky-eyed sister stamped on the cell phone, smashing it into a hundred pieces of glass and plastic. She leaned down, fixing Roxie with one cold eye.

"You need to lie still. Once you're settled he will come and we can begin."

Roxie stared at her, fear flooding through her in an icy torrent. Somewhere in the depths of the house a phone started to ring. Roxie struggled against the straps.

"Begin what?" she said.

Milky Eye clamped the mask over her face. Roxie felt the gas rush into her nose and throat, and then everything went black.

Chilly headed through the kitchen and into his backyard. A barbecue was in full swing. Friends and neighbors were enjoying themselves around a hog roast and some beer. The men were discussing the finer points of transmissions and transaxles while the women danced a sort of funked-up line dance. The music was cranked up high, and people were shouting to make themselves heard. Chilly's house had no immediate neighbors and backed onto a piece of land on which sat various swamp buggies parked up by his fellow enthusiasts. He moved around dispensing pitchers of foaming beer and charred pieces of rib. In the sitting room, a new cell phone lay charging on a table piled high with food. A hungry-looking dog sniffed at the offerings and licked its lips.

Maya watched as Chandler looked around. He'd weakened and called Roxie one more time. The phone had connected but then cut off.

"Looks like you got a no-show," Maya said.

Chandler shrugged. "Seems like she had better things to do."

Maya smiled. "Her loss. But the cell signal's kinda funky down here."

Chandler reached into his jacket and looked at his cell phone. There was nothing on it. He slipped it back into his pocket.

"She'll probably turn up later."

As he said the words, the lizard part of his brain began to stir. He picked up the glass of Southern Comfort and took a sip from it, felt a burning sensation as the spice and whiskey kicked in.

"Oops, wrong one. Give me another orange juice with some ice in it, could you? Thanks."

"Coming right up." Maya filled a glass with orange juice from a dispenser behind the bar and threw some ice into it. "There you go." She put the glass down on the bar in front of him. "Compliments of the house."

Chandler grabbed the glass. "Bottoms up." He took a gulp.

Maya laughed. "Bottoms up—do you really say that in your country?"

Chandler smiled. "It just means you should tilt the bottle into your mouth so the bottom is in the air. Why? What did you think it meant?"

Maya leaned forward on the bar. "Honey, you do not want to know what I thought it meant."

The passageways beneath the Rafetti house echoed with a strange chittering sound, like a mixture of a dolphin and chimpanzee. But it was neither. A blind woman, the fourth Raffeti sister, her translucent white eyes gleaming in the gaslight, made her way carefully through the passageways beneath the house. She clicked her tongue again and moved forward, cradling an ancient shotgun. She paused and made another series of clicks with her tongue against the roof of her mouth, her brain conjuring up a series of crude black-and-white images like sonar scans each time she made the sound. She trilled again and continued down the corridor.

Back at Gumbo's, Chandler was deep in conversation with Maya while Duke was singing a duet with the pretty Creole singer. A girl came up to Maya and whispered something in her ear. Maya smiled and began to punch out from her bar screen. She leaned over to Chandler, an expanse of dark cleavage yawning at him above her low-cut silk blouse.

"I'm checking out now. And as you've been drinking OJs most of the night . . ." She waited as Chandler looked blankly at her. "I could use a ride."

He put his glass down. "Right, er . . ."

Maya smiled. Chandler fished Duke's car keys out of his pocket, looked over and waved them at Duke. Duke gave him a thumbs-up and a broad smile without taking his eyes off the Creole singer.

Chandler smiled at Maya. "You'll have to tell me what to do—er, how to get there, I mean . . . directions . . ." He trailed off weakly, feeling way out of his depth. If he'd been drinking he would have excused himself by saying he was drunk, but he hadn't been, so he didn't. Maybe he was just tired.

Maya took his hand and towed him off the barstool toward the exit. "C'mon."

Inside the boathouse at the back of the Raffeti house, a cell phone screen flashed in the dark, painting its surroundings in a series of grotesque vignettes. Wooden benches in the middle of the room. Dark shapes twitching in glass jars. A half-naked body strapped to a steel gurney. Freddy's sweating and terrified face, steel cannulas and blood-filled tubes trailing from his body. He looked at his jacket that lay in a heap on the floor, his cell phone next to it. Texts were arriving from his friends. He'd arranged to meet up with them later. That wasn't going to happen. Maybe it was Roxie letting him know she was coming for him. Except she had no idea where he was. He tried to speak; it came out as a croak.

"Call Roxie."

The cell phone's computerized voice spoke.

"I'm sorry, I didn't quite get that. Did you want to know the directions to your home?"

Freddy looked over at his phone. More than anything, he wanted to be home.

He tried again. "Call Chandler."

SEVENTY-NINE

LIVINGSTON, LOUISIANA – Present day

CHANDLER DROVE DUKE'S Buick. Badly. He wasn't used to the soft suspension or the heavy-duty power steering that caused the car to weave as he overcompensated. He tried to remember what the flashing right-turn lights meant and ended up following cars or trucks at the junctions, tailgating them, using them to carve a path through the traffic.

He was traveling on what Maya had told him was originally called the Baton Rouge Expressway, but in 1999 had been renamed the Martin Luther King Jr. Expressway. They went the scenic way rather than the direct route. It took them alongside the Mississippi and joined the I-10, which went over City Park Lake before linking onto the I-12. They left the expressway and headed toward where Maya lived, in Livingston. It was about half an hour outside Baton Rouge, but via the scenic route had taken them an hour. She told him Livingstone had originally been a logging community, but nowadays it was better known for having one of the two LIGO gravitational-wave detector sites. Chandler had pretended to be interested in that information, but in reality it was taking all his concentration to keep the Buick in a straight line.

They were soon driving through a quiet suburb, a neighborhood with a few trees and low-level houses. Maya looked over at him, smiled at his efforts to control the car.

"You been driving long?"

Chandler shrugged. "Just not used to driving a boat."

Maya laughed.

"What?" he asked.

"Your accent. Boooat. Boaaat. It's cute. You're cute."

Chandler tried for a bad Southern accent. "Well, thank you kindly, ma'am. I do declare, if you ain't a purty little thing yoself—"

Maya sucked her teeth, shook her curls. "That is so bad! Promise me you won't do that again—ever."

Chandler grinned. "Okay, I promise."

He looked over at Maya. He wasn't sure what was going on with him, or even why he was clumsily flirting with a woman he'd just met. He'd only had some OJ, and two mouthfuls of something from his mystery admirer. So why did he feel so spaced out? And what was he doing driving a waitress home, who obviously wanted more from him than a ride? Was it just because he thought Roxie had stood him up or, worse, was seeing someone else?

His thoughts were interrupted as Maya looked out of the window and said, "We're here."

They were on a small street lined with low-level duplexes and neat lawns. Chandler swerved into the curb, stopping more abruptly than he meant to. Maya lurched forward, her figure strained against her tight blouse as the seat belt cut across her breasts.

She smiled. "So the brakes work." She leaned over and kissed him on the cheek, her lips remaining on his flesh a fraction longer than he expected. "Thanks for the ride. It's been fun. You've been fun." She waited.

Chandler smiled, not sure what to do next. "No, really, it's been all mine."

She smiled again, got out, and closed the door. She leaned down to the window.

"You've been a perfect gentleman. You should be pleased with yourself."

He nodded, not sure what was going on. "Thank you. I do my best."

"Well, you keep it up." She blew him a kiss and walked away.

He stared after her. She wasn't so much walking as undulating. His head was pounding, and his eyelids felt like sandpaper against his eyes when he blinked.

Maya reached her door, gave him a last wave, and went inside. Chandler shook his head, trying to clear it of the mental fog that enveloped him. He was in love with Roxie. What the hell was he doing outside a complete stranger's house like some drunken teenager?

His phone vibrated. He fumbled it out of his pocket, saw a list of missed calls as he answered. The voice on the other end sounded like a dead man speaking.

"Chandler . . ."

He strained to hear, looked at the ID. It was Freddy.

"Freddy? What is it? You sound terrible."

On the other end of the line, Freddy's breathing was shallow.

"I'm at the old Raffeti house. They've got Roxie."

Chandler strained to hear.

"You need to get over here, let Duke and Chilly know . . ."

Chandler shook his head. The evening had descended into a nightmare.

"What's happening? Who's got Roxie?"

Freddy's voice wavered, grew faint, distorted. "I don't know, some women—they're crazy. Quickly . . . you've got to . . . I . . . boathouse—"

The signal started to break up, and then died. Chandler hit "Redial" on the last number.

Freddy's phone rang, the music coming out of it so wrong for the situation. Freddy tensed; he could hear something else. An eerie chittering sound.

The blind sister was headed down the corridor toward the boathouse. She clicked her tongue again and moved forward, toward the sound of Freddy's cell phone, the ancient shotgun cradled in her withered hands.

Chandler looked at the phone as it went to voice mail.

"Shit!"

He accelerated away from Maya's house, hitting "Redial" as he went. Livingston was just off the I-12 and from there Maurepas was under half an hour away. He wasn't sure where the Rafetti house was, or how he got onto the causeway leading to it. But if he could find the road where the dump truck had hit them, he'd be able to see the house from there and navigate his way to it. He stamped on the accelerator, and the powerful engine bayed as it hurled the Buick forward.

Gumbo's was now packed, and people were spilling out onto the street, clutching their drinks and passing cigarettes around among their friends. Inside, some of the customers had started doing karaoke with Duke and the band. In the pocket of Duke's jacket on the back of his chair, his cell phone flashed and vibrated, but Duke's attention was taken up with his music, the ringing drowned out.

Chilly's new cell phone vibrated and flashed on the table in the kitchen. His dog crouched under the table, ready to catch any pieces of food dropped by the guests. Its ears pricked up at the sound of the phone on the table above, its eyes watching as the device pulsated across the surface with each burst of sound. It finally reached the edge of the table and tumbled through the air. The dog clamped the falling cell phone between its jaws and trotted happily away.

EIGHTY

BATON ROUGE, LOUISIANA – Present day

DUKE SHRUGGED HIS jacket on and made his way past the bar. The waitress looked across at him.

"Your taxi's outside. Your English friend took Maya home, so I wouldn't bother waiting up for him."

Duke gave a wry smile. "Thanks, um . . ." He paused, searching his memory.

The waitress smiled. "Chloe."

Duke nodded. "Chloe, I knew that. I think Maya may be in for a disappointment there. Chandler's kind of involved."

Chloe laughed. "Maybe, but Maya can be damn persistent."

Duke nodded. "Yeah, that's for sure, but he's English. They're a little more conservative over there." He winked at her and headed through the club door and out into the warm night air.

The streetlights shimmered as he looked up at them. He rubbed his eyes and took a long, deep breath. A taxi sat at the side of the road. Duke nodded at the driver and climbed into the back before sinking into the seat. The taxi took off, passing a Black Escalade idling in the shadows of the alleyway next to the club.

The cab headed through the streets of Baton Rouge and drove alongside the river. Duke stared out of the window. The colored lights reflecting off the water seared his eyes. He struggled to focus. A cold sweat formed on his forehead. He pulled out a handkerchief, mopped his brow, and spoke to the driver.

"Hey, did I eat some bad gumbo, or what?"

The driver chuckled. "We've all had that gumbo, brother."

The taxi dropped Duke outside the Airstream and drove off. Duke stood swaying on his feet. He'd been drinking from a bottle of iced water for most of the night, but he dimly remembered Chloe bringing him a glass of Southern Comfort from someone in the audience. He'd drunk half of it at the end of his set. He was no longer the hard-drinking person he'd been in the aftermath of Katrina. Now he was through that dark period, he drank less than ever. Still, a single drink shouldn't have reduced him to this state. It had to be something he'd eaten. All he wanted to do now was get some sleep. He reached forward with his keys, missed the door lock, and dropped them.

"Damn."

He picked up his keys and looked around. The lake was a dark pool advancing toward him, while above him the moon was so bright it burnt his eyes. Every nerve in his body was on fire. He drew in a deep breath of the warm, moist air coming off the lake and tried to clear his head.

He let himself into the Airstream and switched on the light. It blazed down on him like a miniature sun. The last time he'd felt like this was at a frat party as a teenager. He'd tried some new mix of weed, and it had been so powerful he'd spent the whole night watching imaginary insects crawling over his body. He started to make himself a cup of coffee. While it was brewing, he looked around the Airstream. It looked odd, as though he were seeing it for the first time. He picked up the picture of himself with Julie, pressed it to his face and kissed it, a ritual he always did before going to bed. He took the photo away from his lips and found himself in a nightmare.

He was standing in the middle of his old house, looking out the window at Julie in the garden. Everything was in hyper-real, saturated colors. His head felt heavy, and he was so tired he could barely stand. He touched the window, looked out at Julie collecting her roses in a small basket. He called out to her, the sound of his own voice deafening.

"Julie?"

He ran toward the door, and the room stretched away from him, the distance to the door staying the same no matter how fast he ran. Outside, the sky was pitch black. The garden and everything in it was bent under the onslaught of a ferocious wind. Julie looked over at him. Her mouth opened, but he couldn't hear what she was shouting. A shadow passed over her. A tree smashed against the back of the house, blocking the door and his view of Julie. The whole house was shaking. Windows splintered and shattered, plaster fractured, stress lines spidered the walls. The house foundation shuddered and creaked. The wind howled.

He heard the sound of rushing water, and through the windows, a gray mass hurtled toward him. Water exploded against the side of the house, pouring through the cracks in the floor, rising up the walls of the house. And as the water climbed, the roar of an engine filled the room. Metal jaws ripped into the side of the house. The water was above his neck in seconds. He saw the trapdoor to the roof above him. He punched it open and climbed up out of the water.

Duke's mind did a backflip.

He was back in the flooded Airstream, fighting for survival. The whole structure was tilting over. Something was ramming it from the outside. The sound of an engine roared. The Airstream was being pushed into the lake. The interior lights died as the power cable was ripped from its stanchion. Only the pale moonlight was visible through the submerged windows as the water closed over Duke's head.

EIGHTY-ONE

SPIRIT'S SWAMP, LOUISIANA – Present day

CHANDLER LEFT THE smooth concrete of the interstate and headed down the side road that led to the Maurepas swamp. It was the same road he'd been down before with Roxie in her Jeep. Moonlight shimmered off the swamp water on either side of him. He saw the site of the crash approaching. There were still pieces of wreckage by the side of the road, and a warning sign had been erected. He passed it and turned down the narrow track that led toward Spirit's Swamp. The faint lights of the Raffeti house were visible in the distance. He pulled off to the side of the track and killed the engine.

He opened the car's glove compartment and rummaged inside. He found Duke's Maglite and flicked it on. It produced a weak yellow beam. He pulled out his cell phone and looked at the screen. There were no signal bars. He put it back into his jacket, cursing inwardly. In the Met he'd prided himself on being ready for every eventuality. Water, Swiss Army knife, fully charged cell phone, and flashlight on him at all times. A change of time zone and a couple of swigs of Southern Comfort, and he'd been reduced to the level of a Stone Age man.

He climbed out of the car and headed slowly toward the house. He wanted to run, but after hearing Freddy's garbled message, he was pretty sure he needed to proceed with caution. Especially as he was only armed with a Maglite and his wits.

EIGHTY-TWO

BATON ROUGE, LOUISIANA – Present day

DUKE'S BODY WAS crying out for oxygen, and his lungs were on fire. Air trickled from his mouth. Silver bubbles floated up through the dark waters that enveloped him. He knew he had less than a minute before he started to black out. He hammered against the large front window of the Airstream with his fists, but it was no good. He felt the last of the oxygen slide through his teeth and a dark fog begin to spread through his system. He knew it was the first and last time he'd experience hypoxia. And as he started to lose consciousness, he saw something gleaming on the floor below.

Swamp water encircled the Raffeti house like a silver bracelet in the moonlight. The back of the house jutted out over the water on wooden supports, forming an integral boathouse. A couple of wooden skiffs were tied up below it. Gas lines snaked up into the building from canisters stacked on a wooden jetty to one side. Mist clung to the surface of the water, isolating the house further from its surroundings in time and space.

Chandler stood outside the front door. The house looked deserted, its rotting wood and peeling paintwork showing years of neglect. He stepped onto the porch and listened. It was silent. He tried the door. It opened to his touch. He stepped slowly inside, his senses on high alert.

Cobwebs and dust covered everything. Unlit gaslights were fixed to the walls. They looked like they'd been there forever.

He panned the torch around the hallway. The walls were filled with black-and-white photographs of the generations that had occupied the house through the years. There were some framed squares of lace embroidered with the iconic belfry of Bruges he recognized from a film set there and starring Colin Farrell and Brendan Gleeson, about some hitmen hiding out in the medieval Belgian city. He looked at a picture of four women. They looked like sisters, all with fixed smiles. But there was something odd about them. They all seemed to have some kind of birth deformity. He remembered Blanche's story about the änglamakerska, the angel makers, and the children bred for the rich and childless. Could these be the ones that didn't make the grade?

Farther down the hallway were more pictures of the women, some with a man who bore a striking resemblance to Tumblety.

Chandler heard a sound and froze. It was a chittering, clicking noise. The sound stopped. He was aware of a smell. The kind of heavy-duty disinfectant smell you get in a hospital. He heard a low moan from behind an old wooden door at the end of the hallway. He headed toward it, pulled it open, the hinges protesting, and went through.

Ahead of him, stone steps led down into a dank and dimly lit passageway. He imagined that many years ago the tiles might have been white. But over the years the dampness had taken its toll, and now they were spidered by veins of green mold. In the distance, he could see other passageways stretching off to the left and right. It looked like they'd been carved out of the rock beneath the house over many years.

He saw a crack of light beneath an old wooden door at the end of the main passageway. He went over to it, turned the door's brass knob, pushed the door open . . . and stepped into a nightmare.

Duke burst through the surface of the lake in a cloud of bubbles. His hand clutched the neck of his steel guitar. He'd used it to smash his way through the Airstream window, and it was looking a great deal worse for wear. He swam toward the shore, his legs pumping, his arms flailing through the water. He made it to dry land and dragged himself out before collapsing on the bank. His wet clothes clung to him as he lay there, shivering in the cool night air.

Patrol cars sat in front of the remains of Duke's Airstream. Their clicking light bars painted the scene in lurid shades of red and blue. Duke sat on a folding seat as paramedics finished checking him over. They'd wrapped him in a foil space blanket, and a young female paramedic shone a torch into his eyes and noted his pupils.

"Sorry to ask this, Duke, but have you been drinking, or . . . ?"

"I only had one drink at the club, but I'm guessing someone spiked it."

The paramedic nodded. "What symptoms do you have?"

"Tiredness, blurred vision, hypersensitivity to light, and hallucinations," Duke answered.

The girl pursed her lips. "I was going to say it could be Ambien, but that wouldn't give you hallucinations. I'm thinking Ketamine."

Duke looked at her. "Surely that would have knocked me out, wouldn't it?"

The girl smiled. "Normally, yes. It's used as a general anesthetic for horses and humans, so a small dose in a drink would pack a powerful punch."

"So how come I'm still standing?" Duke asked.

The paramedic thought for a moment before replying, "It could have been a biphasic."

Duke frowned. "Biphasic?"

"Yes," she said, "a mixture of two different substances that combine to delay the effects of the main drug."

Duke nodded. He'd heard of that. "You mean it wouldn't take full effect until later in the evening?"

"It's not an accurate science. The amount of alcohol you consume, your body weight and temperature, lots of different factors come into play. Even your blood sugar levels can trigger the effects earlier or later.

"So if I was drinking sugary drinks, the effects could show up faster?"

The paramedic nodded. "Yes. A sudden change of temperature, say from air-conditioning to the heat outside, could speed it up too."

Duke thought it through. "The waitress said a man had ordered drinks for me and my friend. He's staying at my place so we were both going home together, but he gave one of the bar staff a ride home, so I took a taxi."

"You think his drink might have been spiked as well?" she said.

"Damn," Duke said. "I should have thought of that. I'd better check on him."

The paramedic packed up her things. "We'll have a more accurate diagnosis when we hear from toxicology."

Duke stood up. "Thanks."

The girl smiled. "No problem." She handed him a small box of pills. "If you get any headaches, take one of these every couple of hours."

Duke smiled. "Thanks. You can never have too many drugs."

"That's one way of looking at it. You take care, Duke."

She headed back to the ambulance and joined her colleague.

Duke sat hunched over on the grass, his eyes fixed ahead, his ruined guitar by his side. The adrenaline in his system was wearing off and being replaced by exhaustion. An officer came over and handed him a cup of coffee. Duke took the cup and sipped it gratefully.

"Thanks, Jim."

The officer nodded. "We got a call from Roxie's mother. She says Roxie never came home this evening." He paused. "Freddy Markus has been reported missing as well."

Duke looked up. "They were both in the same environmental group," he said.

The officer looked serious. "Roxie wouldn't disappear without telling her mom where she'd gone. We'll put out an APB."

Duke stared across the dark waters of the lake. "This is turning into quite a night, isn't it?"

"That's for sure," the officer said, then nodded at Duke and headed off.

Duke looked around the lake, its peacefulness in sharp contrast to the carnage he had recently been involved in. He stood up and went over to where the Airstream lay beached on the edge of the shoreline like a shipwreck. He studied the gouge marks on its side and peered into the doorway at his sodden possessions strewn across the floor. He reached inside and picked up the picture of Julie and him. The glass was cracked, the photograph inside soaked. He wiped it clean and slipped it into his jacket pocket.

Whoever had done this had intended to kill him. They'd gone to a lot of trouble to render him incapable of protecting himself, spiked his drink, and tried to drown him in his own home. In his mind, there was only one suspect: Governor Roman Blackburn.

Chandler was standing inside what looked like an old Victorian operating theater. Roxie was strapped onto a steel table below a gas-lit overhead lamp. She wore a mask over her face, connected to a tube that led to gas cylinders. There were surgical instruments lined up on a table to one side of her. Her eyes were wide with fear. Chandler went over and removed the mask. She groaned, struggled to focus.

"Thank God," she said. "I had no idea if you'd gotten my call."

She took a deep breath as he started to unstrap her hands. Finally she was free. She flung her arms round him, squeezed him so tight it hurt.

"We've got to get out of here," she said. "The Raffeti sisters, they're mad. They've got Freddy, and I think they were planning to cut me open."

Chandler looked around, his imagination working overtime. The atmosphere in the room made his flesh crawl.

"What the hell is this place?" he said.

Roxie shook her head, tried to clear the effects of the gas.

"I tried to leave you a message, but I think I lost the network. We broke into the plant." She saw Chandler start to say something, but she held up her hand. "I know, you were right. It was a stupid thing to do. But we found out what was going on up there. He's running a carbon credits scam. Pretending to destroy a greenhouse gas by-product from a refrigerant he's not even producing, and making millions out of the deal."

"So you were right. It is about the money."

Roxie nodded. "It gets worse. Blackburn shot and killed Amy, and Freddy was wounded by one of the security guards. He's in here somewhere. Amy found out why Roman doesn't want us poking around the swamp."

Chandler looked around. He was getting more nervous with every second they stayed in the house. "Why?" he asked.

"He's been destroying bodies in the decontamination plant—hundreds of them."

Chandler nodded. "Duke found Edward's letters and notes he'd sent to Blanche. There were explosions out at Blackburn's oil field ahead of the storm in 1915. Hundreds of investors and her father died because Adam had faked a survey and covered up the land's instability. There were methane pockets under the ground. The drilling set off a chain reaction that destroyed the oil field the night before the storm hit."

Roxie looked at him. "And that's what he's been covering up ever since. And why he was in such a hurry to clean up the swamp and keep your investigation away from it."

Chandler nodded. "It all makes sense," he said. "But what the hell were they planning out here with you and Freddy?"

Roxie shook her head. "I don't know."

"Where did they go, the sisters?"

"One of them got a call as they were putting me under. When I came to, they were gone," she said. "We need to find Freddy and get the hell out of here."

Chandler looked around. "No argument from me on that score."

There was a chittering sound from outside the door. Roxie froze.

Chandler looked toward the door. The sound came again, nearer this time.

"I've heard that sound before. What is it?" he asked.

Roxie climbed down from the operating table, clutched on to it to steady herself.

"She's coming."

Chandler supported her. "Who's coming?"

Roxie looked up at him. "There are four of them, freaky sisters, one of them is totally blind. Navigates by making clicking sounds. You've got to get out of here. Leave me. I'll take care of her. Go, get Freddy. I'm sure they took him to the boathouse. Go!"

The blind sister shuffled down the corridor, clicking her tongue against the roof of her mouth. Murky flashes of the corridor bled into her brain. The harder the surfaces surrounding her, the clearer the picture was. With each click, she moved closer to the door of the operating theater. Her heightened senses were alerted. She heard voices, and smelled a new smell—a man.

Chandler held his breath and flattened himself against the wall beneath one of the hissing gaslights in the hallway. He hoped the sound and smell from the light would mask his presence. The sister shuffled slowly past him, her translucent white eyes staring, the weird clicking noise she made with her tongue echoing around the dank passageway. She halted a few feet past him, seemed to sense something. Roxie made a low moaning noise from inside the room.

Chandler knew she was putting up a distraction for his benefit. She was a smart girl. He just hoped she knew what she was doing.

The sister stood at the door to the operating theater. She lowered the gun and pushed the door open. Roxie lay silently on the table.

She'd arranged the straps around her wrists as if she were still bound securely. She knew she was taking a risk, but at least she would have the advantage of surprise over the milky-eyed bitch headed her way.

Chandler hadn't wanted to leave her, but she'd assured him she could handle herself. And now she was just praying she could.

Chandler ran down the corridor, past the hissing gaslights, his shadow racing ahead of him. It grew damper the deeper he went. Mold covered the tiled walls like green sweat. He came to a large wooden door constructed with old-fashioned, square-cut raisin-head nails. He reached down and grasped the circular wrought-iron door handle and turned it. The door gave a shuddering screech and swung open.

The blind sister came into the operating theater and stopped, sniffed, and trilled, moving her head to quarter the room as she clicked her tongue. She could see the girl on the table was still asleep. She repeated the clicks to be sure. Flashes of the room filled her head. There was no one else there. She retraced her steps toward the door and sent out another burst of clicks, then followed them back out through the door and into the corridor.

The jagged picture of her surroundings filled her head as she made her way farther down the passageway. Her sisters had covered the walls with tiles while she'd lived below the house. Their hard surface made the reflections clearer and her navigation easier. After a while, her skill with sound and touch became so good, she was able to roam the rest of the house at will.

Earlier in the day, she and her sisters had been moving stuff out from the lower levels of the house. She'd sensed something important was happening when Marsha turned up. They'd loaded things into her vehicle and then returned to continue clearing things out of the lower levels. Because of her blindness, she'd never been allowed that far beneath the house, but she knew it was where they did their work. She would be forced to seek them out if the intruder became a problem. But for now she intended to deal with the problem herself.

She walked carefully down the passageway. She could hear the sound of lapping water coming from the door to the boathouse. It was much louder to her enhanced senses. Too loud. She tightened her grip on the shotgun. If the sound of water was that loud, it meant the door was open, and if it was open, then someone else had gone in there. Someone who shouldn't have. She tightened her grip on the shotgun and headed for the boathouse door.

Chandler shone his flashlight around the boathouse. The weak beam revealed a macabre collection of glass jars on a wooden bench. Pale organs floated in liquid inside them.

He moved closer to the jars. Even in the dull light of the Maglite, he could see what they were. Reproductive organs. He saw tubes trailing away from them into the gloom and bent down to get a closer look. They weren't like the organs he'd seen floating in formaldehyde as a student, and as he peered into one of the jars, he realized why: they were alive.

At the back of the bench was a square earth-filled glass tank. Inside he saw flatworms twisting and turning through the soil. They made a slithering, popping sound as they moved through the castings, their pale skins glistening in the dim light.

He heard a sound from the corner of the room, a rasping noise, like someone struggling to breathe. He swept his flashlight around the room and saw a huddled shape strapped to a steel table at the back. It was Freddy.

Chandler moved across the room to where the teenager lay. There were cannulas with steel needles connected to Freddy's femoral arteries. His blood flowed through tubes that fed into the glass jars on the bench. Chandler leaned down. Freddy's eyes twitched.

"Freddy?" he said.

Freddy opened his eyes, tried to focus.

Chandler touched his shoulder. "You're going to be okay."

He heard a sound in the doorway behind him and turned around.

Two white, sightless eyes stared at him as the blind sister pointed the shotgun into the room. Chandler froze. She clicked her tongue against the roof of her mouth and trilled, scanning the room. Her blank eyes swept across Freddy, strapped to the steel table. She trilled again, searching for something. Her nostrils flared.

She could smell the intruder, but the scent of Freddy's blood was confusing her senses. She needed to get closer to the source of the new smell. She drew in a sharp breath and let it out slowly, cleansing her nostrils of the old smell—letting in the new.

Chandler quickly ducked down and crouched behind the end of the bench in the center of the room. There was a trapdoor under his feet, and he could hear the sound of water sliding past the boathouse supports beneath him.

The blind sister cocked her head and sniffed, trilled her tongue again, sent out a series of clicks that echoed round the room. She was halfway down the bench now, getting nearer with each step. Chandler looked at the shotgun she held in her hands. Even with her lack of sight, she seemed to be on his trail. He had to distract her with something. He slowly reached into his pocket. The sister sniffed the air and listened. He was only going to get one shot at this.

She came to a halt, sensing something. The boathouse filled with a raucous pop tune. The sister screamed with pain of sensory overload, her crude sonar vision overpowered. She trilled desperately, her brain a snowstorm of conflicting reflections swamping her senses.

In the fog of noise she could make out something shifting as Chandler stood up. He slowly began to back away, trying to put as much distance as he could between himself and the shotgun. But before he could take another step, she swung the barrel round—and fired. Lead ripped a jagged hole in the trapdoor beneath him and he plummeted through into darkness.

EIGHTY-THREE

BATON ROUGE, LOUISIANA – Present day

CSI OFFICERS WORKED around the abandoned backhoe in the university grounds. An officer took photographs of the scene while another closed a metal sample case. Duke went over to them.

"You done here?" he asked.

The officers looked at him, wary of his tone and dilated pupils.

"Pretty much. Someone's gonna drive it back to the impound. Are you okay?" one of the officers said.

"Just a bit woozy. Someone spiked my drink."

"Did you get some help with that?" the same officer asked.

Duke nodded, studied the cab of the backhoe. He climbed in and looked around. "Did you find anything?"

The officer with the sample case shrugged. "Just some partials," he said. "Whoever drove this had to be wearing gloves."

Duke flicked a look at the keys that dangled from the ignition. "That figures," he said. He climbed down from the cab. "Well, you have a good night."

The officers looked at him. "You too," one of them replied.

Duke wandered over to where his Impala was parked and climbed in. He watched as the officers finished up at the scene, got into their cars, and drove off. He waited a few minutes and then climbed out and headed toward the backhoe.

In the darkness beneath the boathouse, Chandler tried not to move. He'd landed on an old skiff and smashed through it. Now, he was wedged in the wreckage up to his waist, and his feet were stuck fast in the swamp mud under the boat. He heard the intermittent trills of the blind sister above him getting nearer. He threw his body backward to extricate himself, but only succeeded in smacking his head on the wooden supports above him. He felt blood trickle down into his eyes. He'd watched some documentary where they'd said a shark could smell one drop of blood in twenty-five gallons of water from three miles away. He had no idea if an alligator's sense of smell was as keen as a shark's, and he certainly didn't want to find out.

He ripped a leg free from the clinging mud, losing a shoe in the process. Something soft burst beneath his other foot. He yanked it free from the mud. Putrid gas bubbled up from the water. He'd smelled marsh gas before, but this was worse. Much worse. Something bobbed up beside the skiff. A rotting gray torso drifted past him into the darkness.

His stomach heaved, the acidic bile burning the roof of his mouth. He looked around, listening. He'd ticked all the boxes an alligator could want: a rotting carcass, blood dripping into the water, and human vomit. He might as well have hung a sign round his neck with CATCH OF THE DAY written on it. He wiped his mouth and looked around. If he couldn't get out of the skiff, then the skiff would have to come with him.

He heard the sound of voices and the clatter of feet on the wooden floor above him. It sounded like the sisters were back. He managed to drag himself and the skiff clear from under the boathouse just as someone peered down through the trapdoor. He glimpsed a woman with a twisted face; he'd seen her in one of the pictures in the hall. She poked the barrel of the shotgun through the shattered trapdoor, but couldn't get a clear shot because of the angle. The others were shouting at each other.

Chandler waded through the slimy waters of the swamp, dragging the waterlogged skiff with him. He came to a halt and started kicking at the rotten hull. Finally he managed to tear himself free. He used a wooden pole from the skiff to check for hidden stump holes and began to wade through the swamp, his muscles aching with the effort. He came to a halt, looked through his sodden pockets, and found Zeke's business card. He checked his cell phone and struggled to see anything though the semi-opaque waterproof case, a mixed blessing that he was glad of right now. He could just make out there was no signal. He tried to remember what Zeke had said. Something about texts being like motorcycles on a gridlocked highway. He peeled back the protective case and started to type.

Behind him, burning torches appeared in the dark beneath the house. The sisters were using the remaining skiff. Chandler hit "Send." He looked at the screen. *NO NETWORK. MESSAGE QUEUED.*

The torches were closer now. Three of the sisters were aboard the skiff. They held their torches high and peered out over the water.

He started wading again. Tendrils of vegetation clutched at him, and the swamp mud squirmed beneath his feet. He looked back at the torches. They'd soon be able to see him. He renewed his efforts.

The overhanging cypress trees gave him some cover but made progress difficult in the dark. The moon threw a feeble glimmer of light off the water in front of him. He waded beside the slippery banks of a small bayou, which opened out into the main part of the swamp. He tried to get his bearings and locate the causeway he'd driven in on. If he could find the road, he might be able to double back to his car. In the stillness of the swamp he became aware of the noise he was making. He stopped and listened. At first, there was just his heavy breathing and the pounding of his own heart. Then he heard it: a thick, wet slithering noise, followed by the sound of something heavy flopping into the water with a dull splash. Moonlight flared off a pair of yellow eyes gliding toward him. He realized then that he no longer needed to worry about the millions of alligators that inhabited the swamps of Louisiana.

He only needed to worry about one.

EIGHTY-FOUR

BATON ROUGE, LOUISIANA – Present day

THE FRONT DOOR of Blackburn's house burst open, and the governor and Kale headed out. Blackburn was on his cell. He didn't look happy.

"You're sure? When was this? Okay. Thanks, Barney." He jammed the cell back into his pocket. "Do I have to do everything myself? Lanoix's Buick has been seen near Maurepas. My guess is he's headed for Spirit's Swamp—"

"That's not possible," Kale said, shaking his head. "I gave them both enough ketamine to bring down an elephant."

Blackburn glared at him. "Well, obviously they're not elephants, and now we have a problem."

Kale looked grim. "We can probably cut him off."

"We'll cut him off, alright." Blackburn said. "At the legs!"

They headed for the Escalade that sat in front of the house. Blackburn opened the trunk and stowed his rifle. He gave a low whistle. The two white hounds bounded out of the house and leaped in. He slammed the trunk hatch down, but it flipped open again. He slammed it twice more before the catch caught.

"Damn thing!" he said, before jumping behind the wheel of the Escalade and firing it up.

Kale barely made it into the passenger seat as Blackburn accelerated away.

The Steinway piano gleamed in the muted pool of light inside Blackburn's sitting room. The house was silent. The chandeliers began to tremble, their glass tinkling like wind chimes. The trembling became stronger. The pictures on the walls started to vibrate. One of them smashed to the floor. There was an explosion of wood as the front doors were smashed back into the hallway. The jaws of the backhoe blocked the doorway. Duke sat at the controls.

"Get out here, Blackburn, before I bring this pile of tasteless crap down around you!"

There came no response, just the clatter of the backhoe's engine in the night. Muddy water dripped from its mechanical jaws onto the expensive Persian rugs spread across the wooden floor.

Duke looked around. "Okay, you had your chance."

He gunned the motor and worked the levers that controlled the hydraulics. The shovel swung around and smashed through the wall of the hallway, exposing the lounge. A man ran into the hallway, stopping dead when he saw Duke. The shovel rose into the air and tilted down. Its steel jaws hanging over the gleaming grand piano. Duke pulled a lever. The hydraulics hissed, and the jaws plunged down. But the musician in Duke wouldn't let himself do it. He halted the shovel a foot above the instrument. A single drop of water fell through the air before exploding like a glistening tear on the mirrored surface of the wood.

The man shouted, "Wait!"

Duke looked at him. "Where's Blackburn?"

The man paused. "The old Raffeti place I think. Out at Spirit's Swamp."

Duke looked around, took in the carnage he'd wrought. He was starting to come down from his adrenaline-fueled rampage. Now he just felt tired and old. He looked at the man. "What do you do here?" he asked, climbing down from the cab.

"Housekeeper," the man said.

Duke came over to him. "Well, I could do with some dry clothes."

Twenty minutes later, Duke came out of the house wearing one of Blackburn's Huntsman suits. It wasn't a great fit, but after grabbing a cup of coffee and changing out of his sodden clothes, he felt a whole lot better. He turned toward the sound of an engine. Zeke slammed on the brakes and pulled up next to him in a mud-splattered Jeep. Duke nodded to him and climbed in.

"Thanks for coming. I think I may have burnt a few bridges with the locals."

Zeke smiled. "That's what bridges are for." He floored the accelerator, and the Jeep shot off.

Duke put some dark glasses on. Zeke looked him over.

"I'm not sure about the glasses."

Duke sighed. "It's been a rough night. Somebody spiked my drink and it messed me up. My eyes are still pretty sensitive."

Zeke nodded. "Sounds like Blackburn wanted you out of the picture for good."

Duke slumped low in the seat as a fleet of squad cars raced past them, sirens and lights flashing as they headed toward Blackburn's house.

Zeke watched them in the rear mirror. "I'm guessing Blackburn ain't too pleased with you."

Duke smiled. "Guess not."

Zeke held his cell phone out to Duke. "I got a text from Chandler."

Duke read the screen.

"Need help—irits swap?"

Zeke took his phone back. "Spirit's Swamp. Reception's bad out there. His text message got put on backlog.

Duke looked over. "What's he doing out in Spirit's Swamp?"

Zeke shook his head. "I don't know, but it sounds like he's in deep shit. If we take the tour boat and get near enough, I should get a Bluetooth hit from his cell and we can track him."

Zeke stamped on the accelerator. Duke hung on to a grab handle as the Jeep bucked over the potholes in the road.

"Did you manage to get through to Chilly?" Duke asked.

Zeke shook his head. "I called the station. They've sent an officer round to his house."

Duke smiled. "He always did play his music too damn loud."

Zeke looked across at Duke. "I heard Roxie's gone missing."

Duke nodded. "Yep, and Freddy. Roxie never called in to see her mom. Something's wrong."

They headed over the I-10 and followed highway 22 into Livingston Parish, then continued on through Maurepas. Zeke drove into the Make 'Em Wet Marina, and pulled up at the quayside next to his father's boathouse. Zeke opened up the office and unhooked a key from a board. He went out and checked the boat as Duke climbed on.

"Do you think Chandler's with Roxie?" he asked.

Zeke started the motor and shouted over the roar of the fan blade, "I can't think of any other reason for him to be that near to alligators." He opened the throttle, and the craft accelerated across the swamp.

Blackburn and Kale were racing down the causeway stretching across the swamp when the governor's cell phone rang. He pulled it from his pocket and answered.

"What?" He listened. "What! How bad? Okay—no, I'll deal with it." He stared at the phone and then put it back into his pocket.

Kale looked over. "What now?"

"Damn deputy's got more lives than a cat. It can't have been him in the car—he just drove a backhoe into my house!"

Kale's mouth turned up. "So who's driving his car?"

Blackburn looked at him. "How the hell should I know? Could be the limey detective."

Kale looked over at him. "How's the piano?"

Blackburn gave him a paint-stripping look. "Just shut the fuck up and drive."

Kale floored the accelerator, and the powerful engine hurled the Escalade through the night.

The full moon had turned the swamp waters into pools of mercury surrounding Chandler. He could still remember the size of the huge alligator as it had swum past him earlier. Either he didn't smell right or it had already eaten. Either way, he was grateful he hadn't had to go one on one with it. He felt confident about the outcome of that particular match.

As it was, he was still making slow progress, stumbling into hidden mud holes while mangrove roots tore at his skin. In the distance he could see the sisters crouched in the skiff, the flames from their burning torches blood red in the dark. The full moon made it easier for him to see, but it also meant they could see him.

Wading through the water and mud was exhausting. There was no way he could outdistance the approaching skiff. He was going to have to think of something. And fast. He flattened himself against the gnarled trunk of an ancient cypress tree. He felt a rotting stump beneath him, his feet slipping and sliding off its slimy bark. The sisters were twenty feet away and closing. Every time he moved, it sent bubbles of putrid gas boiling up through the water.

The flickering glow from the sister's torches came nearer, the surface of the water golden in their light. They were almost on top of him. Within seconds they would see him, and that would be it. He could smell the torches' burning oil. Smoke drifted toward him. The skiff slid past him, then one of the sisters held up her torch, swinging it around in a slow arc. She smiled and pointed back at him. The skiff started to turn around and headed toward him. Through his half-closed eyes he saw one of them draw out a gleaming machete.

Chandler's eyes snapped open. He thrashed around furiously, churning the water. His legs kicking beneath the surface—unlocking a flurry of gas around the sisters' skiff and their flaming torches.

There was a roar as the gas ignited and engulfed them in flames. The sisters leaped from the skiff, hit the water screaming. The flames jumped across the surface of the swamp. Gators thrashed below the surface, tipping the skiff over, turning the foaming water pink as they tore into the women. The mangrove trees next to Chandler began to shake, displaced by some force beneath them, and soon their roots were thrashing the air like black tentacles.

Chandler waded away from the massacre. He took a deep breath and ducked below the surface to avoid the searing heat of the flames as they jumped between the pockets of gas that bubbled up from beneath the swamp.

The flames from above sent pulses of red light flaring down through the murky water, and Chandler saw what lay beneath him in a series of flash frames: a subspace of roots and wreckage, torn apart by gas and seismic upheaval; the rusted remains of oil derricks thrusting up through the mud as the swamp floor was split asunder; vague shapes that floated through the water—bodies, faces mottled and leathery, their expressions frozen in horror from back when the oil field exploded. He saw an old motorcar tear itself from the mud beneath him, weed trailing from its bodywork. Inside he saw a corpse, visible through the side window. Its face was blackened, its one dead eye staring into the distance. The car was a Pierce-Arrow. Chandler realized with a start he could be looking at the body of Blanche's father, Louie de Chiel.

He swam back up and surfaced in a sea of flames. He knew he couldn't hold his breath long enough to swim clear of the burning gas. He was out of options. His hair started to steam from the heat. Someone had once told him that drowning wasn't a painful death. What was painful was fighting it; if you just took in a lungful of water, it would all be over much quicker and with far less pain. But then he remembered he was a Travis. And Travises don't give up. He took a deep breath and prepared to dive again when, out of the smoke and flames, a stump reached out. He clutched on to it and within seconds was being hauled into the swamp boat by Zeke and Duke. He coughed out water as Zeke helped him into a sitting position.

Zeke cracked a smile. "Wasn't it Mark Twain . . ."

Chandler managed a halfhearted smile. "I know—the swamp's a cruel mistress."

Zeke gunned the motor, and they raced through the blazing swamp until they were clear of the flames and could see the causeway in the distance.

Chandler looked at the incongruous suit Duke was wearing. "Are we going on somewhere? Because I only have casual."

Duke grinned. "Long story. Someone spiked my drink and trashed my Airstream. Looking at your eyes I'm guessing you got a dose as well." he said. "Do you want to tell me what the hell you're doing out here?"

Chandler coughed and spat out some kind of vegetation. "Roxie's in the old Raffeti house. She's being held in some sort of operating theatre. Freddy's there too. They're using him as a human blood pump . . ."

Duke nodded to Zeke. "We need to get back there now," he said.

The boat rocked precariously as plumes of gas exploded and tongues of flame shot into the sky all around them.

Zeke looked at the burning swamp. "What's causing all this?"

Duke shielded his eyes against the glare from the flames. "The recent hurricane must have disrupted this whole area, shifted the substrata, released gas trapped for hundreds of years."

Chandler nodded. "Mix in the oil pollution, and it was an environmental time bomb. It's uncovering what Blackburn and his ancestors worked so hard to hide."

Zeke shot him a confused look. "What?" he asked.

"One of Blackburn's ancestors faked a survey, started drilling for oil on unstable ground. A lot of people died when the oil field came apart. A storm destroyed the evidence, and the Blackburn family's been covering it up ever since. Until now."

Zeke shook his head. "That's fucked up." He slowed the motor, nodded at something in the distance. "Causeway's up ahead. We can follow it to the Raffeti place."

Duke looked behind him. The flames were arcing across the water, igniting gas pockets as they spread.

Zeke guided the swamp boat slowly along beside the causeway. "Gotta move careful. There's submerged pilings from the original road here in the shallows."

Chandler said, "Whatever the Rafetti sisters were doing up there, I think it's been going on for a long time. I saw pictures on the walls—women with birth defects, Tumblety, Blackburn, and his ancestors. They're all involved somehow."

Duke shook his head. "How could they have worked in those conditions, out in the swamp with no scientific knowledge?"

Chandler shrugged. "Give a hundred monkeys typewriters, eventually they'll write Shakespeare," he said. "They've been experimenting out in the swamps for over a century.

Duke scratched at his chin. "Maybe the sisters' deformities were the results of Tumblety's earlier failed experiments?" he said. "All of the mutations passed down through generations."

Chandler nodded. "That's what I thought. We need to get back to Roxie before the flames reach the house."

There was a sharp crack, and a bullet slammed into the swamp boat's motor, setting it alight. Zeke grabbed an extinguisher and put out the fire with a spray of foam. The boat grounded on the rocks beside the causeway. Blackburn's Escalade slid to a halt above them. Blackburn and Kale jumped out. Inside the vehicle the hounds barked frenziedly, jaws slavering as they pawed against the back hatch window. Kale held a pump-action shotgun pointed at the three in the boat.

Blackburn looked down at Duke. "Nice suit."

Duke said nothing. He looked up and figured out the odds. Blackburn had the high ground, and Kale had a shotgun. Whichever way he ran the numbers, he and his friends came out as losers. He shared a look with Travis. They both had similar training and experience. They were in a hostage situation. But Blackburn wasn't going to hold them hostage. He was going to shoot them and dispose of their bodies, the same way he and his family had always done. During his training, Duke had always been told that if the odds are against you, then you need to change the odds.

Blackburn shook his head. "You couldn't stay out of it, could you? The swamp, the plant—sticking your nose into my business. Still, that's all ancient history now—rather like your investigation."

"You think your problems will go away if you kill us?" Duke said.

Blackburn shrugged. "That's the way it usually works."

"Well, that's not going to happen this time," Chandler said.

"I guess we'll just have to see about that," Blackburn replied.

Kale's finger tightened on the trigger.

"You got yourself in a bit of a jam back in the day," Duke said to Blackburn. "Kale here straightened things out, and now he's on your payroll, making sure that nothing sticks to you, or your campaign. But the money wasn't enough, was it, Kale? You needed a backup plan in case your bromance went sour. So you put all the evidence in a lockbox. Anything happens to you, your lawyer spills the goods on Roman."

Chandler watched Kale's eyes. He saw the tell. Duke had guessed right. This was by-the-book negotiating: divide and conquer. There was no way Blackburn could know what was a lie and what was the truth. Chandler and Duke had to keep them off-balance and hope that between them they could move the odds in their favor.

"He's lying," Kale said.

Chandler smiled. "You're going down in history, Blackburn, but not in a good way."

Blackburn shook his head, eyes bright with madness. "Oh, I'm going to make history. But I'm not going down. I'll be known as the man who opened up the wetlands and brought prosperity to an area crushed by the Evil Wind for a hundred years. I'm going to finish the regeneration Governor Huey Long began—"

Duke shot him a look. "As I remember it, Huey wanted to make money from the oil companies, not give it to them."

Blackburn nodded to Kale, who moved nearer to the edge of the road.

"Times change," the governor said.

Kale leveled the shotgun.

"Wait!" Chandler held up his hand.

"What is this, teacher's question time?" Blackburn asked.

"We know what you're doing up at the plant," Chandler said. "Pretending to destroy a greenhouse gas by-product from something you don't even make, claiming millions in carbon credits without spending a dime on the process.

Blackburn looked at him, a trace of unease on his face.

Chandler went on. "It was all going so well. And then we pulled some century-old bodies out of a carriage in the swamp, and you panicked."

Blackburn smiled. "Why would I do that?"

Chandler said, "Because you thought we'd stumbled on your dirty little secret."

"What dirty secret?" Blackburn said.

"The hundreds of people your ancestor Adam Blackburn murdered."

"That's bullshit."

"I wish it was," Chandler replied. "But it isn't. Adam paid a surveyor to file a report covering up the unstable ground beneath the oil field. On the day of the investor's party, the ground collapsed. Gas trapped beneath the rocks ignited, and the whole place went up. Hundreds died."

Blackburn shook his head. "That's not true. The storm took them. A tragic accident."

"No," said Chandler. "The storm covered up what really happened. But if our investigation had continued, more bodies would have turned up. And that would have brought everything to a halt, wouldn't it?"

Blackburn said nothing.

"The swamp would have been swarming with forensic teams, and the truth about your ancestors would have made front-page news and killed your Senate ambitions."

Blackburn shook his head. "Everybody who knows about that is already dead, and once you're gone, it'll be business as usual."

"No, it won't. Because we have the evidence," said Chandler.

Blackburn gave Chandler a thin smile. "What evidence?"

"The inventory details that show your reprocessing operation is a scam," Chandler replied. "Not to mention the part your ancestor played in the Jack the Ripper conspiracy. That's something you don't want to be shouting about on the campaign trail."

Blackburn said nothing, just stared at him.

Chandler continued. "And then there's the pictures of what really happened that night out at the oil field. Face it, Blackburn, you're finished." Chandler waited to see if Blackburn would acknowledge the existence of the photographs.

Blackburn shook his head. "You're bluffing." He nodded to Kale.

Chandler could see they were all out of options. Kale aimed down at the boat—and then the road started to shake. The ground heaved, buckled and fractured. The Escalade's back hatch burst open as the hounds forced their way out and raced off across the swamp, ears flat against their heads, howling. A huge shape reared up behind the Escalade: an ancient oil derrick, thrust up by colossal forces from beneath the swamp. It smashed back down onto the car, crushing it under tons of rusted steel. Petroleum spewed onto the road beneath the vehicle. Sparks flickered beneath the hood.

Duke, Chandler, and Zeke all hit the deck as the fuel ignited. The force of the blast blew Kale off his feet, sending his shotgun skittering across the causeway. He scrambled up, pulled his Glock 19 out, and started firing. Bullets ricocheted off the metal hull of the swamp boat.

Zeke scrabbled for something on the floor as Kale reloaded. There was a sharp crack as a bullet passed over their heads, then silence. Chandler looked up, saw Kale clutching at a machete that protruded from his neck, blood pumping between his fingers. He fell to the ground, bleeding out.

Blackburn scooped up the shotgun and leveled it at them. There was a blinding flash of light as an incandescent plume of gas enveloped him. Chunks of smoking flesh scattered across the swamp, triggering a feeding frenzy among the alligators. The water boiled with jaws and tails. Zeke shook his head.

"What the hell was that?"

Chandler rubbed his eyes; his retinas still ached from the intensity of the light.

"Superheated methane gas," he said. "That's what hit the investors out in the oil field." Chandler suddenly staggered. It felt like he was on fire, and there was an empty feeling in the pit of his stomach. And then it passed, and he was left with a dull pain throughout his body.

Duke looked at him. "You alright?"

Chandler nodded. "Must be the light. I think I'm still suffering from the aftereffects of that spiked drink. Lucky I didn't have much of it."

"Yeah. I'm not feeling great myself," Duke said. He climbed out of the boat, went over to Kale, and checked for a pulse. "He's gone," he called back.

Zeke joined him on land. "I didn't have a choice. He was going to kill us all."

Duke shrugged. "No doubt about that. But you could do without the paperwork."

He rolled Kale's body off the side of the causeway with his foot and watched as it splashed into the water. Dark shapes swarmed around it and dragged it away. Zeke gave Duke a nod of thanks, scooped up the extinguisher from the boat, and put out the flames from the still-burning Escalade.

There was a flash of orange in the distance. Flames arced into the sky behind the silhouette of a house.

Chandler shouted above the noise, "We need to get Roxie and Freddy out of there, now!"

Duke and Zeke climbed back into the boat. Duke stood up and looked down at the damaged engine.

"Boat's out of action. We'll never make it on foot."

The roar of an engine grew behind them. Headlights flared in the dark as Chilly's Camaro loomed up out of the night. The huge red machine shuddered to a halt, its giant wheels smoking, swamp water up to its axles. Duke's face creased in a smile.

"You took your time," he said.

Chilly shrugged. "I was at the barbecue. Damn dog got my cell, buried it like a bone."

Duke and Chandler scrambled across into the Camaro. Zeke fiddled with the jet drive on the swamp boat.

"The prop engine's DOA. You two go ahead. I'm gonna get the jet drive working, just need to reroute the fuel line. I'll be right behind you."

Chilly gestured at the fires jumping across the swamp as pockets of gas ignited.

"If this gets any worse . . ."

Zeke spat. "It'll only take me a couple of minutes. Go get Roxie and the kid."

Chilly nodded. He hit the starter and the Camaro roared away, its huge tires ploughing through the shallow mud and water beside the causeway.

Flames danced across the water, licking at the sides of the Raffeti house. Inside the boathouse, Freddy moved weakly in the corner of the room. The wooden walls were smoking. One of the jars fell from the bench and smashed to the floor. The organ inside pulsed weakly in the wreckage, blood leaking from a damaged membrane.

In the operating room, the blind sister stood next to the steel table, looking down at Roxie. She gripped the shotgun tightly in her withered hands. Roxie slowly opened her eyes, flicked a look at the medical instruments next to her. She carefully reached out and gripped a metal bowl with her free hand and moaned.

The blind sister clicked her tongue on the roof of her mouth and moved toward her. When she got within striking distance, Roxie smashed her in the face with the bowl. The sister howled with pain, her nose crushed. She fell backward, crashing into a shelf, knocking bottles of liquids and powders onto the floor. Roxie looked down at her lying unconscious.

"Didn't see that coming, did you?"

Roxie jumped down from the table. Her foot landed in a pool of liquid, and her leg went out from under her. She slammed onto the ground and hit her head hard against the stone floor. Her eyes fluttered once, and she passed out.

Chilly gunned the Camaro toward the house. The tires churned through the mud and low-lying vegetation. The engine screamed, exhaust smoke belching from its tailpipe as it hurtled across the swamp. In the distance they could see flames licking the boathouse. Chilly floored the accelerator.

They reached the back of the house in minutes and came to a halt. Chandler jumped down from the Camaro into the shallow water. "There's a trapdoor under the boathouse," he said.

The sound of an approaching engine made him turn. Zeke skimmed toward them in the fan boat and pulled alongside the back of the boathouse before cutting the engine.

"Where are they?" he asked.

Chilly pointed at the boathouse, which was now engulfed in flames. "Still inside."

Zeke spun the boat around so its back pointed toward the boathouse. He tilted the jet drive out of the water and restarted it. The engine blasted a stream of water at the burning structure, dousing the flames and soaking the building behind it, like a crude amphibian fireboat.

Chandler slipped from the buggy and into the swamp, then turned back to Duke in the Camaro.

"C'mon, we don't have much time," he said.

Duke jumped into the water, and they both ducked under the boathouse.

Chandler climbed up through the shattered trapdoor and into the boathouse, followed by Duke.

"Keep your ears open for a weird clicking noise—one of the sisters may still be in the house," Chandler said. "She's totally blind, navigates with the clicks. Some kind of crude sonar."

They heard coughing. They could just make out Freddy in the corner of the smoke-filled room. Duke came over, eyes streaming.

"Christ! What the hell did they do to him?"

Chandler started to unstrap Freddy from the steel table. Duke looked at the cannulas.

"We're gonna need to get some tourniquets going here, otherwise he'll bleed out."

Chandler looked around. "This explains Jonas's torso collection. Once they're finished with their human blood pumps, they chop them up and feed them to the gators."

He reached over to a bench, picked up Freddy's old shirt, and tore it into strips. He took the material and tied Freddy's femoral arteries off. Freddy moaned and moved feebly.

Duke helped Chandler get him off the gurney, then heaved Freddy onto his back and headed for the trapdoor. He set Freddy down before jumping into the water. Chandler carefully lowered Freddy down into Duke's waiting arms. The sound of the water jet drive cut out.

Duke looked up at Chandler. "Go get Roxie!"

Chandler turned and ran out of the boathouse and into the dimly lit corridor. He raced toward the door that led into the operating theater. The corridor was filling with smoke, the acrid fumes making it difficult to breathe. He threw the door open and looked around, saw the empty steel operating table and Roxie lying on the floor. He went over and shook her. To his relief, her eyes opened, and she gave him that smile, the one that always did something to him.

"We have to go," he said, helping her up.

Roxie shook her head. "Where's Freddy?"

Chandler took her arm as she swayed. "He's safe. Where's the homicidal chipmunk?"

Roxie looked around. "I knocked her out—she was on the floor."

Something moved behind them. The blind sister lunged out of the smoke, shotgun swinging toward them as she made the strange clicking sound, scanning for them. They both froze. She swung the gun around, sniffing, listening, clicking.

Chandler looked at the surgical instruments next to the steel table, saw the anesthetist's mask leading to the oxygen canister. He reached slowly across and turned it on full.

The sister cried out, the sound of the hissing gas like white noise in her head, the room a blank canvas. She clicked desperately, but the hiss of the gas pumping into the room blinded all her senses.

Chandler supported Roxie as they ran out of the room and back into the corridor.

They reached the door leading back to the boathouse, and Chandler kicked it open. They fought their way through the smoke. Chandler's foot slid from under him and he nearly fell. Thousands of tiny flatworms slicked the floor. An explosion rocked the boathouse, and the back wall blew off.

"The gas tanks!" Chandler shouted.

He caught Roxie as she stumbled, held her tightly. She looked into his eyes.

"I didn't know you could dance," she said.

He managed a smile. "You should see my mambo."

They saw Chilly's Camaro revving up outside through the shattered wall.

He yelled at them, "C'mon, jump!"

Chandler turned to Roxie. They shared a look and she nodded. They raced across the boathouse floor and launched themselves into space, legs flailing, arms pumping.

Behind them, the milky eyes of the blind sister stared out into the night, her tongue clicking in frustration and anger as she swung the shotgun up and squeezed the trigger. There was a massive explosion as the oxygen in the operating theater ignited, sending flames billowing out behind Chandler and Roxie as they flew through the air.

They landed in the water next to the Camaro and waded over to it. Chilly and Duke hauled them in, and they accelerated away from the house, the remaining gas canisters exploding behind them like fireworks across the night sky.

EIGHTY-FIVE

SPIRIT'S SWAMP, LOUISIANA – Present day

CSI OFFICERS AND firemen moved around the smoking shell of the Raffeti house, picking their way through the debris. Dive teams pulled decomposed remains from beneath the boathouse as Duke and Chandler stood back from the proceedings, next to Jonas. One of the CSI officers over at the house waved at Jonas.

Jonas nodded to Duke. "I'll be back in a moment." He headed back to the house.

Duke looked across the swamp as the sun sank lower. He turned to Chandler.

"So how does it feel? Now that you've solved one of the greatest mysteries of the nineteenth century?"

Chandler looked around at the officers swarming over the scene and thought through the ramifications.

"I think Edward Travis deserves that honor," he said. "We just put the pieces of the jigsaw together. I don't want to be the one telling the world that Jack the Ripper never really existed. I'd spend the rest of my life giving lectures to students on the subject, writing books . . . They might even make me blog." He gave a small shudder. "I'd have my own Facebook page. It's not for me."

Duke smiled. "A few weeks ago, that would have been your dream," he said. "What's changed?"

"Everything. Everything's changed," Chandler said.

Duke looked at him. "Would that be a tall blonde 'everything'?"

Chandler smiled. "It's been a long time since I had a life outside of work. If I expose the Ripper conspiracy, my time will never be my own."

Duke looked around at the carnage and the investigators digging in the swamp, gave a wry smile.

"I think there's a way you can dodge all that and get your life back on track," Duke said.

"I'm listening." Chandler's face was already starting to show some relief.

Duke leaned in to him. "I know some students that would really thank you for giving them a life-changing subject for their theses."

Chandler's face lit up in a huge smile. He felt a sudden lightness in his soul. "That's the best idea I've heard for a long time—right up there with another meal at Crawdaddy's."

Duke looked around at the swamp and the activity at the Raffeti house. "So, do you think we know the whole story now?"

Chandler stretched his back. He'd done more physical activity in the last week than he'd done for years, and there wasn't a muscle that didn't ache.

"I think so," he said. "The conspiracy became a bandwagon everyone jumped onto. Developers took advantage of the Ripper's reign of fear to buy up properties on the cheap, the police were better funded and staffed as a result of the case, and tabloid journalism came of age."

Duke scratched at his chin. "So this secret-agent guy Edward wrote about in his letters—"

"Triton?" Chandler said.

"Yes. Do you think he planned the whole thing?"

Chandler shook his head. "I don't know. It seems he had Queen Victoria's backing. Maybe he saw an opportunity to make some money out of the situation and went with it." He paused, deep in thought. "Now the only unsolved murder is Fay. Eddy's mistress."

Duke nodded, rubbed sleep out of his eyes. "Maybe she was the only real victim in all of this. And whoever her killer was got away with it," he said.

Chandler nodded. "That could be the next subject for a thesis. The Jack that got away."

Duke grinned. "Everyone loves a conspiracy."

They stood there for some time and watched as the officers loaded up trucks with body bags.

"Jonas and his team found more human remains under what's left of the boathouse. Looks like young Freddy had a lucky escape," said Duke.

Jonas came over. He was holding a small blue mug.

"What's that?" Duke asked.

Jonas smiled. "It was in the remains of the kitchen."

Duke looked at it. It was a souvenir mug embossed with a picture of Bruges's Belfort and an old woman sitting on a chair making lace.

"Good to know psychopaths buy the same tourist shit as normal folk," Duke said.

Jonas smiled. "You never know, we may be able to get some prints off it. Might show who else was involved up here."

Chandler looked at the mug, trying to remember where he'd seen a picture of the Belfort before. Then it came to him. The framed pieces of lace embroidery in the hallway of the house.

Duke nodded. "That would be useful. Pretty much everybody implicated is dead now."

"What about Marsha?" Chandler asked.

"I sent a couple of deputies to check out the Future Information Corporation offices. It was all shuttered up, no Marsha, no receptionist," Duke said.

Chandler said, "I expect she saw us coming. After all, that's her business."

A thought came to him. "What about the dogs?"

Duke shrugged. "No sign of them either."

"Maybe they're roaming the swamps like a Louisianan version of *The Hound of the Baskervilles*," said Chandler.

Duke smiled. "I think that would have to be the *dogos* of the Baskervilles," he said.

Jonas shook his head. "Very amusing, Sherlock. You should come and see this."

He led them over to the remains of the house and across to a steel hatchway in the floor, scorched and buckled by the heat of the fire. Jonas peered down into the opening.

"We've rigged up some battery lights down there. Watch out for the steps. They're slippery."

They followed him down the stairs and into a dank vault hewn into the house's foundation, then past walls covered with ancient fossils and through a rough doorway cut into the rock. They found themselves in a cavern stretching into the distance beneath the house. Floodlights bathed the area in cool fluorescent light. A wiry man wearing a bright LED headlamp came to meet them.

Jonas waved a hand at him. "This is Grant, he's an amateur paleontologist in his spare time."

Grant nodded, gave a wry smile. "Not that the coroner's office gives me much spare time." He pointed to the walls. "The original house was built on a limestone spur. You can see the age from the rock striations," he said. He led them farther along the cavern. "This is where it gets interesting."

They halted beside a glass tank set into the wall on a ledge. Something pale floated inside the murky fluid that filled it.

"Is that what I think it is?" Duke said.

Grant nodded. "As far as we can tell, they're arranged chronologically. Must be over a hundred of them."

They continued walking, past tank after tank, the fluid getting clearer as they progressed deeper into the cavern, the shapes floating in the liquid getting larger. Grant touched the wall where a clearly defined fossil embossed the surface.

"That's a brachiopod, and the one next to it is a cephalopod," he said. "Two hundred and fifty million years ago there was only one supercontinent, Pangaea. When that split apart, the Atlantic Ocean and the Gulf of Mexico opened, and Louisiana slowly formed over millions of years from water into land, and from north to south. The limestone bedrock this house was built on was originally under the Atlantic Ocean."

Jonas cut in, "We think this could have been a natural cavern that the sisters enlarged over the years."

Grant nodded at one of the glass tanks. "At first we thought they were medical specimens."

"And now?" Chandler said.

"Now I think we're looking at failed experiments."

Duke looked closer at the tank. "Experiments?" he said.

"Each tank contains a human fetus," Jonas explained. "They range from a few weeks to full term and beyond. When you see what's in the next cavern, you'll understand."

Jonas led the way through a low doorway at the end of the cavern. They entered a smaller room carved deeper into the rock. The roof was lower, and the walls ran with condensation. Against one of the walls was a pile of insulated cooler boxes.

Jonas went over to a low shelf that ran across the far wall. There were three ceramic troughs, like shallow washbasins. Two of them were discolored and empty. But it was the third one that attracted their attention. There was a system of pipes connected to its sides. On one side, two tubes split from a bag of plasma and led down to what looked like a pump beneath the trough, while on the other side a tube drained into a waste pipe leading down to a grating set in the floor.

Chandler looked at the bloody mass that lay in the bottom of the trough, tried to wrap his mind around what he saw.

Duke stared at it. "What is it?" he asked.

"I'm having tests run at the moment to determine whether this is animal or human remains," Jonas said. "Though it may be neither."

Duke looked at him. "What do you mean?"

Jonas took his glasses off and gave them a vigorous polish.

"Have you heard of in vitro meat?"

Duke nodded. "Wasn't that some kind of weird science shit where they made an artificial burger?"

Jonas smiled. "Weird science shit indeed. But the science is actually for real. They take stem cells from animal muscle and culture them with nutrients and growth-promoting chemicals. Within a few weeks, you have millions of cells, and if you feed them with hemoglobin . . ." He paused and shrugged.

Duke looked at the lump in the trough. "Are we talking Frankenstein's monster here?"

Jonas smiled. "Once again, you're almost right. But in this case, you get in vitro meat."

Chandler struggled to catch up. "Don't tell me the Raffeti sisters were making artificial hamburgers down here?"

Jonas pointed to the pink mass. "I'd say they were way ahead of that. The stem cells and the hemoglobin would produce an inanimate piece of meat, but, if you connected it to a blood supply and filtration system, and added neural stem cells, then you open up the possibility of transdifferentiation."

Duke held his hand up. "Whoa, my head is gonna burst!"

Jonas smiled. "It's a kind of stem cell that scientists believe is able to form complex parts of the human body, such as the brain. Some members of the scientific community think that our entire structure, brain, and personality—even our memory—can be grown from the stem cells found in our blood."

Chandler looked again at the inanimate piece of spongy pulp. "Do you think that's what the sisters have been doing all these years, with Blackburn's backing?"

Jonas shrugged. "From what Freddy and Roxie were able to tell us, it looked like they'd been experimenting since the place was an orphanage back in the nineteenth century. Passing their knowledge down from one generation to the next, kidnapping people and using them as human blood-banks to try and grow fetuses outside the womb."

"Do you think they were successful?" Chandler asked.

Jonas shot him a look. "I'll need to investigate further, but if you want my opinion . . ." He hesitated.

"Don't we always?" Chandler said.

Jonas smiled. "I'd say that their aim wasn't to create an adult human. I think they believed that the blood from the fetuses would make them immortal."

Chandler remembered the thousands of tiny flatworms coating the boathouse floor. “Like flatworms?” he said.

Jonas nodded. “I read about that. I guess we'll know the result of that in a thousand years' time. It looks like Tumblety, or Blackburn, was going for a scattergun approach in the hope he'd strike it lucky one way or another. But from what we've found down here, I would say the Blackburns were biased toward blood.”

Duke looked at him. “You think they've been drinking babies' blood for over a century?”

Jonas shrugged. “It's a mythology that's been around forever.”

Duke nodded.

“Dracula,” Jonas went on, “and Elizabeth Báthory, who used to bathe in the blood of her servant girls in the belief that it made her younger . . .”

“Are you saying there may be some truth in the mythology?” Chandler said.

“Maybe,” Jonas said. “In 2014, scientists injected the blood of young mice into old mice and vice versa. Their findings pointed to a definite correlation toward the older mice's brains benefiting from the young blood, while in reverse, the young mice's brain function deteriorated.”

Chandler spoke up. “So Tumblety could have been ahead of the curve with his stem cell research?”

“Yes,” Jonas said. “And apart from murder, kidnapping, and torture, he was a stand-up guy.”

“But would it even be possible?” Duke asked.

Jonas thought about this. “Theoretically, if they developed a protein derived from human blood, an inter-alpha inhibitor, that would allow them to grow human pluripotent stem cells without the need for biological substrates—”

“Biological substrates?” Chandler asked.

Jonas nodded. “Like the artificial hamburger, it takes the human being out of the equation.”

“What happens then?” said Chandler.

“The protein could make stem cells attach to unmodified tissue culture plastic,” Jonas said. “Like growing a human being in a petri dish.”

Chandler looked at the bloody pulp in the third trough. "Or in one of those."

Jonas nodded. "We'll know more when Roxie's finished running her tests. I told her she should take some days off, but you know Roxie."

A CSI officer ducked into the room, nodded at Jonas. "We found something."

Jonas followed him out through a doorway that led into another room. Chandler, Duke, and Grant shadowed him.

He led them to where two more officers crouched over a cooler box on the floor in front of them. They stood up as Jonas approached. The first officer reached down and carefully picked up the box. It was about eighteen inches deep and a foot square. He held it toward Jonas. "Listen."

They all listened. They could hear a rhythmic pulse.

Jonas took the box, placed it back down on the floor, and knelt beside it. "This is an organ care package. It's designed to keep a transplant organ warm and functioning in transit. It has its own battery and pump system."

He carefully unclipped the lid of the box and opened it. They all peered inside.

Duke shook his head. "Damn if I ain't seen everything now!"

Inside the box was a beating heart, connected by tubes to a pump supplying it with blood and nutrients from a self-contained reservoir in the bottom of the box.

They stood looking at the heart. It was Jonas who broke the silence.

"It looks like they were getting ready for the next stage."

Duke nodded. "No more torsos. Or maybe they hadn't tested it out yet."

Chandler's cell phone rang. He picked it up.

"Hi, Roxie." He listened. "Okay. Thanks, see you soon." He ended the call, looked around at their expectant faces. "Roxie's found something."

EIGHTY-SIX

BATON ROUGE, LOUISIANA- Present day

ROXIE STOOD NEXT to Chandler and Duke in the university lab. They were looking at the DNA readout from the MinION sequencer. Jonas had elected to stay behind and continue processing the crime scene.

"So I ran the normal tests to try and establish what we found in the trough," Roxie said. "As you know, DNA is the same double helix shape in humans and animals, but the sequence is very different. It's made up of four different building blocks, nucleotides, and it's the order they're in that tells the cells what proteins to make."

Chandler nodded. "Like IKEA assembly instructions."

Roxie smiled. "Exactly, but obviously not as complicated. It tells the cells whether to make a human leg bone, or an eagle's wing."

"So it's relatively easy to tell the difference between human and animal DNA?" Duke asked.

"Yes," Roxie answered. "But in this case it's not that simple."

Duke smiled. "It never is with this case."

Roxie nodded. "Scientists have been playing around with human-animal hybrid embryos in the laboratory for some years now. It's all pretty controversial, with people worrying about the whole thing turning into a *Planet of the Apes* scenario. It's also an ethical nightmare." Roxie tapped various areas of the readout as she talked.

"I've been able to identify multiple human and animal DNA from the sample we found at the Rafetti house."

"So this is like the in vitro meat we talked about," Duke said.

Roxie nodded. "Yes, but I think we're looking at something more advanced than a synthetic hamburger. I think we're looking at a very real attempt to grow a human being."

Chandler looked at the screen. "But at the moment it's still just a lump of hamburger, except it contains human and animal DNA."

Roxie tapped the keyboard and another sequence popped up. "I can't disagree with that," she said. "I was able to isolate a variety of human DNA sequences. I'm guessing they were from some of the earlier victims, fetal stem cells, and the main donor."

Chandler looked at her. "Main donor?"

Roxie nodded. "Yes. The person I believe they were trying to regenerate, clone, or whatever the right term is." She tapped some keys on the computer. "I sent the sequence to CODIS as soon as I'd isolated it. I'm still waiting to see if there's a hit."

Chandler looked at her. "How would that help us?"

"Well, it would tell us who the driving force behind all of this is—or was. After all, the sisters are dead, and they were the ones running things."

Duke shook his head. "The whole thing's one big freak show."

There was a muted ping from Roxie's laptop.

"We got a hit on CODIS," she said and clicked the attachment in the email. The file began to download, the progress bar headed for 100 percent. The file opened, and the screen filed with the DNA sequence and the name it matched.

"Whoa!" Duke said.

Roxie and Chandler said nothing, just stared at the name: *Roman Blackburn.*

EIGHTY-SEVEN

BATON ROUGE, LOUISIANA – Present day

THEY WERE STILL staring at the screen when Jonas turned up. He'd finished up at the crime scene and had headed over to the lab. He saw from their expressions that something important had happened.

"What's going on?" he asked.

Roxie turned to him. "We got the results from the sample in the trough. It's hybrid DNA, animal and human. And we just got a hit on CODIS."

Jonas stared at the DNA sequence and bent down to look at the name at the bottom of the screen.

"Holy moly," he said.

"Holy moly indeed," Duke echoed.

Chandler shook his head. "So Blackburn was experimenting for his own benefit."

Roxie nodded. "It looks that way. I can't identify all of the DNA that's flying around, especially if it's not in the database."

"How come Blackburn was even in the database?" Jonas asked.

"He wasn't," Duke replied. "We contacted Kale's lawyer and got him to open up his lockbox. There was enough incriminating evidence in it to put Blackburn away for good, including a blood sample taken during his original DUI case, which Roxie fed into the sequencer."

Roxie's fingers flickered across the keyboard. Two DNA sequences flashed up on the screen. She overlaid them and plotted the similarities, then turned to Chandler.

"I don't think you need worry about your missing relative anymore."

Chandler looked at the screen and the names at the bottom of the DNA sequences.

"So . . ." He paused, rubbed his eyes.

Roxie nodded. "Adam Blackburn was the non-paternal twin Mary Kelly gave birth to. Your missing relative. His chimeric DNA was passed down through the generations, from Mary Kelly to Adam Blackburn and on through the other Blackburns, ending up in Roman Blackburn."

Duke shook his head. "Well, he's not missing anymore. He's all over the swamp. And he's not going to be facing any charges."

Jonas smiled grimly. "No," he said. "Not in this lifetime."

EIGHTY-EIGHT

RYKER'S FIELD, LOUISIANA – Present day

THE WARMTH OF the sun on Chandler's face woke him from a deep sleep. He narrowed his eyes against its rays as they spilled through the windows on the far side of the room. Jesse had insisted that he and Duke move into Blanche's house until things had been sorted out with the insurance company and the Airstream had been repaired or replaced. Blanche, far sighted as ever, had put the house in Jesse's name over decades earlier.

Chandler turned to see Roxie's glowing face smiling down at him. Propped up on one elbow with the sun streaming across her mane of blonde hair, she looked more like an angel than ever. Chandler had been smiling so much over the last few days, his face actually ached. He grinned back at her and swept away a random lock of hair that had fallen across one eye.

"How does it feel?" she asked.

"I haven't checked, but I imagine it still works," he said with a smile.

She swatted him with a pillow. "I meant sleeping in a real bed—or sleeping with me, or living in the present rather than the past, or all of the above." And with that she straddled him, taking his face in her hands and kissing him hard as he relaxed beneath her.

He came up for air. "Okay, life's wonderful now, if you're fishing for compliments—which you don't have to, because obviously you're perfect."

He paused, took a deep breath, and launched in. "I have a confession to make."

Roxie looked at him. "Sounds serious," she said.

"Don't worry, it's not that serious. And the fact that my drink was spiked makes for mitigating circumstances."

"Go on," Roxie said.

"While I was at Gumbo's, waiting to hear back from you—"

"I'll ignore the pathetic attempt to guilt me for not picking up," she said.

Chandler smiled. "Well, I may have given one of the waitresses—"

"Maya?" Roxie said.

"Er, yes. How did you know?"

"Lucky guess. Go on."

"Okay. Anyway, Maya may have got the impression that I was coming on to her."

"And why would she think that?"

"I gave her a lift home." Chandler waited.

"Wow. That's certainly borderline seduction," Roxie said.

"As I said, mitigating circumstances. And to be fair, I was feeling a little lacking in attention."

"Because you thought I'd stood you up?"

Chandler nodded. "The lizard part of my brain may well have thought that."

"But the logical part of your brain was able to control your primitive urges?"

"Of course. Though the way I was feeling, I was barely able to control the car."

Roxie smiled. "Yes, Maya said it was an interesting drive home. She'd been serving you OJ all evening and couldn't understand why you were acting so drunk."

Chandler looked at her. "You know Maya?"

"Of course." Roxie laughed. "I'm sorry. You thought you were the only one with low self-esteem? I've had a few bad experiences, relationships that weren't as stable as they might have been. So . . ." She paused.

Chandler looked at her. "You were checking me out? You had Maya come on to me to see if I was some kind of lounge lizard?"

"Guilty as charged," Roxie said.

"Well, I guess we're both guilty if it comes down to it. I thought you'd stood me up, whereas homicidal swamp sisters were holding you prisoner. And you thought I might be a lounge lizard, while I was worried I was going to lose the best thing to come along since God invented that smile he gave you."

Roxie smiled. "I'm a sucker for a silver-tongued Englishman. But for all I knew, you might have just been some limey butterfly looking to land on the next brightly colored flower in the garden," she said.

Chandler suddenly started to smile. And then it hit him. Butterflies. It was always about the butterflies.

Roxie looked at him. "Okay, what is it? I recognize that look. Didn't you and Duke solve everything?"

As usual, she could read him like a book. She rolled off him in a kind of horizontal flounce, but her smile showed she was only toying with him. He jumped out of bed. Roxie closed her eyes.

"Here we go," she muttered.

Chandler shrugged on his trousers. "I won't be long, just need to check something."

Roxie looked at him. "What?"

He grinned. "A forest."

And with that, he was gone.

Duke, Jesse, and Roxie stood in the sitting room of the de Chiel house. Duke had insisted on making some coffee before listening to what Chandler had to say.

"If you're gonna go all Poirot on us, I'm making some decent coffee first," he'd said.

Now, with three expectant faces looking at him, and Duke clutching a mug of his favorite brew, Chandler was ready. There was a knock on the door, and Jonas stuck his head into the room. Chandler waved at him.

"Come in, you haven't missed anything."

Jonas was already polishing his glasses on his shirt in case his opinion was needed. "I didn't want to miss this. After all, it's been a hundred years coming."

Chandler looked around and then launched in.

"Okay, we know what happened back at the oil field in 1915, and we have the negative from the investors' party that Blanche left for Duke so he'd know that Blackburn's ancestors were involved in a cover-up."

Duke gulped a slug of his coffee and spoke up. "Yeah, she was a smart lady. Without her pointing us down that line of investigation, we wouldn't have gotten to the bottom of any of it."

"True," Chandler said, "but she was a lot smarter than we gave her credit for."

Roxie smiled. "Smarter than all of you?"

Chandler nodded. "As it happens, yes. Blackburn's men searched the house, and we've looked everywhere for the missing photographs. When we were talking about conspiracies, Duke came up with the best way to hide one. Do you remember?"

Jonas said, "A tree within a forest."

"Exactly. We thought we'd looked everywhere, but the answer was right under our noses—or, if I could use the Latin, our proboscis."

Duke shook his head. "Please don't. Quite a few of us in the room are under a thousand years old."

Chandler chuckled and moved over to a large bookcase. It sat below a wall covered with small glass display cases containing mounted butterflies.

"Blanche knew that Blackburn's men were going to be looking for photographic evidence of what really happened to the investors ahead of the storm."

"The pictures her father, Louie, took at the oil field during the party," Jonas said.

"Exactly. But he didn't really know if she had those negatives. That's why when I told him about them that night in the swamp, he thought I was bluffing. And I was. I just went with the logic. Because we'd already found one of the negatives, Blackburn couldn't be sure if we knew where the rest of them were."

Duke said, "And if he had known about them, then that would have confirmed they existed."

"Exactly. But quite frankly, I was playing for time."

"Amen to that," Duke said. "If it hadn't been for Zeke and an act of God, we wouldn't be here today."

Chandler went on. "Blanche left some clues that only we would pick up on, because of what she talked about out in Ryker's field."

Duke smiled. "Butterflies."

"One butterfly in particular," Chandler said. He nodded to Jonas.

Jonas handed him a transparent evidence bag containing the small glass mounting case with the blue butterfly inside.

"A *Graphium sarpedon*, or bluebottle," said Chandler. "She left this case for us to find. She used it so we would know where to look."

Duke nodded. "In a blue bottle."

"We were lucky the sun shone through the negative and tipped us off—though I guess we would have worked it out eventually."

Roxie smiled. "Course you would."

Chandler continued. "The picture showed her father with his car at the oil field, so we would know Blackburn was involved, and she hoped it would lead us to the car where she'd hidden Edward's notes and his letters."

Duke nodded. "At least we got that."

Roxie chipped in, "Eventually."

Chandler said, "But we were always missing the other pictures, and that's where this little chap comes in." He slid the box out of the evidence bag. "I'd always felt there was something odd about the way the butterflies were displayed." He walked over to the collection of small boxes containing the mounted butterflies on the wall. "Normally, butterflies are arranged in large cases and are grouped by categories, subgroups, and super families." He held up the small box.

"But though Blanche arranged most of her collection that way, she had a separate arrangement of small boxes like this one. It's three and a quarter inches by five and a half. Postcard size. And if I take the back off . . ." He slid the small piece of card from the back of the box and showed it to them. "You can see there's space inside for just that. Only she didn't put a postcard in the back."

He went over to the small boxes hanging on the wall and lifted one from its hook. "There are nine boxes, ten if you include the one we found. The reason there's nothing inside the box is because she took it out."

Duke nodded. "The negative of the oil field in the bottle on the hoodoo tree."

"Yes. The Graflex 3A uses 122 film and produces ten postcard-size prints."

Chandler reached over to the wall and took down one of the boxes. He slid the cardboard back from it and pulled out a large-format negative. "She hid the negatives that Edward sent her all those years ago behind the butterflies."

The others watched as one by one, Chandler took down the polished wooden boxes and slid the backs open, carefully lifting the fragile negatives out. He placed them gently on a cloth-covered table that held a small lamp and a couple of photo frames filled with relatives smiling for the camera.

Jesse said, "I always wondered why she changed those displays. I was out playing pool at the club one day, and I came back and she'd changed them all." He looked over at the pile of negatives. "She's got a light box in her study."

Chandler carefully picked up the negatives and followed Jesse into the small study. The walls were crowded with framed blow-ups of some of the old black-and-white press photos Blanche had taken over the years. There were some framed front covers from *Time*, *Paris Match*, and *Life*, as well as *National Geographic* and *Harper's Bazaar*. It was obvious that the more serious magazines were what she felt most comfortable working for.

Jesse went over to the corner of the room and turned on the light box that sat there. He pulled the curtains closed, cutting the sunlight out. Chandler carefully laid the negatives on the surface of the box and turned it on. They all stared at the images illuminated from below, picture after picture charting the horrific destruction that took place at the oil field ahead of the storm in 1915.

EIGHTY-NINE

BATON ROUGE, LOUISIANA – Present day

CHANDLER LOOKED OUT across the Highland Cemetery at the dogwood trees' leaves that were turning pink in the fall, and the birds fluttering around their crimson berries. Highland was the oldest surviving cemetery in East Baton Rouge, and the final resting place of his great-great-grandfather, Edward Richard Travis. Edward had wanted to be buried in the same state where Mary had stayed. He'd been allowed to lie at rest there by the university that owned the land. Between Jonas and Duke, a number of strings had been pulled, and the cemetery created a new space for Edward as part of the cleanup operation it had been going through for the last few years.

Chandler bent down to read the inscription on the headstone in front of him. The original gravestone had been tilted at a precarious angle, and the inscription was badly worn, so he'd ordered a new one. He trailed his fingers across the letters. Edward's headstone now bore an extra name beneath his:

EDWARD RICHARD TRAVIS
AND
MARY JANE KELLY.
TOGETHER AT LAST.

Next to Edward's plot were four new headstones. All of the dates ended on October 2, 1893, the day of the Evil Wind. Chandler read their names: Mary Ann Nichols, Elizabeth Stride, Annie Chapman, and Catherine Eddowes. He bent down and brushed some leaves away from a glass-fronted recess set into Edward's headstone. Inside, a hunter-case pocket watch gleamed in the evening light. As he straightened up, he was overcome with emotion, intensely aware that over a hundred years later, the lovers were finally together again.

The sun had become a red orb behind Duke's car. The others had given Chandler some time alone at the cemetery, and now he could see the silhouettes of three figures leaning against the Buick. One of them waved at him as he walked toward them. He didn't need to guess who it was.

Roxie ran over to him and held him close, her eyes shining. They joined Duke, who stood with Georgia, the Creole singer from Gumbo's Club. From the way they were behaving, it looked like Duke had moved on from his monastic existence since losing Julie to Hurricane Katrina.

Duke held out a newspaper. Chandler looked at the front page. CENTURY-OLD CONSPIRACY FINALLY UNCOVERED. There was a byline: STUDENTS HELP LOUISIANA DEPUTY SHERIFF AND ENGLISH DETECTIVE SOLVE OIL FIELD DISASTER MYSTERY. The front page was devoted to a black-and-white photograph of the oil field on the night it was destroyed. The flames, burning oil, and collapsing rigs were all captured in stark detail. Chandler smiled as he read the photographic credit: Louie and Blanche de Chiel.

"Nice touch, giving them both a credit," he said.

Duke nodded. "Check out the inside pages."

Chandler opened the newspaper. There was a double spread featuring the students involved in the Spirit's Swamp investigation. Phaedon, Roxie, and Freddy were all in the line-up. Chandler smiled at the way the international scoop was placed secondary to the locally based story. A byline read, STUDENTS UNEARTH MYSTERY OF JACK THE RIPPER VICTIMS IN SPIRIT'S SWAMP. Chandler looked at the article, a sense of relief in his eyes.

"They've got enough life left to answer all the questions," Duke said. "To give the lectures and Facebook the shit out of it—and do a helluva thesis. And you get your life back."

Chandler smiled. "Sounds good to me. I might just take some time out to fly back and watch Harris eat some humble pie."

Duke nodded. "I get that." He looked reflective for a moment, and then clasped Chandler's shoulder with a bone-crushing grip. "So, do we need to sort you out a visa?"

Chandler looked out across the cemetery at the distant pink waters of the swamp and smiled at Roxie.

"Yes. I think I'll be staying. At least until I get tired of swamps."

Duke laughed, a booming laugh that came from deep within him.

"Swamps, my ass."

Roxie leaned over and kissed Chandler deeply, then they headed around the Buick. Chandler moved the driver's seat forward and followed Roxie as she scrambled into the back. Duke smiled and held the passenger door open for Georgia, before climbing behind the wheel and turning on the ignition. He looked back at Chandler.

"Do you really think we solved it all?

Chandler stretched, ran his fingers through his hair, shrugged. "I think some conspiracies never die."

Duke nodded, churned the starter, and gunned the 7.5-liter V8 engine, blasting a cloud of blue smoke out of the tailpipe.

"Amen to that, brother."

They drove slowly away through the cemetery, past the rows of silent headstones and the dogwood flaring pink in the evening light.

THE END

Look out for the next
Duke Lanoix and Chandler Travis thriller:

BRUGES BLOOD

"Blood is thicker than water."

ACKNOWLEDGMENTS

I'D LIKE TO thank all of the wonderful people who supported the publishing of *Louisiana Blood*. It was truly amazing to get support from readers around the world as well as those from within my own country. I'm also especially grateful for the feedback from my earliest readers, Peter Ryan and Rebecca Rorteseny, and my amazing editor, Sarah Caughie, who along with copy editor Jessica Gardner and proof reader Pamela McElroy at Inkshares made the steep learning curve from screenwriting to prose an easier climb. And finally a massive thanks to my incredible wife, Dorrie, who supported me on this rollercoaster ride.

ABOUT THE AUTHOR

Mike Donald was brought up in Scotland and England. Before going freelance to concentrate on his screenwriting ambitions, he worked for the BBC as a sound mixer, wrote for comedy sketch shows, and developed sitcom ideas. He also worked as a script analyst for a gap finance company and has written many award-winning screenplays. Mike lives in Oxford with his wife Dorrie and a power-hungry Terrier named Bonny May Donald. *Louisiana Blood* was adapted from his award-winning screenplay and is his first published novel.

GRAND PATRONS

LOUISIANA BLOOD WAS made possible in part by the following grand patrons who preordered the book on Inkshares.com. Thank you.

Aleksandra Lloyd
Angela Melamud
Collette Carmichael
Derek Donald
Fred Jodsworth Boak, the Singing Valet
John B. Donald
Doreen J. Wilkins
Sarah Bryant
Steven J. Karageanes

INKSHARES

INKSHARES is a reader-driven publisher and producer based in Oakland, California. Our books are selected not by a group of editors, but by readers worldwide.

While we've published books by established writers like *Big Fish* author Daniel Wallace and *Star Wars: Rogue One* scribe Gary Whitta, our aim remains surfacing and developing the new author voices of tomorrow.

Previously unknown Inkshares authors have received starred reviews and been featured in the *New York Times*. Their books are on the front tables of Barnes & Noble and hundreds of independents nationwide, and many have been licensed by publishers in other major markets. They are also being adapted by Oscar-winning screenwriters at the biggest studios and networks.

Interested in making your own story a reality? Visit Inkshares.com to start your own project or find other great books.